Charles Melville Pepper

To-Morrow in Cuba

Charles Melville Pepper

To-Morrow in Cuba

ISBN/EAN: 9783337379162

Printed in Europe, USA, Canada, Australia, Japan

Cover: Foto ©Andreas Hilbeck / pixelio.de

More available books at **www.hansebooks.com**

To-Morrow in Cuba

BY

CHARLES M. PEPPER

NEW YORK AND LONDON
HARPER & BROTHERS PUBLISHERS
1899

PREFACE

My profession as a newspaper correspondent took me to Cuba in the spring of 1897. With the exception of a short intermission passed with the American army and navy outside the island, it kept me there in the midst of the events shaping the destiny of the Antilles. Impressions of these events as they appeared to me were published in various journals. They were recorded from time to time as they were caught up at the moment.

In the new responsibilities that have come to the American people in the border tropics, exact information is above all things desirable. At the end of more than two years it has seemed to me possible to give information with perhaps more confidence than in the beginning. What is set forth in these pages is not for the purpose of supporting preconceived opinions or of defending any special policy. While the author's views are stated, it has been his aim to set forth the facts on which these views are based. Some persons, doubtless, will reach different conclusions. Whatever opinions may be developed, it is important to know that the problems of Cuba cannot be settled from without. On the surface are the political questions; but deeper than these lie the social and economic problems. It has

PREFACE

seemed to me that if the American people could feel themselves more at home in the surroundings in which all these problems must be worked out, they would be better equipped for the task. As the majority of them cannot see for themselves, I have sought to make them see through other eyes, with the belief that they will be the better able to discriminate between the fretting circumstances which are transitory and the underlying conditions which are permanent. To do this it is necessary to know something of the past, and it has been my aim to exhibit the revolutionary movements of the island in their true perspective.

In conclusion, the utterance of an Italian statesman may be paraphrased, "Cuba is made, but who shall make the Cubans?" and the answer be given, "Themselves." But under what conditions? Perhaps these pages may aid those who seek an answer for the good of Cuba and for the proper discharge of the responsibilities of the United States. C. M. P.

Washington, D. C.

CONTENTS.

TO-MORROW IN CUBA.

PART I
CHAPTERS FROM YESTERDAY

TO-MORROW IN CUBA

CHAPTER I

PROLOGUE TO AUTONOMY

Record of an Experiment—The Pact of El Zanjón—Concessions Which Were Not Autonomy—Grouping into Political Parties—Programme of the Liberals—Loyalists the Union Constitutionals—Echo of European Democratic Movement—Points of Agreement—Disappointment of Autonomists—Promulgation of Constitution—Growth of Autonomist Movement—Alarm of the Privileged Classes—Farce of Cuban Representation in the Cortes—Birth of Reformist Party—Its Members Opportunists—Parties Engulfed in the Waves of Revolution—Influence of Reciprocity Repeal and the Sugar Market.

AUTONOMY was instituted in Cuba on New Year's Day, 1898. Twelve months later to a day Spanish sovereignty was yielded in trust to the United States. The developments of the intervening year were swift. So rapidly had they moved that the chapter with which they began was forgotten. In the broader field of world domain that has opened to the United States as a consequence of the war with Spain, the brief existence of this colonial experiment has almost passed from mind. Yet it was the first attempt of Spain in four centuries to give her colonies a system of self-government. Short as was the period, the story of the experiment is worthy of record.

When the system was decreed in Cuba, the fondness of the Latin intellect for historical sequences caused much philosophical and reflective writing, which traced the series of events precedent as the prologue to a national drama. The real prologue to autonomy in the Spanish Antilles was the Ten-Years' War, which raged from 1868 to 1878. The machete and the torch then gained what peaceful agitation had not been able to achieve. The pact of El Zanjón which brought that insurrection to an end was arranged by Martínez Campos and Máximo Gómez. It affirmed forgetfulness of the past and gave pledges for the future. It was based on promises to Cuba which were to insure to the rebellious island, once more become faithful, distinct political rights. Radical changes were to be made in the organic laws and in the administrative system. Cubans were to be recognized and to share in the government of Cuba. They were to have representation in the Cortes of Spain the same as Puerto Rico.

Spain carried out the letter of the pact of El Zanjón. The organic laws were changed. The restrictive statutes of printing, of public meetings, and of associations or societies were modified and liberalized. A supposedly popular basis of Cuban representation in the Cortes was provided, and the electoral law was passed in conformity with that provision. In the administrative system the statute changes were many. They were carried into effect to the extent of a nominal compliance with the new laws. Mediæval absolutism yielded some of its cherished and hereditary privileges.

Yet neither the spirit nor the letter of the legislation enacted in 1878, and in subsequent years, was autono-

MAP OF THE
CUBAN RAILWAY
SYSTEM
ATLANTIC OCEAN
CARIBBEAN SEA
PINAR DEL RIO
SANTA CLARA
MATANZAS
CAMAGUEY
SANTIAGO DE CUBA
Longitude West from Greenwich

mous. It was as if one of the provinces of the peninsula which had been under a discriminating system of laws and administration had succeeded in getting itself placed on the same plane as the other provinces. For a colony beyond seas requiring a definite measure of independence there was no recognition. A critical study of the statutes and the administrative reforms enacted by the Spanish Government after the peace of El Zanjón produces a plain deduction. A Cuban citizen as a Spanish subject could engage in political agitation with less danger of coming under the charge of conspiracy than formerly. Theoretically, also, his right to a share in the local administration was conceded. With a sincere and honest purpose on the part of the superior authorities a reasonable degree of local and insular government might have been put in force. But the analysis of the legislation and of the decrees of 1878 and subsequent years shows that in essence there was little dilution of what had always been the cardinal principle of Spanish colonial government. This was military rule. The paths were sometimes crooked, the passages wound into labyrinths of cedulas, decrees, orders, edicts, circulars, and bandos. They brought up at the same barrier. The beginning and the end was the Governor-General exercising his military functions as Captain-General. After 1878, Cuba had good, bad, and indifferent Captain-Generals. Their character was reflected in the administration of the island.

It would be an unnecessary task to set forth more in detail wherein the legislation and the administrative acts following the compact of El Zanjón were not autonomous. A comparison with the actual régime of autonomy when established twenty years later is sufficient to demonstrate it. Though the conception of colonial home rule for Cuba was non-existent among the Spanish statesmen of that day, the perception of it was clear on the part of the thinking people of the island. They had felt it when, three years before raising the cry of Yara in 1868, they signed a petition thanking the Duke de la Torre for his motion in the Senate that political rights be granted Cuba. All these things and many more, they said in this document, foreshadowed that within a few years there would be a change in policy, and Cubans would be allowed some voice in the government of their own island. The educated and wealthy Cubans who in 1865 formed themselves into a national party and urged administrative and economic changes upon Madrid felt the lack of understanding among Spanish statesmen. The concessions asked were not a broad application of civil liberties. When their programme was rejected in its entirety they ceased to ask favors. They inaugurated the Ten-Years' war.

Political organization of a mechanical and artificial kind followed the restoration of peace. The grouping was into Liberal and Union Constitutional parties. This formal resolution of the political elements into distinct and opposing groups took place in August, 1878. The first platform or declaration of Liberal principles was a conservative one. It accepted candidly the peace established by the treaty of El Zanjón, and proclaimed the principles which were the bases of that compact. It was an organized, though timid, movement to hold the Spanish Government to the pledges of reforms and enlarged liberties for Cuba. Its programme was comprised under the respective heads of social, political, and economic questions. Its foundation was the liberty of print, freedom of political meeting and association, religious liberty, and the right of petition. Immunity of domicile, of person, of correspondence, and of property was claimed. It demanded the application to Cuba in their integrity of the organic laws of the peninsula, including municipal, provincial, and electoral statutes. Reforms in criminal law were included. It called for a colonial constitutional regimen as a vivification of the lifeless constitution of the monarchy not then promulgated in Cuba. The admission of Cubans to the public offices on equality with Spaniards was also affirmed. Laws which would insure decentralization within the limits of the national unity were indicated. The root trouble was recognized in the demand for a separation and independence of the civil and military powers. An Antillian constitution was declared to be necessary in order that the inhabitants of Cuba might consecrate and organize with respect to its government the principle of responsibility. This was also asserted to be essential in order to reintegrate the possession of the individual rights and the enjoyment of the liberties which were proclaimed in the first article of the constitution of the monarchy as inherent in the condition of the Spanish citizen. The economic difficulty was met with boldness. Suppression of the export duties was demanded. Reforms in the customs were formulated which would prevent the excessive discrimination of the Spanish tariff—a discrimination practised not for the benefit of Cuba, but for the enrichment of Spain. The basis was that the tariff system should be a fiscal and not a differential one. Reciprocity with the United States was particularly specified as desirable. Exclusive white immigration and further emancipation laws for the blacks were favored.

The Union Constitutional party formulated a programme which, in some of its declarations, was the reverse of reactionary. It called for the liberty of the press, the right of petition, of peaceful public meeting, of assimilation in political rights to the other provinces of Spain, of special laws with relation to the particular interests of Cuba, for improved morality in public administration, and for new laws which would be efficacious in securing judicial responsibility. On the economic question it pronounced for customs reforms, special protection for the agricultural production of the island and for the tobacco industry, suppression of export duties, a rational reduction of the imposts, especially on the necessaries of life, and a liberal commercial treaty with the United States on the basis of reciprocity. It favored the abolition of slavery on the terms of the law of Moret, but with modifications suitable to the condition of the country. It also favored immigration under the direction of the government on the basis of free contract.

An echo of the democratic movement in Europe was found in a third platform, but there was no political organization standing upon it. This democratic programme called for free trade, free shipping, free banks, free labor, free teaching, provincial militias, municipal taxes solely, complete abolition of slavery, abolition of the death penalty, and universal suffrage. These planks were in addition to the principles which it indorsed in common with the Liberals and the Union Constitutionals. Spanish laws had not been liberalized to the degree of allowing the propaganda of this theoretical universal democracy. A few Cubans of intellectual strength gave it their approval in the abstract, but it never became an organized political movement. Some of its tenets were subsequently modified and adopted by the Autonomists, and the definite programme was forgotten.

Comparison of the declarations of Liberals and Union Constitutionals does not show a marked divergence. It may be said there were no conflicting principles which afforded a basis for political parties. This is true. In the beginning the difference was simply one of tendencies and of men. The economic ideas were similar, and there was not an essential point of distinction on the social and political articles. Both parties accepted the understanding back of the compact of El Zanjón and the promise of measures to make it effective. The similarity of their creed is the proof that Spain was pledged to grant Cuba political rights which would insure a certain degree of economic independence. The assertion of this understanding was broader and more definite on the part of the Liberals. The programme of the Union Constitutionals reflected more accurately the vice of Spanish politics. There were reservations, checks, and limitations which could be used to defeat the principles that were affirmed. Yet there was recognition of a new regimen under which would be political organizations. The tendency of the Union Constitutionals to become the party of the opposition—not to the authorities in power, but to innovations—was just discernible in the provisos and the checks left in the hands of the peninsula.

With so little cardinal difference in the announced principles of the two groups, the tendencies could be understood only from a knowledge of the men who interpreted and gave them direction. The Liberal party was a Cuban organization, and it so remained. Then and afterwards no leading Spaniards in the island took their stand for autonomy as an avowed creed. The Union Constitutional party might fairly claim the title of conservative from the character of its members. The reactionaries, the Spanish classes who did not accept the concessions to the insurgent elements and who wanted Cuba to continue a dependency of the peninsula without political rights, antagonized it. They were the intransigentes. This term should be understood. For many years the temporary nature of the stay of the Spaniards in Cuba was shown by designating them as *transeuntes*—transients or sojourners. As it was the Spaniards who always stood out against granting whatever Cuba wanted, and as they were the transients, by a Gallic adaptation in political discussion they became known as intransigentes. The etymology is that of Cuban politics. The term is no longer applied solely to the Spanish classes. The instransigente is the irreconcilable, the reactionary, the hopeless Bourbon; the political ostrich who has only one way of avoiding the storm of the desert or the deluge.

The antagonism of the blindly loyal Spanish classes to the enunciated programme of the Union Constitutionals is evidence of its agreement in essentials with the principles of the Liberals. But the inherent tendencies of the two parties developed the difference when interpreted by men of divergent convictions and purposes. The artifical nature of the two organizations formed mechanically as part of a new political regimen was soon lost. Their growth was along natural lines. The Union Constitutionals modified or ignored their original economic precepts. Then they became jealous of the integrity of Spanish institutions in the Antilles. The control passed away from the original supporters. The intransigentes at first had looked with contempt on the group of Union Constitutionals. They began by criticizing its assumptions and combating its principles. They ended by dominating the organization. Whatever party was in power in Spain they were the government party in Cuba. The Union Constitutionals were ministerial under all ministries. Being thus the props of authority, they gradually secured for themselves the official employments, and no Captain-General was strong enough to dislodge them.

The Liberal party celebrated the second anniversary of its foundation in August, 1880, by a reunion of its chief members. The original programme was reaffirmed and broadened. The addresses reflected the disappointment which already had come upon those who had trusted that the understanding back of the pact of El Zanjón would be vitalized and given force. Distrust and suspicion had given way to the conviction that they had been deceived by Madrid. They were discovering that the ruling influence in the peninsula did not mean to concede to Cuba real liberty of political action within even a limited sphere. The ministry of Martínez Campos had fallen in the midst of doubts, perplexities, and hesitation. The ministry of Cánovas del Castillo, always resolute in his opposition to colonial liberties, had taken its place. The Cuban Liberal Autonomists could only deliver addresses voicing their disappointment and their fears. Nor were their voices heard from the housetops. They spoke to one another and among themselves.

The Constitution which had been in force in the peninsula since 1876 was promulgated in Cuba in the spring of 1881. Previous to that there had been prosecution of individuals, usually journalists, who interpreted too literally and too liberally the royal cedulas and the laws enacted by the Cortes following the peace of El Zanjón. Some ayuntamientos, or municipal councils, which sought to apply the new régime to local government too broadly, found themselves stripped of their authority. It was a discouraging experience, which served as a warning and an example to other municipalities. The power of construing the law and the facts rested with the Governor-General, and the construction was commonly on the side of arbitrary power.

The promulgation of the Spanish Constitution did not lessen the prosecution of the journals advocating Liberal principles, though convictions did not always follow. The most notable instance was that of the organ *El Triunfo*, which had not long previously declared that it was not autonomist. The newspaper was charged with attacking the national unity in propagating the autonomist creed or doctrine. Ultimately the judicial tribunal absolved it. Yet the victory for a free press was not a signal one. These prosecutions were effective reminders that the law of imprint had not abolished the censorship of the press. They were meant as warnings against too great freedom of political discussion, and were so accepted. Nor were instances wanting of the arbitrary suppression of journals.

In 1882 the Junta Magna, or central committee, of the Liberal party ceased to apologize and deny that it was autonomist. In April it issued declarations that it favored colonial autonomy under the sovereignty and the authority of the Cortes and the head of the nation. It further demanded identity of civil and political rights for the Spaniards of both hemispheres. This was an effort to propitiate the Spaniards in Cuba, and to obliterate the line which divided insulars and peninsulars. The movement had been growing in strength. With the more open definition of autonomy as a political creed, its vigor spread. The shadow of military government and the press censorship rested over it, yet the organization grew within the shadow. The intransigentes took alarm. They sought to make the political division appear as one between integristas and separatistas. They were the integristas, the defenders of Spanish unity and sovereignty. The Liberals were the separatistas, the traitors who would betray their birthright and encourage the colony to set up an independent government. Autonomy was the viper which, if warmed in the bosom of Spain, would instil the poison that would destroy the national unity. Though the thought was not put in these words, to the intransigentes it was also the monster that would devour the special privileges which made Cuba valuable to Spaniards, if not to Spain.

Students of this period of Cuban political history will find its phases reflected in the newspapers, in manifestoes, allocutions, addresses, and in pamphlets. The addresses, manifestoes, pamphlets, and controversial articles of the journals show a deep knowledge of historical precedents. They go to the root of the causes that destroy empires. They contain all that is true of political and civil liberty in the abstract. In the presentation of these subjects there is more of speculative political philosophy than of practical understanding of the principles of applied government. Beyond this the literature of the day is the ordinary polemics of parties. It is not of the campaign or of the stump as manifested in the United States, for there were no elections of a kind which could give the opportunity for campaign discussion. Pamphleteering was never superseded by newspaper discussion. For the leading Autonomists it is to be said that one true and consistent note is sounded through all the agitation which they carried on for twenty years. This is the warning of the fate which overtakes empires and absolutist governments that refuse to recognize the element of popular representation.

It has been truly said by a Cuban writer,* that "the virile advance of civism among the Cubans through the energetic and spontaneous organization of the Liberal Autonomist party resulted in the awakening of the old intransigente and reactionary party, fearful that the new order of things would undermine the edifice of its interests." The Union Constitutionals rallied against the movement with the passion of tigers whose prey is about to be taken away from them. Yield the first de-

* Cabrera, "Cuba y sus Jueces."

mand of these Autonomists and Spanish sovereignty decrees its own death, was their angry cry. National unity and colonial liberty were analyzed to their ultimate results logically and with ability. The speeches and pronunciamentos of the Autonomist leaders—sometimes radical in talk, as when Antonio Govín, who was in time to become a member of the Autonomist cabinet, called the Spaniards birds of passage—were quoted to show the real purpose of the movement. This was declared to be separation from the mother country.

The Autonomists in their turn would protest, the radical sentiments of individuals would be disclaimed, and the personal controversies would go on. Occasionally these were settled by duels after the French fashion. Throughout the agitation the intransigentes kept steadily before the Spanish classes that whatever threatened or lessened Spanish absolutism threatened their special privileges. It was the *argumentum ad hominem* applied with a tremendous effect. Intellectually, the discussion on the part of the Union Constitutionals was a morass, as discussion usually is in championing vested political wrongs. In this day the historian will not be repaid for losing himself in the bog. The intransigentes were the defenders of the theory of the divine right of Spain to govern the Antilles as possessions rather than as either provinces or colonies. Often, too, they were the inflexible champions of the Church, and charged their opponents with plotting to undermine that support of lawful government.

During this period of political movement, Cuba had representation, of a kind, in the Cortes of Spain. It was of the kind that could be possible only under the system of government which made elections the registering of the will of the governing power. Among the Cuban Deputies and Senators, sometimes as many as half a dozen would be known as Autonomists. Ordinarily one-fourth would be Cuban born, and the remainder peninsulars. Rafael de Labra, the most eminent of the publicists in Spain who advocated colonial government, represented the district of Habana as an Autonomist. Martínez Campos sat as the Conservative Deputy for Matanzas.

How far the Spanish statesmen comprehended the Cuban movement for autonomy must remain undetermined. Emilio Castelar wanted no transatlantic Poland, yet his republican principles did not carry him to the length of advocating complete home rule for Cuba. Moret, who was to formulate the system when it came to be proposed, at that time was giving it little support. Praxades Sagasta, in the regular changes of power which made him the ruler of Spain alternately with Cánovas del Castillo, never suggested home rule for Cuba. The pendulum swung between these two prime ministers; sometimes vibrated with hope of broader and truer parliamentary government for Spain itself, sometimes remained in equilibrium, but never swung loose from the orbit of colonial subjection. Sagasta was up and Cánovas was down: the Liberal party had its vague and hesitating schemes for the Antilles. Cánovas was up and Sagasta was down: the Conservative party had liberal legislation in view, and nothing came of it. If, in the farcical election of Deputies from Cuba to the Cortes, the government in power occasionally permitted an Autonomist to be chosen, it was merely good-natured tolerance. If the Autonomists at times sent delegations to Madrid and were represented by resident committees, this was treated as a colonial chimera not worthy of serious attention. Cánovas had his policy of assimilation by which Spaniards and Cubans were to approach one another in their political rights. But he never yielded his ground that autonomy meant separation of Cuba from the peninsula. And what he called the national actualities, the need of supporting the bureaucratic classes, was always a bar to the real insular government of Cuba by its own people.

In Cuba in time the stubbornness and the aggressiveness of the autonomist propaganda, the steady growth of both industrial and political discontent, produced an effect on what had seemed to be stone. A score and a half of newspapers were advocating the doctrine. The mass of conservatism quavered a little. Then came an era of inquiry. Was it not better to do something to still this perennial discontent? Could not the Cubans be taken into limited partnership in the administration of insular affairs? Could not some of the abuses, the existence of which everybody admitted, be corrected and the system be modified without endangering the national unity? To these questions the majority of the intransigentes returned a passionate No. Yet the agitation, the need of doing something, continued. It came about that the conservatives divided among themselves. The Union Constitutional party had liberal tendencies within its being. It split into right and left wings. The left favored doing something. Its members were known as dissidents. The right favored doing nothing beyond castigating the sowers of sedition. After these divisions came the rapprochements, the reunion of the elements naturally cohesive which had drifted apart. Customarily the basis of reunion was simple. When the irreconcilables found that the reforms proposed in the Cortes were paper reforms, when they learned that the system which to them represented the unity of national sentiment and the preservation of special principles was in no real danger, the dissensions were healed. The Union Constitutional party took back to its bosom the repentant wanderers.

Yet the movement grew. The Autonomist group became as much a political party as it could become under Spanish institutions. Perception of a great truth in human government ultimately dawned upon the more enlightened of the Spanish classes in Cuba. If the agitation would not down, and if the intransigente opposition would make no concessions to this alarming continuance of sentiment, the movement which was going steadily forward might be controlled and diverted into other channels. It was not possible to gain control of the Autonomist party. Had this been feasible, the connection with supposedly separatist principles would have been too marked to permit the Spanish element so to identify itself. The diversion might be made if a new group were formed.

Out of these conditions was born the Reformist party. It had a practical aim. Spaniards who sincerely wanted a more liberal government for Cuba, but who could not afford to join themselves with the Autonomist organization because it was too radical and too Cuban, could shelter themselves under this tenting. The Reformist party embraced many worthy Spaniards and Cubans.

In one respect its aim was definite: it did not contemplate colonial self-government at the expense of Spanish sovereignty. It welcomed the electoral reforms which Maura, the Liberal Minister of the Colonies, proposed in the Cortes in 1890, and in subsequent years. Its members joined the Autonomists in mocking the Union Constitutionals when that party accepted the reforms of Abrazurza offered by the Conservative ministry in the Cortes in 1895.

The Reformist party was formally organized in 1893. It did not advance materially in numbers, but it was a distinct influence, and maintained the shell of an organization till the last. It professed not to favor compromise with the radical tendencies of autonomy, but merely concessions to better government. Towards the end its propaganda was bold and clear. In the despair which was coming over Spanish rule in Cuba with the rising of the insurrection, its efforts partook of the activity of desperation. But there was a fundamental weakness. The poles were positive and negative. The Autonomists affirmed and demanded full colonial liberty. The Union Constitutionals denied and rejected the basis. No magnet midway between them could draw. The Reformists were not a compromise party as compromise had been applied successfully in the United States. They simply favored concessions. At first the name of the Autonomists, the thing to the Conservatives. Later it was a reversal of position with some substance for colonial home rule.

Spanish conservatives who were of liberal tendencies and who foresaw destruction if something were not done joined the Reformists in moments of disgust and reaction from the hopeless Bourbonism of their own party. Timid Autonomists, with the ultimate outcome of separation before them, and face to face with the early probabilities, hesitated, faltered, and turned back. The Reformist standard was their refuge. They, too, became opportunists. The Reformist party pitched its tent on the beach. The waves of revolution were rolling inward. The Reformists raised their brooms to sweep the billows back. The waves broke over the shore, and Conservatives, Reformists, and Autonomists were swallowed in the waters. Their emergence, drowsled and dripping, is the subject for a later chapter of autonomy.

Armed revolt, begun in 1868, had brought the first change in the outward form of Spanish absolutism during four centuries of despotic government. Peaceful agitation following the concessions wrung by the revolutionists of that day had been able to show little further progress in liberalizing the spirit of Spanish political institutions. The energies of the Liberal party in Cuba were absorbed and distraught in seeking to check the reactionary tendencies of parties in Spain which were reverting to the system that had obtained previous to the compact of El Zanjón. When it was apparently going forward the Autonomist party was in reality simply checking the movement backward. There were periods of self-deception and of unconscious deception to the people of the island. Quiescence of the revolutionary elements was mistaken for acquiescence. When the whole world was prospering, industrial prosperity could not be wholly destroyed by official corruption and misgovernment. Sugar production with an abnormally profitable market aided in the temporary quietude. In

1890 it was complacently remarked that the spirit of armed revolution had passed away in the embrace of agitation within constitutional lines by the great Autonomist party. The Cortes was busy with reforms for Cuba. The plans were not for home rule, but they were pledges of improvement which, if carried out, would enable the Autonomists to show that the evolution of colonial self-government in the logical order which they advocated had begun. They were very fond of that phrase, "evolutionary colonial government." Then came the exigencies of Madrid politics, the shifting of ministries and the mockery of the Antillian aspirations for wider liberties. And then, too, came the tariff legislation in the United States, which repealed the Blaine reciprocity legislation and lowered at a stroke the profit of raising sugar-cane in Cuba. The quiescent elements began to move. They were no longer acquiescent. In this inchoate activity was disclosed the abyss which the Autonomists had not been able to bridge. This was the knowledge that the mass of revolutionists of the Ten-Years' war never had been reconciled to Spanish domination.

Antonio Macéo had been a young chief in that war. He had not accepted the regimen of peace, but had consented to depart from the island under a safe-conduct from Martínez Campos. His subsequent life in Central America and the watch which the Spanish authorities kept on his movements are matters of common history. They do not need recounting. Máximo Gómez had retired to his farm in Santo Domingo, and withdrawn himself from participation in the affairs of Cuba. Calixto García, after joining a second abortive rebellion known as the Little War, which raged in Santiago province within a twelvemonth after the peace of El Zanjón, had accepted the friendship of Campos and taken a civil position as a bank officer in Madrid, where he was under espionage. Other leaders of the Ten-Years' war had voluntarily exiled themselves to the United States, to Mexico, and to the countries of Central America. That they did not trust the Spanish promises was evidenced by their actions. Their lack of faith in the success of the Autonomist party was equally clear. Some conspired and plotted. Others merely waited.

The culmination came with the simultaneous failure of Cuban reform legislation in the Cortes and the decrease in the profits of the American sugar market. Economic causes combined with political discontent in keeping the embers of insurrection glowing under the ashes of apparent indifference. The period of freedom from internecine war has been called a parenthesis within a fact. The insurrection of 1895 was the last act in the revolution which began in 1868. There had been an interregnum, nothing more. Armed revolt was coming again.

CHAPTER II

THE WESTERN INVASION

Alarm Bell of Insurrection Sounded—Old Leaders in Arms—Manifesto of Autonomists Reprobates the Insurrection—Subsequent History of the Signers—Activity of Gómez and Macéo—Martínez Campos Takes Command—Battle of Bayamo—Arrival of Spanish Reinforcements—Autonomists Deported—Formation of Revolutionary Government—Gómez' Address to the Cuban People—His Plan for Nationalizing the Insurrection—March to the Occident Begun—Machete as a Weapon—Progress of Insurgents—Campos Quiets Censure of Spanish Classes—Promise of Vigorous Military Operations—Blazing Cane-Fields the Mark of the Insurgent Campaign—Tremor and Turmoil in Habana—Official Orders for Defence—Gómez in the Outskirts—Macéo in the Tobacco Country—The Invasion Gómez' Conception and Macéo's Execution—Spain's Military Power Broken.

TORCH and machete make short work of constitutional agitation. They are not the weapons of political parties. When they were resorted to it was a question whether they would convert the Autonomists into recruits or into enemies of the faith that proclaimed its doctrines by war. A little time had to be allowed before the answer could be given.

It was known in the United States, in the winter months of 1894–95, that something was expected to happen in Cuba. The Spanish authorities in the island were both blind and impotent. They, too, knew that something was going on, yet they did not know where to look for the uprising. One day a small party of insurgents raised the banner of revolt at the hamlet of Ybarra in Matanzas province. Four hundred miles away in the villages of Baire and Juguani, in the province of Santiago de Cuba,* small uprisings also were noted. At Baire the peaceable demand was made for the implantation of the reforms of Maura. At Juguani the demand was for the removal of the local ayuntaimento, or municipal council, because of some alleged malfeasance. At Guantánamo there was an open revolt without a stated grievance.

The movement at Ybarra was premature. The little band of insurgents was quickly dispersed. Some of the leaders were arrested and deported in chains to the penal settlements of Africa, among them the mulatto publicist Juan Gualberto Gómez. Small risings in the province of Santa Clara were also dispersed. But the alarm bell had been sounded. It was to ring through months and years. The night of February 23d, 1895, the printing-presses in Habana were kept whirling with the proclamation of the Governor-General, Emilio Calleja, suspending the constitutional guarantees. This was followed by the official announcement that the provinces of Matanzas and Santiago de Cuba were in a state of war. Then was disclosed the existence of the Cuban revolutionary party with headquarters and branches in the United States, and with a net extended throughout the island the completeness of which was not suspected. All the agencies of secret police and of similar means

* Santiago means St. James. Cubans and Spaniards call the city and the province simply "Cuba."

which were a part of the Spanish system had not uncovered this universal political conspiracy.

José Martí, dreamer, poet, and idealist, had visited Máximo Gómez in his retirement in Santo Domingo, and on behalf of the Cuban revolutionary societies had offered him the command of an insurgent army that was to come up from the earth. Gómez had accepted the command. Antonio Macéo had been communicated with and was ready to aid. The sympathizers in Cuba had been secreting arms, and were awaiting the call. Bartolomé Masó, a sugar-planter at Manzanillo, who had been an insurgent colonel in the Ten-Years' war, was quickly in the field with armed followers. He had the respect of the Spanish classes. Though he had been friendly to the Autonomist propaganda, he had refused to accept the presidency of the party. Masó was said to have taken up arms in order to compel Spain to yield autonomy without granting absolute independence. Minor engagements took place in the Oriente, as Eastern Cuba was called, and within a month the insurrection was in full movement. Spain was sending troops across the ocean, and the leading Spaniards in Habana were calling for more vigorous action by the Government. They were also seeking to place the responsibility for the insurrection. The Union Constitutionals shrieked that the Autonomists had done it all. Insurrection, which meant separation, they cried, was the fruit, as they had warned the loyal classes, of the pernicious doctrines of autonomy.

Thus attacked, the Autonomist leaders through the Magna Junta, or central committee, of the party made vigorous reply. They vindicated their loyalty by offer-

ing their unconditional support to the Government.
They issued an appeal to the country in which they
eulogized themselves and reprobated the insurgents.
The insurrection, they said, had sounded the cry of
revolt at the moment when a new regimen was on the
eve of being inaugurated. They condemned all over-
turning of order because the Liberal-Autonomist party
was a party of legality which had faith in constitutional
methods. Besides, it was fundamentally Spanish because it was essentially and exclusively autonomist.
And colonial autonomy presupposed the reality of the
Metropolis—Spain—in the plenitude of its sovereignty
and of its historic rights. For that reality from its
birth, their party had inscribed on its banner as its
motto, "Liberty, Peace, and National Unity." It also
resented the injurious imputations of its adversaries,
meaning the Union Constitutionals. Recurring to the
rebellion again, the manifesto declared that the insurrection made impossible at that time the liberties which
the Autonomists had conquered. But by good fortune
it would not succeed. All the signs showed that the
rebellion, limited to a part of the eastern provinces, had
with a few exceptions only succeeded in dragging into
it the classes proceeding from the most ignorant and
destitute of the population, who from lack of cohesion
and discipline would soon disperse or give themselves
up. The Liberal party of 1868 had folded its standard
and abandoned its post to the revolutionists of Yara.
The Liberal party of 1878 would not lower its flag nor
cede the field to those who came to undo their laborious
harvest and cloud the perspective of their destinies with
the horrible spectre of misery, anarchy, and barbarism.

By their characterization of the ignorant classes it will be observed that the Autonomist leaders did not consider the insurrection respectable. They themselves were eminently respectable. Their natural opponents, the Union Constitutionals, while denouncing them and their policies, always conceded their respectability. They proved poor prophets, because instead of the insurrection failing from lack of cohesion and discipline, it grew more coherent and put disciplined ranks in the field. But truly the classes who formed its base were not respectable. They were farm laborers, workers in the cane-fields who had never risen to a high condition of education. Nor had they ever given support to the movement for autonomy, because the leaders of that movement, while championing the system of popular government, had no knowledge from experience of the function of the masses in popular government. The manifesto in its reference to the liberties the Autonomists had conquered meant the reforms of Abarzurza. Having been unable to obtain the reforms of Maura, they accepted the diluted substitute as a step in their programme of evolutionary autonomy.

It is instructive to follow the history of the signers of this manifesto, and of other Autonomists not members of the central committee who indorsed it. The majority of them had been for fifteen years and more advocating the principles of the party. They could say with truth that they had cradled the organization. In the years that were to come, some remained unwavering in the support which they had pledged to the Government of Spain. Among them were found apologists and eulogists of Weyler. But others went into voluntary exile, unable to stand between the two firing-lines. Many joined the insurgents in the manigua or brush. Some became involuntary exiles or political prisoners, because they either fell away from the policy announced in the manifesto, or because their support was not zealous enough to satisfy the military authorities.

This manifesto of the Liberal-Autonomist party was published on the 4th of April. The insurrection had been in movement for six weeks. Martínez Campos, the pacificator of the former revolution, had been named Governor-General of the island, and had sailed for his post. Antonio Macéo, his brother José, and a score of companions who formed the expedition from Costa Rica had disembarked near Baracoa on the north coast. A troop of Spanish volunteers lay in waiting for them. There was fighting in the hills, and some members of the expedition were taken prisoners. The brothers Macéo escaped, and Antonio placed himself in command of the increasing bands of insurgents in the eastern regions. Within a fortnight José Martí and Máximo Gómez landed near Guantánamo. Martí was the president of the revolutionary party. He had been a student in Seville and Madrid, and was old enough to be imprisoned during the Ten-Years' war for complicity in that uprising. He was not a military chief. Martí lost his life in combat with the Spanish troops on the banks of the Contraestre River, in the western part of the province, within five weeks after his arrival. Gómez at once took command of the insurgent forces which began coming up from the earth to receive him.

Two days after the secret landing of Martí and

Gómez, General Campos disembarked in the port of Guantánamo. He immediately assumed his office as Governor-General and Captain-General of the island, without waiting to take the formal oath and undergo the ceremonies customary at Habana. At that time the Spanish authorities estimated that the insurgents under arms in the province numbered 5,000. General Campos issued an address to the people, and organized energetic military operations. In proclaiming martial law he enjoined on his own soldiers the recognized principles of humane warfare. His policy was to win back the insurgents by kindness, and to show them that they could trust the indulgence of Spain. At this time he had 27,000 troops under his command. After remaining in Santiago a week he proceeded to Habana.

While Campos was combating the insurrection with the sword in one hand and the promise of pardon in the other, Gómez and Macéo were pushing it westward through Santiago to the thinly populated province of Puerto Príncipe. These Camagüeyans, as the natives of the central part of the island are called, were, like the inhabitants of Santiago de Cuba, perennial foes of Spanish power. The Autonomist party had an organization in Puerto Príncipe which reaffirmed its condemnation of the insurrection and its earnest desire to uphold the military authorities. After drawing to the ranks of the insurrection the leading Cubans of Camagüey, Gómez retired to the southern part of Santiago province. In the mean time General Campos had taken command in person of the Spanish troops in the field, and was directing the movements in that region. The volunteers in many places had been called into action and were supporting the regular troops. The guerillas, or native Spanish forces, organized in the different communities, and the movilazados, or irregular native forces, were also being utilized.

On July 13th was fought the first real battle of this war. It was at Peralejo, near Bayamo. Macéo and Jesus Rabí were known to be contemplating a descent on the Spanish garrison which held Bayamo. The columns under Campos were advancing from Manzanillo. The Spanish troops, according to the statement of the officers, numbered 1,600. The insurgents under Macéo, the Spaniards afterwards said, numbered between 5,000 and 6,000. There may have been 3,000 of them who fell upon the advancing Spanish columns of equal number,—certainly more than 1,600,—attacking them in front and in the rear. General Juan Fidel Santocildes, a distinguished officer and the devoted friend of Campos, was killed at the head of his column. Other officers were killed and wounded. General Campos himself narrowly escaped death. By a strategic movement, turning his rear-guard into the van-guard and changing the course, he succeeded in leading his troops into Bayamo. The laurels of the engagement were with Macéo, and the insurgent cause gained prestige. General Campos, after strengthening the fortifications of Bayamo and increasing the garrison, succeeded in clearing the country in the immediate neighborhood of the insurgents, who confined their activity to the northern part of the province. He then returned to Manzanillo.

Through the remaining months of the summer the insurgent activity was greatest in las Villas, which is the province of Santa Clara, or, as the Cubans call it, Villa Clara. One uprising followed another, and one band after another took to the manigua. The successful disembarkment of filibustering expeditions on the south coast with arms and recruits for the insurgents kept the fires of revolution flaming. The military authorities were energetic, but the bands of insurgents in the province managed to avoid many encounters with the troops. They attacked isolated Spanish garrisons successfully, though in some of the combats they were worsted. In Santiago de Cuba Macéo was active, and his followers had several sharp engagements with the enemy. At Sao del Indio a column of 1,000 Spanish soldiers attacked a force of insurgents under Macéo alleged to number 3,000, and probably numbering half as many, and dispersed them. All this time reinforcements were coming from the peninsula. By the end of summer a total of 80,000 Spanish regulars were in the field. A thousand loyal Spaniards had come from the Argentine Republic and Brazil to the city of Santiago de Cuba, and enrolled themselves as volunteers. Subsequently more Spaniards arrived from South America, and also from Mexico. In Habana the disembarking of the battalions was a weekly occurrence. The Leon battalion, that of the Asturias, of Barcelona, of Valencia, and of other provinces in Spain showed that the army was recruited from all parts of the peninsula. The insurgents may have had 20,000 men in arms and without arms, though this is a liberal estimate.

During this period happened an untoward circumstance. It was a rude shock to the credulous and loyal Autonomists. General Campos began deporting Autonomists to the penal settlements of Africa without civil or military trial and without explanation. In the latter part of September, four leading citizens of Santiago de Cuba were deported to Ceuta by his orders. They were Don Eutaldo Tamayo, president of the provincial deputation and also president of the local autonomist central committee; Antonio Brava, an educator; Alfredo Betancourt, a lawyer; and Desiderio Ortiz, a journalist. Clearly these men did not belong to the ignorant and destitute classes of whom the central committee of the Autonomist party had written in the celebrated manifesto reprobating the insurrection. Their political associates in Habana sought their releases, but the Captain-General denied the request for reasons which were thought to indicate knowledge of complicity in the insurrection. Later, by his direction, other Autonomists were deported. Military executions of insurgent cabecillas, or chiefs, who were captured in arms also began. These chiefs received more consideration than the Autonomist suspects exiled without trial, for they had the benefit of summary court-martial.

The revolutionists, on their part, were beginning to destroy sugar plantations and blow up railroads and trains with dynamite. They also formed their provisional Cuban republic in the woods with Salvador Cisneros Betancourt, better known as the Marquis de Santa Lucia, as President. The possessor of a Cuban patent of nobility and answering all the requirements of breeding and education, a revolutionist of 1868, he had taken into the field with him many young men of the older families of Villa Clara. The insurgent chiefs met and organized an assembly at Jimaguayu, a corner of Puerto Príncipe. They decided that the revolutionary civil government should be kept separate from the military administration. They confirmed Gómez as general-in-chief and Macéo as next in command. Bartolomé Masó yielded his commission in the field to become Vice-President of the provisional government, and he subsequently succeeded the Marquis de Santa Lucia as President. A civil cabinet was also formed. This assembly adopted the first constitution of the Cuban republic. Its creator, the provisional government, sought recognition from the United States. Nominally the provisional government in the woods was the supreme power. It issued commissions and directed the movements of the insurgent army. Nominally, too, Gómez and Macéo and the other insurgent commanders respected and obeyed it. Actually the provisional government registered their plans, or if it did not it was ignored by them. At all times the Junta in New York, of which Estrada Palma was the head and Gonzalo de Quesada the representative in Washington, was the more potent body, for it raised and disbursed the funds and managed the filibustering expeditions. The tribute or tax levied by Gómez on the sugar planters and railroad managers was frequently paid directly to the representatives of the Junta.

Six months of revolt passed before the Spanish Government in Cuba knew that the insurrection had a regularly organized plan of compaign. Insurgent maurading bands, though acknowledging the orders of Gómez or Macéo while engaging in guerilla warfare, did not themselves fully realize that they were working as part of a whole. Macéo knew it, and the veteran chief of the revolution knew it. In the autumn of 1895 his plans began to take form. On assuming command of the insurgent forces, Gómez had issued an address to the Cuban people. It is worth reading in the light of the history that has since been made. Its language may appear verbose and extravagant to the unsentimental American mind. To the emotional people of the Latin and the African races, for whom the address was meant, it was neither verbose nor extravagant. In this manifesto Gómez promised to lead them in the struggle for their liberties. Though the words were glowing, the difficulties and the supreme nature of the task before them was set out with mathematical precision. Spain, he warned them, would never yield Cuba to its people while the land was worth possessing. She would only yield when there was nothing to keep. And the inhabitants of Cuba must be prepared for the sacrifice. Every household, he declared, would have its martyr before the island became free.

In this address Gómez put forth other ideas, though not with the distinctness with which they existed in his own mind. If not local, the Ten-Years' war had been at least provincial. It was confined to the central and eastern part of the island. Barely an émeute had taken place in the west. If Cuba were to be freed from Spain, Gómez knew that the revolution must be made universal. He proposed to nationalize the insurrection. Many young Cubans and some older ones had joined it believing that they could engage in a guerilla warfare in the neighborhood of their own homes. Gómez did not understimate the value of this support. He used this local aid, but did not depend upon it.

Instead, he took the most capable of the recruits and sent them to commands in other localities. From Habana he chose officers for Puerto Príncipe. From Pinar del Río he selected officers for the bands in Santa Clara. The development of this plan was coincident with the broader purpose of nationalizing the insurrection by making war throughout the island. The western invasion began late in the fall, at the end of the rainy season. The insurgents were leaving parts of Santiago de Cuba in a state of comparative calm while their bands were spreading west and attacking the Spanish garrisons. One of these assaults was on the fort of Cascarro, in Puerto Príncipe, which was made notable by the heroic defence of the Spanish soldiers.

As the insurrection developed in intensity, the peninsular classes in the island were alarmed and disgusted by rumors that a peace had been agreed upon with autonomy as a basis. The rumors were without foundation. The Autonomists were in eclipse with both insurgents and the Madrid Cabinet. Gómez crossed the Júcaro-Morón trocha with a force of 1,200 or 1,500 mounted Camagüeyans on the 30th of October. This trocha or trench runs from coast to coast a few miles east of the Santa Clara line, and is known as the railroad trocha. It was established and maintained during the Ten-Years' war, and was again garrisoned as soon as the insurrection broke out. Gómez circled from Sancti Spiritus, in the southeastern part of Santa Clara, to the northwest, in the direction of Remedios, like a hawk. He reduced several small forts and released the Spanish soldiers who were taken prisoners. During November his forces fought with the Spanish troops at

Manacas, Rio Grande, Covadanga, and other villages or sugar plantations. Later he moved eastward again and formed a junction with Macéo, who had advanced from Santiago province through Puerto Príncipe, meeting little resistance. They attacked a Spanish convoy under General Segura at Iguara, and, though having a superior force, were repulsed. Macéo crossed the Morón trocha on December 10th at Ciego de Avila, its central point.

The march to the Occident, the western invasion, was begun. Las Villas—Santa Clara province—was the basis of military operations for this irregular insurgent army which had mysterially mobilized itself. General Campos and his military advisers had foreseen the danger in that region, which was tremulous with the enthusiasm of revolution. They had also seen the signs in Matanzas and even in the provinces of Habana and Pinar del Río. If the insurrection made headway in las Villas they knew they would have to combat more than spasmodic outbreaks in the west. General Campos took command in person in Santa Clara, with his headquarters at Cienfuegos. In that central section of the island he had not fewer than 20,000 troops. Gómez and Macéo divided their bands, and the Santiago negro farmer Quintin Banderas, who had developed capacity for getting small parties over the country with marvellous rapidity, baited the Spanish columns. On the 15th of December was fought the battle of Mal Tiempo. It was one of the genuine combats of the insurrection, though the number of men engaged in it was not large. Mal Tiempo was a village thirty miles northwest of Cienfuegos. Gómez and Macéo watched the engagement and directed it. Part of their forces harassed the Canaries and the Bailén battalions when the Spanish columns were marching through the brush, and galled them with a musketry fire. In the open road a party of insurgents, armed with machetes, fell upon a company of the Bailén battalion and annihilated it. This assault gave the machete a terror to the Spanish troops. In the previous brushes with the insurgents they had learned something of its effectiveness at close quarters, but the annihilation of the entire company was to them a frightful revelation of its possibilities. The machete was more dangerous than the Spanish shortsword, possibly because the insurgents who wielded it had trained their right arms to its use in cutting cane on the sugar plantations. Many of them served through the insurrection without possessing firearms. The weapon was used in other engagements, yet the machete charges by battalions of insurgents of which vivid accounts were related were rare in the actual warfare.

Gómez and Macéo advanced northwest through Santa Clara to Matanzas province. Their movements were aided by a troop of insurgents under General Lacret Morlot, who constantly diverted the attention of the enemy. General Campos sought to throw his columns in a living trocha along the line to intercept them. He could not overtake them with his troops that were scattered through las Villas. Those in Habana and Matanzas provinces were his trust, and they were moved quickly eastward. Experienced generals — Prats, Luque, and Suaréz Valdés—were at their head. The insurgent leaders misled and evaded the Spanish generals. Their forces, partly mounted, appeared unexpectedly in the neighborhood of Colón on the railroad in the eastern part of Matanzas province. Blazing canefields announced their presence. The Spanish troops, including the battalion of the Asturias, were saved from rout in the encounters on the sugar plantations only by bringing up their artillery, which consisted of several field-pieces. The insurgents retired along the road eastward towards the town of Santo Domingo. General Campos himself was at the head of the column on the road between Cimarrones and Jovellanos which it was supposed the insurgents were following; but Gómez appeared in the hamlet of Roque, closer to Colón. The insurgents had outwitted the Captain-General. Three groups or parties were moving for a junction in the hamlet of Coliseo. One was under General Emilio Nuñez, one to the north under Macéo, and the forces of Gómez to the south and east. They entered Coliseo and destroyed it. Campos encountered them in the adjacent sugar plantation of Audaz. The insurgents had their lines resting along the base of the hills in front and in the manigua, or chapparal, flanking the Spanish troops. They barred the advance of the columns and harassed the rear-guard. General Campos himself, for the second time—the first had been at Peralejo—was in danger of losing his life. His adjutant by his side was wounded. Night came on and stopped the engagement. Before morning the insurgents had disappeared. They retired eastward towards the village of Jaguey Grande, as if retreating to Villa Clara.

At Jaguey, Gómez and Macéo reviewed their forces.

The Spanish officers at the time said that they had in all 10,000 men. Later the insurgents declared that their force was larger, but the statement was made for effect. The Spanish troops in active service in Cuba at this time were in excess of 100,000. From March to December 79,500 had been embarked from the peninsula; the regulars previously on the island had been sent to the field, and their numbers had been augmented by the volunteers and the local guerillas. Figures published in the Habana newspapers in the last days of December, 1895, placed the full number of the Spanish forces, active and in reserve, at 189,000. This included the whole body of volunteers, 63,000; but they were largely a reserve force, and did not go out of the cities and towns. While the insurgents had been marching across the country the harbor of Habana had been filled with transports disembarking the soldiers from the peninsula. General Luis Pando, next in rank to Campos, had arrived and had taken command in Santiago de Cuba. General Pando was supposed to have talents as a politician which would be serviceable in dealing with the insurgent leaders in the Oriente. The sugar plantations there were also aflame, and sharp combats between the troops and small bands of elusive rebels were of common occurrence.

The Captain-General returned to Habana, where it was felt that he had suffered defeat. He found it necessary to meet the movement that was arising against him for his ill success in checking the spread of the insurrection. The Autonomists proposed a political manifestation to show that bad fortune had not caused Campos to lose the confidence of the country. The

Reformists joined it, hesitating and doubtful. The Union Constitutionals held back. They were full of resentment towards the Captain-General, yet were not quite ready for a public rupture. Out of the divided opinions among themselves it was finally agreed that they should take part in the demonstration. Their spokesman was Santos Gúzman, a violent intransigente. He referred dubiously to the circumstances, difficult, as it seemed, in which the country was laboring, but promised the loyal co-operation of the Union Constitutionals. Rafael Montoro spoke for the Autonomists, pledging their continued support. A word was also said for the Reformists. General Campos, in responding, felicitated himself on the consoling union of the three parties. He had thought of resigning, he said, because of the apparent lack of unanimity in public sentiment in supporting him; but with these evidences of approval he would reorganize the military operations, and so long as all parties continued to honor him with their confidence he would not separate himself from the island. The clouds were lowering over the head of the pacificator, yet his feet were still on firm earth. The demonstration for the moment quieted the distrust and the growing movement, which was in reality a political conspiracy, to demand his recall.

The insurgents burned their way southwest through the province of Matanzas. They entered Habana province with a pillar of fire by night and black clouds by day. Gómez had said in his address to the Cuban people that Spain would never yield the island while it was worth possessing. He was showing how it might be rendered not worth possessing. Various military proclamations by him had signalized the destruction of the sugar crop as the surest means of crippling Spain's resources. Nightly the skies were lit up by the blazing cane-fields. Tall chimneys in the centre of gaping, scorched plains were all that was left of the great centrales or sugar mills. Blackened walls were all that told of country villas. In the villages and towns the ruins were all that remained of fine residences and substantial buildings. The destruction was not wanton. The insurgents did not riot in it. It was in pursuance of Gómez' campaign against property. They did not seek to take human lives. They released Spanish prisoners when captured, and in their successful march were always merciful to the small garrisons that were reduced. In regular fighting they would have been overmatched and in time their small numbers would have been exterminated. So they applied the most advanced principles of modern warfare by systematic and remorseless destruction of property. It was also said that one purpose of Gómez was to force the plantation workers to join the insurrection by taking away their means of livelihood. Such a course was not necessary. The plantation hands flocked to the insurrection voluntarily, almost spontaneously. Later General Weyler was also to inaugurate a campaign of property destruction and to dispute the mastery of the scorched and barren wastes with Gómez. But in the beginning it was the insurgents under Gómez and Macéo who made the trail of fire from Villa Clara to Pinar del Río.

Martial law was proclaimed in the provinces of Habana and Pinar del Río as a tardy New Year's greeting on January 2d, 1896. The whole island was therefore officially recognized as in a state of siege. The military operations of the Spanish troops in the western regions were paralyzed. The vanguard of Gómez advanced to Marianao, within ten miles of Habana. The insurgents occupied Punta Brava, Hoyo Colorado, and other towns in the vicinity. Cane-fields were burned, railroad stations destroyed, trains given to the flames, tracks torn up, and bridges dynamited. The railroads running out of the city ceased to operate their trains.

Habana was in tremor and turmoil. Though troops had been disembarking by tens of thousands, it felt itself defenceless. Though its fortifications and defences, properly garrisoned, could hold out, as was later boasted, against an invading army of 100,000 American soldiers, the community recoiled before a few thousand half-armed insurgents. Panic stalked its streets. The military authorities were overwhelmed with the pleas to protect the city and its people. To calm the perturbed public mind, show that the defences were sufficient and the army authorities alert, General Arderius, chief of the general staff, issued an order.* This was one of the most remarkable documents of the insurrection. It reprobated the cowardly insurgents for flying from every encounter with the valiant troops, but in order to guarantee absolute tranquillity gave an account of the measures of protection. The signal of alarm, this military manifesto said, would be five consecutive cannon discharges from the Castillo del Príncipe and the raising of the flag on that fort by day, or a streamer under the flag on holidays. By night the signal would be a red light on the flag-pole. This red light would

* The full text may be found in "Crónicas de la Guerra" for 1896.

be displayed also by the other forts when they saw the signal from Castillo del Príncipe. Minute directions were given to avoid false signals. The true signal once given—that is, the cannon discharges and the floating flag or the red light—the various bodies of troops would form in designated places. A caution was enjoined against allowing the cornets to be played while the troops were concentrating. Full instructions for the army formations followed. They filled several pages.

The public alarm was increased instead of being calmed by this official proclamation. Castillo del Príncipe commands the highest hill in the environs of Habana. It did not come about that the flag was raised on its standard and the five consecutive cannon discharges made, yet the inhabitants of the city shivered for days and nights awaiting that signal. Habana had passed through the Ten-Years' war without hearing the echo of a musket discharge from the insurgents in the Oriente. The difference between the two insurrections in their ultimate probabilities is shown by the necessity of giving publicity to the cannon signal. It recalled the measures against English attack one hundred and thirty-four years earlier. Gómez knew where to let the demonstration stop. He never had the purpose of entering within the garrisoned outposts of the city. Yet he did enter the town of Bejucal, only fifteen miles south, burned many of its buildings, and spread terror to the great city northward. Two or three days later in Bejucal again he successfully combated and evaded the Spanish troops under Generals Linares and Suaréz Valdés. For a time thereafter he operated on the south coast.

Macéo and Gómez had divided their followers in pursuance of a specific plan. Macéo was pushing on to the west, not seeking to avoid the Spanish troops at some places, and at others carefully evading them. While Gómez was terrorizing Habana, Macéo entered the province of Pinar del Río. He had a sharp skirmish at the town of Guanajay, near the north coast, with the Spanish troops under General Prats. He ranged through the rich tobacco regions of the Vuelta Abajo as he had done in the sugar lands of Santa Clara and Matanzas. Constantly the insurgent forces were augmented by small parties of recruits. Never before had Pinar del Río been in either secret or open rebellion. Now it blazed with revolt. Macéo carried his standard to the extreme western end of the island. During the last week of January he entered the town of Pinar del Río and held it for a few hours. The following day he fought a pitched battle on the adjacent hills of Taironas, in which, notwithstanding the Spanish accounts, he could claim a victory, for it crowned his purpose. Macéo then turned and led his forces towards the eastern end of the province. On the 6th of February he attacked the railroad town of Candaleria and besieged it for twenty-six hours. The Spanish troops, the Volunteers, made a brave defence and Macéo retired. He next occupied the village of Paso Real. Another genuine battle was fought on the calzada, or highway, leading from this town. The Spanish troops under General Luque had both artillery and cavalry. The artillery was employed with some effect. The insurgents also had cavalry, and it was here as at Mal Tiempo that a genuine machete charge was made. The insurgent horsemen, according to the story of the Spanish soldiers, bore down upon their columns in a crescent with such impetuosity that they were forced back. Finally the Spanish troops were rallied and made a successful stand. The fighting lasted several hours. Macéo led his followers in many charges. The losses on each side were nearly equal—possibly 100 killed and 200 or 300 wounded.

Thereafter Macéo ranged through the southern part of Habana province. He encountered the Spaniards at Artemisa. A week later General Linares attacked him unsuccessfully near Güines. For a fortnight he moved back and forth through the southern part of Matanzas. Later he returned to Pinar del Río. For eight months he combated, in the western part of the island, the heavy reinforcements which General Weyler threw into that section. The trocha running across the narrowest neck from Mariel on the north to the south coast had been constructed in the mean time. Macéo crossed it in December with a small band, and with the supposed purpose of moving eastward to las Villas. He was killed in an encounter with the Spanish troops on the morning of December 7th, 1896, at a point in the woods four miles from Punta Brava, within fifteen miles of Habana. The weight of evidence is that it was a chance encounter, and not a betrayal or an ambush.

Macéo's real work was completed ten months before his death, when he massed his troops for the struggle on the hills of Taironas. He had brought most of them six hundred miles across the country. Some of his officers declare that he had 11,000 men with him when he swept around Habana and into the province of Pinar del Río.   This march sometimes has been described as a mere raid.   Students of military campaigning who follow its course and who examine the number and the disposition of the Spanish troops will give it a higher rank.   It was in verity an invasion.   Spanish officers in the later times showed with pride the decorations which were conferred upon them for engagements with the insurgents under Macéo's command.   To have engaged the mulatto chieftain in combat was a title to distinction.   The glory of the full execution of the western invasion is to Macéo, yet its conception is to the grizzled chief of two revolutions.   Gómez planned it.   The success of his plans nationalized the insurrection and broke the military power of Spain in Cuba.

CHAPTER III

Campos and Weyler

Climax of Conspiracy Against Campos—Madrid Accepts Resignation—Campos' Prophecy of Spain Losing Dominion—Gómez in Sight at the Departure—Two Men Who Understood Each Other—Arrival of Weyler—Welcome by Spanish Classes—End of Policy of Moral Agencies—Culmination of Fighting Period of the Insurrection—Issue of First Concentration Decree—Prison Camps for Pacificos—Failure of Weyler's Military Operations—Attitude of American People—Policy of the Cleveland Administration—Abuse of Naturalization Laws—Consul-General Fitzhugh Lee's Reports—Inauguration of McKinley—Changed Attitude of Spain—Visit of Special Commissioner Calhoun to Cuba—Assassination of Cánovas—Sagasta Ministry Proposes Autonomy.

Columbus piloted the standard of Spain to Cuba. Martínez Campos bore it back. He was not the last of the Captain-Generals, but when he yielded his charge and withdrew from the island Spain's sovereignty in the Antilles was ended. Thereafter what was maintained was the figment of power. The fate of her dominion was sealed.

It was during Christmas week that the movement of the Spanish politicians in Habana against Campos was temporarily checked. Within a fortnight it was blazing forth. It had a degree of popular discontent among the Spanish classes to strengthen it. Yet the discontent was not universal. The Habana Volunteers, who during the Ten-Years' war had dominated Captain-Generals and had speeded their departure from the island, were not antagonistic to Campos. They were not the same aggressive organization that they had been during the previous period of insurrection, though they retained the strength of armed organization and of unwavering loyalty to Spain. The Spanish Casino, which was controlled by the higher classes of Spaniards and which was still a potent influence, was not more hostile to Campos than it had been to other Captain-Generals. The first move did not come from them. The Reformists were the opportunists of Cuban politics. They had advocated reforms and had upheld Campos. But they were weathercocks as well as opportunists. When the opposition began to develop strength the Reformists turned against the Captain-General. Their newspapers were filled with articles inculcating distrust and calling the situation an insupportable one. The Union Constitutionals also became open in their demands for a change in policy and in men to carry out policies. Madrid was deluged with telegrams of a disquieting nature.

General Campos met the emergency like a soldier. He convoked the chiefs or leaders of the three parties in the palace of the Governor-General. Then he demanded to know the meaning of recent affairs. Santos Gúzman, the Andalusian who three weeks before had promised hearty and loyal support, was again the spokesman of the Union Constitutionals. He declared that the party was not in conformity with the policy of Campos. The Reformist spokesman echoed the same sentiment. The Autonomists, faithful among the faithless, renewed their adhesion. General Campos said that he was only a soldier, and that if he had lost the confidence of the elements whose union was necessary he would not remain. He sent a message to Cánovas in Madrid, giving the result of the conference, and adding that the Autonomists believed the policy he had followed should be continued.

The night of January 17th, 1896, it was known in Habana that Madrid had yielded and that the resignation of Campos had been presented and accepted. General Sabás Marín was named his successor temporarily. General Campos, in turning over his office to General Marín, made an address in which he said that the public opinion against concessions to the enemy, such as he had made, existed, but was unfounded. In the Ten-Years' war he had caused the rebels to be executed and they had retaliated in like manner. Now they were following a different course. They wished to raise the structure of independence on the ruins of the country. They burned and destroyed, but they did not harm the Spanish soldiers. They released prisoners and cared for the wounded. Therefore a different means was necessary to combat the present war. He had caused chiefs of the insurrection to be shot, and others to be condemned to perpetual chains, but it was because they had been taken in the acts of incendiarism.

General Campos also spoke of the demands on Madrid for his recall as though they had not been spontaneous. He issued a brief and dignified farewell to the army. After he ceased to be Governor-General he talked to the Habana journalists of the political conspiracy which had made it necessary for him to retire. The traitorship of the Union Constitutionals and Reformists, he declared, was the cause, and he spoke with bitterness of the domineering caprice of certain classes. Of Cuba he declared that which had happened would not have happened if it had been treated as a province of the peninsula. He uttered the warning that if the system were not changed it would confirm once more the historic apothegm, that Spain had lost dominion of America through the fault of the Spaniards. Prophetic words were these. General Campos sailed on January 20th. As he was about to embark he said to those who bade him farewell: "My successor will fail as I have failed." He dictated a message to the Madrid Cabinet, in which he said he had not known how to content all parties, although they had not been just. This was another way of saying that the Spanish classes in Cuba had driven him from power and must accept the responsibility of subduing the insurrection after their own manner. On his arrival in Coruña, General Campos maintained silence in response to popular demonstrations. General Lanchez Bregua, his military friend and voyage companion, said if he would speak his thoughts they would be that on par with vigorous military action must be guarantees of administrative and political reforms, even to autonomy.

The day on which General Campos embarked from Habana, Máximo Gómez with his insurgent followers was encamped on the hills of Lajas on the road to the plain of Güines, almost within sight of the city. It is said that persons in Habana scanning the surrounding country from their housetops with strong glasses were able to see the camp of Gómez. The insurgents knew that Campos was leaving. If ever two men understood each other, they were Máximo Gómez and Martínez Campos; and if ever two men knew Cuba and the Cubans, they were the ones. They had arranged the pact of El Zanjón. Gómez had retired to Santo Domingo; and Campos had returned to Spain, vainly to strive to implant the reforms and even the principles of political liberty which were the basis of that pledge. None knew better than he how shameful had been the betrayal and how complete the failure of the reforms. Knowing that, he could appreciate the intensity of the feeling which animated the Cubans. He also grasped the new plan of campaign which Gómez inaugurated in this insurrection. He knew that the Spanish intransigentes had no conception of its scope and possibilities, and that they would beat against it hopelessly. Gómez, on his part, knew that the recall of Campos ended the possibility that the Cubans would be seduced from the insurrection by conciliatory methods. He knew that the first acts of the intransigente authority, when it should be free to act, would be in the line of greater rigor and blinder folly. The Union Constitutionals thought the recall of Campos was their triumph. They could not perceive that it was a victory for Máximo Gómez and Antonio Macéo.

General Valeriano Weyler, marquis of Tenerife, was appointed the successor to Campos. After an interval of a few weeks he arrived and relieved General Marín. The Spanish classes welcomed him with real enthusiasm. They had an inspiration of what his coming meant. Madrid had heeded their demands. The dependence on moral agencies to combat the insurrection, the policy of conciliation and attraction which Campos had sought to employ, would cease. In its place would come rigorous and relentless action against the Cubans. A score of years had not blotted out the memory of the new Captain-General's record in Cuba when he was first the Colonel and then the Brigadier Weyler, and always the Butcher. The veterans of the Ten-Years' war remembered engagements between him and Gómez. The insurgents' welcome was an attack on the town of Managua, fifteen miles from Habana, and a raid to the gates of the city.

It might almost be said that armed revolution ceased with the departure of Campos, though actually there was some vigorous fighting after Weyler took command. But the Cubans had put forth their supreme fighting ability in the first fifteen months. They could not surpass those efforts, nor could they expect to continue them on the same scale. They had spread revolution in every province and in every hamlet of the island. Now their aim was to keep the insurrection alive until Spain yielded, because Cuba was not worth the sacrifice of blood and money which it was costing the peninsula, or until the United States intervened. The recognition of belligerency would have been grateful to them, but it was of small consequence how the United States came into the struggle, provided it could be actually drawn in.

After the recall of Campos, the insurrection gained absolutely the support of the middle-class Cubans. Though sharing the aspirations of their people for political liberty, they were not certain it could be achieved by fire and musket against the superior forces of Spain, and they were doubtful of the ability of their people to maintain an independent government. Autonomy under

Campos would have held a portion of them to Spanish authority. Under Weyler they all became revolutionists, and the insurgent juntas in the towns and cities were strengthened by their accession.

General Weyler began by publishing the usual bandos, offering amnesty to the insurgents who presented themselves and sought pardon. The first concentration decree was issued within a week after his coming. The story of the reconcentration fits into the last chapter of Spain's efforts to subdue the insurrection. It was the belief in Cuba that the plan was conceived by Cánovas del Castillo, and that Weyler was merely the instrument. Many circumstances supported this view; but the instrument was a willing one, and Philip II. had no more faithful servant in the Duke of Alva than the relentless Premier of Spain had in General Valeriano Weyler.

Of the concentration itself, a paragraph will suffice to tell the story. It was a thorough military measure, but it failed to accomplish military results. And it did not recognize the principles of civilized warfare which require that prisoners shall be fed. The country people—the pacificos—were shut up in prison camps. Often they were herded in settlements enclosed within stockades or trenches, with forts commanding every approach and troops on guard. When they were permitted to wander in the larger towns the bounds were still set by military lines which kept them within the prison camp. No system of issuing rations to them was ever carried out. They were left to live on the charity of the beggared communities in which they were herded. Spain did not recognize the principle of humanity in its treatment of the pacificos—the women and children, the non-combatants who were made prisoners by Weyler's decrees. That was the essence of it all. No apologists could ever alter this fact, and the defenders of military measures could not defend this enforced starvation. But famine did not conquer and could not conquer insurrection, though in time it would have exterminated the non-combatant portion of the rural population. Concentration was the confession of Spain that it could only keep the island without the people.

When General Weyler arrived, Spain had poured 117,000 troops into Cuba. The Cánovas ministry continued to send him recruits. His military operations were active. Since the insurgents had carried the rebellion to the western end of the island, he sought to isolate it and partition it. The building of the trocha from Mariel to Artemisa was one measure. It was not a difficult feat of military engineering to dig ditches along either side of the highway, garrison them with forts and barracks at short intervals, and to unroll barbed-wire fencing on either side. That was the trocha.

General Weyler, in the beginning, threw most of his reinforcements into the province of Pinar del Río. After the death of Macéo he moved heavy battalions into the interior, into Santa Clara. That section had now become the centre of Gómez' operations. After various encounters with the Spanish troops, Gómez retired to the heart of Villa Clara, and from there he directed the scattered forces of the insurgents. The time for opposing the Spanish troops by open encounters was past, and Gómez himself never intended that they should meet in battle. He rarely had with him 500 men, but he kept the insurgent troops moving in small bands in pursuance of a general plan. In Santiago province it might be said that the war was waged on an independent basis, and there was occasional fighting even to the time of the invasion of the province by the American army. General Calixto García, after being wrecked on the Hawkins filibustering expedition, had reached the island, and after Macéo's death he became next in command to Gómez. He conducted all the operations of the insurgents in the Oriente.

The arrival of General Weyler in Cuba was almost simultaneous with the knowledge in the United States that a real war was waging. Lack of geographical knowledge and lack of consecutive news had caused the insurrection as an armed movement to be minimized. Practically nothing was known of what the Western Invasion had been, and in truth not much is known to this day. When the American people came to interest themselves in the fighting there was simply bushwhacking, guerilla warfare, and it never changed its character. The Spaniards continued to complain of the insurgents because they would not come out of the manigua into the open as though the affair were a knightly tournament of the olden times. The insurgents were neither Don Quixotes nor crusaders. They were perhaps a half rabble, and most of them were barefooted and shirtless. But they knew how to prevent the pacification of Cuba, and Weyler never pacified it. He destroyed property as the insurgents had done, and he made desolate what they, by chance or by policy, had left green. He cleared the country by fire, left staring walls as monuments to his military thoroughness, left standing the bare bamboo-poles which, when thatched, had been the bohios or dwelling-huts of the pacificos, and crowned every hilltop with a fortina. But neither by his military operations nor by his reconcentration as a military measure did he end the insurrection. After eighteen months his failure was more conspicuous than had been that of Campos.

In the States the insurrection had received popular sympathy from the outset. It was little understood in its details. Enough was known of Spanish rule and Spanish character and of the history of Cuba to satisfy the public mind that the revolt was a just one. This popular sentiment was at first apathetic. Genuine reforms, honestly applied, might have restrained it within bounds. No genuine reforms were honestly applied, and the sentiment of sympathy grew. President Cleveland, in his message of December, 1896, without asserting specifically the Monroe Doctrine, asserted the right of the United States to intervene in stated circumstances. Previous to that the proffer of the good offices of his administration to Spain in bringing peace to Cuba by helping to establish a system of autonomy had been rejected proudly and scornfully. Spain would subdue her rebellious subjects without the good offices of a friendly nation and without conceding a form of local self-government that would remove the basic grievances. Mr. Cleveland's message was a restatement of the historic position of the United States with regard to Cuba. It was John Quincy Adams speaking again. The message was a declaration of ultimate war between the two countries, and this was recognized more clearly in Madrid than in Washington. Mr. Cleveland, while ignoring the resolutions of Congress recognizing the belligerency of the insurgents, asserted the right of interference, but apparently he did not contemplate its exercise.

But policy must sometimes give way to event. Mr. Olney, as Secretary of State, defiantly fought the Foreign Relations committee of the Senate when that committee reported the Cameron resolution recognizing the independence of Cuba. The éclat of this antagonism may have afforded personal gratification to the Secretary of State, yet its purpose was a public one. This was to assure Spain and the world that the United States had no intention of involving itself in war over Cuba. The contemptuous term of Senatorial jingoism was thought to be sufficient to quiet all apprehension. It might have been sufficient had not other causes been working. Spain felt that she had a righteous grievance against American citizens who were either engaged in aiding the insurrection or who were suspected of aiding it.

The impartial historian must admit that in the international sense the naturalization laws of the United States were grossly abused. American citizenship in Cuba, as a lump or as a mass, was something to cause the republic to blush. But the United States having thrown the mantle of its citizenship over this mass, could not shame itself before the world by denying protection to those who could lawfully claim the shelter of its flag. The State Department, under the direction of Secretary Olney, did the best it could to discourage recognition of this class of citizens. In doing so it clouded the rights of all American citizens in Cuba. The Spanish authorities under Weyler became as intolerant as they had been during the Ten-Years' war, which had culminated in the butchery of the *Virginius* prisoners. The forbearance and indifference of the State Department led them to the presumption that American citizens could be treated as Spanish subjects were treated. Suspicion was allowed to take the place of evidence. Treaty rights were ignored. President Cleveland and Secretary Olney were not willing to go to war in order to enforce the American construction of the Cushing protocol to the treaty of 1795.

The treatment of American citizens by the Spanish officials continued with a high hand until an untoward event brought the climax. General Fitzhugh Lee, of Virginia, had been selected by President Cleveland for the delicate position of consul-general to Cuba. One avowed purpose in his selection was to enable the administration to have the benefit of the presence of an experienced military observer. It was not publicly stated that he was to report on the military situation, but in time it became known that he credited the insurgents with a strength in the field and in reserve of 50,000 men.

The correctness or incorrectness of this numerical estimate was not a vital question. The significant feature of the consul-general's reports was the reiterated statement that Spain was making no real progress in subduing insurrection. The purport of these communications may have been known to Madrid and to the Spanish authorities in Habana. The actions of the latter showed resentment towards the consul-general. His own Government was not upholding him with the vigor which he thought was due to his official position. The culmination in his relations with the Spanish officials came in the death in the jail at Guanabacoa, across the bay from Habana, of Dr. Ricardo Ruiz. Dr. Ruiz was a dentist who had been educated in Philadelphia, had been naturalized as an American citizen, and had returned to Cuba to practise his profession. There was less ground to distrust his good faith in becoming a citizen of the United States than existed in the majority of cases. His character was excellent. In January, 1897, some insurgents under Nestor Aranguren stopped a train on which Spanish officials were returning to Habana, made a prisoner of the paymaster, but released the officers. It was one of the demonstrations which the insurgents were in the habit of making in order to show their contempt for the pacification of the province by the Spanish troops. Dr. Ruiz was arrested for alleged complicity in this affair. He was thrown into jail and kept incomunicado as prescribed by Spanish practice. The first information the consul-general had of the military arrest and imprisonment of this American citizen was when the news came that he had been murdered by his jailers. Whether Dr. Ruiz was actually murdered or whether he was driven to madness and beat his brains out against the walls of his cell has never been satisfactorily determined.

In its bearing on the relations of Spain and the United States the incident was reduced to the fact that Dr. Ruiz was dead in circumstances which created great popular indignation in the United States and fixed public attention afresh on what was happening in Cuba. The

Cuban question was in suspension during the brief remainder of Mr. Cleveland's term. The reasons which actuated Mr. Cleveland's policy were unquestionably patriotic, but in its historic aspect only one conclusion can be reached. By his administration Spain was given every opportunity and every aid towards putting down the insurrection. Her sensibilities were respected to the point of withdrawing American war-vessels from West Indian waters and keeping them withdrawn. The consuls of the United States in Cuba who began making reports on the actual conditions, including the first death-fruits of the reconcentration, were ignored and discredited by their own Government. That weakened them with the Government to which they were accredited. The State Department forbore to press the treaty rights of American citizens. That forbearance was misunderstood. Passed into review, it may be said that during the Cleveland administration the attitude of the United States towards Spain, with reference to Cuba, was one of indulgence which was barren of results. The assertions of the right of intervention made in Mr. Cleveland's messages were barren because of the indulgent attitude that preceded and followed them. His administration had done its best for Spain. It had done nothing for the United States in so far as would place the army and navy on a footing to carry out the right of intervention which Mr. Cleveland affirmed, and it had done nothing for Cuba.

When Mr. McKinley was inaugurated, with his customary acute penetration of the popular sentiment he outlined a policy for his administration which served a twofold purpose; it freed him from the embarrassment of specific declaration of intentions, and satisfied the unquiet public mind to await future developments. The protection to American citizens which he announced was a broad statement. Its application was narrow. It meant American citizens in Cuba. From the 4th of March, 1897, no consular representative of the United States in the Antilles lacked support in maintaining the rights of American citizenship. Nor were their reports of the conditions of the country discredited.

The astute minister of Spain in the United States, Mr. Dupuy de Lome, was quick to grasp the situation. He saw that American popular sentiment might not become dangerous if it could be kept in certain channels. Sympathy for the Cubans would not cause an American administration to be driven into war. When their own citizens were touched the prospect was changed. The irritation over these instances would cause a clamor which could not be brooked. Mr. Dupuy de Lome was able to present this fact so forcibly that Premier Cánovas modified the arrogant stand his ministry had taken. General Weyler, who was plunging violently to a collision with the United States by his arbitrary actions, was checked. Thenceforth American citizens in Cuba were given the fullest protection due them. This protection extended to some individuals of whose unworthiness as American citizens there could be no dispute; but they had the shield of citizenship, and that could not be tarnished.

Mr. McKinley followed this definite evidence of the administration policy with another step. The death of Dr. Ruiz called for investigation. Spain professed its willingness to co-operate with the United States in ascertaining the truth. Judge William R. Day, the friend and neighbor of the President, was selected to go to Cuba, in a legal capacity, to aid Consul-General Lee in the investigation. Actually it was known that he would be also a special commissioner to gather information about the real conditions. Before the time set for his departure, Judge Day became Assistant Secretary of State, and Mr. William J. Calhoun, of Illinois, who also possessed the friendship and confidence of the President, was chosen for the Cuban inquiry. Mr. Calhoun reached Habana in May. The Ruiz investigation followed the usual lines. One report was made to the Spanish Government exculpatory of the Spanish authorities, one to the American Government, incriminatory. Mr. Calhoun did little travelling. It was said at the time that one trip to Matanzas, sixty miles distant from Habana, and a visit to the reconcentrado settlements there, sufficed him. His temperament was judicial and his actions judicious. He sifted all he saw and heard.

Mr. Calhoun returned to Washington in June. His report to the President was a private and unofficial document. In a general way it was known that he indorsed the consuls as worthy of credence. He, too, saw the first death-fruits of reconcentration. He also gained information which negatived the claim that the insurrection was maintained by bandits and the lower classes of negroes. He got a passing glimpse of the degree to which it had spread among all classes of Cubans. Mr. Calhoun noted that General Weyler was not pacifying the island so that peace could be assured at any definite time in the future. His own conclusions were understood to be that Spain could not subdue the insurrection and that the insurgents of themselves could not end the power of the peninsula. At the period of Mr. Calhoun's visit another chapter in legislation for Cuba had been taken in Madrid. New reforms had been proposed by Cánovas. They had not secured confidence in Cuba and General Weyler had not promulgated them. They were never promulgated, and their analysis is not worth the while. While hints of Mr. Calhoun's confidential report appeared, they were only hints and could have no official standing. The answer from Madrid to these hints was an official statement to the Spanish minister in Washington that the Queen Regent would retain the Cánovas ministry and that General Weyler would not be recalled.

General Stewart L. Woodford, of New York, had been appointed minister to Spain. It was known that his instructions contained urgent representations on the imperative need of Spain adopting a policy which would bring prompt amelioration in Cuba. Diplomacy covered the ultimatum with feathered phrases. Provoking delays in the arrival and the reception of the American minister followed his appointment. It was August when his credentials were presented. For a month Premier Cánovas made no sign. Then the assassin ended his career. The most resolute enemy to colonial liberties that Spain had produced was no more. A temporary ministry was formed with General Azcarraga as Premier. It was a weak attempt to continue the conservative policies and traditions. With the further months allowed him General Weyler had made no visible progress in pacifying the island. The irritation over the treatment of American citizens in Cuba was stilled, but the public feeling against Spain had not lessened. During this time the horrors of the reconcentration in Cuba were continued. The American people were slowly learning what it all meant. They had disbelieved at first, because it was incredible. When they believed and knew, their wrath was menacing to the peace of two friendly nations. Moreover, timid commerce was beginning to demand that something be done to end the situation which destroyed substantially all trade between Cuba and the United States.

The Queen Regent of Spain formed a new ministry with Praxades Sagasta at its head. As Liberal Premier during the previous terms of power he had never proposed self-government for Cuba. In the month of October, the year 1898, he proposed the experiment. Weyler was recalled and Ramón Blanco was appointed to succeed him. A complete system of autonomy for Cuba was outlined with the promise of its early enactment. All this came to Cuba not from a conviction which had caused the rulers of Spain, and of such fraction of the nation as had a voice in the Government, to change their policy into one of enlightened justice. Autonomy came from without, from the pressure exerted by the United States with diplomatic inflexibility on the Madrid Cabinet and the monarchy. The insurgents of 1895 had not been able of their own strength to compel either autonomy or independence. They were strong enough to create and to continue a condition which was bound to cause the intervention of the United States.

CHAPTER IV

Wooing the Lost Colony

Olive Branch Brought by Blanco—A Cold Reception—Measures of
Amnesty—Concentration Decrees Revoked—Interest in McKinley's Message—Analysis of Autonomous Decrees—Insular Parliament and Its Powers—The Cabinet and the Council—Veto of
Governor-General—Comparisons with Canada—Defects in the
Light of Experience—System Accepted by a Remnant of Autonomist Party—Allocutions and Addresses—Adhesion of Reformists—Opposition of Union Constitutionals—They Adopt
the Retraimiento—Rejection of Policy by Cubans—Formation
of Autonomist Cabinet—Its Personnel—Historic Oath-Taking
Scene—Aspirations of the Past.

Cuba was lost to Spain. It was lost when General
Ramón Blanco came to the island with autonomy as
a peace-offering to the armed revolutionists and their
unarmed supporters. The task before him was to win
the island back to its allegiance. Conciliation was to
supersede concentration. Recourse was to be had once
more to the moral agencies.

The instrument of the new policy was a good representative of the better type of the soldier of Spain.
Ramón Blanco had been Governor-General of Cuba
from the beginning of 1879 until the end of 1881, succeeding Martínez Campos. He had served in the Ten-
Years' war as a colonel and had reached the rank of
general. The period of his authority in the island was

the era of mild agitation for autonomy. As Governor-General he had tolerated the movement, but had never shown a leaning towards its principles. The first year of his administration had been marked by the guerra chiquita—the little war—in the province of Santiago de Cuba. He had stamped it out. Though he had shown the military spirit in dealing with political movements during his term of office, he had left no harsh and bitter memories. What was remembered of his rule awakened no feeling of resentment deeper than would have been felt for any former Captain-General. He was not odious to the Cuban people for any conspicuous act of tyranny.

General Blanco arrived from Madrid in the early days of November. His welcome was not a generous one. The partisans of Weyler, the Spanish classes, were sullen. The Autonomists were waiting further information before committing themselves to the new administration. They were now a very small body, but were still respectable. The mass of the Cuban people were distrustful or indifferent. The community was benumbed. It had no faith. When not critical it was cynical. The public was apathetic. The presence in Habana of the celebrated bull-fighter, Mazzantini, excited greater popular interest than the promise of autonomy.

The acts of Captain-General Blanco were an earnest of the intentions of the Sagasta ministry. *The Official Gazette* was filled with decrees modifying, suspending, or annulling previous decrees. On paper the reversal of the policy of Cánovas and Weyler was complete. The reconcentration bandos were modified so as to permit the reconcentrados to leave their prison camps within an extended zone of cultivation under the approval of the local military authorities. At the time it was erroneously supposed that the decrees were absolutely revoked. The difference is not of historical moment. If there had been power enough in Spanish authority as personified in the Captain-General to enforce the modification of the reconcentration bandos, the world would not have known that they were not revoked in their entirety.

Proclamations of amnesty to those in arms against Spanish sovereignty followed one another. The fullest pardon of past offences was offered on the sole condition of those in arms laying down their arms and accepting the new regimen. Political prisoners who for real or suspected complicity in the crime of rebellion had been deported to the penal settlements of Ceuta, Chafarinas, and Fernando Po, or shut up in the prisons, were freed and returned to their homes. This release was not universal, for after the peace between the United States and Spain hundreds more of Cuban political prisoners in the penal settlements or in the prisons were released. Yet the amnesty was general enough to give proof that it was genuine. The military executions in the Laurel ditches at Cabaña fortress ceased. After Blanco took command no Cuban patriot puffed his last cigarette, nodded to the spectators gathered on the hill above the fortress, and cried, "Viva Cuba libre!" while awaiting the volley of the firing squad.

The royal decree implanting autonomy in Cuba and Puerto Rico was affirmed by the Queen Regent in

Madrid on November 25th, 1897. The same day were affirmed the decrees establishing universal suffrage, the laws of political equality, and the adaptation of the electoral laws of Spain for the Antilles. The promulgation of the decrees in Cuba was made by Captain-General Blanco when the official text was received in the early part of December. As the new system was enacted through the pressure of the United States, it was of momentous consequence to Spain and to Cuba to know what would be the position of the national administration. This position was shown in the message of President McKinley. Spain could not complain. Having tacitly acknowledged the right of the United States to dictate colonial reforms in the interest of humanity and of peaceful commerce, she could not object to the temperate language in which the executive statement outlined the American policy. The best construction was put by the President on the system as meeting the demands of the hour, and credit for good faith and sincere intentions was given in outlining or sketching the decrees. An argument meant for Congress and the country was made against the recognition of either the belligerency of the insurgents or the independence of the provisional government for which they claimed an existence. The balm for Spain was soft, and the ointment was sweet. Yet there was vinegar, too. The message in its strongest terms reaffirmed the paramount right of intervention by the United States.

The administration of Mr. McKinley having given Spain the benefit of the assumption that the system was genuine colonial self-government and would end the conditions of chronic insurrection in Cuba, the examination of the system itself remains, as also its reception by the Cubans and the Spaniards in the island. The decree of November 25th provided that for the government and administration of Cuba and Puerto Rico respectively there should be an insular parliament divided into two chambers and a Governor-General, representative of the Metropolis, who should exercise in the name of Spain the supreme authority. The legislation of colonial affairs should be the function of the chambers concurrently with the Governor-General. The parliament should be composed of two bodies possessing equal powers—the Chamber or House of Representatives and the Council of Administration. The Council should consist of thirty-five members, of whom eighteen should be chosen after the manner prescribed by the electoral law, and seventeen should be designated by the Crown through the nomination of the Governor-General. The Crown representatives should serve for life; the elective ones for five years, unless the Council should be dissolved. The members of the House or Chamber of Representatives should be chosen in the proportion of one to each twenty-five thousand inhabitants, and their term should be for five years.

The legislative powers defined were substantially those of an insular assembly with reference to local affairs. The colonial parliament was to control the colonial budget. To the Cortes of Spain it was reserved to determine what were the obligatory expenses inherent in sovereignty and to fix the revenues necessary to cover them. Regarding foreign commerce—a root subject, a fundamental necessity for genuine colonial home rule—whether the initiative negotiations came from the insular government or the central authority in Spain, delegates especially authorized by the colonial government were to participate in the negotiations. The treaties of commerce in which the insular government had not intervened were to be communicated to it in order that it might declare whether or not it adhered to the stipulations. The framing of the tariff of both import and export duties was conceded to the insular parliament. These were the cardinal provisions of the legislative powers. There were reservations. After the definition of the powers and functions of the parliament, note the definition of the Governor-General's authority: "The supreme government of the colony shall be exercised by a Governor-General." He could suspend the constitutional guarantees and apply the Law of Public Order, which was martial law. He was to be the viceroy patronate, exercising the faculties inherent in the patronate of the Indies. He was to be commander of the army and the navy, the delegated representative of the ministries of state, war, navy, and colonies in Spain. All the authorities of the island were subordinated to him. He was responsible for the order and security of the colony. His veto power allowed him to suspend parliamentary legislation, referring the veto to Madrid for confirmation or rejection.

The cabinet was to consist of five members or secretaries with portfolios and a president without portfolio. The secretaries could be members of either the Camara or the Council, could take part in the discussions of both bodies, and could vote in whichever body they held membership. They were responsible to the parliament. The debt incurred in the Ten-Years' war and in the then existing insurrection was left subject to future adjustment.

This system of colonial government proposed by Sagasta and drafted by Moret was a laborious effort to apply to the Spanish Antilles the autonomy of Canada as it could be learned from the books. In his exposition of the subject to the Queen Regent, Sagasta declared that the Autonomist constitution was not exotic, was neither copied nor imitated, yet the student will search in vain through the pages of Spanish national or colonial history for evidence that it was indigenous. The system could not be analyzed merely from the written text. Its nature was to be gathered from the circumstances in which it was proposed. Its application and interpretation had to be in the light of past events. Experience with Spanish administration of previous reforms could not be overlooked. When the critical examination was finished, the conclusion was strong that Spanish statesmen did not know the meaning of colonial self-government. In the ultimate analysis all powers centred in the Governor-General as the viceroy of the Crown and the representative of Spanish sovereignty; and notwithstanding Sagasta's declaration that the Autonomist constitution was not exotic, the chief recommendation of its sponsors was its resemblance to the Constitution of Canada.

A literature of annotation followed the publication of the decrees. This literature went into laborious comparisons to show the points of resemblance and also the improvements. The difference was fundamental. The constitution of Canada is interpreted and applied in the spirit of free institutions. All parties to the compact understand parliamentary government. The foreign office, the British Parliament, and the English people know the weakness of the reserve powers if their exercise should ever be attempted. A comparison on paper of the respective functions of the Governor-General of Canada and the Governor-General of Cuba was an absurdity. Spanish statesmen had no conception of executive power falling into forgetfulness through disuse. To their minds power was conferred only to be exercised.

The people of Cuba were of a similar mind. They had no conception of authority reserved to a supreme power and not being exerted. Their knowledge was the knowledge drawn from experience. Their experience had been with one Captain-General after another who construed the laws to suit his own notions and executed them with military rigor. The composition of the Council was the broadest evidence of the lack of faith in colonial home rule. With the Crown creating seventeen life members, a condition could not arise in which it would be unable to secure the additional member, and thus having a majority, block absolutely all popular government. Taken in addition to the veto powers of the Governor-General, this Council was an exhibition of how easily Madrid could continue to control Cuba against the interests of the island. Leaving the debt unsettled was to leave an irritant which in the future was certain to cause dissensions between the peninsula and the island, and possibly foment another revolution. But it was the system itself which was submitted to discussion rather than the debt, which properly lay outside of autonomy. And the discussion had hardly begun before the end was seen. Moret had joined his name imperishably with the emancipation law of 1871, which was crowned in 1886 by the complete freedom of the slave race. His fame was not to be joined imperishably with the constitutional autonomy which would save the Antilles to Spain.

The adhesion of the Autonomists who had not joined the insurgents in the field, been thrown into prison, deported to the penal settlements, or gone into voluntary exile was made clear after the promulgation of the decrees of autonomy. Madrid was waiting to know how the system would be received by the different political groups. Naturally the Autonomists were the first ones to be considered. Individually they published manifestoes, allocutions, and addresses pledging their support. They exchanged felicitations among themselves and sent congratulatory telegrams to Madrid. The Autonomists in Paris were also satisfied. Those in the United States, with a very few exceptions, were silent. Speaking collectively, the central Junta of Autonomists issued an address telling the people of Cuba to prepare for the elections without fear that the verdict of suffrage would be falsified. This was an indirect way of characterizing the former elections as fraudulently controlled by the Spanish authorities, which was simply history. The local juntas were requested to begin the preparation of the regimen of autonomy. The central Junta adopted as its sentiments an article in its newspaper organ * which declared that the new system was the realization of their doctrine of 1881. Former reforms were slighted in the statement

* *El Pais.*

that the system proposed by Sagasta was not the administrative and economic decentralization previously offered by Liberal governments. This which was now presented was the genuine autonomy—representative autonomy with responsible parliamentary government, the ultimate evolution of the process which the Autonomist programme had formulated.

What was lacking in minor details, the Autonomists said, was unimportant. The system in its entirety conceded all that they had sought. It gave Cuba home rule without impairing the national unity. It was a tie that would forever bind the island to the peninsula not in chains, but in free will. Under it the mother country and the erring child would walk again hand in hand. Peace and prosperity would come again. Cuba had been rebellious; her aspirations for political liberties had been discouraged, and some of her children had unfortunately taken up arms. But now that autonomy was to be implanted the past would be forgotten, and they would return to the ways of peace and cultivate its growth. The annexationists in the United States would redouble their efforts, would again talk of manifest destiny, but the Cubans would not be deceived. At the bier of the decrepit ancestor—absolutist government—they would imitate the heralds who preceded the funeral car of the French kings, and would cry, "Long live autonomy!" Dead the fault which had caused discontent, would die also the spirit of rebellion. Autonomy meant the definite failure of the insurrection, already broken by arms. The central Junta appealed to the patriotism of the insurgents. It knew that the eternal revolutionists, the anarchists, would not be satisfied. No matter.

Autonomy would satisfy by its fruits. The arch of the new alliance between Cuba and Spain, it affirmed the indestructible sovereignty of the mother country in the love, the gratitude, and the liberty of the colony. The shades of the Autonomists who had died—most of them in exile, it was parenthetically observed—were saluted. "Long live Cuba—long live Spain!"

But Spain in Cuba had not long to live, and a new life was unfolding for Cuba.

The Reformists also proclaimed their adhesion. Nothing had been heard of them during a twelvemonth and its half. In the elections for deputies to the Cortes, which were held two months after General Weyler took command of the island, they had been retired along with the Autonomists. Their treachery to Campos was fruitless. The Weylerites kept them under the ban of suspicion. Now the weather-vane had shifted. The wind was north by northeast. Being opportunists, the Reformists turned with the weather-vane. Autonomy was more than they had ever asked or wanted. It was something they had not believed in. But it was the programme of the day, and they would accept it. They sent effusive telegrams to Madrid, exchanged felicitations among themselves and congratulations with the Autonomists. They would co-operate with the latter in making the new system effective. Liberal leaders in Spain and the organs of their opinions were deceived by this effusiveness. They discussed it as a fusion, as though two great and powerful political organizations differing in principle had coalesced and would form a cohesive unit.

It was left to the intransigentes dominating the Union

Constitutionals to demonstrate once more that they were the unchanging element in Spanish power in Cuba. When autonomy was proposed in October, 1897, the intransigentes were what they had been in 1879, when the proposition had been made to carry out in spirit and in letter the compact of El Zanjón. Their importance and their influence could not be decried. They ostracized General Blanco. He dwelt in isolation among his own race and his own people. They received the first suggestion of autonomy with distrust. This gradually grew into violent opposition. The sentiment was unified and consolidated when the Union Constitutional party called a convention for the third week in December. These Spanish Tories in Cuba had claims to be called representatives of public sentiment. They showed the vigor of party organization in delegated assembly. The Autonomists had been content with the declarations of adhesions from the local juntas. Three men might constitute a junta. The Reformists had been satisfied with the approval of small groups. The Union Constitutionals were numerous enough to hold a convention to which delegates were chosen by the various local juntas. Some of these delegates were from sections of the island in control of the insurgents. It was the only political assembly held in Cuba in five years.

The symptoms were stormy. Captain-General Blanco was making a shrewd and persistent effort to gain control of the organization. The president of the Union Constitutional party was the Cuban-born Marquis de Apezteguía, who possessed more liberal instincts than the Spanish classes of whom he was the representative.

Blanco sought to make the conservatives more auton-omist than the Autonomists themselves. The Marquis Apezteguía was in sympathy with the plan. It was a conception of high politics. But the majority of the Union Constitutionals were not fitted for high politics. They thought the mission of their party was to preserve Spanish sovereignty, and they believed colonial self-government would destroy this sovereignty. "Author-ity, not autonomy," was their watchword. The deter-mination of their leaders was to make a demonstration of the rejection of the new colonial policy which would be echoed in Spain and would overthrow the Sagasta ministry. They were not satisfied with their experi-ence in forcing the withdrawal of General Campos. In the preliminary private meetings of the Habana dele-gates these cried out anathema to autonomy.

The convention was as intolerant as conventions usu-ally are when conservatives become radicals in the violence of their opposition to a stated course. The central Junta, which had shown receptiveness for Cap-tain-General Blanco's schemes, was repudiated. Mar-quis Apezteguía was rebuked, shorn of his power as president of the party, and then left in that position. The Queen Regent was congratulated in entire sincerity on the restoration of peace in the Philippines. Violent speeches were made against the United States, Presi-dent McKinley, and Congress. A telegram was sent to General Weyler which was meant to show that the con-vention was in sympathy with him and with his policy. The official attitude of the party was expressed by formal resolution which made opposition to autonomy a party creed. Sedition was condemned, and as loyal Spaniards the Union Constitutionals would not hint at armed resistance to the programme of the Government. They would not themselves become rebels by talking sedition, but they would have none of the responsibility for the new system. Instead, they adopted the Retraimiento. This meant the drawing within the shell. It pledged the party to retire from participation in public affairs and to take no part in the elections. The Autonomists spread the table, the Reformists ate the feast, and the Union Constitutionals were asked to pay the bill. Never. This action was taken in order that the non-participation should not be interpreted as lending moral support. It was passive resistance in the most sullen and embarrassing form. The Government was drawing nearer the precipice. They would not be the ones to push it over.

After these declarations had been made specific and the attitude of the party defined, some leniency was shown the central Junta, whose membership had been altered. This directory was given power to act if developments later called for drawing out of the shell and participating in public affairs. But the great end of the intransigentes was accomplished. The powerful Union Constitutional party was placed on record as inflexibly opposed to autonomy. The intransigentes did not believe that autonomy would conciliate the insurrection out of existence; they did not believe it would succeed, and they meant that it should not succeed.

There was no insurgent political party to which the Madrid authorities could turn in seeking support for autonomy, yet there was something which in a degree represented the insurgents. This was the Junta in New

York and the secret revolutionary committees in the Cuban towns and cities. Weyler had not succeeded in breaking up the latter. Blanco did not succeed; but it was thought that they might be persuaded out of existence by securing the support of leading Cubans who were suspected of being in sympathy with them. A very small number of Cubans did join themselves to the Autonomists, but the majority of the Cuban people not in the field remained as determined in not accepting the new policy as were the actual insurgents. They had become revolutionists to the core. The American Junta also repudiated the system. Its effort was given to showing that the autonomy proposed was not genuine. It made comparisons with the colonial government of Canada; pointed out the defects in the regimen prepared for Cuba, and showed especially the danger of the reserve powers. All this was meant for American public opinion. The time had gone by when the actual provisions of autonomy—parchment autonomy, they called it—were of consequence to the Cuban revolutionists, whether in the United States or in Cuba. They were waiting for events to determine the limit of the near future foreshadowed by President McKinley as determining American intervention.

Immediately after his arrival, General Blanco began putting the new policy into effect. The Weyler officials throughout the island were removed. Influential Cubans were invited to take office. Here was met the first difficulty. It was a responsibility which most of them sought to decline. In some instances what was called gentle compulsion was used. José Bruzon, a leading lawyer of Habana, was persuaded to accept the office of civil governor of the province. His position was defined as waiting while Cuba drifted to its destiny. The insurgents showed no resentment towards him. It was commonly believed that compromising documents in the hands of the Spanish authorities induced him to take the post of governor in preference to involuntary exile to Chafarínas. In Santa Clara province Marcos García was prevailed on to accept the office of governor. Marcos García was an insurgent colonel in the Ten-Years' war, in which he was associated with Gómez. He had not been suspected of active sympathy with the last insurrection. For the other provinces fairly good men were secured, and in the municipalities changes were made in the alcaldes, or mayors, by selecting either Cubans or Spaniards who had not been too closely identified with the Weyler administration.

The royal decrees provided for an insular cabinet. Until elections could be held and the full system of autonomy be got in working order, the cabinet necessarily would be a provisional one. Captain-General Blanco and the officials in Madrid gave the composition of this body careful thought. It was developed that though the Autonomists were not numerous, they were broken up into factions. One faction was known as the historic Autonomists. The other faction was less historic and more radical. The Reformists also had to be taken into consideration. The comment at the time was that they showed a greedy eagerness to get office. Ultimately the cabinet was arranged. Madrid approved and Habana smiled.

The cabinet was inaugurated on the 1st of January, 1898. It was an historic scene in the throne-room of the Palace—the same room which exactly a year later was to be the scene of the yielding of Spanish authority to the United States. All the foreign consuls, the official representation of Spanish authority, and the dignitaries of the Church were present. Captain-General Blanco, after the members had taken the oath of fidelity to Spain, the Queen, and Spanish institutions, addressed them. Peace and the welfare of Cuba, he told them, formed the best propaganda they could make in behalf of autonomy and against the revolution, which, although it was never justified, would thereafter have no pretense whatever to exist. He closed his address with the exhortation, "Long live Cuba, forever Spanish." At the conclusion of the ceremony, mass was celebrated in the chapel of the Palace by the bishop of Habana. A few hundred of the populace were gathered outside. They made a feeble demonstration when the new cabinet appeared. The community as a whole showed little concern in the ceremonies. Military precautions had been taken against an outbreak or an unfriendly demonstration.

The new cabinet might justly be called representative of the aspirations and agitation of the Autonomists of the past. The president, without portfolio, was José María Galvez, a lawyer and political orator. His name was attached to the first manifestoes issued by the Autonomists, in 1879. It was attached to the manifesto issued in 1895, reprobating the insurrection, deploring its effect in postponing Autonomist reforms, and predicting its failure. The leading figure in this Autonomist cabinet was the secretary of the treasury, Rafael Montoro. His had been the consistent career of a constitutional agitator. A student in Madrid, he had been educated as a lawyer and had shown force as an advocate. He was the most accomplished orator in the island. His admirers called him the Cuban Castelar; and he was such, if allowance be made for the difference between the man of talent and the man of genius. Montoro's public addresses and writings are voluminous. His name appears to the introduction and prologues to many books by Cuban authors on politics and on literature. He was one of the founders of the Liberal-Autonomist party. He signed the manifesto of 1879, and afterwards was an Autonomist Deputy to the Cortes, where he sat in obscurity. Montoro's name appeared at the head of those who, in the name of the Liberal-Autonomist party, repudiated the uprising of 1895. He indorsed the reforms proposed by Cánovas, and was rewarded by the bestowal of the title of marquis. From that time his influence with the Cuban people ceased utterly. They forgot his past services, and characterized him as Weyler's partisan and parasite.

Antonio Govín was named as secretary of justice and administration. He was a forcible personality. He was both an historic and a radical Autonomist. He was the secretary of the party in its early days, one of the signers of the first platform, and the author of documents which were put forth in its name in explanation of the principles of autonomy. Govín was capable of making enemies, and during the period of the active agitation for autonomy his boldness arrayed the Spanish classes against him. He signed the manifesto of April, 1895, but he never permitted himself to be identified with Weyler's acts. Ultimately he sought voluntary exile, and settled with his family in the United States. He did not reach Habana in time to take the oath of office with his colleagues. Govín was a prominent freemason, and it was thought that his influence might be potential with the masonic organizations, which were filled with the revolutionary spirit.

The Reformists were given a member of the cabinet. He was Eduardo Dolz, a lawyer, who had shown some talent for arranging compromises. He was a Deputy in the Cortes. He came direct from Madrid, and it was said that he would represent Spanish sovereignty in the bosom of autonomy. Autonomy never warmed to this representative of the monarchy. Francisco Zayas, an educator who had the public respect, was made secretary of public instruction. Laureano Rodriguez, a peninsular from the province of Santiago de Cuba, became secretary of agriculture, industry, and commerce. The irony of these latter departments caused only a passing sneer. The actual functions of the Autonomist cabinet were never clearly discernible. The cabinet was chiefly useful as a shield for the unpopular acts of the Spanish Government.

CHAPTER V

EPILOGUE TO AUTONOMY

COLONIAL home rule was finally in function, as the
Castilian idiom has it. The insurgents in the field had
shown little disposition to assist in the functions. A
glance backward is necessary to understand their attitude. When the system was first proposed, Gómez,
Calixto García, and the other insurgent commanders
made known positively that their demand was for independence, and they would not consider autonomy. It
was abundantly and conclusively proven that they represented the feelings of the ragged soldiers who acknowledged military allegiance to them. The insurgent
army, as an army, would not permit autonomy to be
talked. It was held that to propose it was a violation

of the Cuban constitution and required the proponent to be passed through arms—that is, executed.

Coincident with the promulgation of the decrees of autonomy the Spanish authorities began what they called their moral campaign. This was a campaign of bribery and persuasion. They were very persistent in seeking to disintegrate the insurrection individual by individual. Every inducement was offered to the Cubans in arms to present themselves. The list of presentados began to be followed with interest. But those in arms who presented themselves were discouragingly few. The insurgents in the field, by an understanding among themselves, permitted the presentations of their sick. This enabled some of their numbers to die among friends and relatives rather than in the camp. A few chiefs did present themselves, some of whom held the rank of colonel. The invariable explanation of these presentations by the Cubans was that the officer had been deprived of his command or degraded by Gómez, and that his presentation was in revenge. While this was not true in every instance, it was the fact in a surprising number of cases. A few of the minor chiefs who were among the presentados undoubtedly did so in good faith. They were weary of the long struggle and were willing to accept the promises of the Spanish Government; but these were the exceptions rather than the rule.

All of Spain's efforts to secure the adhesion of the insurgents in the field were made by private messengers and emissaries. They were not envoys. Frequently these were relatives who were forced to undertake the doubtful mission. Towards winning the moral support of public opinion of the world, which might have been had by an honest effort to present the policy of autonomy to the insurgents, Castilian pride was an insuperable obstacle. The last shred of territory gained in centuries of conquest was at stake, yet Spain could not bring herself to recognize that the revolutionary force which had brought 200,000 of her soldiers to Cuba to combat it was a force in arms. No conference was asked, no truce proposed to discuss the proposition of autonomy, and no white flag shown. Instead, dependence was placed on secret messengers. That some of these emissaries were executed by the insurgents is beyond question.

The Ruiz case was the best known. Joaquin Ruiz was a colonel of the Spanish engineers in Habana, and was of a winning personality. The military authorities sought to disintegrate the band of Nestor Aranguren through him. Aranguren was a young man who had made reputation by his daring in attacking and annoying the Spanish forces close to the city. He had been employed in the office of a firm of contractors which constructed the water works, and this had brought him in relation to Colonel Ruiz, who was the engineer in charge. If Aranguren could be reached it would have a great effect in Habana and among the insurgents in that province. Colonel Ruiz undertook the task. He opened a correspondence with Aranguren—a less difficult matter than might be supposed. Former personal ties and family relationship kept up communication between many Spaniards and insurgents in the field so long as no efforts were made to treat of the insurrection. Ruiz sought a personal interview with Aranguren. The latter agreed to it if he did not come on a political mission, and warned him that if he came proposing autonomy it would be at his peril. Ruiz' first attempt was unsuccessful. Subsequently he succeeded in reaching the camp of Aranguren, in defiance of the latter's warning, with his propositions from the Spanish authorities. The story of the insurgents who were in the camp was that on Ruiz' appearance Aranguren burst into tears, and asked him why he had come to certain death. Then an insurgent summary court-martial was held and Ruiz was executed. The full story was never told, but the common belief was that he was macheted.

Rumors of Colonel Ruiz' disappearance reached Habana. The authorities feared for his fate, but did not dare let the truth be known. Finally it was arranged that a foreign consular representative in Habana who was a personal friend of the reckless colonel of engineers should ask General Lee's aid. The United States consul-general, in his unofficial capacity and with the consent of the Spanish authorities, despatched a messenger to the camp of the insurgents. When the messenger reached the camp Aranguren was absent, but the officer next in command sent a message that Ruiz had been tried and executed. Intense excitement was caused by the news, and the officials sought to make capital of it in the United States, where some weak sentiment was shown, and the execution of Ruiz was denounced as an act of savagery.

A dispassionate study of the circumstances of the case does not uphold this contention. Colonel Ruiz bore no white flag and no safe-conduct to the insurgent camp. He went against warning. He sought to serve his Government, and that service would have been rewarded by military promotion. The service could only be performed by securing the treachery of Aranguren to his comrades in arms. Back of the attempted interview with the young insurgent was the purpose of creating distrust and suspicion among the revolutionists of one another. The mere fact that a Spanish emissary had sought to visit Aranguren in his camp was relied upon to arouse distrust among the other insurgents. The military authorities professed that they had letters which would show that Aranguren's course was barbarous and treacherous. They never disclosed such letters. Instead, Aranguren himself made public the documents. These were a conclusive showing of the plot to discredit him and to spread dissensions among the insurgents. The plot recoiled, and the death of its agent was the sequel. Colonel Ruiz was called the Cuban Major André. The difference was that young Aranguren was not a Cuban Benedict Arnold. Weeks afterwards Aranguren was surprised in the hills of Tapaste by the Spanish troops and killed. His whereabouts were betrayed by a camp follower. His body was brought to the morgue in Habana. He was buried in the cemetery of Columbus. His grave is a few yards away from that of Colonel Ruiz.

The execution of Ruiz took place in the latter part of December, 1897. A month later Augusta Morales, the alcalde of a village in Pinar del Río, penetrated the camp of the insurgent general Pedro Diaz, near San Cristobal. He brought propositions for autonomy. Morales was tried by a court-martial. Dr. Hugo Roberts, a young insurgent officer, defended him. He was condemned as an emissary of the enemy and was executed. This ended the visits of secret messengers to the insurgent camps.

The army of Spain in Cuba was the last to be heard from regarding the new system. By the army was always meant the officers. The privates, dumb beasts of burden and abuse, were not taken into account. The army never had been for autonomy. That was perfectly well understood. But its opposition heretofore had been passive. Military discipline was lax and the military commanders in the different districts were supreme. Where they happened to be in sympathy with General Blanco, a little support was given the new policy by not throwing insurmountable hindrances in the way of extending the zones of cultivation and aiding the reconcentrados. These cases were not numerous. Usually the military commander nullified every effort to relieve the starving population. The army was not in its own understanding disloyal to Spain, but it did not want the insurrection to end just then. That would end also the double pay, the pensions and promotions, the decorations, and the monstrous system of corruption which prevailed. The army had not been fearful of autonomy succeeding, and therefore did not fear the early end of the insurrection. All it wanted was to be let alone. But it was not let alone, and this precipitated the demonstration which showed that the army was not for autonomy.

The restrictions of the Weyler rule had been relaxed in so far as affected the freedom of the press. The censorship was not abrogated under Blanco, yet a certain latitude of comment was permitted the newspapers.

Some of them, professing faith in the sincerity of the more liberal policy, ventured criticisms of admitted abuses. A newspaper called *La Discusion* had been suppressed by Weyler because of its insurgent leanings. It had been an organ of radical autonomist tendencies. The paper reappeared under Blanco. It began to call attention to gross abuses of the army, and to demand their reform. Another paper of less character than *La Discusion*, which had adopted the title of *The Reconcentrado*, was also sensational and personal in its criticisms. The army officers took alarm. One night groups of them dropped into a café and did not leave till after midnight. The next morning a score or more of these officers in uniform went in a body to the office of *The Reconcentrado* and wrecked it. Then they proceeded to the office of *La Discusion* and began to demolish it. The office of this journal was on the Prado, opposite Central Park, in the very heart of the city. Soon the officers had a mob back of them which completed the wreck. Many members of the Volunteers were seen among the mob. The officers, having started the demonstration, retired and left the rioters to finish their work. The Orden Publico, the military police of the city and the finest body of regulars in the service of Spain, sought to drive them back by gentle means. They were not allowed to use their swords or firearms. The rioters flouted them, and mob orators addressed the populace, inciting them to greater activity. The authorities were powerless.

It was a Wednesday morning, the morning of January 12th, when the rioting began. There was a lull during the midday, but in the afternoon the mob rallied. It made little demonstration, however, and was content with throwing stones and breaking windows. But the city feared something more. It was known that the authorities had been unravelling several supposed conspiracies, and that at all the recent bull-fights extraordinary precautions had been taken to prevent an outbreak. In Spain the popular uprisings usually begin at the bull-ring. That afternoon the feeling was as if a black cloud had settled over the city. It was like waiting for the thunder-storm on an oppressive summer day. General Parrado, who was next in command to Blanco, personally took command of the police forces. Orders were given that all shops should be closed, and within half an hour the doors were locked and the iron shutters fastened. People were warned off the streets. The Guardia Civiles, or military rural police, were brought in to reinforce the Orden Publico. Then some of the regulars began to arrive and make their evolutions in a public square. After them came the Fifth Battalion of Volunteers, suspected of disloyalty, who were stationed in the palace of the Governor-General half a mile away from Central Park, where the rioting had begun.

In the evening the mob rallied. The narrow streets leading to the Palace were choked with rioters. The plaza in front of it was filled with them. They cried "Long live Weyler!" "Down with autonomy!" "Death to Blanco!" Captain-General Blanco and the members of the Autonomist cabinet who were with him in the palace could hear these cries. After a while the troops succeeded in clearing the plaza and the streets leading to the palace, and holding them against approach. Their instructions were to be gentle. The disorderly crowds were permitted to roam almost at will through the streets, crying long life to Weyler, to the Volunteers, to Spain, to the army; death to Blanco and death to autonomy. Sometimes they had sharp colloquies with the troops. One group cried, "War to autonomy!" and the captain of the guard which had been brought in from the country afterwards told how he had heard that cry before. It was when a band of insurgents had laid an ambush for his men and had borne down on them crying, "Death to autonomy!" The night was passed without bloodshed.

The following day General Juan Arolas, recently named as military governor, took commmand of the forces. He had just arrived from Santiago province. Artillery was brought in from the country, and the garrisons were reinforced by the addition of 8,000 regulars. In spite of this heavy force the mob made several demonstrations during the day, but without any set purpose beyond baiting the troops. At night there seemed to be actual danger. The rioters gathered in numbers on the Prado on each side of Central Park. The troops frequently charged them, sometimes with the cavalry in the lead, sometimes with the infantry on the double quick. The soldiers were not allowed to use their firearms unless a shot should be directed against them. Happily this did not happen. The hospitals were filled with people suffering from bruises and sabre cuts, but they had not drawn the fire of the troops. The belief at the time was that if the order had been given to fire it would not have been obeyed. The word ran around that Spaniards would not fire on Spaniards. It took four days for Habana to resume the semblance of order, and this semblance was not reached until the artillery was placed in position to command every point.

The events of that week constituted a real siege, and Habana was garrisoned against the rioters by thousands of regular troops. But they were not a bloody mob, and this caused a misapprehension of the serious nature of the uprising. During the days of rioting it was observed that the rioters seemed to be incited by persons not taking part, and the presence of the fraternal spirit between them and the military forces was also manifest. Yet Habana was on the brink of bloodshed all the time, and 8,000 troops could not have prevented it if there had been one musket discharge on the mob.

When the tension was relieved the Spanish authorities gave themselves up to explaining that the rioting had been trifling and had no meaning. But it had a deep meaning. It was a political demonstration of the army against autonomy, and it served its purpose. Three or four score of the officers who precipitated the rioting were placed under military arrest, but they were never punished. Not one was court-martialled. Pretexts were found for releasing most of them within a few days after their arrest, and they were returned to their commands. This was the significant confession of the weakness of Spanish authority in Cuba. Captain-General Blanco did not dare to discipline the insubordinate and rebellious army officers. Instead, the Spanish authorities disciplined the press, which was held responsible for the trouble because it had attacked the honor of the army. The Captain-General issued a decree which, without superseding the already rigorous laws against the freedom of the press, placed the censorship absolutely in the hands of the general staff of the army. Persons who transgressed the censorship, in addition to their liability for the penalties of the law were held guilty of the crime of rebellion; and the crime of rebellion was punishable by either death or exile in chains to the penal settlements. And this was done with an Autonomist cabinet in nominal power and under a regimen whose first principle had been the liberty of the press. The army ended autonomy.

The influence of the outbreak on American public opinion was pronounced. The people of the United States were not deceived when the news was published as to what had happened. The censorship of cable messages prevented the history of the days of siege from reaching the north until the vessels could carry the true story. Then it was felt that the army officers and the rioters had uttered a true cry in their "Death to autonomy." The rioting had been at no time directed against Americans, but there was inquietude and a natural fear of further trouble. It might be said that the American public was convinced of the failure of autonomy. There was at once a demand for the reports of the consuls and for full information regarding the actual state of affairs in Cuba. The condition of the reconcentrados was one of the subjects on which information was wanted. Their relief had been part of the promise of Spain that went with autonomy. In the generous impulses following the promise of that system a proposition had been advanced that the American people aid the starving population. Captain-General Blanco proudly rejected it, declaring in an official telegram to the Madrid Cabinet and to the Spanish minister in Washington, that Spain could care for her own. Within a fortnight he was compelled to admit that Spain could not care for her own.

President McKinley issued a Christmas appeal to the American people for help. At first the responses were slow. The American people wanted the aid, if given, to reach the starving Cubans, and they were not willing to trust it to Spanish officials. But back of this was their perception that this kind of relief could only be temporary, and that no permanent alleviation could come until the circumstances were changed. They saw that until the cause was removed the distressing conditions would continue; and the cause, they were convinced, was the inability of the Spanish Government to govern the island satisfactorily. Nevertheless their hearts and their purses gradually opened, and within a few weeks American aid was pouring into Cuba, and continued to pour in until war between Spain and the United States was declared.

Captain-General Blanco's Government was able to make appropriations which ultimately reached $250,000 in silver for the relief of a suffering population of half a million. All the functions of Spanish sovereignty were paralyzed and it could do no more. This was one cause of the continued refusal of the Cuban people to believe in autonomy. Material relief was promised with it, and this relief did not come. The consuls of the United States could not have reported honestly that progress was being made in relieving the distress. Nor could they report that autonomy was making progress. It was not even standing still. It was going backward. The consuls could see what was going on in the vain effort to implant the new system. They could see the exploradores, or pilot engines, preceding the trains with armored cars and troops for guards. This was railroad travel in a pacified country.

They knew other things that could not be treated of publicly. With one exception, every consul had lists presented to him of Spaniards, generally of the commercial classes, who wanted Cuba annexed to the United States. They had private and confidential statements made of the movement which had begun in October among the sugar planters of Habana and Matanzas provinces for the intervention of the United States. These classes had absolutely lost faith in the ability of Spain to maintain her sovereignty. As the failure of autonomy became more apparent, they became more pronounced in their desire for American intervention. They could not take overt action because they were Spanish subjects. Such action would have made them amenable to the statutes against sedition, and placed them in the category of the insurgents who were charged with the crime of rebellion. But they managed to let their attitude be known. The United States consuls in giving their judgment had to take account of these indications. They could also note the full effect of the sullen and passive opposition of the Spanish classes to autonomy as manifested in the attitude of the Union Constitutional party. The intensity and the influence of that opposition could not be fully understood in the United States. It had to be measured in the atmosphere and in the midst of the events which were in process of development.

It was a question how fully Spain understood the

desperate conditions at the time of the army riots. She had been watching the experiment of autonomy in ignorant hope. The capacity for national self-deceit was apparently illimitable. Yet the reassuring accounts, without practical results, were beginning to cause distrust. The query in the peninsula was why greater progress was not made in securing the support of the Cubans. Her statesmen were afraid to tell the people the truth. Blanco was not winning Cuba back to Spain. Conciliation had failed, and autonomy must be implanted by the sword. The Captain-General was unable to make a vigorous military campaign. Weyler had left the army in a state of suffering and demoralization second only to that of the pacificos. General Blanco began its improvement at once like the trained commander that he was, but it was certain that the troops could not be got in condition for service in the field till the rainy season came on. Then there could be no real campaigning, and the insurgents would ask the United States if the reasonable time given Spain in which to implant autonomy had not expired. Blanco did one thing which showed that he intended to employ the army. He called for more recruits. The Madrid press spoke of it as the last sacrifice; but the 15,000 fresh troops were started, and the last detachment of them reached Cuba just in time to form part of the defensive force against invasion from the United States.

The exact position of Spain was exposed in February by the letter of Dupuy de Lome, with its coarse abuse of the American executive. Military successes were imperative. The best possible efforts were made to manufacture these successes. General Jiminez Castellaños started out from the town of Puerto Principe with 2,500 troops. They reached the mountain hamlet of Cubitas, where the Cuban provisional government had had its wandering existence. The government was gone, and the place in the woods was not worth taking. Eight hundred of the insurgents harassed the troops, and a few were killed and wounded on either side. Then the columns returned to the garrison at Puerto Príncipe. That was the nature of the military successes which the Spanish troops were achieving at this critical period.

General Blanco left Habana in the latter part of January and made a trip through the island. He went by the south coast to Santiago de Cuba, and returned by the north coast. His journey could not be called taking the field. It afforded him a full insight into the despairing state into which Spanish sovereignty had fallen. When he returned to Habana the *Maine* had been in the harbor for ten days. The condition of the Spanish mind was one of irritation and disappointment. It was seeking to hold the United States responsible for the failure of autonomy because the Junta was not expelled from New York and because occasional filbustering expeditions were successful. The Spanish authorities in Madrid and in Cuba were willing to forego their irritation and to forgive the United States if it would undertake the task of forcing autonomy on the insurgents. The proposition offered by Mr. Cleveland, which would have placed the United States in a position of guaranteeing the Spanish flag in the Antilles, would now have been accepted with eagerness. But with the knowledge that the American Government would not coerce the people of the island into keeping allegiance to that flag the resentment was fierce.

The Spanish warships were ordered to Habana harbor to keep the *Maine* company. When that vessel was blown up the feeling in Cuba was hysterical and Spanish authority bordered on anarchy. To one living in the midst of those events as was the writer a plain conclusion was inevitable. With the passions born of that hour of national sorrow stilled, and with every circumstance reviewed in the calmer moments of reflection, I have not changed that opinion. A very large element of the Spanish classes in Cuba rejoiced in the destruction of the *Maine*. It was not alone the ignorant populace. The feeling was manifest among the army officers. Outside of the possible conspirators none might know whether the explosion was due to accident or design. But the satisfaction felt was the same. The higher officials from the Captain-General down deplored it in itself and in its consequences. Many of the Spanish merchants were sincere in their sympathy. Yet this did not obscure the more common sentiment of satisfaction. The violent anti-American circular which was distributed the day a breakfast was given by Consul-General Lee to Captain Sigsbee and the officers of the *Maine* is sometimes cited as evidence of the plotting that was going on. My own belief is that this circular was like others of the same character, an invention. It was a coincidence. Genuine circulars were occasionally circulated, but they were of a different kind. They were short, and usually typewritten or struck off from a hand-press. The resentment which was capable of the deliberate destruction of the *Maine* was too deep for utterance in inflammatory circulars. Regarding the higher officials, while they sought to exculpate Spain, my impression was that they did not feel sure of their own ground. They hoped the explosion was due to an accident, and they advanced the grounds for the theory of an accident, yet with the apparent fear that there were Spaniards capable of causing the destruction of the American warship.

The violent intransigente classes were in earnest in wanting war with the United States after the report of the naval board of inquiry was made. A part of the military and naval element, as well as of the official class, believed in war in order that Spain might lose Cuba with honor. Her honor would not permit her to accept a guarantee of $200,000,000 from the United States and concede independence. But she would go to war and take the consequences rather than make a trade bargain for the most precious of her colonial possessions.

It was impossible for the people of the United States to understand that the Spaniards in Cuba believed that in the event of hostilities there would be another war of secession and the Southern States would revolt. Yet that delusion existed. It found utterance in the newspapers and in numerous pamphlets. These pamphlets described supposed invasions of the North American nation, and their repulse. Some of them were filled with contempt for the bargaining Yankee. They are interesting reading now as showing that the delusion did exist. One pamphlet told how the North Americans achieved success after success over the Spanish in arms, but were finally compelled to withdraw, because the spirit of Spanish resistance was impregnable. Other pamphlets were filled with Don Quixotism. The knight of La Mancha really seemed to walk abroad. More important than this supposed secession sentiment in the United States was the belief in European intervention. That was found in the pamphlets, in the newspapers, and among the army and navy officers, and the representatives of the Spanish Government. Spain would yield Cuba with honor; but perhaps it would not be to the United States, and perhaps it would be after a general war had been precipitated. This was both the spoken and the unspoken sentiment.

All this time the overtures to the insurgents were redoubled. Autonomy could be cast aside and Cubans could have the island if they would keep the flag and leave the forts and the garrisons to Spain. Govín and Dolz of the Autonomist cabinet were encouraged to press these overtures on the insurgents. Radical Autonomists were aided and indorsed in formulating a new set of propositions for Gómez. These were a dozen or more in number. They failed. Gómez and the insurgent chiefs who were invited to share in the government treated the overtures with contempt. Whenever Spain would concede independence as the basis they would open negotiations. And with independence as the basis they would welcome the intervention of the United States, and whatever terms it made would be accepted.

It might be said that the last chapter of autonomy was written when the *Maine* was blown up. But there was an epilogue. Elections were held. The preparations which were commenced in November proceeded slowly. An electoral census had to be taken. It was completed in March. It was a remarkable census. Though the official reports showed that people had been dying by the hundreds of thousands, this demonstrated that there had been no diminution in the number of inhabitants. The island was divided into districts. This first election under autonomy took place the last Sunday in March. The Union Constitutionals had been satisfied to let affairs drift. An arrangement had been made by which they were to have one-third of the deputies to the Cortes to be known as the opposition, and the Autonomists, or Government, two-thirds. The arrangement was not carried out to the letter, for two or three of the conservatives were rejected, and the Government was charged with treachery. It was the old story. No one cared to deposit a ballot, and the authorities arranged the election.

In April there were also elections for members of the insular chambers, that is, the House of Representatives and the Council. Previous to that time Galvez, as president of the Autonomist cabinet, issued a public appeal to President McKinley in the name of autonomy, urging the American executive not to let the system, which was on the eve of success, be made a failure through American encouragement of the insurrection.

The chambers were inaugurated in May, and the provisional Autonomist cabinet also became a permanent cabinet. President Galvez declared that the programme of the colonial government should be to defend the Autonomist constitution. Of this Autonomist congress, few names are known unless they are gathered from the official list. In the flowing Castilian idiom it is said of them that they celebrated sessions, pronounced discourses, and adjourned. But they also passed laws. After the signing of the protocol between the United States and Spain they held no sessions. In October Captain-General Blanco declared the chambers dissolved. The Autonomist cabinet was dissolved a fortnight before the end of Spanish sovereignty. Autonomy would have been better thought of by the Cuban people if it had never been formed into an insular government.

AIRPIT.

CHAPTER VI

Transition to Local Home Rule

Groundwork in Autonomous Constitution—Spirit of Spanish Local
Institutions—Paternal Edicts of Governor-Generals—Cuban
Municipality Similar to Township and County Government of
American States—Details of Organization—Illustrations of
the Geographical Basis—Minority Representation—Alcalde the
Chief Functionary—His Position and Power—Attributes of the
Ayuntamientos—Creatures of the Central Authority—Former
Military System—Lack of Knowledge by Citizens—Autonomist
Modifications—Changes Under American Military Authority—
Sources of Income.

ARMED revolt of Cubans brought autonomy when too
late for Spain. Armed intervention of the United
States ended the experiment which had failed. As a
system, the breath was out of the body before vitality
could be discerned. From the beginning autonomy
was pulseless. Has it then left no trace?

The question cannot be answered in the negative.
Most of the Autonomists who consistently opposed the
insurrection and who took office under the Spanish
Government were old men. The unpopularity which
was visited upon them by the masses of Cubans may
die out, but none of the leaders among them will be
called on to direct the destinies of the new government.
Their day is gone. Yet it cannot be said that their
work was in vain. They gave Cuba the only political
education in its history. The propaganda which they

maintained for twenty years was a preparation. Under centralized Spanish authority, with the traditions and inheritance of absolute power, the failure of autonomy was certain. With free institutions under the guidance of the American republic it may not be said that the principle is worthless. It is already the hope of Cubans and Spaniards who fear either annexation or independence. The foundation of the Cuban commonwealth was laid in insurrection, but it may properly be said that autonomy furnished the scaffolding for the new structure. The Cuba which came to the United States in trust was under an autonomous constitution, legitimately proclaimed by recognized Spanish sovereignty though never put into complete operation. It is therefore as much an inheritance as the Spanish code of civil and criminal laws.

In the administrative sense autonomy may be called the basis of the future Antillian state. It recognized the political and geographical division of the island into six provinces, it affirmed the principle of decentralization under provincial government, and it provided for a new basis of municipalities. It also provided that in pursuance of the autonomous constitution, laws should be enacted for local self-government. The stage was never reached at which these laws could be enacted, or the pledge of enacting them be neutralized by the Spanish authorities as with the compact of El Zanjón; but their formulation should not be difficult. The system of geographical divisions gives an excellent groundwork for home rule. The groundwork exists to-day, and on it may be built a popular system of home rule administration. This possibility is the first inquiry made by American statesmen who have practical notions about the building of commonwealths in the tropics. For that reason I analyze it first, though this is not the process of the Cuban political philosophers. They would build a republic in the clouds and set up a complete structure at the very beginning of independence. Its present discussion is also contrary to the natural order of the Spanish system, for that began with centralized authority, and what there was of local government came from above.

But before the municipal statutes are the municipal institutions. The spirit of Spanish local administration as it existed for a hundred years is breathed in hundreds of orders, edicts, and circulars of the Captain-Generals. It must be sought there, instead of in town records and in the histories of village communities. The Spanish régime in its relation to the individual—the individual was a subject rather than a citizen—for three-quarters of a century is embodied in the Bando of Good Government of Governor-General Gerónimo Valdés. In a degree it is the regimen up to the present day. The compilation is both curious and instructive. This bando or edict was published in 1842. It was republished at intervals up to the end of the Ten-Years' war. It is something more than a codification of laws, regulations, and customs. It is a living exposition of a system of government without the popular element. It reflects the political existence of the Cuban people under absolutism—sometimes administered by a benevolent and progressive despot such as General Valdés, oftener by a miltary tyrant such as Valeriano Weyler.

Though a score of years have passed since the Spanish Constitution was extended to the Antilles and municipal legislation enacted, to a large proportion of Cubans and Spaniards the old system is better known than the new one. Their transition will be as much affected by the old traditions as by the present municipal statute system. Furthermore, while the new system was embodied into statutes the former practices continued. So the gap is not so wide as a reading of the written local laws would lead one to think. The spirit of Don Gerónimo Valdés walked abroad through this old body of laws, customs, regulations, edicts, bandos, decrees, circulars, orders, and injunctions which he gathered together and vitalized. The regulations relating to slavery are the only ones that entirely disappeared.

The titles of the bando relate to Religion and Public Morality, Order, Health, Security, Theatres, Cleanliness, and Decoration. It required two hundred and sixty-one articles to define the relation of the citizen to the government or the municipality with respect to these headings. A special chapter is devoted to the pédaneos, or petty law officers. The instructions give an insight into the entire lack of personal or civil liberty reserved to the individual. The pédaneos and their assistants, the cabos de rondas or roundsmen, were real Paul Prys of the State. The list of cases in which they could acquire fees is a long one, and they could impose fines in compliance with specific articles of the bando. They were practically charged with the regulation of both the public and the private morals of the community.

The regulations are wearisome in their minuteness, from their prohibition of the picador at the bull-fight pricking the animal when in the centre of the ring, to the requirement that the bodega keepers should have a basin of water standing in front of their shops so that the dogs which ran through the streets might drink as they listed, and thus avoid the danger of hydrophobia. But through them all runs the authority from above, and it is the very highest authority. Long after Don Gerónimo Valdés had gone to his reward, the Captain-General and his Council of Administration continued to fix in detail the regulations for the cock-fight. The existence of this supreme authority and the extent to which it was exercised in the most trivial subjects should be kept in mind in reaching an understanding of local government under the general municipal legislation, the basis of which was the provisional law of 1878.

In the Spanish meaning the term municipality has a territorial significance broader than that which is given it in the United States. The county in one of the States of the Union corresponds to the municipality in Cuba. There is little distinction between city and country government. The city and county of New York answers to the municipality of Habana. The present system, in its administrative features, dates from the municipal law of 1878. After the enactment of that law the municipal life of a Cuban community, whether village or urban, underwent little change, because Spanish administration did not change materially with the modification of the statute. But the system had a recognized legal existence which is the existing basis. It is a good working basis, too, for the development of local self-government. The island was divided into 132 ayuntamientos or municipalities. In the United States it would be said that there were 132 counties. By provinces, there were 25 municipalities in Pinar del Río, 37 in Habana, 23 in Matanzas, 28 in Santa Clara, 5 in Puerto Príncipe, and 14 in Santiago de Cuba. The municipal termino, or district, is the extent of geographical territory over which the administrative action of the municipality extends.

For the creation of a termino municipal these were the exact conditions: first, not less than two thousand resident inhabitants; second, territory proportionate to the population; third, ability to sustain the obligatory municipal expenses out of the resources which the law authorized to municipalities. Every termino municipal forms part of a judicial district of a province. The census of population determines the number of concejales—aldermen or county commissioners—and their division is into the two classes of lieutenant alcaldes, or assistant mayors, and regidores, or ordinary councilmen. There are grades of municipalities based on population. Cities possessing a population of forty thousand and upward have an ayuntamiento or council composed of thirty members, and this is the maximum number. Habana, Matanzas, and Santiago de Cuba are the cities of this class. Under the statute definition, a municipality is the legal association of all people who reside in a termino municipal or district.

The original law of 1878 also provided for a body known as the junta municipal. This was composed jointly of all the members of the ayuntamiento and of vocales or special delegates in equal number chosen by the electors. This junta municipal was in effect an auditing committee, as it was charged with the revision and censoring of the ayuntamiento accounts. This form of organization underwent various changes; but the junta municipal was never a real factor in local administration. The members of the ayuntamiento were elected theoretically by the residents who possessed the electoral right, which was based on both property and personal taxes. The concejales selected three of their number, from among whom the civil governor of the province, subject to the Governor-General, could choose the alcalde or mayor if it so pleased him. If not, he designated some one else. Generally it was some one else.

The grades of communities still recognized are ciuades or cities, villas or towns, pueblos or villages, and caserios or hamlets, and urban districts and rural districts. Aldea, which is the name in Spain for a small village, is seldom used in Cuba. Lugar, the Spanish designation of a town or place, is rarely heard. Bayamo, with a population of 17,000, is a ciudad, as are Habana, Cienfuegos, Matanzas, and other places. Bejucal, with 8,000 inhabitants, is also a city. El Caney, where the first attack was made by the American troops in seeking entrance to Santiago, is a villa or town. Dos Caminos, with 500 inhabitants, is a pueblo. Guani, in the tobacco country around Remedios, in Santa Clara province, has 200 inhabitants, and is a caserio. El Cerro, one of the suburbs of Habana, is a barrio urbano. Guamo, near Bayamo, has 700 or 800 inhabitants, and is a barrio rural or country district. Barrios, rural or urban, consist of territory which for any reason is not organized into a municipality. Aguacate is a municipality of the province of Habana and belongs to the judicial district of Jaruco. Its area is 121 square kilometres, or 75 square miles. The municipality is divided into four barrios or districts, which are the pueblos of Aguacate, Campastizo, Reoj, and Zabaleta.

The pueblo of Aguacate is the headquarters of the municipal district of the same name. It has 600 or 700 inhabitants, and is a barrio urban or town ward as distinguished from a barrio rural or country township. The pueblo has a municipal judge. Jaruco, with an area of 253 square kilometres—157 square miles—is a partido judicial or judicial district belonging to the province of Habana and to the audiencia or general court. Jaruco has eight municipal districts or terminos, including that of the same name, which is a ciudad or city. The officials are the alcalde and members of the ayuntamiento, a primary judge or judge of the first instance, a municipal judge, and a register of property. Batabanó, with a population of 8,000 and an area of 147 square kilometres, is a municipality of the province of Habana, belonging to the judicial district of Bejucal. It has six barrios, of which the pueblo of Batabanó, with a population of 1,700, is one. It has a municipal judge. Bejucal is a judicial district in the province of Habana, and depending from it are eight municipalities, the largest of which is the municipal district of the same name, which has a population of 7,900 and an area of 400 square kilometres. The municipality is divided into four urban barrios and seven rural barrios. It has a judge of the first instance, and also a municipal judge and a register of property.

Other illustrations might be given, but these may

suffice to show the geographical basis of local government in Cuba. The municipalities, as stated, correspond as closely as can be under different political systems to the counties in the American States. The barrios rural are the townships. Before the insurrection and the reconcentration wiped out whole communities, there were a dozen more than 700 barrios rural or townships in Cuba. By geographical divisions there are still that number, but scores and scores of them are without a living inhabitant. The official statistics formerly gave 600 caserios or hamlets, but these have no political meaning. Usually the caserio is administratively part of the barrio rural. In perhaps thirty instances the caserios and the rural barrios or townships are identical in boundaries, but in the general sense the caserio may be ignored in seeking to determine the basis of home-rule government. The whole question of future local administration lies in these 700 townships and the 100 or more city districts which combined form the 132 ayuntamientos or municipalities.

Under the law a census of the inhabitants of each municipal district was directed to be taken every five years. This provision was rarely observed. The concejales—aldermen, or members of the county board, as they would be called in some parts of the United States —were chosen by the citizens of the municipality in accordance with the electoral law. As before explained, the grouping of the rural population was into barrios or country districts, each of which had an alcalde or township governor named by the superior authority. It was the same with the urban barrios, except that they had celadors or police magistrates.

Minority representation was recognized in the provision that when three concejales were chosen, each elector should vote for two out of the three, for three out of the four, four out of six, five out of seven, and in that proportion up to the limit. Half the membership of the ayuntamiento ceased every two years. The members were subject to fines for absence from the sessions. In actual administration it was not common for the alcalde named by the aldermen to be approved by the civil governor or the Governor-General unless the wishes of these officials had been ascertained in advance. The Governor-General having the power "when he believed it convenient to the interests of the locality," often rejected the entire list of nominations and named an alcalde who did not belong to the municipality. In the larger cities the teniente alcaldes, or assistant mayors, who had jurisdiction as municipal sub-rulers over different districts, were named from among the aldermen. The alcaldes de barrios, or township rulers, were named by the alcaldes of the municipalities from the territory in which they exercised their functions.

Sometimes difficulty was encountered. A notable case was that of the municipal alcalde of Mangas, in the province of Pinar del Río. He refrained from naming alcaldes in the rural districts of Pueblo Nuevo and Guamanor because in them there was no elector who knew how to read and write. The case was taken up to the Governor-General's Council of Administration, being too knotty for the intermediate authorities to settle. The Council of Administration found no precedent and no analogy. After mature discussion it resolved that there being no electors within those two country districts who could read and write, the alcaldes could be selected from electors who could not read and write. The decision stood, and the selections were made. On the part of the central authority there seems to have been some idea that the office of alcalde should be considered a non-partisan one. The Madrid decree of 1880 directed the governors of provinces to prohibit alcaldes from assisting at reunions of a political character, and also from acting as editors or directors of newspapers. The primary application of this order was to the provinces of the peninsula rather than to those of the island.

A visitor to any rural community of Cuba is impressed with the evidence that the alcalde is the local authority and the only authority. He is so clearly the functionary that inquiry is seldom made for other functionaries. It is he who receives the higher officials, who meets the stranger, and who dispenses the honors of the town. In American towns due regard is paid the official position of mayor, but he is not allowed to monopolize the honors. In a Cuban village these privileges are conceded unhesitatingly to the alcalde because he represents political power commensurate with them. A beneficent instance of this power may be seen in the proclamations reducing the price of bread when it becomes too high. His proclamations enforcing public order contain frequent references to the culture and good name of the people. In the plays at the theatre which represent Spanish customs the alcalde is always a leading character. It is the same in Cuba.

The governors of the provinces could suspend the

alcaldes, this act being subject to the approval or disapproval of the Governor-General. Similarly they could suspend the assistant alcaldes and the regidores, or ordinary councilmen. Regarding the superior authority, it was specifically declared that the alcalde was the representative of the state. Being so, he could not be the representative of the people of the community. In everything relating to the political government of the municipality, the authority, duties, and responsibilities of the alcalde were independent of the ayuntamiento. Likewise the assistant alcaldes and the alcaldes of the country districts were under the direction of the municipal alcalde as the representative of the government. They did not represent the people.

Under the system in force until the legislation following the peace of El Zanjón, there were thirty-one gobiernos, or political districts, in the island, each of which had an ayuntamiento; while the villages which were the heads of jurisdictions had local councils whose members were named by the civil governor of the province and were nominally responsible to him. Actually, they were responsible to the military authority. The elective officials in the larger municipalities were justices of the peace and collectors of fines who were known as syndics. Besides their responsibility to the military authority, the civil governor, and the Governor-General, the auyuntamientos had also a central administration with a jefe or chief residing in Habana. The main functions of this central administration were the control of the rural police.

In spite of its defects, the law of 1878 was in one sense a concession to popular government. Before that time many municipalities had consisted simply of military districts whose absolute rulers were the military commanders. And the commander, though described as the captain of the district, was always a lieutenant ruler of some military official higher in power. When he was a benevolent and energetic despot he gave a good local administration; but it was a military, and not a representative one. Where the military commander was a bad or an indifferent despot, the municipality reflected his character. This law also did away with the regidores perpetuales, or aldermen who held their offices for life. It may be said to have made a clearing in the jungle of centralized municipal government. But its application was limited, and the majority of the people had little conception of the system. To-day a question put to intelligent Cubans or Spaniards regarding the details of municipal government in past years is usually met with an apology for ignorance. They never knew much about it.

The attributes and functions of ayuntamientos included the usual municipal services: opening of streets and parks, enrolment of residents, draining and sewerage, bridges, water supply, baths, slaughter-houses, markets, sanitation, public construction, policing, and local public works generally, including the roads. Also charitable institutions and hospitals of their own or administered through benevolent societies. Penalties were provided for the infraction of municipal ordinances by fines. The ayuntamiento had power to require from all males between the ages of sixteen and fifty not to exceed twenty days' labor on public works. This is in another form the road tax of many of the States in the

American Union. The teniente alcaldes in the larger towns and cities were acting mayors in the absence of the alcaldes. Each also had a district in which he exercised the administrative municipal functions under the direction of the alcalde. The ayuntamientos selected from their own numbers one or two members who as procuradores sindicos, or attorneys, represented the corporation in all legal proceedings, and also revised the local bills and estimates. The ayuntamientos named their employes. The income of the municipalities came from goods owned by them, taxes on personality and realty, taxes laid for maintaining the police, fines for violations of ordinances, assessments upon the citizens or landowners, and imposts upon articles to eat, drink, and burn. Where the town was large enough to maintain a market, that was owned or controlled by the municipality. Generally it may be said that the chief source of income was the slaughter-house tax, which was from two or three cents a pound on beef. Habana had power to lay other imposts.

A brief critical examination of the municipal law of 1878, independent of its administration, is sufficient to show that under it there could be little growth in local self-government. The clear statement of the centralized conception appears in the declaration that the alcalde is the representative of the central government; that in everything relating to the political government of a municipality his authority, powers, and responsibility are independent of the ayuntamiento. The appointment of the alcaldes by the Governor-General, frequently not residents of the community, was the affirmation of this fact. A further check on the independence of the ayuntamientos was devised in their subjection to the provincial deputations and again to the civil governors. The law underwent no organic statutory modification. It was interpreted and construed in the first place by royal orders and decrees from Madrid applicable to the municipalities of the peninsula. Then there were the circulars and decrees of the Governor-General construing and interpreting it, often in contradictory instructions. The saying that Spanish government in Cuba was government by decree found its aptest illustration in the municipal administration.

Under the Spanish system everything came from above and from without. Spain began its administration of the colonies on the principle that they should be treated as directly subject to the throne, commercially and politically. One was the corollary of the other. Columbus memorialized their Catholic Majesties for permission to appoint an alcalde in each grouping of population. The Council of the Indies and the House of Trade were created within a few years after Columbus' discovery to secure and insure commercial monopoly. They exercised all the functions of civil administration, legislative, executive, and judicial. In that age was constructed the framework of the Spanish colonial administrative system, which endured with little fundamental change until no colonies remained. This power began with the viceroys and Captain-Generals. It ended with the municipalities. Captain-Generals ruled in Cuba for four hundred years. In the beginning they nominated governors and mayors. They were doing the same thing when the last Captain-

General but one took the office in order to implant autonomy. Obedience to the superior authorities was exacted as rigorously in 1897 as in 1527, and with less power of local rule to the municipalities.

All that the people of Cuba knew of municipal or of rural government is embodied in the statute. Less of actual knowledge was gathered by them from the system in operation than from reading the law, because the application was at the will of the Spanish authorities. These officials contrived to bring it into harmony with their own ideas of administration. Few abuses were corrected. Elections were made farces, so that good citizenship found no encouragement. In a municipal election of Guanabacoa the registry list was posted up as required. Three electors voted. The officials returned the whole list as voted, though some of those whose names were on it had been tenants of the grave-yards for months. The same thing was done elsewhere.

The Autonomist constitution made important changes.

Instead of the alcaldes being nominated by the Governor-General or the civil governor, it provided that the election by the ayuntamientos should be final, and that the alcaldes should exercise the active functions of the municipal administration as executors of the ordinances of the ayuntamientos and as their representatives. Instead of two thousand inhabitants for a termino municipal, the municipal organization was made obligatory on every group of population of more than one thousand. This provision was never carried into effect. The Autonomist legislation is useful as suggesting changes which may be made on a basis of the old laws for genuine local self-government.

The American military authority through decrees of Governor-General Brooke modified and enlarged the sources of municipal income. They abolished the imposts on killing cattle which were known as the slaughter-house tax, along with those on food for articles of consumption, and on wood and charcoal for burning. That is, the power of making the necessities of daily life dearer by local taxation was taken away. In recompense the municipalities were allowed to utilize the state share of direct taxes upon town and country real estate, and also the industrial tax. Some minor sources of income were further transferred from the central authority of the state to the muncipalities. The local imposts on alcoholic or spirituous beverages were not disturbed. These changes were necessarily provisional, and subject to the readjustment of the internal fiscal system of the entire island.

Under the American military authority a reapportionment of the municipalities in their boundaries and classifications was also outlined. Its provisional and temporary character renders valueless a detailed examination of its effect on the local political organisms of the island. To a proper understanding of the future system of municipal self-government a knowledge of their relation to the provinces is necessary.

CHAPTER VII

Provinces as a Federal Framework

MIDWAY between local administration and the central authority was the provincial government. It will be of more importance in the future of Cuba than it was in the past of Spain. Its former relation was hardly definable. The provinces were facts of geography and fictions of administration.

They did not grow out of any system of town and country government. With the insight afforded into the municipal administration of Cuba, and even with the modifications proposed by autonomy, the investigator will not find much of local self-rule. He will search in vain for the genesis of the New England town meeting. His quest for something resembling the newly formed community of the West in the pioneer days, coming together by natural movement, calling itself into being, and providing for the management of its own affairs, would be barren. One reason would be that Spanish colonial government is old and there was a precedent for every condition that might arise. And as the precedents were not favorable to the self-ruling instinct, the ideas which would be encountered on this subject would be primary, hardly rudimentary.

Jaruco, in the province of Habana, has a connected municipal history of one hundred and forty years, but there is no record of a town gathering to consider public improvements or of an indignation meeting to protest against acts of public officials. Trinidad, in Santa Clara province, has an historic banner going back almost to the foundation of the town in the early part of the sixteenth century, but it has no memorials of local government. The town of Villa Clara has a history filled with incident, but the incidents are not of the community's management of its own local affairs by elections and by free discussion. Matanzas has a municipal organization recorded stage by stage from the opening of the seventeenth century to the present day. Its leading chapters in local administration are the measures it organized at various periods for defence against the pirates and the filibusters. Puerto Príncipe tells the same story, and its most luminous chapter is the heroic defence of the alcalde and the citizens against the land incursion of Morgan and his buccaneers in 1668.

Habana's early history is filled with similar incidents. When the English assaulted the city the regidores, or aldermen, were in charge of the garrisons. Habana at that time was a larger city than the Boston which held the tea party or the New York which a dozen and more years later expelled Lord Howe. It was almost as large as the Philadelphia in which the Continental Congress met. It complained righteously that its municipal basis had continued since its primitive creation that of the smallest councils in the peninsula. In the first quarter of this century it remonstrated that it had no power to control municipal government, that its council was in shackled hands. There was, nevertheless, more local or municipal liberty, though not of free discussion, during the first three centuries of Spanish government of Cuba than during this last century. The need of measures of self-defence was one. The Council of the Indies was also concerned with the commercial benefits arising from liberal treatment of the municipalities, and the dangers of political revolution were not great. But in those times the provinces of Cuba did not exist as geographical or political divisions.

Rising from the subject of local and municipal government to that of provincial or territorial government, it may be said that there was none in the American sense. The provinces did not have that degree of independence which is conceded to territories in the United States. There was nothing that approached the idea of a provincial legislature. No conception of such a function could exist in a country where there was no national legislature; where the Cortes across the sea legislated, and the agents of the crown administered according to their own will. For a series of years Cuba was divided politically into territorial provinces each with a lieutenant-governor appointed by the Captain-General. There were also military, judicial, regional, maritime, ecclesastical, and economic divisions. Their spheres and functions are indicated by their names, except possibly the economic division, which is better described as the real hacienda, or royal treasury. It was the fiscal department of the island. These departments interlaced as it were in a network, without clear distinction between administrative and other branches; but since the Spanish system was essentially military, they all converged in the Captain-General, called in his civil capacity the Governor-General.

By the royal decree of 1878 the provinces of the island were fixed as they exist to-day, the division being into six civil jurisdictions, which took their names from their respective capitals. With these provinces in mind, the other divisions into maritime, regional, ecclesiastical, and so on may be ignored. The administrative authorities of each province were the governor, the provincial deputation, and the provincial commission or junta. The governor was named by the supreme authority. He had a substantial veto on the acts of the ayuntamientos and of the deputations. He supervised elections. To him was especially intrusted the administration of public order in the province. Genuine provincial government was lost somewhere in these centralized functions of government and administration. To find it again and restore it to its proper place and rightful function is one of the tasks of the future.

The political entity of the province was recognized in the provincial deputations. Their similarity to the same bodies in the peninsula was often quoted as evidence that Cuba enjoyed as much civil liberty as did the mother country herself. Cuba, it was declared, had local parliaments, and could ask nothing more without placing herself on a higher plane than the provinces of the peninsula. But the parliamentary character of these provincial deputations does not disclose itself on inquiry. They were anachronisms. They were merely another check on local self-government. They were neither provincial legislatures nor provincial councils. The deputation was composed of deputies selected by the electors who voted for concejales. Three were chosen from each judicial district of the province. Their term was four years. The deputation was especially charged, first, with the improvement of the roads, irrigation canals, provincial public works, hospitals, and instruction; secondly, with the administration of provincial funds and the general management of the fiscal affairs. Educational establishments might be created or sustained by the deputations, subject to the general law regarding public instruction. With relation to the municipalities the deputation enjoyed the faculties conferred upon it by the municipal law, which were of a general supervisory character.

Then there was the provincial commission, which was named by the Governor-General from the members of the deputation. Its membership was five. The commission was assumed to hold regular sittings at the capital of the province. It answered to the Governor-General's Council of Administration. Its members were lawyers, and they gave opinions upon the laws and regulations submitted to them by the governor of the province or by the Governor-General. It decided disputed elections, and the eligibility of deputies when this was questioned. It acted as the provincial deputation in emergencies when the full deputation could not be got together. In practice the commission, created out of the body of the deputation, served a useful purpose as instrument of the central authority. By chance or by neglect it would sometimes happen that the majority in a provincial deputation would be Autonomists. The superior power would feel obliged to check their too dangerous gropings after liberal government, and their tendency to exercise to the limit the narrow prerogatives which the statutes gave them. This was done by the Governor-General in naming the permanent commission. There could always be found five or six members who would be subservient to the powers above. And thus what little good was in the provincial deputations was destroyed.

The provincial commissions underwent an organic change in the law of 1890, but the change is not important now. Under the autonomous constitution of 1897 they were declared to be of a permanent character. They were given essentially judicial functions. The provincial magistrates of the audiencia, or general court, were to preside over the commissions, which were to be known as provincial juntas. These juntas were to be composed of fifteen vocales, or delegates. By virtue of their being provincial deputies, the president and vice-president of the deputation and the oldest ex-president were to be vocales. There were also to be four tax-payers chosen by lot from among those who paid the first quota of the industrial tax, four from among those who paid the first quota of the land tax, and four citizens who had official titles showing their professional or academic standing.

The autonomist decrees made the deputations autonomous in everything relating to the creation and dotation of establishments of public instruction, charitable institutions, provincial rights of way, maritime or fluvial, and the budget. The decrees also authorized both the municipalities and the provinces to establish freely the taxes to cover their expenses without other limitation than that these should be compatible with the general taxing system of the island. The resources for taxation of a province were declared to be independent of the municipal resources. In the election of members of the ayuntamientos and the deputations, provision was to be made for minority representation. From these provisions some hints may be had for the future, but that is all. The provincial deputations were so utterly useless that they were abolished by the American military administration. They are not likely to be re-established under any system of government that may be adopted.

In describing the municipalities, reference has been made to the judicial districts. In Spain's colonial administration the judicial district seems to have been the political unit. At one period it was almost synonymous with or meant the same as the military partido, or district. The laws following the compact of El Zanjón made no important change in the judicial system of the island. There were 33 judicial districts then, and the number has been increased or decreased by one or two at different times. The judicial districts in the island number at present 34. They are divided among the provinces as follows: Pinar del Río, 5; Habana, 7; Matanzas, 6; Santa Clara, 6; Puerto Príncipe, 3; Santiago de Cuba, 7. Each judicial district is the cabecera, or head, of a number of municipalities. Sometimes, as in the case of the city of Habana, there is only one municipality, but most of the districts have included in their jurisdiction half a dozen municipalities. Each district has a judge of the first instance, except that of Habana, which necessarily has more than one. This judge of the first instance, or primary judge, might be designated variously as a county, district, or circuit judge. The judicial partido would be known in the United States as a circuit rather than as a district. What are known as the municipal judges come closer to the definition of county judges and justices of the peace. They are more numerous than the judges of the first instance, numbering two hundred. The municipal judges have the ordinary functions of local magistrates and possess police powers. The judges of all classes were appointed by the higher authorities.

The audiencias, or general courts, as commonly understood, would be called appellate courts in most of the States of the Union. Under Spanish sovereignty the final appeal was to the courts in Madrid. Originally in Cuba justice was administered from the ancient audiencia established in Santo Domingo. When that island was ceded to France in 1795, the judicial tribunal was translated to the city of Puerto Príncipe as the most midland one of Cuba. It began its functions in 1802. In 1838 a second audiencia was established in Habana, and with a pretorial character which was lacking in the Puerto Príncipe tribunal. For the administration of justice the aim was to adapt the judicial districts to the political and military boundaries. Till recently Habana constituted the superior audiencia; but Puerto Príncipe was a royal audiencia to which pertained civil jurisdiction over Santiago de Cuba. Formerly the division was into twenty-six judicial districts, known as the territory of the royal pretorial audiencia, or general courts. Each of these judicial districts had an alcalde mayor or ordinary judge who had auxiliary alcaldes or local judges. The appeal lay direct from these courts of conciliation and counsel to the audiencia sitting in Habana.

Each province of the island is a criminal audiencia in itself. The judgments of this criminal court may be appealed to the criminal section of the Habana audiencia. The audiencia of Habana includes the province of that name and the provinces of Pinar del Río, Matanzas, and Santa Clara. While each municipality is supposed to have its municipal court, there are some places not municipalities which have their municipal judge. Habana is divided into districts with different branches of the audiencia having jurisdiction. Under the American military authority, a supreme court was established to take the place of the Madrid tribunals, which were the courts of last resort. The Supreme Court of Cuba consists of a chief-justice and six associate justices. An independent court had previously been organized in the province of Santiago without reference to the former pretorial audiencia of Puerto Príncipe, of which jurisdiction it was part. A question was raised whether this Santiago court was final in its decisions or whether they could be appealed to the Supreme Court of the island. The only logical answer which could be given to this question was given, and the Santiago tribunal was declared a subordinate one. This sketch of the administrative organism of the judicial system is presented here without reference to the laws themselves, because the courts are a part of the local and the provincial régimes as of the general government.

Another organism is that of the registry of property. These do not follow the lines of the municipalities or county divisions, as is customary in the United States, but in a general way follow the boundaries of the judicial districts. Actually they are not so numerous. By royal decree of July 4th, 1879, twenty-five registries were established for the whole island. In most instances the boundaries are coincident and coequal with the boundaries of the judicial districts; but Habana City has one register for its three districts and for its suburb of Marianao; and in the eastern provinces there are also consolidated registries. This accounts for the number of registries not being equal to that of the judcial districts. It may be said that the registries of landownership and the records of property transfers are well kept. Contrary to the common belief, titles in Cuba are easily traced, and are, if anything, more secure than in the United States.

From what is and what has been, an idea may be gained of what the internal political and administrative framework of the Cuba of the future may be. For the present it is not of moment to discuss the external aspects of the prospective state, or whether it shall have departments of foreign relations, of the army, and of the navy. Cuba may be considered as a federal body with central authority and central administration. The difference in the future will be that the central authority will rest on a foundation of local and provincial government, instead of the provinces and municipalities depending on it and from it. The old conception of centralized authority will disappear. Though the Captain-General was the supreme power, even before the implantation of autonomy he had his Council of Administration which advised him in regard to the interpretation of the colonial statutes and their application to the island, or to its provinces and municipalities. The only point was that he could enforce his own arbitrary construction whenever he chose. This freedom of the executive from responsibility is one of the defects of the past system which is certain to be remedied. Whatever form the future government of the island may take, Cuba will have a judiciary department coequal with the executive branch. It has seen too much of the subordination and the prostitution of the courts ever to consent to placing them on a lower plane than the executive power.

For what might be called the internal federal administration, autonomy made little change in the outward system. The Autonomist cabinet in practice was little more than raising the departments of the treasury, public works, and education to cabinet positions, with separate functions which also embraced the administrative features of the courts and of agriculture. The American military authority created a provisional advisory cabinet for the four departments respectively of the treasury, of state and government, of public works, and of justice and education. These departments are the central power in what might be called internal administration, for the control of the customs was kept so largely within the American military authority that it could hardly be called a part of the actual jurisdiction of the provisional treasury department. The department of state is a misnomer. In the provisional arrangement it is the department which regulates the relations of the municipalities and provinces to the general government. In the evolution of the commonwealth of Cuba its functions are decidedly the most important of all the departments.

The six provinces will probably exist in the future as they exist to-day geographically and politically. Various suggestions have been made of rearranging their boundaries and consolidating them. The natural division would be into the eastern, central, and western provinces. The Spanish authorities in their military and judicial divisions split the island into two districts. Pinar del Río was also at one time joined with the province of Habana. But the inhabitants have become accustomed to the present boundaries, and they are a people who cling strongly to that to which they are accustomed. Each province has its history, its local usages, and its traditions. Each province has a capital of the same name. When General J. C. Bates fixed the military headquarters of his department at Cienfuegos, a mere military convenience, strong feeling was aroused in the little city of Santa Clara, which under Spanish sway was the centre of both political and military administration. The people protested against the removal of the ancient capital of the province. Trifling as was the incident, the intensity of the protests showed how difficult it would be to enter upon a series of changes which upset old boundaries and did violence to ancient memories.

Some of the Cuban revolutionary leaders have worked out a plan of five provinces to replace the existing division. The first Cuban revolutionary assembly divided the island into four jurisdictions, with prefecturas and sub-prefecturas as the subordinate administrative districts. But this was for the military operations of the insurgent troops, and never came to the knowledge of the masses of the people. They are attached to the present divisions and may be depended on to oppose a change.

These six provinces are also to be considered as six states or territories within a nation, rather than as six great counties within a state. But this is within definite limitations. The wisest among the Cuban leaders already appreciate the importance of nationalizing the sentiment while decentralizing the administration. The provinces will have elective civil governors—that can be readily foreseen. The uncertain question is how much further they will go. The uselessness of the provincial deputations has been disclosed, and at this day there is little disposition to revive them. A provincial parliament in the sense of a twofold legislative body corresponding to the American State legislatures is not an apparent necessity even as a part of the education in popular government. With the laws uniform for the whole island, as they will be, there does not appear to be a wide sphere for provincial lawmaking. The administrative functions are the important ones.

It may be that the doubt will ultimately resolve itself

into the creation of councils something like the territorial councils in the early history of the Western territories of the Union. These councils may possess mixed executive and legislative functions. They may become the general board with reference to the municipalities, but not in the sense of the veto power possessed by the old provincial deputations. An understanding of the sentiment as it exists to-day will make this clear. The people of the various communities have a real longing for home rule. They may not know much about the system in operation, they may not do it so well as higher authority would do it for them, but they have a full determination to do it themselves without the veto of provincial assembly, provincial governor, or Governor-General. Some general legislation will undoubtedly be enacted which will simplify their work. Probably the line between town and country government will be drawn more distinctly, so that the confusing term municipality—confusing to Americans—will not have its present wide application. But the organization of either country grouping or of town inhabitants will be on the basis of self-government within the administrative organism of the province. The municipalities, whether city or rural, are units of the future provincial administration. The provinces are the units of the decentralized federal authority that is to be evolved into a commonwealth.

The physical features of the various provinces may be said to have a bearing on the political characteristics of their inhabitants; yet these are not marked enough to develop strong differences. Most of the mineral wealth is in the eastern section of the island, and the tobacco districts are the central and western regions. Beyond this there is a general similarity of products. No dangerous diversity is likely to spring up among people who follow similar pursuits. Like the Spaniards in the island, the Cubans have their distinctions of localities. With the blacks of Santiago there is a slight mixture of Jamaica negroes, while Haiti and Santo Domingo also have representation. The mulatto element there is the result of the crossing of French blood. Around Baracoa and the towns on the north coast are yet traces of the habits and customs of the French refugees of Santo Domingo. These French refugees were the most progressive industrial element that ever entered into the life of Cuba. The Camagüeyans, the inhabitants of the central province of Puerto Príncipe, are fond of calling themselves the genuine Cubans; and in this part of the island it must be confessed there is little of Spain, though sometimes a trace of Africa appears in the blood. Santa Clara, more particularly the eastern part of the province, also claims the distinction of being purely Cuban. As with the Camagüeyans, its men are superior physically to those in the western part of the island. From Matanzas west through Habana and Pinar del Río there is more *mezcla* or reunion of Spanish and Cuban blood.

The Spanish writers called this provincial sentiment, when applied to the people of the various provinces of the peninsula, regionalism. It might be translated into English by the word sectionalism. Whatever danger of sectionalism exists is in the two eastern provinces of Santiago de Cuba and Puerto Príncipe. They were in constant rebellion against Spanish authority, and the query is whether they will not insist on having independent governments of their own rather than be parts of a central political organism. Santiago province especially is credited with this possible ambition. The city of that name in a small way is a rival of Habana. The province is geographically almost disconnected from the rest of the island. Symptoms of opposition to the general government were shown under the American control. At regular periods protests would be made against the customs receipts being distributed throughout the island, instead of the dues received at the Santiago ports being disbursed exclusively in that province. This attitude was indirectly encouraged by the American officials who were administering the affairs of the province as an independent department. Santiago, as it happened, came under the American control several months before the remaining provinces. So much was accomplished there under the wise direction of General Leonard Wood, that it was perhaps naturally his part to seek the fullest freedom of administration, as though the eastern end of the island were a separate country.

Should the popular currents run for annexation when the time comes to determine the form of stable government which is to prevail, a revival of this feeling may be looked for in the request of Santiago to be joined with Puerto Príncipe and be erected into a separate state. But in the presumption of an independent island government too much stress should not be given temporary outcroppings of regionalism on the part of Santiago or Puerto Príncipe. The building of the central or backbone railroad will draw these provinces into closer industrial and commercial relation with the western provinces, and their political interests are in any circumstance identical with the rest of the island. The free institutions for which all aspire are the same. To check the spread of regionalism or sectionalism all the provinces should share equitably in the central administration. With uniform general laws, and with the municipalities acting as independent local organisms within the provinces, the latter will have a distinct function in the commonwealth. They should form the administrative federal framework on a decentralized basis.

CHAPTER VIII

The Race of Color

Señor Don a Gentleman—Official Definition of Civil Status—Spanish
Law Affirmed by American Authority—Nightmare of Black West
India League—Analysis of Statistics of Population—Comparison
with Jamaica—Relative Decrease of Blacks—Temporary Relative
Increase as the Result of Reconcentration—Colonization Improb-
able—Value of Negro Labor on Plantations—Higher Industrial
Plane than in the United States—No Color-Line—Dispropor-
tionate Number of Criminals—Ñañigoism a Misleading Term
for Crime—Advance of Blacks Under the Spanish Civilization
—Future Standing that of Political and Industrial Equality.

A staring interrogation is better answered when first
met. What of the black race? The question cannot
be evaded. The existence of the blacks must be reck-
oned with in every phase of the reconstruction of the
island. Consequently their standing and their prospects are now discussed with the simple reminder that
Cuba has social and economic problems to solve as
well as political ones. The African population has a defined status socially, industrially, and politically. The
black race has no future separate from that of the other
inhabitants of Cuba. It is essentially and integrally a
part of that future.

The negro or the mulatto may call himself "Don,"
and ask that others use the prefix in addressing him.
This is more than the simple "Mister" of American fa-

miliarity. "Señor" answers to that meaning. "Don" is the "Esquire," the old English designation for gentleman, the title of courtesy, and it is translated by the dictionaries as the Spanish name for gentleman. The colored man is not simply Señor So-and-So: he is Señor Don So-and-So. The prefix was the possession of the proudest grandees of Spain, and it is still supposed to carry with it a certain dignity. The Captain-General of Spain, whose titles filled half a page, was always "Don" in the beginning of his official dignities and honors. And under Spanish law, by formal resolution of a Captain-General, the humblest negro in Cuba was decreed as rightfully using the same prefix.

The distinct recognition of the civil status of the African race under the Spanish law was formally proclaimed by Captain-General Calleja in 1893. It was, in effect, the interpretation and indorsement given by the Council of Administration in affirming previous decrees. This action is sometimes described as a mere authorization of the blacks to use the title of "Don." In reality it was far more. The story of this definition of the civil rights of the race of color under Spanish law is instructive. Various societies of blacks petitioned the superior authorities that they direct the governors of the provinces and the presiding judges and fiscals, or prosecuting attorneys, of the courts to communicate to their subordinates the decrees and official dispositions previously made affirming the right of the colored classes to enjoy equal rights with the white classes, and prohibiting the establishment of distinctions by reason of color. The official dispositions previously made forbade the proprietors of cafés or similar public places to discriminate against persons of color, and affirmed the privilege of the blacks to travel on the railways on the same terms as the whites.

The Council of Administration under Captain-General Calleja did not consider instructions to the courts necessary, but it granted the other requests of the colored societies.* The basis which it affirmed was an official disposition made by the governor of the province of Pinar del Río in 1885. A negro complained that the proprietor of a café refused to serve him because of his color. The government thereupon issued an order directing that the penalties be enforced and that the discrimination cease. This order recited that "if customs were the fruits of the ideas which inspired the laws, it was the duty of the supreme authority, mindful of its own, to combat the prejudices in the minds of the people from usages and opinions born of times which had disappeared, never to return. For the success of such important ends it was competent for the superior authority to consecrate itself to the maintenance and the respect of the rights which the Spanish constitution guaranteed to every Spanish citizen, and which reposed in the principle of equality." This declaration stands unchanged. Under the Spanish rule few instances arose in which this enforcement was necessary.

After the American occupation a mulatto chief of the insurrection was refused entertainment in a café kept by Americans. The Spanish code of civil rights, cited above, was invoked and was enforced. However distasteful it may be to American prejudices, the code will be enforced. Nor will there ever be discrimination

* *Gaceta de la Habana*, December 19th, 1893.

on account of color in the privileges of railroad travel. The American military authorities from the outset showed a scrupulous regard for the civil rights of the blacks. So far as their official acts went, they studiously ignored the color-line and discouraged race prejudice. The social toleration which was so natural for Spaniards and white Cubans did not prove difficult for the military commanders. But their example was not always followed by their own countrymen.

The idea of a black West India republic has been both a dream and a nightmare. It haunted the English historian, James Anthony Froude, like a spectre, and conjured up for him visions of a mongrel nation of negroids. In moments of despair American statesmen have dreamed it as the solution to the problem of the African race in the United States. To more of them it has been a nightmare, a fear that the Antilles would become, if not a menace, at least a bar to the civilization of the continent. Haiti, on the map hardly bigger than a man's hand, in the Antillian sky became a portentous cloud. The cloud is a psychic, not a physical phenomenon. It disappears on analysis. In the early part of the century, when Humboldt * began to differentiate the population of the West Indies, the blacks in Cuba were in excess of the whites. The figures as then collated were as follows:

* After Humboldt, the most complete analyses were given by Arboleya in his "Manual de la Isla de Cuba," published in 1859, and by Pezuela in the "Diccionario de la Isla Cuba," published in 1863. The fullest analysis of the subsequent censuses may be found in "La Revista Cubana" in a series of articles by Señor Coppinger. While perplexed by confusing figures and unreliable official statistics, all the authorities substantially agree in their conclusions.

	1811.	1817.	1825.
Whites....................	274,000	290,000	325,000
Blacks	336,000	340,268	390,000
Total	610,000	630,268	715,000

A discrepancy between the statistics of 1811 and 1817 is chargeable to imperfect census-taking. It is also noted that from 1811 to 1825 the jurisdiction of Habana received 185,000 negroes brought by the slave traders from Africa. With respect to other countries in 1825, the population of Cuba was almost double that of Jamaica. By color, thus:

	White.	Black.
Cuba.....................	46 per cent.	54 per cent.
Jamaica.................	6 "	94 "

Taking the greater Antilles as a group, Humboldt found that, excluding fractional percentages, the pure blacks were 68 per cent, the mixed blacks 15 per cent, the whites 17 per cent. These estimates are simply relative, the exact proportion not being determined. A generation may be passed over without special observation, and the statistics gathered in 1855 be analyzed. During those thirty years the slave trade had not been seriously restricted, though Spain was party to the treaty with Great Britain for its abolition. Here is the relation of the two races in Cuba in 1855:

Whites	498,752	47.65 per cent.
Blacks	545,433	52.35 "
Total	1,044,185	100.00 per cent.

A fractional reduction of the black percentage and a corresponding increase of the white percentage appear, yet so slight as to indicate no real change in the relative position of the two races. Arboleya, taking the years 1827 and 1854, analyzed the statistics which he considered trustworthy a little differently. He placed the percentage of whites in 1827 at 44, and of blacks at 56. In 1854 he made it, whites 47 per cent, and blacks 53. Another ten or twelve years, and the change had begun which has since continued. The census of 1867, taken a twelvemonth before the outbreak of the Ten-Years' war, and before the gradual emancipation of the slaves commenced, shows:

Whites......................	764,750	55.09 per cent.
Blacks	605,461	44.91 "
Total	1,370,211	100.00 per cent.

Here is an apparent increase in the number of whites of 326,000, while the increase of the blacks is only 60,000. Actually it was less, because the Chinese, vaguely enumerated, were included. In 1877 the total population had grown to 1,509,291. Leaving out 40,000 Asiatics and 8,400 foreigners, and making the correction of the Madrid statistics for transients and absent residents, we have a difference of 7,000.

Whites	973,725	67 per cent.
Blacks......................	480,166	33 "
Total whites and blacks	1,453,891	100 per cent.

These figures show an actual, as well as a relative decrease in the number of blacks. It is so large as to be puzzling. The Spanish statisticians explain it on the ground of imperfect census-taking. This is always a justifiable explanation in dealing with Spanish statistics. It does not alter the known fact that the relative decrease of the blacks had begun, and that a large increase of the whites was taking place, partly from immigration and partly from natural development. Coming to 1887, the last regular census that was taken, the results show:

Whites	1,102,889	69.46 per cent.
Blacks	484,987	30.54 "
Total	1,587,876	100.00 per cent.
Asiatics....................	43,811	
Grand total..............	1,631,687	

Foreigners, who had grown to exceed 32,000, are included among the whites. They were relatively so large an element that they may properly be considered in balancing the races.

Here is an actual decrease in the percentage of the blacks during the ten years. If the figures are in error, it is possible to accept the conclusion that the blacks were stationary while the whites were progressing. There was a large increase by white immigration from Spain during this period. This steady decrease of the negroes under the most favored conditions seems to be conclusive as to the natural ascendency of the whites by force of numbers. It is true that the censuses taken were all based on slave conditions; but the emancipation of the negroes had been going on, and there is nothing to show that the increase of population has been larger during the years of freedom. In the first quarter of the nineteenth century, 54 per cent of Cuba was black blood, 46 per cent white blood. In the middle of the century practically the same conditions obtained. At the beginning of the twentieth century relatively 30 per cent black and 70 per cent white blood is the proportion.

The census of to-day may show a larger percentage of negroes and mulattoes, due to artificial causes. Every observer noted during the period of reconcentration that the black victims of Weyler's policy stood it better than the whites. The blacks formed the larger element of the surviving country population. But this is a temporary condition only. The broad fact can be stated that at the beginning of the nineteenth century the black population of Cuba was 54 per cent and of Jamaica 94 per cent. At the end of that century normally it would not be greatly in excess of 30 per cent. Actually, as a result of the reconcentration, it may prove to be 40 per cent. In Jamaica it is 99 per cent. In Cuba, two whites for one black; in Jamaica, 99 blacks for every white. Some writers classify the blacks in Cuba into various divisions of natives, Africans, and mulattoes or mixed blood. Spaniards and Cubans do not talk of the black race. With them it is the race of color. In some of the censuses taken, distinction of mulattoes and blacks is drawn; but it is not necessary in determining the number of whites. Whether of the Latin race born in Spain or born in Cuba, the proportion of white to colored blood is as two to one.

The mixture may be traced through all grades and through a wilderness of statistics in slavery and since slavery, but for half a century there is the steady decrease of the African race relatively to the white race. Superficial observation is so often relied on to settle this question, and the conclusions drawn from this observation are put forth with such positiveness, that it is fair to measure these conclusions by the history of a century as shown in the census statistics. Before them, assumption falls to the ground. Unless artificial conditions arise, the history of the last fifty years seems to show that Cuba is in no danger of becoming a negroid nation, which means a preponderance of black and yellow blood.

The possibility of an artificial movement can be judged in the light of what has happened. For a quarter of a century there has been a free movement of the blacks throughout the West Indies. They could come to Cuba from Jamaica, from Haiti, from Santo Domingo, and from the Bahamas. A sprinkling of all these classes of blacks was found among the insurgents—the Bahamas and Santo Domingo furnishing the greater number of them. This free movement will doubtless continue, though after the American occupation it was temporarily checked by the application of the immigration laws of the United States. This was due to exceptional circumstances in the eastern end of the island. It prevented the influx of idle blacks from Jamaica.

No reason exists for thinking that the free movement of the West Indian population will have a greater influence in the future than in the past. The industrial conditions may call for harder work, and that assuredly will not invite a heavy immigration from the other islands. It is evident that the black population of Cuba can only be swelled by colonization or immigration on a colossal scale. Both whites and blacks are opposed to negro colonization. If a heavy black immigration is to be sought, it can only come from the United States. Such a thing might happen as a million or more American negroes, wearied over the continued denial of their political rights, taking their flight across the Florida straits, but it is not an hypothesis based on probability. The American negroes, as a class, have not given up their destiny in the United States. Small projects of colonization may be attempted; some negroes in the Southern States will inevitably drift to Cuba; but the physical surroundings will not be substantially different from the cane-fields and the cotton-fields of the South. Moreover, while they will find themselves among people of their own color, the tongue will be a strange one to them. Nobody who knows the habits of the Southern negro and his sociable nature believes he will long endure this isolation. The scheme of negro colonization has been broached in the United States, but the American negroes have shown little disposition to encourage it, and it finds no support among their race in Cuba.

In the industrial sense the value of negro labor in Cuba has not had full justice done to it. Agriculturally, it is essentially of the sugar plantation. Admittedly the black does not do well at fruit-raising, and the intricacy of tobacco cultivation is too great for him to become a successful veguero, or tobacco farmer. In the cane-field he is at his best as a laborer. The right arm that wielded the machete in cutting cane was more feared by the Spanish troops than the arm which sighted the Remington rifle. The estimates of the sugar planters vary, but out of a sheaf of such estimates it is possible to form the conclusion that fully one-half of the plantation laborers are black. On some estates they have remained with little change since slavery times. They do not work hard enough and long enough in the sun to suit the plantation owner, especially if he be an American or Englishman. Labor, whether white or black, in the tropics will never sweat quite enough to please capital. Knowing the wealth of the soil, the capitalist frets at his inability to gather the fullest fruits of its fertility.

The negro field-hand is not always willing to work six days out of the seven, though the oxen which may be his own and the cart which is his would lend their aid to continuous productiveness. His traits in this respect are not dissimilar to those of the negro in the South and of the white laborer everywhere under the burning sun of the tropics. But under sympathetic management the race is fairly industrious. The Cuban negro has a marked trait in the instinct of landownership. It is one of the standard complaints of the sugar planters that he clings to his cabin and his patch of ground to the detriment of successful cane-raising. He does not care to be swallowed up in the big plantation, and usually his wish for a bohio or palm-hut of his own in preference to quarters in the plantation barracks has to be gratified. Under encouraging circumstances this drawback may be surmounted. The way lies open. It is to increase the negro's wants by educating him up to a higher standard of consumption. Then he will exert his strength more in order to meet that standard. It is also worth noting, as every traveller in the West Indies does note, that the Cuban negro supports his family. The negro women do not work on the roads and in the fields as in Jamaica. The men perform that labor. The women care for the children—always a numerous brood.

In the industrial life of the towns and cities the Cuban negro is on a higher plane than is his brother in the United States. It may be that the African has no aptitude for the mechanical arts. Cuba is hardly the field for determining that question, because it is not a manufacturing country; but in such light manufactures as it has, the negro works on an even plane with the white man of the border tropics. The cigar factories of Habana attest this fact. Between twenty and twenty-five per cent of the cigar-makers are blacks. They work at the same bench with the whites. They receive the same pay. They have the same voice and the same influence in the labor unions. In the shoe shops there is the same equality in labor. The white lad and the black lad work side by side. The negroes are found in the tanneries and in the shops where saddles are made. They are in the building trades, many of them as masons and painters. No complaint is heard that the black artisans do less work than the whites. They hold their own in the less skilful grades of labor. A fair proportion are also clerks. The broad generalization can be made and confirmed by observation that in the industrial life of Cuba, whether agricultural or mechanical, the negro shows an equal aptitude with the white man.

The outline which has been given of the industrial condition of the blacks and the mulattoes has inferentially carried with it a statement of their position in the social organization. That there is no color-line is re-marked by every traveller. Caste feeling is not absent, social equality does not exist, but there is social tolera-tion. The presence of the negro is not an offence to the whites. Race prejudice is not rabid. It is further noted that the African race in Cuba is homogeneous. The mulattoes are not antagonized by the blacks. The military leaders who gave the race its share in the honors of the insurrection were, with few exceptions, mulattoes. The pure black knows that he shares their honors, and is content.

This sketch of the position of the negro in Cuba would be incomplete and misleading if it failed to note the blemishes. A controversial literature exists in which Spanish and Cuban authors discuss the relative statistics of crime with reference to peninsulars and insulars. With the African race such a discussion is not necessary. A disproportionate number of crimi-nals are black. The chain-gang which may be seen daily going through the streets of the cities under armed guard is made up of blacks. The Ñañigoes, frequently cited as a society of banded criminals, are chiefly of blacks. Nevertheless it is doubtful if these Ñañigoes are as entirely criminal as is generally as-sumed. The Spanish authorities made it out so for their own convenience. The American police officials who organized the Habana police force did not describe the organization as a distinctly criminal one. What they found was that criminals of all classes and of all colors took refuge under the shadows of the Ñañigoes. Whenever a crime was committed, it was said to be by the Ñañigoes. Originally the society had no criminal element in it. It was formed by the Africans brought as slaves from the regions tributary to the Gulf of Guinea. Bryan Edwards, in his volume on the British West Indies, published a century ago, notes a similar society in Jamaica. The classes who were most prominent in its formation were from the districts of Africa known as Carabali. They brought the superstitions of their tribes with them.

The first organization of the slaves, in 1836, as Ñañigoes was permitted by the masters as something entirely harmless. The rites of Voodooism were practised, and natives not born in Africa were not admitted. Subsequently separate societies of Cuban-born negroes were formed, but not on the same plane as the ones born in Africa. These various societies were known as Juegos. They had their ceremonies of initiation and of burial—grotesque and superstitious. In time these Juegos became imbued with the criminal element, and personal vengeances were executed. Ultimately Juegos of white Ñañigoes were also formed. As it existed in its greatest vigor, the society had no central organization. Each Juego was independent. These Juegoes were sometimes at war with one another. The Spanish police claimed that the Ñañigoes had a ritual of crime and assassination, that the ceremonies provided for the commission of crime as a condition of initiation. The Ñañigoes had seals or signs for each Juego or society. This was tattooed on the wrist, while the Ñañigo mark was tattooed on the shoulder. A society of professed criminals would hardly take this means of identifying its members.

At a period when crime was prevalent in Habana,

assassinations and robberies of daily and nightly occurrence were attributed to the Ñañigoes. Punishment was difficult, because it was said that many of the officials charged with administering the laws had been in their youth Ñañigoes and were fearful of the vengeance of the society to which they belonged. The more probable explanation was that the criminals, understanding the process of the Spanish justice, bought immunity from the magistrates. During his rule, Captain-General Weyler gathered up all the criminal classes of Habana, and deported them as Ñañigoes. By this means he was enabled to exile hundreds of non-criminal Cubans suspected of complicity in the insurrection.

After the signing of the protocol, the Spanish Government returned the criminal classes of Cuba from the penal settlements of Africa. Some of these were undoubtedly Ñañigoes, but the majority were ordinary criminals, without membership in any criminal society. A few of the Juegos were formed again after the return of the deported criminals. It is doubtful whether these societies are as criminal as represented. They are as likely to be groupings of the superstitious negroes in whom the rites and practices of their ancestors have not been effaced. Cabildos, or processions of Africans, were forbidden in the days immediately following the American occupation. In olden times these cabildos often carried a snake as a symbol. They are never without their drums. The African dance is also a feature of Cuban life. All these things go to show that inherited superstitions, and practices, and ignorant customs, and usages have not been completely uprooted. But it gives an unfair idea of the Cuban negroes to identify Ñañigoes solely with them, and to assume that all crime is committed by organized and banded negro criminals. Ñañigoism has come to be the general term for crime. This should be borne in mind whenever the doings of the Ñañigoes are reported from Cuba.

It is not my purpose to enter into a full discussion of the future political standing of the race of color in Cuba. Their place in the industrial element is of infinitely greater consequence, but it is worthy of recording that the industrial progress has been coincident with social toleration and civil recognition. The blood of the Latin races does not repel the African blood so violently as that which runs in the veins of their fellow-Caucasians of the Saxon stock. Amid the ruins of Castilian empire, Spanish civilization has left one enduring monument in the Antilles. It has not denied opportunity to the black man, and the black man has risen to his opportunity. He has assimilated to the toleration of the Latin civilization, and his position to-day is a refutation of the theories of the pessimists.

It is probable that after a few years, when the currents of immigration flow in natural channels, the relative importance of the race of color, black or blended, will decrease, because relatively the proportion of the colored population will decrease. The culmination of their influence may be marked in the calendar of to-day. But this is not the end of opportunity. Unless an overwhelming wave of Americanism with race prejudice on the crest sets in, the future opportunities will continue as in the present and as in the past. That there is distrust at this period is undeniable. It has been created by Americans urging their own ideas of inferiority, and telling the white Cubans that the only hope for them is in ignoring the African race. Towards this aggresive movement the blacks and the mulattoes have shown a natural resentment.

On the resumption of peaceful relations between the United States and Spain, the Cuban blacks manifested no antagonism to the American authority. Their leaders complained that they showed too great an indifference to their own future in the island whose freedom they had helped to win. The mulatto insurgent General Eligio Ducasse, issued an address in which he regretted the indifference of the race of color, which was due, he said, to the lack of civic valor. It was necessary for them to turn their faces to the light. He urged upon them the indefatigable propaganda of democratic theories, and proposed that they form a group and unite in order to work in accord with the white Cuban element.

This appeal and similar ones met with little response until the American newcomers, most of them of the kind without influence at home, raised the color-line. Then the solidarity of the race of color began to show itself. It might be converted into a harmful influence, for while not dominating the whole island, there are sections in which the blacks are numerically preponderant. In Santiago province, in the period from 1877 to 1887, the blacks increased four per cent, and in Puerto Príncipe two per cent, though they decreased in the other parts of the island. This is one reason why the white element in Santiago is to-day fearful of the experiment of independence. But with the understanding of the purposes of the United States Government and the knowledge that individuals who seek to raise the color-line do not reflect the views of the American people, this solidarity of the race of color will not continue. It is defensive rather than antagonistic.

The figment of a black republic, of a West Indian league, vanished in the air when Antonio Macéo fell at Punta Brava. When the news of his death was confirmed, the Spanish authorities in Habana sent up rockets as signals of rejoicing. Every rocket was a dart which pierced the hearts of the Cuban patriots in the city. Yet in their anguish the wisest of them felt that it was an agony not in vain. Macéo brought to the revolution the support of his race. Under him the Santiago blacks fought their way across the island. They were enlisted to extermination against Spanish rule. In their leader were the military potencies of the African race. Had he lived, the notion of a black league might have grown and spread. Macéo died sword in hand, and the blacks fought on as part of the insurgent forces, looking for their share in the future government of Cuba that was to come out of the chaos of revolution. Those who feared and doubted lest negro supremacy might succeed were encouraged to fight by the side of the blacks. There was no color-line in the revolution, there need be none in peace. A monument will be raised to Macéo. His deeds will be celebrated by the Cubans not as whites or blacks, but as Cubans. His memory will be cherished by the blacks as one of their own heroes. He raised them to his own level. Their political and their industrial standing in Cuba for all time to come is that of equality.

CHAPTER IX

The Spanish Colony

Strangers in the Country of Yesterday—Description of Themselves by Spanish Classes—Composition of Colony—Madridleños and Andalusians—Catalans the Masterful Latin Element—Asturians the Town Population—Castilian Yankees—Gallegos Widely Distributed—Other Provincials—Benevolent Societies—Instinct of Nationality—Change in Feeling Towards United States—Reciprocal Relations of Cubans and Spaniards—Present Political Attitude, the Retraimiento—Temporary Isolation—Status Under Treaty of Paris—Strangers in the Cuba of To-morrow.

STRANGERS in the country of yesterday. Thus in bitterness and in anguish the intense Spaniards described themselves when the flag which for four centuries had floated over Cuba was lowered forever.

Though they called themselves strangers, the Spanish classes did not care to be known as aliens. That would be too great humiliation. It would convey a false impression of their affection for this Antillian land and of their concern in its future. They meant that they were strangers to the new surroundings and the new institutions. They chose to treat themselves as guests of the United States accepting its protection. No longer masters, they would not be the servants of the natives of the island. By a natural impulse they formed into the Spanish colony. In places they grouped themselves into an organization under this name. In other sections they kept the old name of the Casino Español, or Spanish club or circle; but whether they formed into societies or not, they took the designation of foreign subjects. Cuba was no longer a territorial possession of Spain, and they assumed the attitude of a colony in a foreign territory.

The Spanish colony was a spontaneous development. It was the outgrowth of the instinct of nationality. It reflects the sentiment and the aspirations of a people rather than of a class. Its members have the common basis of language, usages, tradition, and religion. They all have kin across the sea. Since this Spanish element is to be for a time a separate unit, its composition is worthy of analysis. First are the natives of Catalonia, then Galicia, and Asturias. After them the people from the adjoining districts of the Cantabrian Mountains, as also from the Basque provinces on the slopes of the Pyrenees, the Montañeses from Santander, the Aragonese from Aragon. Spanish officers and soldiers who settled in the island gave all of the provinces of the peninsula representation; but these did not affect the main tide from the northern provinces.

The provincial customs of the peninsula are still seen in all their literalness, and the proverbs which describe the usages and peculiarities are heard as in Spain. The Madridleños were the most cultured class. They were the office-holders, the bureaucrats, the leeches and the locusts. They were strong because of their intrigues and their influence with the government in Madrid. Almost the same may be said of the Andalusians. They, too, lived on the offices and were leeches and locusts. At one time they had a society of natives of the province. It was not strong in numbers, but its members included the violent and irreconcilable Spaniards who opposed every concession to popular government in Cuba because popular government threatened their privileges. Until an immigration movement sets in, the Andalusian element in the Spanish colony in Cuba is not likely to be of moment. The natives of Andalusia are the scorn of the other provincials. "As lazy as an Andalusian;" "an Andalusian said it" (meaning a doubtful statement); "the women for beauty, the men for wit, and all Andalusians for lying;"— these are the proverbs most commonly heard. They show the estimation of the Andalusians by their fellow-peninsulars.

The Aragonese are numerically not a large element, but they are a good one industrially. They carried their hard heads and their stubbornness from Spain to Cuba. Runs the saying in the island, "when an Aragonese says two and two make five, don't dispute it; for in Aragon two and two make five." The natives of Vasco-Navarre are also a small numerical element who brought their customs unchanged to the island. They are seen on holidays in the red-and-blue caps of their province. Formerly they possessed political influence which came from their clannishness. The natives of Castile and Leon have sought to preserve their identity under the designation of Castilians. At one time they had a society, but it was not influential. They were mostly poor people, neither strong in numbers nor aggressive in public affairs.

Following the natives of the provinces back to their birthplaces, it will be seen that Catalans, Asturians, and

Gallegos have lost little of their individuality. Their charitable societies in all parts of the island are monuments to their spirit of union and to their thoughtfulness for their own. The memorial chapels to their patroness are evidences of their religious fervor and their devotion to Catholicism. The Catalans are the masterful Latin element in trade and in politics. They are synonymous with commercial enterprise. Of all the provinces of the peninsula they have left the deepest impress on the island of Cuba. In many places the Catalan is still spoken of when a Spaniard is meant. Some of the colloquialisms of the Provençal tongue are preserved among them. They have always been the most independent politically, and their demands on the peninsula for legislation in the interest of Barcelona have always been heeded. In government administration they have been prominent more for their influence in shaping economic policies than for holding office. In that respect the difference between them and the Madridleños and Andalusians has been a radical one. They have been the intellectual life of the Spanish element in the island, and have dominated in journalism and in the Church. From them have also come suggestions of political anarchy and of labor proletariatism.

The Catalan peasant is as sturdy in the labor of the fields and towns as his fellow-Catalans of higher grade are in commerce and in public affairs. He has the same traits of dogged perseverence and of unyielding opinions. In spite of these strong traits, the Catalans have been numerically a decreasing class in Habana and the western part of the island for the last score of years. The opportunities in trade and in commerce have not been wide enough for them. Their influence and their numbers have not been impaired in the eastern provinces. In Santiago de Cuba they are still the dominating force, and their enterprising and adventurous character has found full play there. The Santiago Catalans gave some recruits to the insurrection.

Aside from the commercial privileges which made the Catalans aggressive Spaniards, they have shown themselves possessed of progressive and liberal ideas. They yet dominate the Spanish press of the island. The Central Union and various other societies in Habana had at one time ten thousand members, with branches in other cities. In Matanzas the votive chapel to the Virgin of Monserrate is a testimonial of their devotion. In Habana an hermitage or memorial to the patroness of the province was projected, but never finished. In whatever concerns the Spanish colony of Cuba the Catalan influence will be strong, but its independent character will be preserved. It has shown no disposition to yield the field of commerce and industry which it has held. Instead of bowing to American competition, the Barcelona merchants prepared to meet it on the even ground of Cuba instead of in the unequal territory of Spain. They will not give up what is theirs without a struggle.

The Asturians are the most numerous element of peninsulars in Cuba. It was they who crowded the Catalans in Habana and the western provinces. They are estimated to form forty per cent of the Spanish-born population. They were the most loyal of loyalist Spaniards, and their sentiments have undergone little change. When the insurrection broke out, of 63,000 enrolled volunteers in Cuba, 26,000 were born in Asturias. The Asturians have the largest and most powerful provincial society in the island. It is known as the Centro-Asturiano of Habana, and has branches in Cárdenas, Cienfuegos, Matanzas, Sancti Spiritus, Camajunani, Pinar del Río, and other places. The society of clerks known as La Sociedad de los Dependientes de Comercio is also made up largely of Asturians. It is within the last twenty years that they have gained such power. Originally they were engaged chiefly in the retail business; but they soon mounted to wholesale trade, and gained a strong foothold in the tobacco industry and in financial enterprises. In recent years they have had many influential men who have divided political and commercial influence with the Catalans.

The Asturians are essentially a town population. Barely a fraction of them are engaged in agricultural pursuits. They are the most potent and the most representative Spanish class. Their patriotism is the patriotism of ignorance. The majority are also zealous churchmen. Our Lady of Covodanga, the patroness of the province, has a splendid memorial chapel in Habana, and in the smaller towns there are also memorials. The Asturians have transplanted all their Spanish traditions. Gil Blas would be as much at home among them as among his kinsfolk in Oviedo. Their characteristics are thrift and trustworthiness. For this reason they make good clerks and tradesmen. They also furnish the largest criminal element among the peninsulars in the island. This may be due to the fact that they are inhabitants of the towns. Several years ago when a Scotch sociologist made systematic inquiries regarding the inmates of the jails, the number of Asturians was reported as exceeding all the other natives of the peninsula.

The Asturians are also more given to drink than their brother Spaniards. Drunkenness is so rare that it seems invidious to single out any class; but the Spaniard of whatever province will say that the Asturians are the drunkards of their race. In trade they have sometimes been called the Yankees among the Spaniards. A nasal twang in their speech has been cited as further evidence of their kinship with New England. The major portion of the shops and stores in Habana are owned by Asturians. This ownership is advertised, and the patronage of the natives of the province is solicited and secured on these grounds. The Asturians are gorged with Spanish pride. They are at present the most compact element; but being townspeople, they are not likely to increase in numbers by immigration until conditions change. They are tenacious of their trade and will not readily be driven out by American competition. Their thrift and industry make them a most useful factor in the industrial ranks of the island.

The Gallegos are next to the Asturians in numbers. They are widely distributed in both town and country. Commercially they have little foothold, and are not to be considered on the same plane as the Catalans and the Asturians. Their acquisitive instincts are not marked, and they have not exercised a controlling influence in either trade, politics, or in the army. Apparently they have fewer material interests in Cuba than the Catalans and the Asturians. In the towns their labor is what would be called unskilled. In the country they work in the fields. They are employed in all the shipping ports. Most of the boatmen in the Habana harbor are Gallegos. Many of the inhabitants of this northwest corner of Spain drifted from the merchant marine of the peninsula to the shipping trade of the island. The Gallegos are also employed in the mines of Eastern Cuba. They have been called dull intellectually, but this may be because of their indifference to material comforts, for to a stranger they seem quick-witted. The Gallegos have shown the same tendency towards organization as their brothers from other provinces. The central society in Habana is an unusually good one, and has been noted for its efforts to popularize education. The probability is that the Gallegos will continue to increase in numbers, though they suffered greatly during the insurrection and the war, and lost some of their unity. They show less regard for the past and greater adaptability to new conditions than the other natives of the peninsula.

The Canary Islanders, the Isleños, are called Spaniards, for their speech is that of Spain and many of them were born in the peninsula. Nevertheless they have been less Spanish than the other Castilians. It might be said that their feelings were neutral as between the peninsulars and insulars. The similarity of the climate of the Canaries to that of Cuba induced an immigration which was assisted for selfish reasons. During the slave times, when England was in the habit of reminding Spain of its obligations to suppress the traffic, Spaniards in Cuba were wont to retort that British shipmasters were engaged in a system of white slave traffic from the Canary Islands. The Isleños had a society in Habana which was charitable and useful. Most of the haughty Spaniards looked down with contempt on the Canary Islanders, who were engaged in minor employments, such as peddling and raising vegetables. In the tobacco country of the Vuelta Abajo, the Canarians are admittedly the best industrial element. They have never been a compact political force. They make good laborers in the fields, and many of them have small tobacco farms of their own. Every year the large tobacco plantations bring laborers from the Canaries, who return when the crop is over. In the future the effort will be to keep these islanders in Cuba. There is work for them on the sugar plantations as well as on the tobacco farms.

It should be observed that the various societies of the provinces have their newspapers. These are not political journals, yet while maintaining the traditions of the province they contribute powerfully to preserve the idea of Spanish nationality. They are given up chiefly to news from Spain. They tell what is going on in Coruña, in Barcelona, in Oviedo, or in Santander, as the case may be. That is to say, they keep the people informed of what is happening in their old homes. Some of them also give space to the literature of the provinces. This is especially true of the Galician newspapers. After the conclusion of war with the United States some of these journals voiced very accurately the conditions in Spain. They contained articles which the censorship would not have permitted in the journals published at home, but which showed the real feelings in the provinces.

The reciprocal relations of Cubans and Spaniards

cannot be fully determined in a single year. In the past, the animosity and the antagonism have been undeniable. It was a psychological problem to determine just when this antagonism of two classes of the same race began to develop. In Cuba all persons born on the island, whether white or black, of native or of foreign parentage, are Criollos or Creoles. The child of a Spanish father born of a Cuban mother was a Cuban from the cradle. The child of Spanish parents born in the island sometimes became a Cuban in the first generation. General Calixto García was born of Spanish parents.

Commonly two generations would pass before the Spanish offspring ceased to be a Spaniard. Invariably in the third generation the offspring would be Cuban in sentiments and aspirations. The Spaniard was wont to say: "What is best in Cuba is our work. See us. We are hard-working, frugal, thrifty, peaceable, developing the riches of the soil, conserving its productiveness for other generations, sowing that which the spendthrift Cubans may cast to the winds. And we pay our debts." Retorted the Cuban: "See yourselves. You labor but it is not in the fields. The Spaniard works in the shade. You grow rich on the labor of others. Your government, which is not our government, gives you the advantages. You save that you may spend away from the island that which you have drawn from it. You do not bring your families. You demoralize our morals. You are birds of passage who would carry away the seeds of prosperity. We are the true economists, for we both produce and consume."

As in most disputes, the truth was midway. The

Spaniard unquestionably was the middleman. He monopolized the shipping trade partly by reason of his inclination for commerce and partly by official favoritism. The trade conditions in Cuba had their beginnings in the old monopolies granted by the Council of the Indies to Cadiz and Seville. Barcelona's heritage of these monopolies was a natural one; but in the retail trade it cannot be said that a Spaniard became the merchant through special privileges. His superior ability as a trader placed him in that position. With the end of Spanish sovereignty the commercial conditions changed along with the political system. The Cuban is on an equal plane with the Spaniard in everything that belongs to industrial enterprise, and politically he is a little higher up. Cubans and Catalans in the new circumstances may be left to assimilate the industrial virtues which they have in common. I shall have occasion to write of the industrial phases with reference to the Spanish element in discussing prospects and sources of immigration. The position of the Spanish colony as an influence apart and by itself is of present concern.

When the Spaniards in Cuba declared themselves strangers in the country of yesterday, they had been for six months aware of their condition. In the first burst of passion following the conclusion of peace they turned to the conquering nation. They would owe allegiance to the United States rather than to a government of Cubans. If opportunity had been given to declare themselves they would have been unanimously American because that was the only means of being anti-Cuban. Then came the American military occupation and a change of feeling. The Spanish classes liked the Americans less among them than at a distance. They began to doubt whether they could get along better with them than with their own Latin blood.

At this period the feeling of resentment and revenge was very strong among the Cubans. A voice came from the woods which stilled it temporarily. Máximo Gómez risked his popularity and challenged the radical elements by preaching peace and concord. He accepted invitations from the Spanish casinos, declared that the insurgents had fought against the Spanish Government and not against the Spanish people, and that all classes must join together in the industrial reconstruction of the country. This was not new doctrine with him. He had preached it in the height of the insurrection. His words were received gratefully by the Spaniards and respectfully by the Cubans.

Afterwards there were periods of proscriptive agitation against the Spanish classes and of demands for them to leave. Some left; but it must be taken into account that the parasites of Spanish bureaucracy and militarism were numerous. They could not all get away when the troops left. Others went because they felt there was no opportunity remaining for them in Cuba; yet in estimating the departures for Spanish ports regard must be had for the arrivals in Cuba from Spanish ports. The mass of the Spanish population in the island—the Asturians, the Catalans, and the Gallegos —have not made up their minds to leave for good, and the streams of immigration have already begun to flow back. It is a simple explanation. The opportunities are better in Cuba.

In present conditions a numerical estimate of the number of Spaniards who remain in Cuba could only be a guess. Without making that guess, it is enough to know that the number is considerable. Spanish newspapers all over the island reflect the existence of the Spanish colony. The financial and commercial classes, the merchants and the planters who secretly sought American intervention when Spain was trying to implant autonomy, want annexation or indefinite military occupation, which they look upon as the same thing. Nothing is likely to change their views. Some of them have been encouraged in the belief that though Spain has ceased to govern Cuba, the island will continue to be governed for the benefit of Spaniards. Others simply fear, and fear sincerely, that a Cuban government would be a failure, and they are not willing that the experiment shall be tried within their own lifetime.

While this is the feeling of the distinctively commercial element, I have never been able to discover by what process of reasoning the conclusion was reached that it was anything like the unanimous sentiment of the Spanish classes as a whole. It is encouraged politically by some of the old-time Reformists, weathercocks as ever, who have tried to create a Spanish party. But as in the days of the Autonomist agitation, followers are needed to build up a political organization, and the former Reformists are lacking in that respect. The Spanish element is not to be judged by a few men. The bodegueros—the grocery keepers and retail merchants—and their clerks are a distinct power. They have had violent spasms against even the temporary presence of the American troops. They have been the most passionate in their opposition to the change in forms of government and in laws. They stand for old customs and usages, whether good or bad. The appeal to preserve the Latin civilization from the brutal aggression of Anglo-Saxonism is addressed to them, and they are responsive to it. Their Spanish nationalism is sincere and intense.

The present attitude of the majority of the Spanish classes is their favorite one, that of the "Retraimiento," the drawing within the shell and disclaiming responsibility for whatever may happen. They acknowledge their debt to that portion of the Cuban press which combats the intolerant tendencies of the rabid Cubans. They declare their faith that the policy of peace and concord and union of all the Latin elements will ultimately prevail. But they are not willing to trust themselves to it just yet. And from their "Retraimiento," despite the representations of individuals, the majority of the Spanish classes still look with distrust on American influence. They want to be withdrawn from it as much as from Cuban politics.

Out of this retreat there is only one path. It may be regretted, but that does not affect the controlling forces. It leads to the temporary isolation of the majority of Spaniards in Cuba in so far as relates to the policies which are to be determined. Some of the newspapers hint at political action as a means of annexation, but these hints are received coldly. For a while the idea prevailed that they could elect to remain Spanish subjects and yet have a voice in establishing the government which is to obtain in Cuba. It grew until the belief became a delusion that, though Spanish sovereignty was gone, the Spanish classes would continue to rule Cuba through the United States. But with the understanding of the terms of the treaty of Paris this vanished.

All peninsular-born inhabitants of the island now know that by April, 1900, they must decide whether they shall renounce their nationality, because that will end the year from the time of interchanging the treaties. The certainty is the creation of a Spanish colony in Cuba similar to that which exists in Mexico and in the countries of South America. The registry of Spaniards as subjects of Spain will not be universal. Some prominent ones among them will elect to take the uncertainties of the immediate future in the belief that the authority of the United States will ultimately prevail. Others of the bodeguero class and of small landowners in the country will cast their lot with the Cubans. But the majority of the Spanish residents will elect to continue their allegiance to the peninsula. On the part of the commercial and professional classes of Spaniards this will be simply the affirmation of the position they have always held. They came to the island to better their fortunes and then return to Spain. Permanent residence has never been their intention. The paucity of registrations after the Spanish consul-general opened the registry for Spanish subjects should not mislead. The majority of them will wait until the last month.

What the course of the Spaniards may be in the years to come, when the political incertitude is ended and possibly immigration is flowing from the peninsula, is conjecture not worth wasting time on now. In the formative period of the future government of Cuba their attitude is that of the Retraimiento. The beginning of American sovereignty in trust found them, by their own characterization, strangers in the country of yesterday. By their own choice the members of the Spanish colony remain strangers in the Cuba of To-morrow.

CHAPTER X

IMMIGRATION AND COLONIZATION

Prospective Greatness of Habana—Agricultural Population the Basis —Economic Epitome of the Reconcentration—Acclimatization of White Men in Border Tropics—Spanish Immigrants Not from Southern Provinces—Comparison of Latitudes—Madrid Government's Policy of Encouragement—Drawback in Political Institutions—Failure of Plans to Keep Spanish Soldiers in Cuba— Little Prospect of Farm-Hands from the United States—Evils of Proposed Systems of Colonization—Former Experiments—History of Chinese Coolies—Probability of Exclusion Measures— Treaty Between Spain and China—Family Immigration for the Future.

OF the people who once were in Cuba it is not difficult to write. Of those who remain it is even less difficult, for they are fewer. Of the race that will be, it is too early to write comprehensively. But an exploration must be made in search of those who shall till the fields.

Whatever race and national characteristics are developed, the leading traits must always be those of an agricultural people. Habana will become a greater and a more magnificent commercial mart. It will show the possibilities of the civilization of commerce in the tropics. Seventy-five years ago Humboldt placed it with Rio Janiero as one of the five great tropical cities of the world. The Cuban metropolis then had 100,000 inhabitants; Rio Janiero, 135,000. Habana lies in north latitude 22°. The parallel of south latitude 22° passes close to Rio Janiero. The latter city has in this day a population in excess of 600,000. Habana rises a little above 200,000. Yet with the establishment of a stable government it is possible to look forward to a day not so far distant when the commercial capital of the Antilles will equal in size and importance the metropolis of Brazil. With its progress other ports will grow and spread, and Cuba's coasts will be lined with as many flourishing ports as once lined the coasts of the Mediterranean.

The basis of these *entrepôts* of trade will be the land, because Cuba is so essentially an agricultural country. Its development will be such as comes from the harvests of the soil. The mines will give up their wealth. The forests will be cleared. And when it is all done the island will be more than ever before the land of the farmer. Light manufactures will spring up, and they, too, will lean on the soil, not as a crutch, but as a prop. It is, then, of an agricultural people, and of the commerce and trade which develop from agriculture, that the future must be written. Hence the initial question is of field-labor immigration.

There is in the first place an artificially created gulf to be closed. It is the void that exists in the productive agencies of the island—the void that will be years in filling. I wish to write here of the reconcentration only in its economic effects. It was meant to extirpate the people from the soil in which they had taken root. The rooting out was partially successful. The victims included the heads of families, the children whose arms would have been bent within a few years to the tilling of the land, and the women who would have borne other children. The strongest, if not the fittest, survived. Probably in the eye of political economy they were the fittest. More women than men also survived—not exactly the reconcentration, but the events leading up to reconcentration, because many of the husbands, fathers, and brothers were killed by the Spanish guerillas. Two illustrations from widely separated points may suffice. In the six months from July 1st to December 31st, 1897, in the community of Sancti Spiritus, in Santa Clara province, the births were 202 and the deaths 1,944. In the rich agricultural district of Güines, in the province of Habana, within defined limits the population was 15,000. In the two years from January 1st, 1897, to January 1st, 1899, the deaths were 9,802, the births 319; the excess of deaths over births, 9,483. This page from the story of Güines is the economic epitome of the reconcentration.

Recent discussion has reopened the whole question of the acclimatization of the white man in the equatorial regions and in the border tropics. Assumption has given way to investigation. Distinguished naturalists, among them Alfred Russell Wallace, have challenged assumption in the light of experience. Specialists in medical science have also challenged it. Its latest exponent * may find it necessary to go beyond generalizations in upholding his theory. The effect of Cuba's climate cannot be fairly demonstrated until modern sanitation has cleared away the artificial hindrances. When the yellow fever becomes in Cuba

* Benjamin Kidd, "The Control of the Tropics."

no more an epidemic than pneumonia in the United States, the experiment of acclimating the white man in the border tropics will be fairly entered upon. Malaria will always exist there, just as it exists in immense regions of the United States. Calentura or breakbone fever will not be destroyed any more than ague can be destroyed in the United States. But medical science may continue to check it and mitigate it in Cuba as in the United States.

Applied to Cuba, two criterions may be set up without intricate analysis. They are experience and common sense. The natives of the Iberian peninsula are of the white race. They have shown that they can work in the fields with equal endurance with the blacks. The Spanish soldiers who have settled on the island have always proved good laborers. The peasants from Catalonia and Galicia are admittedly of the best class of laborers. And in spite of all the talk the descendants of the Spanish peasants, the Cuban peasantry, are hard workers in the field.

In describing the Spanish colony in Cuba I have stated that it was composed substantially of the natives of the three provinces of Catalonia, Asturias, and Galicia. Those who have not studied the subject will be surprised when they take their geographies and follow the streams of immigration to the source. Though the Council of the Indies sat in Seville and in Cadiz, giving those towns the monopoly of the trade, Andalusia did not people Cuba. Nor has the immigration tide, whether at ebb or at flood, been from that province of olives and oranges to the land of palms and oranges. The fertile regions of Southern Spain were not deserted for the more fertile lands of Cuba. The industrial immigration came from the northern provinces. Allowing for the moderating influences of the Mediterranean and the Bay of Biscay, the inhabitants of the peninsula who settled in Cuba came from regions which, nevertheless, cannot be called tropical. The damp and cold mountain-lands of Northern Spain, the high plains which are swept by the cold winds, have contributed the bulk of the Spanish inhabitants in Cuba. First they came from the commercial mart of Barcelona and from the surrounding districts of Catalonia. Later they came from Asturias, Galicia, and the mountainous provinces of the north.

The beginning of immigration from Galicia in a systematic manner was half a century back, when the great poverty prevailing among the inhabitants of the province caused measures to be taken to assist some of them to emigrate. Now it is to be observed that Catalonia lies, roughly speaking, between north latitude 40.5° and 42.5°, that Aragon extends from the parallels of 40° and 43°, and that Asturias and Galicia are north of 43°. They are in the latitude of Middle New England, New York, Northern Pennsylvania, Ohio, Indiana, Illinois, and Iowa. Allowing for the softening influence of the Mediterranean on the bordering provinces, the broad deduction remains unchanged. A line drawn laterally from continent to continent shows that the bulk of the white immigration to Cuba has come from north of latitude 41°, and latitude 41° takes in the great wheat-growing regions of the American continent. There is no wheat to be grown in Cuba, and the question becomes one of how far people from the wheat-growing latitudes can raise products in the tropics. The answer is given in the agricultural development of the island. The laborers who have been a leading element in it have come from the wind-swept plains and the barren mountain regions of the north of Spain.

In a blind way the Madrid Government encouraged Spanish immigration to the Antilles. It was the one instinct of national polity which it showed. The voyager in the waters of the West Indies sometimes puts into Man-o'-War Bay at Great Inagua Island, midway between Eastern Cuba and Haiti. The English customs officer, who receives him courteously, tells him that there are four white families on the island who administer the affairs of the fifteen hundred black inhabitants. The same is true of the Bahamas and the other British West Indies. England has never sought to people these islands with her own colonists; or when she has done it, has given up in dismay. Jamaica is the most striking instance. The development of the future will show the defect of this policy, strong in its administrative features and weak in its economic basis. Spain, in the midst of unutterable errors and deficiencies of political administration, did manage to avoid the economic error. A progressive government would have given the island 5,000,000 inhabitants at the beginning of the twentieth century, four-fifths of them of Spanish blood. An unprogressive government managed to insure a population of 1,600,000, two-thirds of Spanish blood. The instinct was correct. The drawback was bad political institutions.

When, during the decade from 1880 to 1890 the tide of immigration from the peninsula to the Argentine Republic and other South American countries alarmed the Madrid ministry, various explanations were sought for it. One Spanish writer said the potent reason was that the emigrants from the peninsula were seeking new institutions rather than a new country. He declared they would have gone to Cuba in preference if it were not that they would encounter their own bad government in even worse form than at home. At this time there was an actual halt in the immigration to the Antilles, and for a while more people were returning to Spain from Cuba and Puerto Rico than were coming to those islands. This was in one sense the climax of the system which did not settle Spaniards in the island permanently, but only to draw from it wealth enough to return in comfort and ease to Spain. While the bureaucratic policy of the Government upheld this system, it nevertheless groped about for a means of feeding the industrial deficiencies by immigration. The various provincial societies also aided immigration. The Cuban and Spanish authors who in multitudinous array have written of the island have differed radically regarding political liberty and administrative government, but they have always agreed that the number of inhabitants was never sufficient to utilize the natural richness of the soil. This phrase, "the natural richness," is found in all their writings.

When the movement of population to the South American countries was at its height, the Government issued various decrees relating to immigration which had for their object the encouragement of immigrant families settling in Cuba. State aid was advanced, and privileges were given families similar to those which were granted to soldiers whose time expired and who settled on the island. Immigration was stimulated somewhat, yet not in great degree, because of the fatal defect in Spanish administration, which is its lack not of formulating, but of executing national policies. With it, "la inertia" is what "la guillotine" was to the French people at a period of their history

The future coming of Spanish immigrants to Cuba in the first instance will be dependent on the government which is set up in the island. The hypothesis of political stability is necessary to all discussion of economic and industrial prospects. If the policy of peace and concord succeeds, and the Spanish who remain in Cuba are well treated, there is encouraging probability that the Spanish peasants will come in numbers. They will gain advantages which cannot be secured to them at home. If the Cuban government proves stable and liberal, they will find both new institutions and a new country in which they will not be strangers, because they will be among people of their own tongue and their own race. Galicia has 100 inhabitants to the square kilometre. The land is poor and thin. In years past its inhabitants have spread into Portugal, and even to Andalusia and the southern provinces, competing with the laborers there, and under this competition doing better than they could do at home. And in Andalusia the laborer's wages are rarely more than 20 cents a day. The Gallegos have also gone by the tens of thousands to South America. Cuba offers them far greater inducements in soil and opportunities. They have shown their capacity for every kind of labor—in the fields, the mines, and in the merchant marine.

Asturias, from the fact that it contributes a town population instead of farmers and field laborers, is not apt to be a source of immigration for many years to come. But Catalonia is a fountain of agricultural and commercial industry, and the prospect is for an increased immigration from that province. The island can receive no more valuable contributions than these sturdy and independent Catalans. Probably the earliest source will be the Canary Islands, because the movement of immigration and settlement from them is already under way. But the Canaries have a total population of only 250,000 inhabtants, and from that cannot be drawn a heavy increase for Cuba. When the insurrection broke out immigration had been started from the Basque provinces to renew the labor of the sugar plantations. The men were strong and excellent laborers. This experiment was promising. It may be renewed under more favorable conditions. It is also possible to look for a permanent and steady immigration from Andalusia in place of the scattering settlement that has heretofore taken place. The similarity of climate and products affords a natural economic basis. It may be that within a few years the olive, which heretofore has not been cultivated for commercial purposes, will be under cultivation by thousands of Andalusian peasants and farmers in Cuba.

When the Spanish troops were evacuating the island a prospect was held out that a definite number of the soldiers, sometimes placed as high as 20,000, would secure their discharges and remain. They were of the classes whose terms of military service expired during that period. These soldiers would have been an immense addition to the depleted labor population of the island. They were from all the provinces of the peninsula, and belonged to the soil. But it was found that the promises made them of their pay would prove worthless if they stayed in Cuba. The Spanish Government, which at first had been well disposed to the plan, became indifferent, and various causes contributed to its failure. A few hundred Gallegos went to the mines in Santiago, but it is doubtful if 2,000 Spanish soldiers remained on the island. So the problem of immigration from the peninsula has to be taken up as a new question.

It may be asked where the encouragement for immigration from the United States is to come from if the labor is to be drawn from the provinces of Spain. I am not one of those who look to see Cuba Americanized in that sense. It is my belief that climate will not be a bar to the men of the temperate zone seeking homes in the island. The wiser ones will push aside all fancy schemes and seek a stake in the land. A fair number of American farmers will undoubtedly engage in 'fruit-raising successfully. They are certain to work into tobacco cultivation as into coffee plantations. In time the readjustment of the sugar industry will be likely to find many Americans raising sugar-cane extensively on their own capital for the central mills to grind.

This may happen without changing the prospects as a whole. It is not probable that the farm-hand from an American wheat-field or corn-field will seek employment in cutting cane in Cuba. That labor can be drawn from the blacks and from the Spanish peasantry. Agricultural labor will be leavened by what it receives from the United States, as will other industrial elements; but this does not alter the probability that the labor supply of the fields as a mass and in a mass will be drawn from other sources. It is the fashion to talk otherwise, to assume that in a few years American farm laborers and unskilled town laborers will be spread over the island like the industrious ants; but there is little ground for this talk. Of the 35,000 American soldiers who were stationed in Cuba during the winter months, and who therefore saw it under the most favorable conditions, a percentage which cannot yet be guessed will gather together what resources they have and return to settle there. Others will follow, but not as hired hands, and the bulk of immigration to Cuba for a long series of years must be that of farm-hands.

Colonization differs from immigration. As applied to the present and future needs of Cuba, it is undesirable, for it contemplates a continuance of the old evils in disguise. These were the treatment of Cuba as a temporary settlement incapable of maintaining a permanent population on a high, civilized plane. Some prospective employers of labor have looked longingly to Chinese colonization. They have imagined the employment of coolies to be the solution of the industrial problem. If the island could be treated as an immense farm or plantation to be farmed by aggregation of capital from the outside, this might be possible. But such a plan will never succeed. It finds lodgment with many unthinking Americans who have only this notion of labor in its impersonal sense, and who do not know the real conditions. They have the idea that labor might be imported and exported like any commodity.

This idea was held by some Spanish publicists. Half a century ago Don Urbano Sotomayor,* a great landowner and capitalist, planned an extensive scheme of the kind. It was at the time that the Gallegos at home were suffering the keenest industrial distress, and in a small way were being aided to emigrate to Cuba. Don Urbano Sotomayor looked on Cuba as an immense plantation with only a transient population convenient to Spain and the island. He was a very patriotic and loyal Spaniard, and he rejected with horror the idea of a permanent settlement because, though it might be of Spanish origin, he saw that ultimately it would breed rebellions subjects. So he proposed that the island should be forever an enormous farm with gangs of men brought from the peninsula to work it, and then returned at intervals of five years, while their places should be taken by fresh gangs. He rejected absolutely the idea of bringing men to stay or women to raise families. His plan was the formation of a patriotic mercantile society which should bring the Gallegos and natives of the other provinces under contract, and should return them in as good condition as they were brought. Don Sotomayor believed in white-race colonization because of the slave traffic then being interdicted and labor importation being necessary to satisfy the requirements of agriculture. His delusion as to the probability of enforcing this scheme of transient labor population was no greater than that of some Americans of to-day. Don Sotomayor also declared that Chinese immigration was not a success. He had tried it, and had reached the conclusion that

* "Inmigracion de Trabajadores Españoles," Habana, 1853.

the social, hygienic, and economic objections were fatal.

This Chinese immigration was begun in 1847. It was part of a corrupt and money-making scheme by Spanish officials in Madrid and in Habana. The Chinese coolies were brought under contract, but it was virtual slavery. In the beginning many came from the Philippines, and all the immigration was from the ports of Southern China. Many of the coolies were kidnapped. China and Spain still have an unsettled diplomatic controversy growing out of the claims of Chinese subjects who were thus abducted. In 1860 there were 16,000 Chinese in Cuba. The Madrid Government at that time took measures for facilitating the importation of the coolies, and in 1877 the Chinese on the island numbered 40,000. Ten years later their numbers were 43,000. Their introduction was continued through government corruption in the face of warnings of the bad effect of this element.

It cannot be said that the Chinese immigrants were worthless. They were a fair agricultural population, and contributed their share of employment in other occupations. They also made a little headway in trade, and the Chinese genius for conquering the civilization of the conqueror began to manifest itself. They did not spread over the whole island, but were massed in Habana, in Cárdenas, and other sugar-growing regions on the north and south coasts. In some places they became numerous enough to form a social element of their own. They erected casinos or clubs. In Habana they still have a fine casino and theatre.

The Chinese suffered greatly by the insurrection. They were a neutral class, with the friendship of neither the Spaniards nor the insurgents. They lost heavily by deaths, and those who were able to do so got away from the island. A population of 43,000 dwindled, according to the estimate of the consulate, to less than 20,000. While the Chinese as an industrial element were fair, the moral results were inevitably bad, because the immigration from the beginning was one of males. The criminal population among them was also unusually heavy, and in the present day they have a very large proportion of beggars. This, however, is declared to be solely the outgrowth of the war, because formerly a Chinese beggar was rare. The Chinese quarter in Habana was not as bad as Chinatown in San Francisco, even in these enlightened days. Before the thoroughfare was purified by the American authorities, the stranger might stroll along Zanja Street and sometimes catch the fumes of opium or peer into rooms and see shocking sights. But with the exception of the opium-smoking he could see equally shocking sights in other quarters of the city.

Spanish civilization made no impress, one way or another, on the Chinese in Cuba. In few instances the Chinese contracted regular matrimonial alliances, and the offspring of these alliances have not proved a vicious class. But naturally the bulk of the alliances were illicit. Many of the Chinese who left Habana managed to find shelter in the United States in spite of the exclusion law. The tendency among those who remained is yet to seek this stealthy shelter; but an effort has been made to revive the immigration into

Cuba of contract laborers. Inevitably whatever Cuban government is established will antagonize these attempts.

The agitation in the United States which resulted in the Chinese exclusion laws of 1889 and 1890 found a reflex in Cuba among Spaniards and Cubans alike, but no legislation was enacted. The rights of the Chinese in Cuba under Spanish sovereignty were protected by the treaty of 1864, which was fairly liberal in its provisions. Though Cuba was regarded as foreign territory under American military control, the exclusion laws of the United States were not enforced against the coming of small groups of Chinese. The immigration rules of the Treasury Department, which are of a general character, were applied without reference to the nationality of the objectionable immigrants.

The possibility of an influx of coolies excited the cupidity of the speculators. Some steps were taken to replace the depleted Chinese population. Immigration of this kind, for a year or so, will do no lasting harm. It will bring back to the wasted industrial fabric of the island good working blood. But when a permanent and unrestricted movement is indicated, the question becomes a momentous one. In the temporary status of Cuba some delicate international questions are involved. The consul-general of China sought to have the treaty of 1864 recognized by the American authorities. That treaty was a reciprocal engagement between Spain and China. While the United States inherited the obligation to protect the rights of the Chinese in Cuba, it did not inherit the commercial privileges and advantages granted to Spain. The ground on which it can be asked to continue this treaty in force is not clear. The clause relative to emigration permitted Chinese subjects to make contracts with Spanish subjects for labor in the Spanish colonial possessions and to embark from designated ports of China. Many of the Chinese having come direct from the Philippines, this provision was not necessary to them.

Whatever form of Cuban government is established, a restrictive treaty or an exclusion law undoubtedly will be enacted. This will not grow out of racial hostility, for there is little of that among either the Cubans or the Spaniards. It will grow out of the instinct of self-preservation and of national advancement. Chinese immigration to Cuba must always be an immigration of males. Its nature was disclosed in the census of 1877, which gave 77 females among a total of 40,000 Asiatics. That is why Chinese colonization in Cuba on a grand scale will be discouraged. If the civilization of the millions of Caucasians on the Pacific coast was threatened by Asiatic irruption, the probable effect on the mixed races of Cuba can be judged. The reason for restriction is a thousandfold stronger. The industrial gain would be lost in the social demoralization. Because of its social and political bearing, Chinese coolie colonization cannot be looked upon as a means of supplying workers in a mass. At the most it will be simply a help, and not a source of labor supply.

With this fully understood, the Sugar Planters' Association, which knows the agricultural needs of the country, has held steadily to white immigration. The Autonomist party in its first declaration of principles was specifically for white immigration. And the few enlightened Spanish leaders who gave the subject attention took the same ground. In no case was the hostility to the race of color the reason. The relation between whites and blacks was proof of the lack of hostility as a motive. The governing cause was the fear that with the incoming of blacks and without white immigration the whites would be absorbed by the race of color, and that the common level would sink. With the white immigration kept preponderant, Latin civilization has brought the African race up to a high standard. In a previous chapter I have indicated the belief that no scheme of negro colonization in Cuba will lower it.

But whatever the color of the laborers, the people of the island realize that the hope of the country for to-morrow lies only in the immigration that is based on the family. They will be true to that instinct, though it may disappoint projects of venturesome and impatient capital. They will be exercising the principles of the broadest statesmanship and the most enlightened patriotism in whatever measures they may enact to protect themselves from an immigration that does not bring with it the family of the immigrant.

CHAPTER XI

Shadow of Beet-Root Competition Not New—Comparison with Cane Production—Cost of Labor—Effect of Hawaii's Free Market—Local Conditions of Cuban Industry—Modern Methods in Use—Latest Crop—System of Colonos—Improvement Probable—Large Capital Requisite for Growing Cane-Sugar—Contrast of Tobacco Production—Field for Small Capitalists—Family-Group Labor—Control of Crop Not Likely—Statistics of Exports—Prospective Revival of Coffee Cultivation—Fruit Raising and Its Opportunities—Commercial Productiveness of Soil—Mineral Resources—Value of Forests—Stock Raising a Profitable Field—Extent of Small Landownership.

REVOLUTIONS of government do not revolutionize the soil. Industrial ruin was the inevitable consequence of the Cuban insurrection. In the distress which followed, the prophets of dismay declared that the stricken cane-sugar industry never could meet the new conditions of competition and production which were arising. Nevertheless, Cuba is the greatest natural sugar plantation in the world.

The decadence of the cane-sugar industry is not a new topic. In the year 1812 A.D., cane was the subject of a series of vaticinations, and a dozen years previously it was observed that the introduction of the beet-root plant in Germany was a menace to the sugar-growing islands of the West Indies. The industry was so profitable that during the first half of the century the change from coffee raising to sugar planting began— a change which continued steadily, and reduced the coffee production to a comparatively small number of cafétales, or plantations, in the eastern end of the island. Yet the shadow of the beet root lengthened, for the stalk was growing. In the 'fifties it was the beet root, not in Germany, but in France, that was causing concern. Pezuela, the learned and laborious author of the "Dictionary of the Island of Cuba," writes of it as a "prejudicial rivalry." The complaint was that this "prejudicial rivalry" had begun in 1828, when the sugar of Cuba was preparing to take greater value. At that time France had ninety refineries of her own and supplied the whole French consumption. Pezuela also remarks that as an offset to losses in the French market, Cuba gained by the decline of the sugar production in Jamaica which the freeing of the slaves caused. Little note is taken of the steadily increasing consumption in the United States, and the market which was then widening for Cuba as an offset to the European exclusion.

In 1830, when, in spite of the French beet-root competition, the development of the cane-sugar industry in Cuba really commenced, a negro plantation-hand was accounted worth $400, a yoke of oxen $135, and a horse or a mule $60. The negro cotton-hand on a plantation in the United States had a greater worth. In 1857 Pezulea estimated the value of the 2,000 sugar plantations on the island at $239,000,000, of which the land was figured at $80,000,000 and 150,000 slaves at $105,000,000. The balance was made up of the plantation animals and implements. New inventions were also utilized to increase the production. The number of separate ingenios, or plantations, diminished by absorption into larger ones.

In 1860 the production of cane-sugar in Cuba was 1,127,348,750 pounds. The aguardiente, or cane-brandy, and other by-products also had to be taken into account. In that year the production of cane-sugar in all countries of the world was 2,750,496,950 pounds. The beet-sugar production was 449,999,943 pounds, divided between France and Germany in the relative proportion of two-fifths to three-fifths. Coming down to a later period without intermediate analysis, the situation may be seen at a glance, and the changes that have taken place be understood by the following comparative figures of cane and beet root:

	Cane.	Beet.
1887–88	2,541 tons	2,407 tons.
1896–97	2,452 "	4,772 "

Cuba's quota had fallen abnormally on account of the insurrection, and the percentage of cane production was therefore not trustworthy. But this deficiency did not obscure the steady increase of beet production. Since then some further changes have taken place, due largely to the tariff legislation of the United States intended to foster its own beet-sugar industry. Cuba's future must be examined in the light of all these changed circumstances.

During the worst years of the insurrection the Cuban sugar planters were confident that when peace should be re-established they would be able to meet the beet-sugar competition. They never feared that the cane of

Cuba would lose its market. All their hopes were dependent on the United States. This is so obviously the correct view that it does not need elaboration. The United States is fostering beet-root production by a relatively high protective tariff. The growth of the industry has not yet reached the proportions which justify the belief that the Western farmers will go into its production extensively rather than to continue raising bread-stuffs for the sugar-producing West Indies.

Investigations made by the United States Agricultural Department show that in Puerto Rico cane-sugar can be raised for two cents a pound of the same standard that it will cost the producer of the United States three and one-quarter cents a pound to produce beet root. The limit of production in Puerto Rico is so small, being not over three per cent of the total consumption of the United States, that it is not an important factor. In Cuba it is different. A careful examination will show that in the new conditions cane-sugar cannot be produced there much below two cents a pound. The margin may be one cent a pound between that and the beet-root production in the United States when beet-root production cheapens. The cost of labor is relatively high. This cost will increase rather than diminish in the future, because the Cuban plantation laborers are likely to reach a higher standard of living. Cane-sugar production in Cuba at one and one-half cents a pound is due to exceptional advantages. It is not general. It is probable that in its elementary stages the beet-root industry of the United States and the Louisiana interests will prevent the free introduction of Cuban sugar. They will not be able to prevent that liberal reciprocity which is so essential to the Cuban cane production, especially since a concession has been made to the British West Indies. The steady increase in consumption in the United States will justify broad reciprocity. A spoonful of beet root for the morning coffee from the home product, a saucerful from Cuba for other household purposes, will be the relative proportions for many years to come.

Hawaii has the advantage of the free market forever secured by annexation. Its production is undergoing an abnormal stimulus. No reason exists for placing the ultimate Hawaiian production beyond 300,000 tons annually. Under the free market afforded by reciprocity the greatest annual output was 237,000 tons. All the economies of production and new methods have been utilized in Hawaii for years past. The area of soil suitable for cultivation is limited. Because Hawaii once thought 100,000 tons the limit of her productive capacity does not prove that 300,000 is not the limit.

Jamaica and the British West Indies, under the present policy of the British Empire, are not apt to see the revival of their cane-sugar industry. The British imperial policy changes slowly. Grants-in-aid are farthings tossed to a ragged beggar. Though Jamaica has secured partial reciprocity with the United States, her recuperation must be slower than that of Cuba because the conditions of the recuperation are not so favorable. Cuba has more to fear from the development of cane-sugar in Mexico and perhaps in the Philippines than from the reconstruction of the industry in Jamaica and Barbadoes.

These are what may be called the external conditions affecting sugar production in Cuba. They give fair basis for the assumption that a profitable market may be assured for the next few years, possibly until the former production of 1,000,000 tons annually is reached. In the mean time the conditions under which this production must go forward become important. Sugar planters in debt, with years of non-production and of wreck and ruin behind them, were not in position to make a vigorous start. Probably many of the mortgaged plantations will pass into other hands. But the soil is there, and if the American market can be assured the redevelopment will come, first to the planations closest to the sea-coast, then of those farther back in the interior, and finally there will be new plantations. In this development the revolution in methods of production which has been going on will be continued. Already machinery has effected a saving of twenty per cent in production. The economic basis of production may be modified, so that there will be practically no wastage, and these new processes must serve as the compensation for the relatively high cost of labor. One fact seems to stand out. This is that while capital will be cautious, it will not find the beet-sugar competition too dangerous to prevent investment in Cuba. In 1905 the Queen of the Antilles may be producing as large a quantity of cane as she produced in 1895, but under different conditions and at a less relative cost of production.

It is a common mistake that the prodigality of nature destroyed systematic cultivation of sugar-cane in Cuba. Pen pictures of the planters spending the riotous earnings of their cane-lands in Saratoga and Paris while the plantations produced and reproduced without management were often drawn. These pictures gave a false idea. Some of the Cuban planters were as extravagant and as improvident as those of Louisiana in former days. In time the mortgages ate the substance of the soil, and the plantation-owners were ruined. It was also true that they did not act together as one body in establishing a scientific basis of production as the Hawaiian planters have done. The latter by their organization have brought cane cultivation to an exact science which assures the fullest return of natural wealth from every acre of land.

But improvidence was not true of the whole class of Cuban planters. After visiting the few estates which were enabled to plant and grind during the worst period of the insurrection, it came to me to visit the leading plantations in the islands of the Hawaiian group and to observe the methods of production. During a subsequent stay in Cuba further opportunity was given to study the cultivation there when peaceful industry reigned. I did not find a single process in Hawaii, with the admitted perfection to which the use of improved machinery has been brought and the economic devices for preventing waste, that was not understood and practised in Cuba. The progressive planters of the Antilles knew how to utilize every product of the sugar-cane. The difference was that while the rule of scientific production in Hawaii was universal, in Cuba it was followed simply by individual planters. Needless to say it must become universal in Cuba also before the sugar industry can recuperate on a lasting basis. The day of the prodigal planter is gone. I might add that he was not always a Cuban. In the province of Habana the plantation which is usually cited as an example of modern methods and of keen business administration is owned and managed by Cubans. In Santa Clara province a magnificent estate which may fairly claim to be one of the finest sugar plantations in the world is the property of a noted Cuban family. The supposedly prudent Englishman in the rôle of a planter ruined by his own extravagance is too often seen in the West Indies to charge that quality solely to the Latins.

The sugar crop of 1898–99 was a disappointment to unthinking persons. They imagined that with the return of peace the scorched cane-stalks which spread for hundreds of miles over the island would at once bear sap. The net production for the year was 304,-360 tons of 2,240 pounds against 290,028 tons the previous year. Eighteen months are necessary from the time the cane is planted until the first crop is ready for grinding. Then the soil produces seven years without renewal. The planters needed first of all oxen, then laborers, then money for machinery, and all the time money for interest on the accumulated mortgages. Some of them by the closest figuring of which they were capable declared they could not replant their ruined estates under $30 an acre. Others in favored localities thought they could do it for $15 an acre. The owner of a small estate of 1,700 acres which came within my notice said he could replant for $23,000, or a little less than $14 an acre. He had the seed-cane available, and this was not included in the estimate.

With a proper understanding of cane-sugar cultivation, no one will look for a heavy increase in the crop before the season of 1901. By that time an output of 500,000 tons may be in sight. One general fact must be kept in mind. A maximum of two cents per pound must be allowed for production. The profit is in the fraction below that figure. Ultimately this fraction will be assured in the reciprocity granted by the United States as a compromise between the pressure of the sugar-refining interests for free raw product and the opposition of the beet-sugar producing interests to any lowering of the duty.

Whether the system of colonos will remain is a problem. In the beginning it seemed an ideal system. A large plantation, in addition to the land worked by the owner, would have a dozen or more tenant producers. The cost of production was largely lessened by having one great central mill grind for the surrounding country. Machinery which on separate plantations would cost $2,000,000, on a single plantation at an investment of $500,000 could do the same work. Production was unquestionably cheapened. It is certain that the cane will continue to be ground by the central mill. The practical difficulty is in the adjustment of the relations of the plantation-owners and the colonos, or tenants. Under the old system, on a big plantation in return for so many tons of sugar-cane brought to the central mill the plantation-owner would return to the colono a definite quantity of raw sugar. The profit to the mill lay in the amount or quantity of sugar taken as compensation for the grinding. Naturally the colonos claimed that the mill wanted too large a proportion. That is a difference of opinion which will always exist.

The real difficulty lay in the fact that the colonos leased the lands from the plantation-owners. The latter were always large borrowers, and in return they made advances of money to the colonos. With a debtor loaning to another debtor, the unsatisfactory results were certain to follow. But the system is clearly capable of improvement. It is possible to imagine a time when the central mills will grind the product of sugar-farms which vary in area from a caballeria to two hundred acres, the land either owned or leased by the farmer, who can raise enough farm products for the support of his family, and devote the rest of the land to the cultivation of cane to be ground at the central mill. On the larger scale the colono system will also be developed. An ambitious American may lease 2,000 acres and upwards for a period of five or six years. If he has his own capital with which to do that and can secure his own labor, the central mill will become his servant and not his master.

Though the great planters are not encouraged with this prospect, and though the sugar industry in Cuba must always be dependent on large investments of capital, the failure of the colono system cannot be affirmed. It demands a new trial under new conditions. The planters apparently have not considered the probability of the industry shifting to a new basis. The amount of capital required to be invested in a central mill is large, ranging sometimes from $500,000 upwards for the machinery. There seems to be no inherent obstacle to the mills representing capital independent from that which controls the plantations, just as the great flour-mills of the Northwest are independent of the wheat-fields.   In some form it is an industrial possibility.

In the economic history of the island the old writers note that cane-sugar became a profitable industry when negro slaves were introduced in numbers.   They re-marked the progress made during the short period of English occupation in 1763, when 5,000 slaves were added to the stock of human blood which the island already possessed.   The slaves came from Jamaica and the other adjacent islands.   The English went, but the Africans remained.   The slaves whom the English left gave a marked impetus to the sugar plantations.   This growth continued until the beet root caused inquietude and until the prophecies were made on the prospective ruin of the industry.   The beet root did not cause the fears of the planters to be realized.   Sugar-cane con-tinued to add to the wealth of the Pearl of the Indies. The aggregate of slave labor increased, keeping pace with the increase of sugar production.

When the African slave trade was restricted under treaty agreement and failed to fill the void, Chinese coolies were introduced.   This experiment was not a promising success.   The influence of the Chinese im-migration is discussed elsewhere, but the fallacy of the slave-labor necessity was shown after the Ten-Years' war, when the progressive emancipation of the blacks was in operation and sugar production increased.   It was a demonstration again of the greater productiveness of free labor over servile labor.   The years of greatest production were those following 1886, when the remnant of slavery was abolished.

This, however, may be said to be shifting the labor issue instead of meeting it. The question to be met is whether sugar production can continue on a profitable scale under conditions which are not substantially servile labor. The coming industrial life of Cuba is so largely one of immigration that the bearing of immigration on sugar production calls for a word. It may be taken as a maxim that white labor from the United States is not going to work in the cane-fields. Western farm-hands who show little willingness to exchange the freedom of the wheat and corn fields for the more tedious labor of beet-root cultivation will not transfer themselves to the cane-fields of the Antilles. The labor of the cane plantations in the future will be drawn from the same sources as in the past. It will be made up of black and white Cubans and Spanish peasants. Capital will find the means of securing labor, and the island will benefit in the collateral branches which come from handling the sugar crop. If, however, the future of Cuba were for it to be simply a huge sugar-cane plantation, that future would be dark politically, socially, and economically. Happily the promises for development are along other lines which will be parallel with its sugar production and will offset its drawbacks.

The smoke of the Vuelta Abajo curls upwards from millions of cigars in Europe and the United States and in every corner of the known world. The conditions of the tobacco industry in Cuba are not limited by the uncertainty of tariff duties. The effect of these must be weighed, but they do not permanently restrict the output. It might also be said that the production of cheaper tobacco, following the laws of natural economy, has not reached its limit. Its growth will be accompanied with greater economic developments and with fewer drawbacks than the redevelopment of the sugar-cane production. It benefits, too, the artisans of the island as well as the agricultural laborers. With the increase of tobacco production, the number of cigar factories in Habana is certain to increase. This is the kind of light manufacturing suitable to the tropics. It pays to have an Habana brand on the tobacco of the Vuelta Abajo and Partidos districts. Remedios, in the central part of the island, may ship its strong products to the United States, and the poorer grades raised in Santiago may go to Germany without affecting this fact.

Centuries of privilege did not destroy the Government monopoly of tobacco which Spain enforced. From the time when the Government factory was established in Seville by the Council of the Indies to the end of Spanish sovereignty in the island, both production and distribution were regulated by the authorities. When the royal decree of 1817 was promulgated, it showed the reluctance which the Spanish Government yet preserved to making the cultivation and manufacture of tobacco entirely free. During the insurrection the export duties were moulded to suit the Barcelona monopoly. Under an independent government or an American protectorate they will be shaped so as to lighten the burden of the producer.

The leading characteristic of tobacco production in contrast with sugar-cane is that it is emphatically an industry for the small capitalists and farmers. The island is in little probability of becoming a vast tobacco plantation controlled by a trust or syndicate with the power to regulate production. Capital in this form or in other forms is of immense benefit to Cuba, but it has its limitations. The tobacco industry may become, in the regions which have tobacco soil, an immense grouping of small farms. The uncertainty of the crop, the difference in grades, the necessity of manufacturers having a variety from which to choose, militate against a monopoly of production. To control the production of potatoes in the United States would be as simple as to control tobacco production in Cuba. While the syndicates or companies which own the factories may also own large plantations, the conditions of production are such that it does not pay them to work the plantations as a single tract.

Experience may be needed to demonstrate this fact. The vegas or small farms, whether leased to the producers or owned by them, are to the interest of the factories as well as to the producers. Where the veguero needs money, the amount is small compared with that which the sugar planter must advance to the colono, and the risk of losing its return is less. In 1858 there were 8,250 caballerias of tobacco land under cultivation, and the production was 1,700,000 arrobas of 25 pounds. In 1894 the number 8,875 was given as plantations, rather than as caballerias. The number of people employed directly and indirectly by the industry was 80,000. Of these there were in Pinar del Río—the Vuelta Abajo district—26,000 men and 10,000 women and children. Aside from its economic and industrial value, tobacco raising will be of great worth in the transition of political conditions and in its effect on rural prosperity. Its labor is of the highest type, which is that of family-group labor.

Ordinarily four or five years are needed to learn the science of tobacco growing. It is also an art. One man may grow nine bales, or about 1,000 pounds, of tobacco. The plants are placed in the ground from October to January, and the harvest is from January to April. The first cutting is for wrappers and the later cuttings are for fillers. Tobacco is thus a three-months' crop. When it is in the drying-house, corn or some other cereal is planted and a crop had from the same soil.

The foreign demand for Habana cigars and Cuban leaf tobacco is not likely to be met for a long while because the consumption grows steadily. The prohibition of exports and the lack of leaf for local manufacture during the insurrection make an accurate comparison impracticable, but a general idea may be gained from the cigars and the leaf tobacco exported for a ten-years' period. This is afforded by the following table:

Year.	Cigars.	Tobacco. Pounds.
1889	250,000,000	30,000,000
1890	212,000,000	....
1891	197,000,000	17,000,000
1892	167,000,000	16,000,000
1893	147,000,000	18,000,000
1894	134,000,000	22,000,000
1895	159,000,000	23,000,000
1896	186,000,000	30,000,000
1897	123,000,000	Prohibited.
1898	98,000,000	9,000,000

Coffee promises to become what it was in the early years of the century, a staple for all sections of the island. At present its cultivation is limited to the eastern province, and the excellence of the plantations

around Guantánamo is well known. The French refugees from Santo Domingo who established the industry
there also carried it to the western end. Until they
were abandoned for cane growing, the cafétales in Habana province were very productive. Their re-establishment is probable. Uplands from 1,000 to 2,500 feet
above sea-level abound in Matanzas, and also around
Alquízar and Artemisa in Habana, and this height in-
sures a good crop. The capital invested in coffee production must wait four and possibly five years for its
full return. The field is not, therefore, one for the pell-
mell investment which wants one hundred per cent.
within a twelvemonth; but when the fever of this kind
of speculation passes away and normal inducements are
followed, the increase in plantations will be seen. The
coffee industry has a great advantage in that it does not
require large capital, and while a plantation is being
brought to the point of market productiveness the land
affords other means of support for those who cultivate
it. With a coffee-consuming population such as the inhabitants of Cuba will always be, and with a soil capable of producing almost unlimited crops, the importation of coffee from Puerto Rico and the United States
is bound to cease. A better quality can be produced at
a cheaper price than it can be imported. The Santiago
grade commands a premium in the markets of the isl-
and. In a few years Habana will probably be supplying its local consumption from the cafétales within forty
or fifty miles of the city.

Fruit raising may be engaged in earlier than coffee
production. American interests are understood to be
supplementing their successful development of fruit

growing in Jamaica by purchases of land in Eastern Cuba, where Banes and Baracoa are the ports of export. There is opportunity for the small fruit farmer also. Sugar planters are discovering that the raising of bananas, pineapples, cocoanuts, and oranges may be carried on in connection with sugar production. Those who are in a position to do so are willing to try the experiment. This does not mean that oranges will cease to grow in Florida. It means that the productiveness of the Cuban soil is likely to be further diversified in such products as find at their door the markets of the United States.

The fertility of the soil of Cuba is so boundless that exaggerated estimates of what is worth producing are sometimes made. The tables of the leading authorities on industrial subjects are taken in their literal meaning as though applicable to all the cultivators of the soil. But this is not the commercial productiveness. Their figures show the limit of capacity of a caballeria, or $33\frac{1}{3}$ acres, and the number of families which may be supported from that area of land. Sugar, coffee, tobacco, cocoa, corn, hay, potatoes, rice, yucca, or starch-plant—which stayed the hunger of Columbus and his mariners—even wheat, cotton, bananas, and other fruits may all be raised on one farm, besides the pigs and the poultry which can be fed; but the limitation of this productiveness in practice must be noted. Cotton grows on trees instead of bushes, but it is not going to be produced in Cuba to compete with that raised in the Southern States; nor will wheat be coaxed from the ground when it is cheaper to ship sugar and fruits to the Mississippi Valley and import flour and cotton goods in return.   The diversity of products is great, but in the lifetime of the producers of to-day they will not be producing everything that they want to eat.   Corn alternates with tobacco beneficially to the soil, and other crops rotate with advantage; but they do not reduce cultivation to a minuteness vastly greater than that of the farm lands in many portions of the United States.

Homely calculations have been made of the increased area which was brought under cultivation on American farms when the barbed-wire fences straightened out the corners lost in the elbows of the rail fences.   The estimate of the wheat and corn and vegetables which might be raised on all the railroad rights of way would be an interesting one.   In the same way the generalization might be made of the increase in production when every caballeria of Cuban land is under cultivation of crops diversified scientifically and mathematically; but it would have no present bearing.   The thing to be known about the soil of Cuba is that its cultivators need never be dependent on one staple, as the Western farmers are dependent on wheat and corn.   The value of this condition is in the probability that, while sugar-cane will not lose its supremacy, agricultural industry will be diversified by the increase of lesser farming.

The mineral wealth of Cuba has been prospected with passable thoroughness.   Imbernó,* one of the best of recent authorities, says that besides the country immediately adjacent to the city of Santiago de Cuba, there is iron in the region around Holguín and Baracoa in the same province, in various parts of Santa Clara, near Jaruco in the northeastern part of Habana province,

* Guía Geográfica y Administrativa.

and in Pinar del Río, especially near the coast along Bahia Honda. Copper he locates chiefly in Santiago, but he refers to the deposits near Minas in Habana. These deposits are now owned by Americans. Plumbago, he says, is found with iron in Santiago, and antimony with lead in the Holguín district. Coal he locates in the region of Consolación, del Sur in Pinar del Río and in Matanzas province; gypsum in Pinar del Río, magnetic ore around Guanabacoa, which is across the bay from Habana, in the hills of Trinidad, around El Caney near Santiago, and in other districts. The marble in the Isle of Pines is extensive, but it is of inferior quality.

The best report on the asphalt and bituminous oil deposits was made by the Spanish official engineer, Pedro Saltarian, in 1883. He located bituminous wells in various sections of Santa Clara province, and the asphalt beds in the Cárdenas district as well as several in Pinar del Río were described by him. Some of these have been partially worked with divergent opinions as to their commercial value.

Americans who prospected in Eastern Cuba thought they saw the greatest possibilities in the manganese and copper mines, with some encouragement for lead deposits. Discoveries of this kind became as common as the location of silver mines in the Western States. Some of the prospectors were doubtless mistaken; yet the authorities who are competent to judge do not differ in their opinions regarding the value of the copper deposits and the uncovered wealth of the Sierra Maestre range of mountains in Santiago.

Trustworthy information concerning the iron ore

deposits, the Bessemer hematite, is given by the large amount of duties paid into the United States treasury by the American companies which work these mines. Of recent years they have been shipping ore also to Europe. The following table shows the productiveness of iron ore in Santiago by tons:

Year.	Tons.
1884	23,997
1885	80,095
1886	110,880
1887	94,810
1888	204,475
1889	255,406
1890	356,060
1891	261,620
1892	320,859
1893	346,341
1894	153,650
1895	377,041
1896	405,671
1897	452,559
Total	3,443,464

It is a question whether there are the 10,000,000 acres of virgin forests in Cuba that have been vaguely estimated. Sometimes the innumerable groves of royal palms, the most useful tree known to the tropics, are included in this guess. Experienced Americans who for a year travelled over the island seeking to determine the most valuable timber locations became doubtful of the extent of the wooded area, though the eastern province seemed to them a single forest. But the area is great enough to take many years to clear it. The cedar from which the cigar-boxes are made is found in Pinar del Río as well as in Santiago. The mahogany close to the coast has been thinned out, but further in the interior it is untouched. The other hard woods are of great variety. Their commercial value is uncertain until systematic lumbering as known in Michigan and Wisconsin is developed. In the building of railroads the ties may be taken from the woods which it will be necessary to clear.

Stock raising in Cuba offers one of the most profitable fields for a quick return on invested capital. The high rolling land which begins in Santa Clara and extends into Santiago affords the best ranges. Much of this grazing land is capable of sugar cultivation, but many years must pass before this can be engaged in to advantage. The central province of Puerto Príncipe is a vast grazing region. Its Cuban name, Camagüey, means a cattle-pasture. Hundreds of thousands heads of cattle disappeared during the insurrection. To-day the traveller may journey from sunrise to sunset and see no signs of live stock; but this barrenness will not last. The grazing ranges are bound to be restocked not only with cattle, but also with horses. Animals from the United States may be imported to help restock them. Heretofore they have been imported simply as live beef for daily consumption. The supply, however, will not be solely from the United States. In securing oxen for the sugar plantations it is found that Mexico, Venezuela, and Honduras are the main sources. Live stock from the United States will have to be crossed with animals from those countries and with the native stock. It is the common experience that the stock runs out in three generations unless it is renewed by breeding with imported animals.

The landownership instinct is very strong with the mass of the Cuban population. This means that it was strong with their Spanish progenitors and will be strong with the Spanish immigrants of the future. This is shown in the government reports, which were, for Spanish statistics, fairly trustworthy because on them were based the taxes. The last enumeration which was made before the insurrection broke out showed that in the whole island there were 1,119 sugar plantations, 4,214 stock farms, 375 haciendas or large country estates, 188 coffee plantations, 8,485 vegas or tobacco farms, and 22,224 sitios or estancias. A sitio is simply a place, and an estancia is a small farm. The number of city, town, and village real-estate holdings was 76,402. These fincas urbanos, as they were called, shaded off into land-holdings capable of cultivation. It will be several years until an exact estimate can be had of the products of small farming in Cuba.

CHAPTER XII

TRADE AND TAXATION — RAILWAYS AND INTERNAL DEVELOPMENT

Some Primary Principles—Adjustment of Purchasing Power of Products by Reciprocity—Tariff Dues and Their Capabilities—New Sources of Revenue—Decay of Spanish Shipping—American Markets for Tropical Products—Unwarranted Expectations of Merchants—Railway Building and Its Limitations—Systems in Operation—The Backbone Line—Value of Existing Railroad Property—English Ownership—Water-Way Competition—Harbor Improvements—Good Roads the Coming Question—Cheap Labor Not Found—Prospect for Agricultural Banks—Strikes Not a Recent Development—Artificial Monetary Basis — Ultimate Supremacy of American Financial System.

TRADE and taxation in Cuba may be reduced to a few simple formulas. The elaboration of these formulas into economic treatises is not difficult. When the elaboration becomes wearisome and confusing the return to the starting point is easy. There is really little need of wandering far away from it into the wilderness of speculative economics.

The island for all time will have to supply the wants of its inhabitants by what they can get in exchange for a bag of sugar, a bale of tobacco, a sack of coffee, and a cargo of fruits and nuts. The adjustment of this purchasing power of sugar, coffee, tobacco, and fruits so as to bring back the largest quantity of flour, lard, and bacon, the greatest amount of agricultural machinery, and the most extensive assortment of cotton and other dress goods is the problem of trade and also of tariff taxation. The United States consumes everything the island produces. It produces everything that Cuba consumes. The doors open one to the other. There is the whole question of Cuban commerce, and its basis is reciprocity.

It is shown since the American control of the custom houses that an impoverished people not numbering much more than 1,000,000 can pay $1,000,000 monthly in customs duties. This is done by light rates on articles of commerce and consumption. With the restoration of prosperity the rates can be further shifted to articles of luxury, because the Latin-American's fondness for luxuries when able to gratify itself pays tariff tribute willingly.

A hitherto untouched source of internal-revenue taxation exists. It is ample enough to supplant most of the present unsatisfactory internal taxes. This source of revenue is in the tobacco that is consumed in Cuba and in the by-product of sugar known as aguardiente or cane-brandy. Everybody in the Antilles smokes, and smokes countless cigars and packages of cigarettes. Under the Spanish system the wax tapers which were used for lights paid an internal-revenue duty, but the infinitely greater income from cigars and cigarettes was neglected. The aguardiente, besides its use as a beverage, is employed in a variety of household ways. It takes the place of a score of toilet articles which in the United States pay an internal-revenue tax. Internal taxation of this kind would easily replace the income lost by the prohibition of the lottery and would also replace the vexatious industrial tax, which was literally an impost on progressive industry and enterprising commerce.

When the Blaine reciprocity provisions were in force, the harbors of Cuba were filled with vessels flying the American flag almost to the exclusion of the ships of other nations. After Spanish sovereignty ceased, ships continued to enter Cuban ports under its flag, but the cargoes they carried were small. With the artificial restrictions removed the peninsula had little to sell to the island, but it was not itself independent of the products of the Antilles. Its exports dropped to a cipher. That may not be a permanent nothingness. Cuba will buy some things of Spain, and the traffic from Barcelona to Buenos Aires by way of Habana may not entirely cease. The Barcelona merchants are already making an aggressive struggle to keep their Antillian trade. But with no discriminating tonnage dues, and with no preferential tariff forcing Cuba to receive the products of the peninsula at a low rate while its own products pay a high import duty into the peninsula—that was the basis of the Spanish system—Spanish shipping, it might be said European shipping, must remain near the vanishing point which is represented by the cipher. There have been years in which 95 per cent of Cuba's exports were sent to the United States. Those years are coming again, and under conditions which render it certain that American vessels will not enter or leave Cuban ports in ballast.

The great country to the north is so little to the

north that the vessel twenty-four hours or thirty-six hours out from a Cuban port may start the distribution of products over an area of 1,500,000 square miles and among 50,000,000 consumers—all the region from the Mississippi valley to the New England coast. Habana can ship its freight to reach New York, Chicago, St. Louis, and Cincinnati within four days. The American markets await the tropical products which 5,000,-000 inhabitants of Cuba can supply. These border tropics will not encroach seriously on the products of the temperate zone. The crevices between the rocks in New England will be sprouting hand-nurtured blades of grass when the caballeria of rich Cuban land is yielding its maximum of sugar, coffee, and fruits, but not of wheat in competition with those blades of grass or with the prairies of the West.

On the part of merchants in the United States there was keen disappointment because they did not find a market of 5,000,000 consumers awaiting them within three months after Cuba ceased to be a possession of Spain. They did not stop to reflect that the inhabitants had been reduced in four years by at least 25 per cent, and that consumption could not make a quick stride forward until the surviving population was recuperated. The Mississippi valley was surprised that the demand for bread-stuffs was not vastly larger than when the flour had to be shipped by the way of Barcelona, while the Atlantic coast was disappointed that the $100,000,000 of Cuban commerce which was in vision when the insurrection broke out did not immediately sweep into its ports. A little thought was needed to recall that industrial recuperation has its limitations of time, and that increased commerce can only come from increased development and increased population. And the basis of these is internal development.

The question recurs to the resources of the island and the means of unfolding them as the prelude to the growth of commerce. A quaint Spanish author once wrote of Cuba as an island "whose population and whose richness were a drop of water in the grand ocean of Spain's colonial treasure." The grand ocean has dried up. Shall the water-drop become a stagnant pool or a fountain fed, by steady streams? The answer is again to be sought in the uncovering of that natural richness and in the population which uncovers it. What is of first concern is the lines which the development will follow in the lifetime of the young men of to-day. The market is assured.* Capital starts with that certainty. Its next movement is for the quickest and largest returns where there is the least competition and not too great adventure.

The clearing of the forest lands and the building of railways and ordinary roads for a time will go forward evenly with the reconstruction of the sugar plantations. The island to-day has 1,135 miles of railway, exclusive of the narrow-gauge lines on the sugar plantations which serve to bring the cane to the central mills. When 1,300 or perhaps 1,200 miles more are built, railway construction will be ended, because there will be no need of further means of rail communication. In its industrial aspects the Cuba of the past must be viewed almost as a stationary body. The building of

* See Appendix B.

railways was a slow work. A description of the island in 1900 would vary little from a description in 1845. The towns in 1850 were what they were in 1895. The means of travel were the same, the roads were the same, and few new highways of commerce were opened during half a century. The first railroad was built from Güines to Habana within a few years after George Stephenson told the poking Parliamentary committee which quizzed him, that the locomotive he had invented would undoubtedly prove an inconvenient thing for the cows which happened to get in its way.

The 1,200 or 1,300 miles of railway which are yet to be constructed will join the city of Santa Clara with the city of Santiago, closing a gap of less than 300 miles. It will have feeders to the north and south coasts to Nipe, Gibara, Baracoa, Sancti Spiritus, Santa Cruz del Sur, and Manzanillo. When this construction is finished the backbone or central railway across the length of the island will be a fact, because existing lines will complete the links. The narrowness of Cuba forbids parallel roads, except for short distances. This backbone railway was for fifty years an inviting project; but the English and the French capitalists who organized companies, made surveys, and secured what they supposed were Government concessions were always foiled in the end by the Spanish shipowners. Only the memory of banquets to the government officials remained to the capitalists; but that will not be the case in the future.

The railways in actual operation in Cuba to-day, as given by the American military authorities, are as follows;

Name.	Miles.
United Railways of Habana	244
Western Railway	109½
Marianao Railroad	9
Habana Terminal Railway (American military line)	6
Regla and Guanabacoa Railroad	2½
Matanzas and Sabanilla Railroad	172¾
Cárdenas and Júcaro Railroad System	248½
Sagua la Grande Railroad	88
United Railroads of Caibarién	57¼
Trinidad Railroad	22
San Cayetano and Viñales Railroad (narrow gauge, 2½ feet)	15
Zaza and Sancti Spiritus Railroad (narrow gauge, 3 feet)	22½
Júcaro-Morón Railway (military line)	40
Nuevitas and Puerto Príncipe Railroad	45
Guantánamo Railroad	10½
Gibara-Holguín Railroad	9½
Santiago Railroads	33
Total	1,135

Of the systems, the Júcaro-Morón Railway belongs to the future Government of Cuba. It is an inheritance from Spanish sovereignty, being the old military trocha. It passes through a thinly populated region, and its commercial value has been doubted because neither of the terminals has a good harbor. Nevertheless the country which is tributary to it is very fertile and capable of great development, while branches may be built from the main stem to good ports on both the north and the south coast. This line cost the Spanish Government $1,152,800 in gold. The Habana Terminal Railway, so called, is a belt-line running from the docks at Triscornia and intersecting the lines which enter Habana. It was built to facilitate the movement of the troops and the handling of the supplies. When the

United States ceases to have use for it, this belt-line will be valuable to the existing roads, and if sold to them should bring a good price.

The present ownership of the Cuban railways is chiefly in London. English capitalists were heavily interested before the insurrection broke out. They built the Western Railway running from the city of Habana to the town of Pinar del Río, through the tobacco country. Surveys have been made to extend this line 30 miles farther westward. English capitalists also control the United Railways of Habana, which enter the city from both east and west, though the most of the lines run eastward. Cubans and Spaniards were the chief stockholders in the sugar-carrying roads known as the Cárdenas-Júcaro and the Matanzas-Sabanilla systems. After the signing of the protocol, in order to get money with which to work their plantations or for other purposes they sold their holdings to the Englishmen.

At one time American capital seemed likely to control the Cuban railways. It had the opportunity, but the chances of manipulation, of reorganization committees, and of new issues of stock and bonds apparently were not great enough to appeal to the daring financiers of New York. So the American capitalists retired and left the ground to their English rivals. It was another illustration of American disgust because Cuba was not a promising field for "quick returns and double money." Some financial interest is still held by Americans, but the supremacy is in London. The English owners, after they gained control, sent agents to the United States to offer a profitable share in the enterprises to public men whose political influence was thought desirable.

In a general way it may be said that it does not matter whether the capital invested in the Cuban railway system is from the United States or from Great Britain. The English owners will buy their material in the States if they can get it there cheaper than in England. Nevertheless it is to be regretted that enterprising American railway managers will not operate the Cuban railways. The slow and conservative management of the Englishmen is not suited to the new industrial life of Cuba. Under the Spanish system railway charges, both freight and passenger, were exorbitant. Both the theory and the practice were a limited business and high charges. The English capitalists follow the same plan. During the insurrection both freight and passenger business paid a war tax of 20 per cent in addition to the regular government impost of 10 per cent on passenger business and 3 per cent on freight traffic. The English management does not seem likely to get out of the old rut. It looks forward to continuing to collect 7 cents a mile in American gold for first-class passengers and 5 cents for second-class passengers. Freight tariffs are enormous. The burden for the sugar industry is too heavy to be borne. A fall in rates must come either by the voluntary action of the railroad companies, which is improbable, or by the action of government.

There is something of a political side, also, to this European ownership of Cuban railways. Controlling the system from Pinar del Río to Santa Clara, it is natural that the English capitalists should want to control the backbone railway to Santiago when it is constructed and the branch lines to the coasts. No one supposes that the main stem, or trunk line, between Santiago and Santa Clara will be in itself a paying one, or that there will ever be much through freight from Habana to Santiago unless the Florida straits and the Caribbean Sea dry up. Nevertheless the extension will be valuable in a way. At the present time the projects of the English capitalists are combated by interests which are said to be American. These interests claim to have acquired certain rights with reference to the Cuba Central Railway, partly by the action of Generals H. W. Lawton and Leonard Wood during the early military occupancy of Santiago province, but chiefly by acquiring the rights of the French company which organized the project for the backbone railway in 1881. The surveys made by the French engineers were the most complete and valuable of any that had been attempted. As to the precise rights regarding the projected railway, either Congress or the future Government of Cuba must determine. The most important point is not to delay the construction of the road too long.

The telegraph and the telephone systems of Cuba were owned by the Spanish Government. The telephone privileges were leased to a private company, but the telegraph system was operated in connection with the post-office. Under the American military authority, the lines have been repaired, extended, and improved. They will be valuable property to the State or the Republic of Cuba, but they are better operated in connection with the railway system than independent of it.

The existing 1,135 miles of railway are valued at $43,000,000 Spanish gold, according to the stock and bond issues. This would not amount to $40,000,000 in American money. While some of the stock and bonds were quoted above par and some below par after the restoration of peace, the general average would bring the total value up to the capitalization, regardless of temporary fluctuations due to the efforts of rival interests to obtain control. These lines have been described by American experts as equal to the worth of any similar length of railroad in the United States; and it is probable that when the island has a complete system of 2,500 miles, this system will be equal in value to any 2,500-mile system in the States.

As they stand in the present day, the Cuban railroads must spend large sums of money in betterments and in repairing the destruction caused by the insurrection. This work will be completed by the time political conditions reach the stage at which there will be some authority capable of granting the franchises necessary to the construction of new lines. Once entered upon, ten years will be enough for constructing all the railways Cuba will need, for clearing the forest lands of the eastern provinces, and for opening up the mines of the Sierra Maestre Mountains which are yet untouched. The laborers engaged in railway construction may be drawn from the inhabitants, or they may be of a class of immigrants who will settle down as a part of the agricultural population. When the construction is completed it is a simple process to estimate the number of people who will be engaged in the administration and operation of 2,500 miles of railway.

The Cuban railroads will always have water-way competition. They will have no rivalry in hauling sugar to the sea-board; but in the general commerce of the island, and especially in the local commerce, geography is against a monopoly. Under the Spanish rule the Caribbean Sea, the Gulf of Mexico, and the Atlantic waters were a monopoly because the coasting trade was a privilege. It was made the more valuable by the obstacles which were interposed to railway construction. But with the artificial limitations of government removed there can be no monopoly, and with the coasting trade free a permanent alliance of railway and vessel interests is improbable. Too many American skippers can engage in it for the big steamship lines to control the coasting trade.* Every fishing-smack is a competitor. Most of the towns are on the coast or so short a distance inland that electric lines are also certain to compete with the steam railways for passengers and even for light freight. A few years will be enough to demonstrate the opportunities Cuba offers to the merchant marine of the United States. When the island has 5,000,000 inhabitants relatively no more people will be engaged in the midway occupations than to-day. Light manufactures will increase proportionately, while the shipping at the ports due to increased commerce will give further employment. When this is stated there is no disturbance in the balancing of natural occupations which grow out of the turning over of the soil, seed-time, and harvest. In its broadest sense the subject of internal development ends with the agricultural population, though it does not begin there.

* See Appendix B.

The domestic commerce of Cuba, as well as its foreign shipping trade, if shipping trade with the United States can be called foreign, makes the question of the water-ways one of the earliest of public improvements. The island may never have a river-and-harbor bill such as regularly floats through the Congress of the United States, because there is only one navigable river. This is the Cauto, in the province of Santiago. But when it comes to improvements, harbors supply the deficiency of rivers. Their betterment and maintenance will be at once an encouragement to commerce and a temptation to extravagance on the part of the State. Private enterprise will be sufficient to supply every need and to meet every deficiency of the shipping interests in so far as relates to docks, wharfs, and piers, but the actual control of the water-ways, and therefore the improvement of the harbors, will remain the function of the commonwealth. Bahia Honda, Cabaña, Matanzas, Cárdenas, Sagua, Caibarién, Nuevitas, Nipe, Baracoa, Gibara on the north coast, Santiago, Guantánamo, Mazanillo, Santa Cruz, Trinidad, Tunas de Zaza, Cienfuegos, and Batabanó on the south coast are the leading ones, but there are a large number of smaller havens which the coral reefs do not render entirely inaccessible.

The most important public improvements in the future of Cuba are the roads. To insure its success the work must be that of the central Government rather than of the provinces or the municipalities. A system suitable to the development and the permanent interests of the island can only be carried out under a central plan and by a central authority. Good roads are the industrial and in a degree the political future of Cuba, and good roads cannot be limited to a province or to a municipality. National turnpikes are the promise of the island, and the Cuban statesman who emulates Henry Clay's championship of the old Cumberland road will be its true benefactor. Whatever form of government is adopted there will be nothing in the Cuban constitution which the strict constructionists will be able to invoke against this form of public improvement.

The calzada, as it is called, will be the Cuban turnpike or national highway running in all directions across the country. The extent to which the building of roads was neglected and even discouraged by the Spanish Government has been so often recounted that it does not bear repetition in detail. The military road was always a good one. The others were of no importance. There are caminos reales, king's highways, on the maps of Cuba by the hundreds, but neither king nor peasant could find them in actual travel. Where not trails they are wagon-ruts which in the rainy season are entirely lost. The real highway of internal commerce and of agricultural intercourse is the calzada, or macadamized road. When once constructed it resists the changes of the seasons and is easily kept in repair. Four of these calzadas lead out of Habana. The longest one is 40 miles, and extends southeast to the plains of Güines, the market-garden of the city. The shortest one runs south to the village of Managua, 15 miles away. The town of Pinar del Río has a calzada connecting with its port, Coloma, 15 miles south. Santiago has a few miles of good roads, and other

cities have short calzadas, but there is no general
means of continuous communication in any section of
the island. When good roads furnish this system of
continuous communication, not only will an industrial
advance of one hundred years be made, but brigandage,
the commonest form of rural crime, will be destroyed.

Whether it be in railway construction, in road building, or in tilling the soil, the cost of labor is relatively
high in Cuba. The probability that it will continue
relatively high, especially agricultural labor, cannot be
argued away. But what is commonly lost sight of is
that the profits of capital are both relatively and absolutely high. Well-paid labor cannot be considered an
unhealthy industrial condition when well-remunerated
capital goes with it. Nor can it be looked upon as
a discouragement to investment in lands or in commercial and industrial enterprises. Sugar plantations for a
series of years paid 12 per cent on highly secured
loans, and were not depleted. The individual usurers
in the country districts drew their 18 per cent from the
farms of the neighborhood for long periods without the
opportunity of foreclosing on the land. It was too
much. It drew the life-blood from the small farmers,
but their endurance of it showed what the capabilities
of production were. In time agricultural banks will
come, and in displacing the individual usurer will be an
immense gain to the industrial life of the country.

The agricultural banks will not be established until
a stable government is beyond the sphere of experiment
and the old Spanish laws relating to debtor and creditor and mortgages are codified into a general banking
law. That may not be so far off. When it is reached,

the country banks will be able to exact an annual interest of 8 per cent, while performing their functions of loans and deposits in the community, without interfering with the prosperity of the people or becoming the masters instead of the servants. I have made the statement of 8 per cent as a probable rate of interest from a large number of individual calculations without going into the intricate details on which they are based. Two crops a year on much of the land is one basis. Americans hardly conceive of a community of 15,000 people, such as Güines, engaged in varied and profitable forms of farming without a bank, or of the town of Pinar del Río, in the centre of the tobacco-raising country, without one. That is, however, true of these places as of many others.

It does not seem to be an unwarranted assumption that a country which can pay 8 per cent on banking capital conservatively loaned in the rural regions can pay fairly well for labor. Farm labor in Cuba is usually accounted at $20 per month throughout the year where the laborer finds his own "keep." On the sugar plantations in the season of cutting and grinding the cane it is accounted higher. The planters are always willing to pay $1 per day, and hands are in demand just as they are on American farms during the harvest season. In talking with many planters, perhaps a majority will give the amount of $1 a day as what they pay for nine months out of twelve; but the average $20 per month is commonly accepted as the basis for farm labor in Cuba.

Unskilled day labor on the streets and roads and on public works generally may be said to command $1 a day also, though sometimes 80 cents is the maximum. The day's labor begins at six in the morning and ends at four in the afternoon, with an hour for breakfast, making a day of nine hours. This, of course, does not apply to the plantations, where work begins at sunrise. Formerly the wages were paid in Spanish silver, which was usually at a discount of 18 per cent from gold; but the common necessities of life were also measured in silver. Considering that the laborer in Cuba does not have to lay up fuel for winter, that less clothing is required, and that all the means of existence are more easily procured than in the temperate zones, it is clear that $15 to $20 a month in the country and $25 in the city is good pay. After the military occupation began, American contractors who had contracts for public improvements did not find it possible to secure labor at cheaper figures. The laborers who were employed directly by the military authorities received substantially the same. The dollar-a-day basis is not likely to be materally modified under prospective conditions. Artisans, railway employes, and skilled labor of whatever kind receive higher pay, the cigar-makers being the best paid. But the development and the reconstruction of Cuba are in the land and in public improvements, so that unskilled labor in the mass is the real basis for computing the cost.

In the industrial readjustment following the American occupation, a series of strikes occurred in Habana and in other cities. These were cited as evidence that American methods had been introduced, and that labor disturbances were thenceforth to be expected as though they were something new. Strikes may be looked for in the future of Cuba just as they may be looked for in the United States; but they will not be a new development nor due to new institutions. They occurred under Spanish dominion with all its rigor of military repression. The most determined of these strikes were by the cigar-makers and by the stevedores, or longshoremen. There are numerous gremios, or trades-unions, but the majority of them are benevolent and social organizations. Under the Spanish authority the cigar-makers' unions were partly political conspiracies against the Government and partly centres of theoretical socialism where collectivism and the collective labor life were taught somewhat in the manner of the French theorists. After the exit of the Spanish rulers the Socialist or Workingmen's political party was organized in Habana with the avowed purpose of incorporating socialist principles into the industrial and political government of the island. It gained vitality in Habana, but did not spread to the other towns. The majority of its members were from the cigar-makers' unions. The movement did not give promise of becoming a formidable organization.

Most of the strikes after the American control was assumed were based on demands for the scale of wages which obtained before the insurrection, or for payment in United States money or its equivalent.

It is unsafe to guess when the artificial monetary conditions in Cuba will work into natural channels. The only safe course for Americans who are making investments or engaging in enterprises is to follow the example of their Government and base their transactions on the money of the United States. A dislocation must come at some period when the inflated value given the Spanish and the French gold coinage by decrees of the Spanish Government will cease. It served the good end of keeping abundant gold in the island; and though silver was in common use, the white metal was a subsidiary coinage and always so recognized.

The amount of American money in circulation may be estimated at the end of the first year with some degree of accuracy. Then a judgment may be formed of the time when the bankers who received deposits at the inflated government value of Spanish and French gold coinage will pay the deposits back in the equivalent of the American standard, and when the value of debts incurred on the old basis can be computed in the money of the United States. The requirement for the payment of customs duties in American money or its equivalent at a valuation which ignored the inflation of the European coins, the disbursement of the expenses of administration and of public improvements in American money, the distribution of the $3,000,000 to the insurgent troops, the resumption of commerce with the United States, the payments for the sugar crops—all contributed to the one end of establishing a uniform currency of the American standard of value.

In the city and the province of Santiago it did not take long for the American money to establish its supremacy. In Habana and throughout the island as a whole the change was not so rapid. By all natural laws Spanish silver ought to have depreciated, but instead it appreciated. This was partly due to speculative manipulation and partly to a genuine need of the silver in commercial transactions. But with the steady influx of United States currency in the circumstances noted above, it is possible to foresee the disappearance of the Spanish silver. When that happens the period cannot be a long one until the Spanish and the French gold pieces will circulate at parity with the money of the United States on their bullion value. Cautious financiers who peer further into the future, and who also take a glance backward, may see the shadow of an irredeemable paper currency. They may recall that the various Cuban constitutions adopted by the assemblies which met in the woods all provided for the issue of paper money. But the shadow need not take the outlines of spectre. There were mitigating circumstances for those revolutionary assemblies in devising means of support for the insurrection.

With what has been said of commerce and internal development, in conclusion it may be worth recalling the primary formulas. Cuba will have no expenses of sovereignty and no budget of a huge debt to maintain out of her customs collections. The expenses of sovereignty were the burden with which the peninsula broke the back of the island. The million dollars a month from customs receipts which the present population seems capable of contributing will be so far in excess of the expenses of administration that the bulk of it may be devoted to internal and external improvements. If the ratio of increase in customs collections does not keep pace with increasing population, it will at least show a substantial growth. In the utter demoralization and impoverishment of the finances of the provinces and municipalities the American authorities applied a portion of the customs revenues to provincial and municipal purposes. That was a temporary measure. Ultimately it will be unnecessary.

The question will then be with regard to the applications of the customs revenues to island purposes, public improvements, and the like. They may be large enough to discourage the laying of an internal impost upon cigars, cigarrettes, and aguardiente. Yet this means of raising revenues is so easy and would be so little felt by the consumer that it will hardly be overlooked. It is not in any sense a tax on agricultural production as were the Spanish export duties. Looked at in any light, the subject of revenue and taxation in Cuba is a simple one. The matter of the purchasing power of a bag of sugar and a bale of tobacco is not quite so simple. In it are involved both the future commercial and the future political relations of the Cuban commonwealth to the United States.

CHAPTER XIII

Religion as a Withered Branch

Reflections of a Spanish Captain-General—Scarcity of Native Priests
—Statistics of Shepherds and Their Flocks—Historical Review
of the Roman Catholic Church—A Part of the State—Provisions
for Its Support—Ecclesiastics Against Toleration and Civil Liberties—Freemasonry as a Foe—Sketch of the Institution—Con-
flicts with Authorities—Controversies with Champions of the
Church—A Protest Against Intolerance—State of Religion in
Cuba Summarized—Dregs of Spanish Priesthood—Popular Conception a Low One—Exaction of Birth and Burial Fees—Obstacles to Future Usefulness.

Can the Roman Catholic Church in Cuba call again
the day that is past? The dry branch withers. The
living branch puts forth fresh leaves.

Half a century ago Don José Guitérrez de la Concha,
who had been twice Governor-General and Captain-
General of the island, wrote his memoirs. During his
term of office he studied the maladies which threatened
the life of the Spanish possessions in the Antilles. In
1846 he found 458 ecclesiastics, curés, and sacristans
to administer to the spiritual needs of nearly 1,000,000
inhabitants. Many parishes were without priests.
The clerical households of the archbishop of Santiago
and the bishop of Habana were not included in this list,
as he was estimating the parish priests. Fifty years

earlier Humboldt had incidentally noted, according to Concha, that 1,500 ecclesiastics guided the spiritual paths of 500,000 inhabitants.*

General Concha was impressed by the falling off in the number of the parish priests. As became a devout and reflective churchman he deplored it, and he analyzed the sources of the Church's decay. The lack of interest on the part of the Government in Madrid he criticised. One cause of the decay, he said, was the indifference to the education of the clergy. An ignorant priesthood, was his pained comment. He urged immediate and sweeping reforms which would insure educated priests. He wanted the Government to look specially to the welfare of the Church. The memoir-writing Captain-General also noted the paucity of Cuban priests. At that time the right of the native-born inhabitants, or insulars, to share with the peninsulars in administering the secular affairs of the island was not admitted. To trust them with spiritual authority was suggestive of sedition. Yet General Concha courageously gave this proscription of Cuban priests as one of the causes of the low state into which the Church had fallen. He wrote frankly and warningly of the bad results of excluding the natives. He advocated an educated Cuban priesthood which would vitalize the Church by keeping it in sympathy with the people. So far from this course being dangerous to the authority of the

---

* The Paris edition of Humboldt's work, published in 1827, says that the number of ecclesiastics did not exceed 1,100 according to the official census which he had, but gives the number of churches as 224. He speaks of the clergy as neither numerous nor rich, except the bishop and the archbishop.

mother country, he believed it would give the priests the confidence of the people and would encourage loyalty. This was a plain hint that the Spanish shepherds were not trusted by their flocks.

Preceding and succeeding Captain-Generals might have written memoirs, and might truly have said what General Concha said about the state of the Church in Cuba. Don José García de Arboleya, a layman, writing a few years later, drew a more complacent picture. He noted that in all the island there were 364 temples or places of worship, of which 173 were hermitages and oratories. He recited that there were 41 parishes in the jurisdiction of Santiago de Cuba, with 68 places of worship and 128 parishes in the Habana diocese. Each diocese had a conciliario, or theological seminary, for the education of priests. In all he estimated 700 persons consecrated to the service of religion, including the monks. As General Concha had not included the monks in his estimate, it is probable that when Arboleya wrote there had been no increase in the number of parish priests.

In 1864 the Government budget made provision for 106 cures and sacristans in the eastern diocese and for 244 in the western jurisdiction. At that time in Habana diocese the parish churches numbered 137, with 8 auxiliary chapters, 32 oratories and hermitages, 6 convents for monks, and 8 convents for nuns. The appropriation for maintaining the Church in the Santiago diocese was $186,000, and of that in Habana $345,-000. In 1872 the "Guide for Strangers" placed the parish clergy, cures, coadjutors, and sacristans in the Habana diocese at 240, and in the eastern diocese at

75—a stationary condition in Habana and an apparent decrease in Santiago.

General Francisco de Acosta y Albear, writing from his estates in Spain during the closing years of the Ten-Years' war, enumerated the causes of the trouble in Cuba. He had long been a resident of the island, and was familiar with its internal affairs. One of the causes of the trouble, he declared, was the lamentable results of religious abuses. Religion in Cuba, he said, was a myth. It was a useful agency to the political party which secured its influence for national integrity, but it was grossly abused. The parish priests, he declared, were models least of everything of the virtues necessary for the good discharge of their sacred mission. The example of their bad conduct was demoralizing to people favorably disposed to religion. He himself knew their exactions from personal experience, they sometimes demanding four times the regular fees for baptisms and burials. A concurrent cause in perverting the moral sense of the Cuban people, he said, was the lack of religious belief.

In 1898, according to the official figures, there were 110 parish cures and sacristans in the diocese of Santiago and 216 in the diocese of Habana for whose support provision was made out of Government funds. The amount set aside for the support of the Church was $352,000. This was not a heavy draft out of peace revenues which some years reached the total of $26,-000,000, though it was more than was appropriated for public education, that amount being $250,000. The salaries of the parish priests were good, ranging from $500 to $1,500. It is more than the majority of country clerymen of Protestant denominations in the United States receive, though they have families to support. The budget figures three or four years earlier, at the beginning of the insurrection, were substantially the same. There were not as many church edifices devoted to worship because some of them were barricaded and turned into garrisons for the Spanish troops.

When Spanish sovereignty in the Antilles ceased, the Pope designated the Very Reverend Archbishop Chapelle, of New Orleans, as apostolic delegate to Cuba and Puerto Rico. Cuba, which had once formed part of a diocese with Louisiana and the two Floridas, thus again came into relationship with Louisiana. The bull of Pope Leo X. in 1518 erected a bishopric in hitherto unknown Cuba with the seat at Baracoa. A Franciscan friar, Juan de Witte, of Flanders, was named the first bishop, but he was not able to go to Cuba to take possession of his mitre. By the pontifical bull of 1522 the seat of the diocese was transferred to Santiago de Cuba. Other bishops were nominated, but did not administer the diocese, and it was not until 1537 that the island enjoyed the presence of its bishop. He was Miguel Ramaricz de Salamanca, a Dominican friar. His successor was a Carthusian monk, Friar Diego Sarmiento, of Seville. Then there were a few bishops who were not monks; after them the monks again, mostly from Valladolid; and then prelates who were natives of Mexico.

Don José Hechavarri, the first bishop of Habana, was translated from Santiago. His diocese included the Floridas, Louisiana, Cuba, and Jamaica. In 1788, Cuba, having lost more than one-half of its jurisdictional territory, was assimilated to the political and military territory. It was divided into two dioceses. In 1804 Santiago was created a metropolitan archiepiscopal diocese, which it remains to this day. Habana was made a suffragan bishopric of Santiago, but each diocese served as a court of appeal from the other. The geographical division was by a line running from coast to coast through the western section of Puerto Príncipe province; so that Habana, while a suffragan diocese, had the larger territorial area and much the greater population and wealth.

The spiritual and temporal regimen of the Roman Catholic Church in Cuba was embodied in the sinodo diocesana, the synod celebrated in 1681 by Bishop Juan García de Palacios. This was approved by Royal pragmatic, and with some modifications has since remained in force. Under Spanish dominion the ecclesiastical authorities were part of the State. The bishop of Habana was a member of the Governor-General's council. The ecclesiastical tribunals were respected, and the ecclesiastics did not hesitate to oppose the secular authorities in insisting on the rights of the Church. Both Santiago and Habana have cathedrals, with cathedral clergy and the privileges thereto appertaining. Each has also a theological seminary for the education of priests. Under Spanish rule the secular or temporal head of the Church in Cuba was the Governor-General, and as his delegate in the archbishopric of Santiago the general commanding that military department. The archbishop and the bishop were appointed by the Vatican on the nomination of the Madrid Government.

Arboleya, in the edition of his manual published

forty years back, observes that the Church was poor, especially in the archbishopric. The acts of worship were celebrated with some pomp, although there were no sumptuous processions. He thought the royal cedulas, issued a few years previously, would contribute without doubt to the aggrandizement and decorum of worship. These royal cedulas fixed definitely the charges of the Church and its ministers on the royal treasury, and also fixed the salaries of the priests and their assistants. A computation of income and efficiency was to be made every five years. If the income were in excess of the salary, the excess was to be apportioned among the assistants and to the maintenance of the church edifice. If deficient, the deficit was to be made up by the royal treasury. One-third part of the canons, prebendaries, and sub-prebendaries when vacated, were to be filled from parishes whose cures had at least twenty years' service, reserving to the dioceses of the peninsula a certain number of prebendaries and dignities in the capitularies of the two dioceses, or in the parishes in which they had options.

Arboleya gives an interesting list of the church fees, and these were not greatly modified during subsequent years. He also notes as one of the softening influences of the Church on slavery that in addition to the 52 Sundays there were 20 church holidays on which the obligation was to hear mass and not to work, so that the slaves had actually 72 days of rest. The 20 church holidays were known as the days of two crosses because they were thus marked in the calendar. The days of one cross on which it was obligatory to hear mass and permissible to work numbered 22.

With respect to civil reforms and to liberal political movements, the Church in Cuba was what it was in Spain—always reactionary. Clerical intransigentism became a phrase as common as political intransigentism. It opposed innovations. The Spanish conservatives in Cuba joined it in complaining that religious toleration and free study encouraged the separatists and fomented disaffection towards Spain. They, too, deplored what they called the vacuity of the religious sense in the island; but they laid this to the concessions and the tolerations that were granted. The statutes protected the Roman Catholic Church as the state religion. The penal code provided that those who in offence of state religion broke or profaned objects sacred or devoted to worship should incur the penalty of traision correctional. A similar penalty was applicable to whomever made ridicule of the Roman Catholic religion by word or writing, by publicly contemning its dogmas, rites, and ceremonies. The Church opposed civil marriages. In defending in the Cortes the toleration which the constitution of 1876 extended, Cánovas, rigid churchman that he was, declared that three hundred years of intolerance had so brought it about that religious indifference was the distinctive character of the Spanish society of the age. But the clerical intransigentes would not have it so.

In Cuba as in Spain the Church was against freedom of worship. The religious toleration extended by the Constitution of 1876 was promulgated in the Antilles several years later. It was confined within the narrowest limits. The Baptist mission which was established in Marianao, a suburb of Habana, by appealing to the higher authorities secured the reversal of a ruling by the alcalde who had held that public religious services were within the restrictions of the law of public meetings. By statute provisions, dissenting sects were limited to precincts or places set apart for them, and within those precincts were protected from interference or disturbance by ordinary police regulations. The provision was not broad enough to have covered the Salvation Army. Under it the Baptist mission was maintained in Habana, and a Protestant cemetery under the same denomination was secured. The Presbyterians had a small mission in Matanzas, and there were missions in two or three other places of the island, but they never had a vigorous growth.

The ecclesiastical influence was exerted strenuously against the more liberal provision of the law which permitted civil marriages. The Church combated this in inception and in operation. As late as 1894 there was a dispute between the bishopric and the civil authority regarding the certificates of baptism required in order to contract civil marriages, and it was necessary to issue a legal process against Juan Bautista Casas, ecclesiastical governor of the dioceso.

The Spanish ecclesiastics laid much of the irreligious condition of Cuba to Freemasonary, ignoring the degree to which their reactionary tendencies encouraged that institution. Toleration they declared to be an evil to the State, and toleration of Freemasonry they held was an encouragement of a foe to the Church and to the State. The history of this movement is worthy of a brief review, and it comes as much within a chapter on the Roman Catholic Church as within an analysis of the political side of Spanish dominion.

Freemasonry * was introduced in Cuba by the French refugees from Santo Domingo in the first years of the century. Lodges were formed by the immigrants who established coffee plantations in Santiago province, and also in the west in the country around Habana. Hostile public opinion growing out of Murat's attack on Madrid in 1808, during the war between France and Spain, caused the French colony to emigrate a second time. Its members went to Louisiana, and with them the lodges disappeared from Cuba. It was not until ten years afterwards that lodges were again formed in Cuba under charters from the grand lodge of Pennsylvania. In the same period the grand oriente of France authorized the founding of lodges in Cuba, and the conferring of the thirty-two degrees of the Scottish rite. A few years later the grand oriente Spanish American Symbolical of the Island of Cuba placed itself under the jurisdiction of the grand oriente of Spain, but shortly afterwards declared its independence. A fusion was effected of the various lodges in Cuba, and in 1822 they numbered 67. It was the time of political conspiracies and revolt from Spain by the South American countries. The Captain-General of Cuba, Francisco Vives, protected the masons, not because he was one of them, but because by introducing the official element into them he was able to check their tendencies towards political treason. After his recall Freemasonry came under the ban of the Spanish Government, and a dozen years later, through the vigorous

* "La Masoneria en la Isla de Cuba," Inza. Habana, 1891.

prosecution of the aggressive Captain-General Tacon, the masonic lodges disappeared from Cuba. A score of years passed and they reappeared with the vigor of a new growth.

When the cry of Yara portended the Ten-Years' war, it was disclosed that some of the leading insurgents were prominent masons. The lodges in Santiago de Cuba were disrupted in consequence, and those of Habana came within the suspicion of the authorities. When one lodge was celebrating a memorial session the police and an armed force of Volunteers surprised the meeting and took fifty-two members prisoners. Those who were Spanish subjects were kept in prison nearly four months. They were finally released by direction of the Madrid provisional Government, which was then under the Presidency of General Prim, himself a mason.

The Spanish authorities in Cuba were in constant dread of the lodges as centres of conspiracy. In the closing year of the Ten-Years' war there was another police descent on a lodge meeting in Habana, and two hundred members were arrested while celebrating a memorial session. Captain-General Jovellanos was a mason. By his direction the members were paroled, instead of being imprisoned; and though they were kept under surveillance, no further consequences were visited upon them. At all times the lodges had among them officers of the army and Spanish civil officials. After the peace of El Zanjón the lodges reunited and Freemasonry had a fresh growth. There were 60 lodges with a total membership of 2,800. Three years later, more than a score of new lodges had arisen, and the membership was 3,800. Ultimately it reached 7,000. What was known as the Law of Associations, promulgated in 1888, enabled the grand lodges and the subordinate lodges to be registered as lawful societies. Nevertheless the Spanish authorities always feared them as cloaking conspiracy.

At various periods the Cuban lodges had controversies among themselves and with the Spanish grand oriente for attempted usurpation of authority. They always resented this usurpation. When the masonic fraternity of Spain split, the Cuban lodges celebrated a mutual compact of recognition with the faction of Don Praxades Sagasta, so often Prime Minister of Spain. Though Cuba was a political dependency, a possession of Spain, the Cuban lodges uniformly asserted that the masonic confines did not run with the political confines. The Cuban grand lodge regularly reaffirmed that it was a masonic potency, free, independent, and sovereign. Previous to the last insurrection, masonic newspapers were published in Habana, and a school was maintained. The lodges ceased to exist to all public intents and purposes during this insurrection. The large majority of their members were Cubans. This meant that they were in sympathy, either actively or passively, with the revolt. So prudence and the frown of the authorities kept them from holding sessions. Moreover, most of the members were either in the field with the insurgents or in exile. Some of the leading chiefs, incuding Calixto García, were Freemasons.

From this sketch of Freemasonry in Cuba the inference might be drawn that it was considered solely on its political side. This would be incorrect. Its progress was opposed by the Church on twofold grounds.

The main one was that it was a secret society, and in contravention of the doctrines of the Church. The other objection was that its tendency and even its aim was to weaken the civil authority of which the Church was the beneficiary and the bulwark. Clerical intransigentism opposed it as vigorously as did political intransigentism.

Following the revival which Freemasonry had in Cuba after the peace of El Zanjón, a fierce dispute raged over its tenets and its tendency. A notable controversy was carried on between the masonic writers and Don Rafael de Rafael, the ablest Spanish editor of the leading conservative paper. Rafael de Rafael was a Catalan who believed that Freemasonry had initiated and fomented the insurrection of Yara, and that its object was the destruction of the Church and of Spanish sway. Its character, he sought to prove, was revolutionary alike towards established government and established religion. Since in the Spanish dominions the two fundamental institutions which served as a base of society were religion and monarchy, he reasoned that masonry was the special enemy of Spanish institutions. Other journals continued the controversy, which lasted for several years; and the Church authorities persistently opposed the progress of the society. But with Premiers of Spain and Captain-Generals of Cuba themselves Freemasons, it was not always easy to make out that the fraternity was the enemy of the State and of the State religion. Some Cubans of intelligence joined the lodges as much as a protest against ecclesiastical intolerance as from fondness for the principles of masonry.

The fruitage of a century of Roman Catholicism in Cuba bears a simple analysis in so far as it relates to the spiritual welfare of the masses. It may be studied without prejudice and without bias. All that is bad that may be said of it has been said by those whose faith it is. The state of religion in Cuba, if not retrogressive, was at least stationary, while the movement of population was progressive. The parish clergy who ministered to the spiritual needs of 1,600,000 people were fewer by at least one-fourth than those who administered to 800,000 souls. Cuba, not being *in partibus infidelium*, was not the object of missionary zeal. Its inhabitants were Catholics from the time the Conquistadores exterminated the native Indians and immigrants from the peninsula filled the void. The Africans whom the good Las Casas thought it merciful to import into human servitude in order that the soil might yield its fruitfulness also were converted, and in time came within the pale of the faith.

With entire homogeneity of the language and predominant homogeneity of the Spanish race, the conversion of the inhabitants of Cuba was not an incentive during this century that could be urged on zealots or missionaries in the peninsula. The stream of faith was allowed to grow sluggish and become a stagnant pool. Perhaps the trouble was in the fountain from which it was fed. The Catholic Church in Spain has its rancorous critics, its sturdy champions, and its apologetic defenders. They may all bury their differences in the acknowledgment of a craggy fact, and then dispute the cause. The Church in Cuba was not responsive to the aspirations of the inhabitants. Church and

Crown were one. By its union with the State, the Church became identified with the oppression and misgovernment of Spanish dominion. Out of this condition came the refuse of the priesthood as ministers of the spiritual wants. Often they were in ecclesiastical exile from the peninsula because of offences which forbade their exercising their sacred offices among the people who knew their offences. Before the last insurrection, in the popular mind the Spanish priesthood in Cuba as a class personified ignorance, cupidity, and indifference to their holy office. This is a harsh judgment. It has been pronounced in calmness and sorrow by Catholic observers.

The popular conception is shown in the theatres. In the best of the plays the foibles of the cures or parish clergy are received by cultivated audiences as suggestive of something grosser. In the low variety theatres the grossness of the stage representation makes the suggestion unnecessary. The escapades of the cures are a stock subject. The nephews and nieces of the priests are sometimes given in polite company their rightful relationship. It does not need a moral essay to show that these ideas would not prevail or would not be tolerated if they were baseless. The slanders and insinuations of the scoffer are ignored where holy living enforces the respect due to the holy office. A representation of Catholic priests or of Protestant clergymen such as finds favor in Habana would be flat and dull to a depraved American audience because of their consciousness of its falsity. In the Habana variety theatres the sauce comes from the truthfulness of the suggestion. It was the same in the vile literature.

Americans are sometimes momentarily shocked when they see a priest in his vestments sitting in a café; but this is an exaggerated sentiment. For the priests to smoke in public or to lounge in a café does not offend the customs of the country or degrade religion. The degradation comes from a deeper cause. A priest in one of the suburbs was in the habit of gambling in public with the Spanish officers. He invariably won. One night the game broke up in a fight. The officers accused the priest of cheating. In another village the parish priest played regularly, and won the money of the officers. Knowing his habits, the insurgents knew when the officers were occupied and took advantage of it. During the blockade of Habana by the American fleet, public gambling was licensed and the license fees used for the benefit of the poor. At one of the most notorious places a priest in vestments nightly tempted fortune at the roulette wheel. These were individual instances of which the writer had personal knowledge. The American military commanders, when they took control, also had a chance to inform themselves. In one of the most prominent towns the American general sent to his superiors a peremptory demand for the bishop to remove the parish priest because he was a drunken old vagabond.

Here is a portraiture of the Spanish priest in Cuba painted by what may be called an unfriendly hand,* yet it cannot be called the hand of an enemy of the Church, for it is that of a native-born Cuban priest: "Cuba, like all of Latin America, has been the refuge of the Spanish clergy expelled from their dioceses, the

* "Veritas" in the newspaper *El Grito de Yara*, December, 1898.

filon of ambitious prelates. Here they have come in totality, least of all to preach the dogma, to make Catholic propaganda, to moralize. They have betrayed the design of domination; for hope, they have substituted lucre and usury; for charity, tyranny; the god of the majority of priests has been the vile metal. In their time of power they were not seeking to save souls or to administer the sacraments, but to make money, to dominate, to collect dues. Not to educate, but to prostitute."

It is the general testimony that under Spanish rule the Church fees for marriage, baptism, and burials were mercilessly exacted. The people paid tribute from the cradle to the grave. Some controversy occasionally is heard in the United States about the abuses of the priestly office and the exaction of these Church fees. There could be no controversy in Cuba, where the fact was one of prominent experience. Whoever wishes to understand the feeling of the masses of the population towards the Spanish priests because of these exactions has only to select a given community and judge for himself. The good priests remitted or moderated the legally authorized tithes; but the good priests were few. By the majority of cures the parish was administered for its commercial gain. The Church thus became the partner in the abuses of the Spanish political system.

During the insurrection, in some parts of the island it was the belief—a belief which remains to this day—that the secrets of the confessional were betrayed to the Spanish authorities, and that insurgents were sent to their deaths from the altar. That belief may be baseless, yet its existence cannot be ignored. Of other acts, conjecture is not needed. Some Spanish priests, without sympathizing with the revolt, labored nobly to mitigate the horrors of Weyler's reconcentration. Others were indifferent, and some abetted it and gloried in it. The memory lingers in certain parishes of priests who told their flocks that the enforced death of women and children by starvation was the judgment of God because the husbands and fathers rose up against lawful authority. Physicians of Spanish blood honored an honorable profession by their ministrations to the sick and dying without thought of political passion. Too often the spiritual physician was reproachful in his ministrations. So the obstacles to the future usefulness of the Spanish clergy are clearly discernible. They are gross ignorance and lack of the sympathy and confidence of the Cuban people.

CHAPTER XIV

Cuban Priests the Living Branch

Native-Born Clergy in Sympathy with Their People—Persecutions—
Movement Against Spanish Bishop and Clergy—Manifesto of
Cuban Priests—Hint to Vatican Against Italian Intrigue—De-
mand for Ecclesiastical Home Rule—Pastorals of the Bishop of
Habana—Acceptance of the New Conditions—Jesuits' Adapta-
bility—Appointment of Native-Born Archbishop in Santiago
Diocese—Alienation of People Not Permanent—Freemasonry
Not Virile in Opposition—Weakness of Religious Orders—Un-
grounded Fears—Conservative Action of American Authorities
—Protestant Evangelization—A Religion of Deeds.

THE morning of promise which came to the island
when its political freedom was assured was not her-
alded by a sunburst of ecclesiastical rejoicing. To the
mass of the Cuban people, the Church as it remained to
them was hateful. It was identified with all that was
bad in the buried Spanish domination. If not hostile,
they were indifferent. Yet the withered tree of the
Church has a fresh branch. This is the Cuban clergy.
Through all periods and through all phases of Spanish
authority this small Cuban priesthood interpreted the
feelings of the people and was true to their aspirations.
With it rests the future of the Roman Catholic Church
in Cuba.

The Cuban priests came out from the shadows into
sunlight. Don Manuel Santander y Frutes, the Span-

ish-born bishop of Habana, is credited with describing them as mutinous and pugnacious. From the standpoint of superior ecclesiastical authority that may be a proper designation of their defiant and aggressive stand in these days. In the former period it would hardly fit. The opportunity was lacking for them to be pugnacious and mutinous, but they were intensely and consistently patriotic in the Cuban national sense. They were with their people in all the struggles for freedom. For their national instincts they suffered contumely, discrimination, ecclesiastical persecution and exile, political deportation to the penal settlements, and even death by military execution.

The story of Padre Escambre is known to every Cuban priest. In the Ten-Years' war he blessed a flag for the insurgents, and within twenty-four hours was shot by the Spanish troops. Padre Luciano Santano was present at a political meeting in Santa Clara. Cespedes, its leading spirit, afterwards raised the banner of revolution. Padre Santano was taken to Habana a prisoner and deported to Santo Domingo. Padre Yera, of Esperanza, in the province of Santa Clara, blessed a Cuban flag. He was arrested, fined, and only through the influence of the colonel of Volunteers who arrested him was enabled to go into exile of his own choice instead of to the penal settlements. The colonel of Volunteers had personal reasons for his course. Eight priests were deported to Fernando Po. One of them died on the voyage. It was charged that he had been poisoned.

In the last insurrection no Cuban priest was subjected to military punishment, but some were driven into exile, and others were made to feel the superior ecclesiastical displeasure. The few who had churches were changed to other parishes. It was known that some of the flags carried by insurgent troops—the flags were not numerous—received the blessing of patriotic priests, though their identity was not disclosed to the ragged, bushwacking troops who carried them. In the village of Artemisa, in the province of Habana, when the church was occupied by Spanish soldiers, the priest got arms and ammunitions past them in a coffin to the insurgents. It is possible to suppose that this was not the only instance of the kind. In known instances the sacraments were administered to dying insurgents when to visit them was governmental and ecclesiastical peril. This encouragement of rebellion was contrary to the teachings of the Church. It was sedition against the Spain which sustained the Church. But it is over. The revolution triumphed, and through it comes lawful government not under Spain.

After the termination of Spanish rule in Habana and the ending of the press censorship, articles on the relation of the Church to the new conditions began to appear in the newspapers. Some of the violent sheets, which were demanding a boycott of everything Spanish, named individual priests (Malos sotanas—evil robes) whose removal was demanded because of their crimes against the Cubans. Most of the articles were of a different character. Though acrid in tone, they were not attacks on revealed religion nor on the Roman Catholic Church. A sceptic or a free-thinker could not have written them. They were in purpose and in substance an attack on the Spanish priests in Cuba and on the bishop of Habana. They were also a notice to the Vatican that something different was expected. Their authors were known to be Cuban priests.

The essence of these articles was that religion, the Roman Catholic religion, in Cuba had fallen into a low state through the fault of its bad ministers who had corrupted the purity of doctrine and of discipline. The first obstacle to the revival of Catholicism in Cuba was its Spanish representatives. In peace the attitude of the Spanish clerics had been to collect dues, live well, and to mix in politics. In war, to encourage the shooting of Cubans, betray the confidences of the confessionals, and to deny Christian burial to the reconcentrados and the insurgents. The religious communities—the Jesuits, the Dominicans, and the Franciscans—it was charged, had followed in the rut. The Paulists were especially censured for their violent denunciation of the insurgents.

The persecutions of the Cuban clergy, both by the civil and the military authorities, were made the basis of a special indictment. Bishop Santander was bitterly assailed. The pastorals in which he abused the Cubans for their patriotism were recalled and analyzed. He had contributed $1,500 to the Spanish navy, had encouraged converting the churches of God into barracks and garrisons. He should not try to seduce the Cubans. Rather he should remember the pastorals in which he calumniated them when he changed the frock of the shepherd to the sword of war. He had done nothing to alleviate the miseries of the reconcentration. It had been stated that he did not approve of the principle of the reconcentration. Where was the evidence? When he should have protested against it, he was shut up in his closet dreaming of Spanish victories. The conclusion of all these articles was that the Spanish clergy from the bishop down, having been identified with the odious Spanish rule, and having made themselves odious champions of it, should go because Spanish sovereignty had gone. The sons of the country should be called to represent the Church. It was not possible for the Spanish priesthood to continue directing the Cuban conscience.

Preceding this series of polemics appeared the manifesto of the Cuban clergy. It, too, furnished the text of newspaper articles. In some of the journals the document was treated as apocryphal. It was not apocryphal. It was written by Cuban-born priests of the Habana diocese. Some authorized their signatures directly, and some gave their adhesion to a general statement, not caring in what language the utterances were clothed. A very few of the Cuban priests disapproved of the doctrine. Several avowed to the author of this volume that they indorsed it in every line.

From either the ecclesiastical or the political standpoint, this manifesto was a remarkable document. It declared that divine Providence had made to shine resplendent the inalienable right of the Cuban people to liberty. Coincident with the establishment of the Cuban republic would be necessary the rejection of a foreign and a hostile clergy. Now was the time, the manifesto insisted, for the Spanish clergy to renounce spiritual sovereignty over a people not its people. The same reasons that the Cuba people had for rising in arms, the native clergy had for not wishing to be dependent on the Spanish clergy. "We, the most humble of the citizens who compose the little nucleus of the suffering and persecuted clergy," said these things. They reviewed the history of the struggle for Cuban independence. The seminaries overflowed with Gallegos, Asturians, and peninsulars from other provinces of Spain. Was it strange that the Cuban families should dissuade their sons from the priestly calling when to the priestly peninsulars were the roses and violets and to the insulars the thorns?

The manifesto rejected energetically the idea of a schism from the Roman Pontificate, but it was a bold hint that Italian intrigue would not be tolerated. Respecting dogma, the Cuban priests feared nothing, because the canonical law permits dissidences with the divine end that the Catholic clergy be advised. They would obey faithfully the Pope because they were persuaded that never a Roman Pontiff such as Leo XIII. would impose upon a free people other clergy and prelates than those which the sacred canons and the sovereignty of that free people held respectively— that is the duty of granting and the right of having. In the actual circumstances the Cuban Church must enter the new orbit of reorganization. The first step was that the Spanish ecclesiastics should go. They proposed that the spiritual administration should be conducted by means of two delegates appointed to organize and direct the Catholic Church in Habana and Santiago de Cuba dioceses. These two delegates should be chosen from priests of the native Cuban clergy of recognized fitness, and indorsed by the most conspicuous defenders of the liberty of the island, and should not be members of the Spanish Catholic clergy, which always had been a political organization of the Spanish Government, and which was greedy for spiritual domination in Cuba to compensate in a measure for the lost temporal sovereignty, the one being as fatal as the other.

The purpose of these Cuban priests was to impress on the American authorities and on the Vatican the right of the Cuban priesthood to the administration of the Church in Cuba. Its aim was also to accentuate the demand that the Spanish priests depart. The manifesto and the articles in the daily journals caused a mild controversy. Some of the moderate Cuban newspapers in an apologetic strain, while approving the principle, deprecated the polemical and personal tone in which it was couched. They eulogized the worthy attitude of the Cuban clergy who did not subscribe to the violent language. It appeared, nevertheless, that the Cuban priests were in full accord on the capital points of the manifesto. All the native clergy aspired that the Catholic Church in Cuba should be as free and as expansive as in the great American nation.

The manifesto was censured by the Spanish press for its uncharitable and unchristian sentiments, and for the contempt it showed for ecclesiastical authority even to the degree of heresy. The Spanish papers also pointed out that it was directly contrary to the political doctrines of Máximo Gómez and other insurgent chiefs who were urging peace and concord among all classes, Cubans and Spaniards, forgetfulness of the past and union for the future. The Spanish priests as a body made no answer. Silence was their best if not their only defence.

The bishop of Habana did not reply directly to the contumacious Cuban clergy. His displeasure was shown by mild rebukes in his pastoral letters, and by his efforts to put them in the wrong before the American authorities. He appeared as a grieved prelate, deprecating the violence and the uncharitableness of his enemies.

What the Cuban priests said of the bishop's Spanish partisanship was true. He had been the most zealous of loyal Spaniards in combating the insurrection. When war with the United States was portending he made an Easter offering of the goods of the Church, and during its continuance he exhorted his flock to the lawfulness of resistance. Notwithstanding the harsh judgment of the Cuban priests for his failure to denounce the reconcentration, Bishop Santander was generally credited with opposing the Weyler policy, and with exerting himself to relieve the suffering it caused. But his opposition to the Spanish military authorities taking possession of church property, such as hospitals and asylums, was credited with being more pronounced than his exertions for the victims of enforced starvation. He accepted the American control without question and counselled full obedience to it. Although, he said in his pastoral letters, the heroic flag of Spain had ceased to wave over the country she civilized and evangalized, and though they would never cease in their love and feeling for the mother country, the will of the Lord should be fulfilled. This pastoral letter was also conciliatory towards the Cubans and the prospective Cuban Government. Afterwards the bishop issued other pastorals reciting that the union of Church and State no longer existed, that consequently the Church must be supported entirely by voluntary contributions from the faithful, and exhorting them to this support.

The bishop's attitude towards the American authority was correct if not cordial. He was aggressive in defending the property rights of the Church, and his protests were prompt and vigorous when the first suggestion was made of the municipalities taking control of the cemeteries. He steadily opposed all changes looking to lessening the privileges and perquisites of the Church in fees. Naturally he was against broadening the law of civil marriages. Distrust of American influence was shown in one of his pastorals which guardedly warned his flocks against educational movements outside the Church.

The bearing of the Spanish priests towards the United States authorities was sullen, but not defiant and meddlesome, as in Puerto Rico. They realized their helplessness. A few whose bitterness towards the Cubans had made their positions unbearable took the first opportunity to leave their parishes, but the majority preferred to remain and trust to the bishop to make provision for them. The religious orders, with one or two exceptions, were distrustful of the American influence and of prospective Cuban control. The Jesuits showed their traditional acuteness and adaptability. When General Gómez emerged from the woods and made his journey to Habana, the Jesuit priests were among the first to visit him and receive his words of encouragement that religion was necessary to the State. When there was hesitation in Habana and its suburbs by the Spanish colony to receive the American flag, the Jesuits promptly raised the stars and stripes in welcome of the new authority.

The Habana diocese forms so important a part ecclesiastically of Cuba and its relation to the United States is so close that it has been taken as a mirror of the Roman Catholic Church in the island. This is correct, for the conditions were not dissimilar in the archbishopric of Santiago de Cuba, and the tendencies and the influences there were the same. Nevertheless the eastern diocese is worth a word by itself. Notwithstanding that it was a superior diocese ecclesiastically, less was known of the Santiago jurisdiction because of its isolation geographically and its feebleness in comparative wealth and population. Though the Spanish predominance was maintained, this was less pronounced because in the intensely Cuban provinces of Santiago and Puerto Príncipe it was impossible for the Church to be so thoroughly out of sympathy with the people and retain any hold on them. When the Spanish authorities were making their last and desperate attempt to save Spanish sovereignty by proffering the insurgents further propositions for amplified autonomy, one of these propositions was that the archbishop of Santiago de Cuba should always be Cuban-born.

The archbishop of Santiago de Cuba, when the revolution broke out, deplored it as a fratricidal struggle. If not in direct condemnation of the Weyler policy of reconcentration, his voice at least was raised frequently deploring the results and pointing out the unmerited suffering of the innocent classes. When the American army lay in the trenches before Santiago, after the heights of El Caney and San Juan had been taken, his message was the first one which went to Madrid invoking the surrender of the city in the name of humanity.

The feeling among the Cuban priests of the Santiago diocese does not seem to have been friendly, though it may not have been so intense as among the priests in the Habana diocese against the bishop. The Santiago journals began to publish articles calling for a change. The archbishop was defended mildly by some of the priests, yet it was apparent they would not be content with a Spanish ecclesiastic as their superior authority. Archbishop Saenz himself was too intense a Spaniard to remain under American administration and in the face of Cuban opposition. He returned to Spain. On the suggestion of Archbishop Chapelle as apostolic delegate, the Vatican named the Rev. Francisco de Barnada, a native-born Cuban priest, for the vacant diocese. This was the first step of Rome towards putting the Church in Cuba in harmony with the new conditions. After a struggle of nearly a year the bishop of Habana also resigned. The Cuban priests charged that in resigning he sought to perpetuate his influence by persuading the Vatican to name his own choice for a successor.

The extent to which the Cuban people have fallen away from the Church is recognized by American Catholics. Whether it is a permanent alienation must be determined by events. The author's opinion is that the alienation is not permanent. The Cuban women were all violent revolutionists. They lost their confidence in the Spanish priesthood even as an impure vessel which might hold the crystal water of the pure faith without corrupting it. Yet they did not lose the faith.

It is rare to enter a Cuban household and not find a crucifix, a print or a picture of the Virgin Mary on the wall. During the bitterest period of the insurrection, in the families of Cubans it was not uncommon to hear from the men the remark, "Our women are not, like us, free-thinkers. They do not go to church, but they pray in the morning and they pray at night." The rosary in their hands would frequently witness the truth of this saying. The humble colored women, sometimes of the outcast classes, keep the tapers burning in oil to mark their saints' days. On the church holidays or celebrations, throngs of these black women may be seen gathered at the sanctuary, awe-struck and devout. Their devotion is mingled with superstition, it may be removed only a degree from fetichism, but to the zealous churchman it is a basis of belief, and it is infinitely more hopeful than indifferentism.

The lack of faith has sometimes been cited as evidenced by the poor attendance at the churches. Observation does not support this assumption. At the early morning mass at any of the churches of Habana or of any of the larger towns, or at the later services, attendants are not lacking. The churches are usually well filled with worshippers. The absence of men may be noted, and it may be said that the services are more a social reunion than a devotional exercise; but the same thing is said with equal truth of both Protestant and Catholic congregations in American cities. After the American military occupation began, in some places the parish priests blessed the Cuban flags anew. In the village of Jaruco, *Te Deum* was chanted in the Church. At Alquízar mass was said on the anniversary of the death of Macéo. In Santiago de Cuba mass was also said as in other towns. When Gómez entered Habana on the fourth anniversary of the insurrection, three Cuban priests rode with him.

The intellectual life of the island has been variously described as agnostic, infidel, and free-thinking. A majority of the men call themselves free-thinkers to describe their mental attitude rather towards the Catholic Church than towards religion. They revel in the philosophy of Herbert Spencer; but speculative political philosophy has more attractions for them than speculative theology. The influence of Freemasonry is not likely to be a serious bar to the efforts of the Church to regain the confidence of the people. The institution has not shown great vitality since the change in political conditions. Unquestionably its secret character drew to it many Cuban patriots who saw in it the means for furthering their aspirations for independence. That inducement no longer exists. Without the stimulus likewise of prosecution and opposition the probability is that Freemasonry in Cuba will not be a potent factor outside of its social features. While it will remain under the condemnation of the Church, the antagonism is not likely to be strong. The Cuban priests in their national aspirations sympathized with it, and their condemnation of its members was lenient. This leniency may distress the superior ecclesiastical authorities, but it will continue during the lifetime of this generation of Cuban priests.

The religious orders were stronger in Cuba in the earlier eras than in the later days. The nominations of the monks as bishops was proof of this fact. Their powers waned and rose in the Antilles with the varying fortunes of the religious orders in the peninsula. Dominicans and Franciscans got the strongest foothold. It was the church of the San Franciscans that was profaned by English military occupation in 1762, and thereafter was given over to the secular business of the customs service. The convent of the Dominicans became the property of the university of Habana when that institution was secularized in 1837. Forty years ago there were sixteen convents for monks, and five for nuns in the diocese of Habana, with seven or eight in the jurisdiction of Santiago de Cuba. In Habana there were the monks of Santo Domingo, San Francisco de Asis, la Merced, San Augustine, San Felipe, San Juan de Dios, San Lazaro, Jesuitas, and Escolapias. The nunneries were of Santa Clara, Santa Catalina, Santa Teresa, and two of Santa Ursulina.

At present there are eight religious congregations in Habana and vicinity—those of San Felipe, San Francisco, Santo Domingo, San Isidor, Mission of St. Paul, Escolapians, and Jesuits. The mission of the two latter orders is declared to be especially for the instruction of youth. The Jesuit college of Belen in Habana has been honored by the astronomical discoveries of Father Viñez, who has contributed his share to higher education. The Jesuits also have a college in Sancti Spiritus. The Escolapians have schools in Guanabacoa near Habana, and in Puerto Príncipe. Yet it cannot be said as a whole that the religious orders have done much for public education in Cuba.

The convents of nuns include the Urbanistas of the Franciscan order, Santa Clara, Santa Catalina, the cloistered Carmelites, and the Ursulines. The Sisters of Charity have charge of various hospitals and charitable institutions in all parts of the island. At various times there has been an agitation against the ecclesiastical authorities for keeping the cloistered nuns as prisoners shut up against their will. All the religious orders have property, but the title to some of it will have to be settled by legal process. The formal title to the convent of Belen was conveyed to the Jesuits by the Spanish authorities after the signing of the protocol. Scandal was thereby caused, though the procedure was alleged to be simply recording the title which already existed. All the religious orders showed antagonism to the establishment of societies from the United States. Nevertheless, in Habana, the Augustine Brothers established a chapel where services are conducted in English.

Roman Catholic prelates in Cuba and elsewhere were fearful after the war lest there should be hostile legislation and confiscation of church property if an independent Cuban government were established. The dispute over the title to church property shows a possible ground for this belief. It may be as well that this question is to be settled by judicial process during the American control. The other fears were born of the temporary resentment of the hour, and took no account of the restraining influence of the Cuban priests. A few individuals in what was called the intellectual element of the Cubans talked of a philosophical state without religion, but their talk was the empty echo of French reading. One of the assemblies in the woods which adopted a constitution for the Cuban republic included a provision making civil marriages alone valid; but this came from the freshness of the memory of the Church's opposition to legalizing civil marriages. Such a provision could not secure support in a regularly constituted assembly legislating for the island. Whenever a Cuban congress comes to be chosen and enacts laws for the commonwealth, it will unquestionably exercise the complete divorcement of Church and State. There is no danger of it going further than this, and enacting proscriptive legislation against any creed or sect.

From the outset the attitude of the American authority was clear. The union of Church and State ended with the end of Spanish sovereignty. None of the revenues collected by the American Government could be applied to the support of the Catholic clergy or of any religious sect. The Church holidays were not recognized as State holidays, though in deference to long-established custom on some of these days official business was not transacted. Absolute freedom of worship was guaranteed the same as in the United States. The assurance was given that the property rights of Roman Catholics would be protected, and this assurance was broad enough to quiet all fears. Disputed titles to property, such as the Jesuit church of Belen, were left for future judicial adjudication. No other course was open. The American authorities on the one hand could not afford to confiscate church holdings, nor on the other hand could they confirm a clouded title and possibly rob the municipality of its vested interests.

The most delicate question was that of the cemeteries. The popular resentment against the Church for its monopoly of the burial of the dead was strong. This Church ownership of the cemeteries and the resultant abuses were among the causes which weakened its hold on the people. The municipalities in various places declared for the right of free burial, and proposed to make the cemeteries free regardless of assumed property rights of the Church. The American authorities could only decree that where the complete ownership of the municipality was clear, the burial grounds should be free; where the title was plainly in the Church, it should so remain, and subject only to Church regulations. Where it was held in joint ownership or was in dispute the respective rights should be left to judicial process. Where the municipalities had taken possession of the cemeteries before the American occupation, that action was allowed to stand subject to judicial action. In time all the towns and villages of Cuba will have free burial grounds.

The embarrassment which the Roman Catholic Church will meet will be in its stand on popular education. Under the American authority what could be done towards establishing a school system on the basis of the former Spanish system was done, and in the teaching religion is ignored. In a country whose inhabitants are at least nominally Roman Catholics this may be called an unjust course; yet the American authority in assuring religious freedom could not do otherwise. The reversal of this policy may be sought by the Catholic Church when Cuba comes to manage its own affairs, but nothing is more improbable. A legislative assembly may have a majority of members who are devout churchmen, but they are not likely to make provision for religious instruction in the schools. The popular mind is firmly, irrevocably fixed on keeping the schools apart from the Church. The religious instruction of the Cuban youth must be within the portals of the temples and within the homes.

Protestantism was quick to seize upon free Cuba as a promising field of evangelization. Under the old control the discouragement and the obstacles were too great. After the signing of the protocol, even before the American occupation began, Habana was invaded by the apostles of rancorous and sensational theology. A brief experience was enough to show that the little headway which Protestantism had gained would be lost by this kind of propaganda. It received no encouragement from those who had sought to inculcate a faith other than the common one, and it fell from its own weakness. The people might not hold the Catholic creed in venerated affection. At least they were not ready to accept a gospel which reviled what religious instincts they did possess. After this experiment came the more earnest effort of the various Protestant denominations, several of which established chapels in Habana and missions in other towns.

Protestant ministers travelled over the island studying the prospects. They could not fail to see that the field for evangelization was a vast one. Some acquired the grotesque misinformation which is common in superficial observation made to carry out preconceived notions. The majority laid hold of the cardinal fact that the religion which would make progress in Cuba must be the religion of deeds. They showed the strength of Protestant evangelical work in their organization for the relief of the suffering population and for the support of orphan asylums and hospitals. They also grasped the depth of the popular feeling against the Roman Catholic Church for its taxes on birth and death, and their first promise was free burial grounds. The utterance of a young Cuban, "Protestantism cannot be bad, because they baptize you free and they bury you free," was the keynote with which they sought to reach the conscience of the masses.

Both Spanish prelates and American ecclesiastics were averse to the idea of Protestant evangelization of Cuba. The bishop of Habana, in his pastoral accepting American authority, said that those who were happy in the thought that the Church would lose its influence and be vanquished by the Protestants had no cause to be happy at such a thought. It is certain that the various evangelical denominations will not withdraw from the work upon which they have entered. There is no occasion for a conflict of creeds in Cuba. The majority of people will be as in other Latin American countries at least nominally Catholics. If the liberal policy of the apostolic delegate succeeds in making them genuine Catholics, the incentive furnished by evangelical Protestantism may be credited with a share in the work.

The Cuban clergy will not be content until the Cuban parochial priests are the custodians of the Cuban conscience. They will also insist on lessening the Spanish influence in the religious orders. It is doubtful whether either Protestant missionaries or Roman Catholic ecclesiastics from the United States appreciate the thoroughness of this movement or the degree to which it may be invoked in winning the masses back to the Church.

In the lapse of years, when this national instinct has worked its mission, immigration from Spain may bring Spanish shepherds with the flocks from the peninsula, and the history of the French in Canada in their devotion to the faith may be repeated. But that is not of the present day.

CHAPTER XV

MANNERS AND MORALS

Ingenuous Social Life—Reserve Towards Strangers—Immemorial
Customs and Habits—Grosser Amusements—Bull-Fight and
Lottery Disappearing Institutions—Gambling as a National
Trait—Geography and Climate—Statistics of Illegitimacy Not a
Criterion—Unmorality and Immorality—Habana as an Antillian
Paris—Vice on Exhibition for Visitors—State Regulation of
Prostitution—System Accepted by American Military Officials
—Recruits for Iniquity from Abroad—Causes of Social Demor-
alization Traced—Disproportionate Number of Males—Change
for Better in Social State—Habana Not a Moral Mirror of the
Whole Island—Healthful Influences.

POLITICAL institutions reflect the character of social
institutions. No government in the border tropics
which seeks to place itself above and beyond the customs and habits of the people can succeed. How far
immemorial usages are to be deemed a reflex of the
moral station is not worth stopping to discuss. The
manners and customs and the amusements are all mir-
rors of Latin traits. Naturally the climate has something to do with them.

Much of the social life is in the open air. Cubans
and Spaniards are indifferent to the scrutiny of their
neighbors. There is an unconsciousness, even a naï-
veté, about their methods of living. It might be said
that they live in public. The courtyards of their

houses, the rooms opening directly on the street, make it so. Publicity is not annoying because nobody is curious about that which can be seen so readily. Family groups at the open windows are indifferent to the passers-by. In the evening, when the heat of the day is past, it is customary to leave the house for the plaza or park where the band is playing. A stroll of an hour or two, a meeting with friends, the interchange of little gossip among the women make these evening strolls in reality social reunions. There is also the theatre to attend, and half an hour in a café with all the members of the family, and then the return home. Because of this habit of recreation in public and of the groups in the cafés, impressionist American observers form their conclusions of the lack of home life among Cubans and Spaniards. Nothing could be more misleading. The custom is in itself a tribute to the moderation and temperance among all classes which is so general as to be almost universal. The climate helps to enforce temperance; but the simplicity of the social diversions, the innocence of the recreations, could not exist among a people predisposed to grossness.

Cuban social life has lost some of its reserve, but it does not yet conform to American notions. The visitor from the United States does not readily understand why the men whom he meets in business affairs or in official intercourse do not invite him to their homes. At the balls or dances which he attends as a guest the constraint shown by the sexes appears stiff and unnecessary. Some of the older usages are disappearing. After the return of the Cuban families which had been in exile in the States, the women began to appear in the

streets and in the shops without being accompanied by
the duenna whose presence had always been considered indispensable. They also showed their independence of other customs with which previously they had
been hedged. These innovations may all come without a real change in the social usages. It will be a long
time before the visiting stranger will be received into
the families of his Cuban friends with the same freedom that he meets with in the United States. More
than the crust of reserve has to be broken. Cuban hospitality is a proverb, but it is hospitality after the
manner of a Latin country. Until he is on more familiar terms it is well for the American not to judge too
confidently of the family life of which he is ignorant.

Manners do undergo a change and not always for the
better. American brusqueness has already modified
the politeness which was always met with in public, in
the cafés, the theatres, and the tramways. It was perhaps superficial, and there may have been too much
servility for the independent and self-asserting native
of the North. Yet the habit of being courteous should
not be too readily accepted as a mark of an inferior
civilization.

The amusements of the Latin races do not always
conform to American ideas. It is to be said for the
Cubans that in spite of the sombreness of their political
history they do not take their amusements sadly. The
rural diversions are both simple and joyous. Music is
the soul of these diversions. The serenade is the popular form. The calendar of Church holidays, feast days,
is a full one. Its length sometimes appalls the em-
ployer of labor. The people are always ready to ob-

serve the calendar not so much in the devotional frame of mind as in the holiday spirit.

The robust and grosser sports are to be considered. There is the cocking main. This is not a noble sport, but it is distinctively a Cuban one. Nor is it the amusement of the lower classes alone. The neat latticed structure in the form of an amphitheatre which is seen on the outskirts of many of the villages is the cock-pit. A similar structure is found on private estates. In the country the amusement is a favorite one. Its final disappearance is not of the immediate future. The most that can be expected for a time is that the Cubans who have been decrying the sport as a brutal and degrading one will find greater encouragement in their efforts to banish it. A Captain-General of Cuba once kept a cock-pit in the courtyard of his official residence. Another Captain-General declared that game roosters made it easy to rule the Cuban people. The Spanish authorities licensed and encouraged matching the game roosters because of the revenue it brought the Government. This knowledge, among the Cubans who were bitterest in their opposition to Spanish rule, is a moral argument which has greater weight in banishing the amusement than its brutality.

It was a question of many observers who judged from the South American countries whether when Spanish sovereignty was gone the bull-fight and the lottery would also go. In Cuba, so far as this generation is concerned, the answer is clearly foreshadowed. The bull-fight and the lottery were part of the Spanish institutions against which the fiercest resentment was shown. Educated Cubans charged that they were maintained by the Government for the purpose of debauching the moral sense of the people. By one who has not lived in the midst of them the intensity of this feeling would not be understood. It was strong enough to give assurance that these institutions once gone would not be revived without determined resistance. Moreover, the bull-fight was the especial sport of the Spaniards. The majority of its patrons were always from their ranks.

The lottery was a more subtle evil. Its existence was among a people who are declared to be gamblers by nature. That both Cubans and Spaniards are inordinately addicted to gaming there can be no denial. How far the Government was responsible for encouraging this instinct by maintaining the great gambling scheme of the lottery as a State institution may be a matter of individual opinion. Outside of this, the Spanish laws against gambling were very severe—quite as severe as the statutes and the police regulations in the United States. When the Spanish lottery fell, the mass of the people, though they had been in the habit of buying the tickets regularly, did not seem to miss it. Some surreptitious schemes of lottery drawing found their way into the island—just as similar schemes existed in the United States after the Louisiana lottery was driven out. But they did not secure patrons in the overwhelming numbers that would justify the belief that the people could not get along without the drawings.

The time since the stain of the lottery was on the escutcheon of the United States, the agitation which was necessary in order to secure the passage of an act of Congress outlawing it from the mails, are so recent that it hardly lies in the mouth of Americans to be too critical of the Latin toleration. They will find to-day a pronounced public sentiment against the lottery which promises to continue strong enough to prevent it getting a foothold under whatever form of government prevails. And in any given community in Cuba quite as strong a feeling will be found against gambling and quite as urgent a demand on the authorities to enforce the laws as exist in any given community in the United States. This does not mean that gambling will be eradicated. It does mean that it may be lessened among a people who recognize that it is detrimental to their own welfare and demoralizing to their morals.

These questions of manners, customs, and amusements have a bearing on the relation of the social institutions to the political institutions, yet they are not the core. That is one of usages and habits in their effect on the morality of the people and their capacity for maintaining good government. Public morality is the closed book of Spanish rule. Though never practised in the past, it is compatible with representative government in the tropics. But what of private morals? Cuba comes within the geographical zone of supposed contamination. The state of civilization has been represented as one of gross immorality.

It is proper to inquire how far this impression is correct, and what is the actual and the prospective state of morality among this people crossing the threshold of nationality. After that comes the inquiry into relative morals, into the causes that have produced the present conditions and whether they are ineradicable. That is to say, whether the morals of the border tropics are a temporary condition, or a fact of geography and climate, a natural rampart of vice and incapacity for good government which can be neither scaled nor beaten down. These might bo considered subjects for the closet rather than for open discussion, but unfortunately they cannot bo settled in the closet. In making the inquiry I do not propose to take the statistics of illegitimacy as the premises of any conclusion. The reason is that they do not furnish the basis from which just conclusions can be drawn.

Illegitimacy is not confined to the tropics, and is not a product of the tropics. Acrid religious controversy may grow out of the discussions over Protestantism and Catholicism, or over the relative vice of the Anglo-Saxon as shown in London or of the Latin as shown in the rural regions of other countries. But on its theological side Cuba may cite Jamaica with an annual birth-rate of 76 per cent of illegitimates, and Habana may bo compared with a dozen other cities. And if the religious instincts of the American people are done violence to through this apparent indifference to the sanctity of the marriage rite, they may find sober thought in their own statistics of divorce. If tho statistics of illegitimacy are their basis for measuring the capabilities of the tropical Antilles for self-goverment, why may not statistics of divorce be taken as a proper means of determining the standard of American civilization? Who shall take the measurements? The state of *unmorality* in Cuba is deplorable, but this is not immorality nor the immoral basis of a commonwealth.

Habana is the Paris of the West Indies. Its immorality is worn on the sleeve. The American visitor may learn more of its vices in a week than he has known of the dark shadows of his home city in a lifetime. He may go without apology or without disguising his identity to one of the public balls during the carnival season. When he encounters there acquaintances whom he has met in other spheres he need not be shamefaced, and seek to explain that he is observing the customs of the country. No explanation will be expected. He may attend social functions of the best society, and wonder at the *insouciance* of the refined ladies who dance what he is told is the Cuban national dance. If his mind is prurient he may dwell on its possibilities; but this impression will not continue after his familiarity becomes more extended. The Cuban dance will fade away as the waltz and schottische fade away.

At the public ball he may see the national dance exaggerated and vulgarized in a manner that the good women whom he met at the social function do not know to be possible. The probabilities are very great that he will see nothing more; and the hours will wear away into the gray morning to the thrumming of the music without variation and the monotonous motion of the dance without other incident. His desire for some excitement is almost sure to be disappointed. At the variety theatres of the lower order his experience will be more varied. The stage indecencies may be more pronounced than may be seen in the low variety theatres of the large cities in the United States, but this is doubtful. Much of the performance will be dependent upon an intimate knowledge of the Spanish language, its colloquialisms and the double meaning which can be given to so many of its words.

The traveller may look twice at the comely, graceful woman with the chocolate complexion who passes the hotel or the café where he is seated. He may assume that he is in Savannah or New Orleans. He may wonder if it is the eternal doom of the mulatto to be *declassée*, and if she is to know no other fate. If he has the opportunity to study the social life of the middle classes fully, he will learn that the struggle against this fate is going on, and that the mulatto race is not accepting the decree. But he will not know this in the beginning. The visitor will not see the strange women in the street as he may see them in Chicago or New York. But they will peer at him from the windows and the doorways of their habitations, and will resent his refusal of their hospitality. Their trade is the open trade of the outcast everywhere. It is lawful. The State recognizes it.

The visitor may read in the newspapers municipal orders about the location and other regulations for the houses of tolerancy. He will probably be told that the indifference to their home surroundings is one of the characteristics of this branch of the Latin race, and that their lack of morality is shown in their toleration of neighborhood surroundings of that kind. It is true that the Spaniard or the Cuban builds his residence for himself and not for the outside world. Its exterior gives little idea of the interior, and this sometimes causes the fine house to be near a foundry, a shop, or something not so harmless. Yet the visitor who reads the newspapers will find constant complaints against the authorities for permitting the houses of tolerancy to go beyond their prescribed limits and invade respectable neighborhoods. This assuredly does not indicate a lack of moral sensibility. Being recognized by the State, they have their metes and bounds laid down by official orders, and the protests against their overlapping the bounds are usually numerous enough and emphatic enough to impress upon the authorities the enforcement of the regulations.

If the curiosity of the visitor develops into legitimate inquiry, he may glean knowledge that will unsettle previous opinions. He will find a complete code of civil regulations for prostitution enforced by special police and re-enforced by medical inspectors. He will learn of the system of license fees, and will not fail to hear of the horrible abuses which grew out of that system under the Spanish administration. In comparison with these abuses, police blackmail of the unfortunate classes in American cities becomes a luminous spot in this dark shadow. The American military authorities accepted the system as they found it, which was as a measure of hygiene and not of reformation. Some of them approved the principle of licensing the social evil, but they would have preferred a different practice. Others indorsed it both as a general measure and for the special protection of the soldiers. Under military administration the enforcement of the regulations was rigid, but no effort was made to give them other than a hygienic character.

Some phases of the subject are better fitted to a chapter on medical sociology than for popular information; but the system in so far as legalizing immorality is concerned is not different from that of other countries which adopt the same principle. Neither this official

recognition of the social evil nor the abuses in connec·
tion with its regulation are chargeable to the morals
of the tropics. Moreover, notwithstanding the toleration of public sentiment, State licensing was at all times
opposed by a part of the community. Vicious practices in the United States might be exhibited in their
deformity because the American military authorities
enforced the license system for the protection of their
troops with the same justice as to set forth its existence
as evidence of a low condition of morals in Cuba.

But the stranger may learn other things. He may
meet many persons who will tell him that it is hopeless
to expect a pure home life; that the mixture of races
forbids; that the climate produces social demoralization,
and that climate cannot be conquered. He may follow
his inquiry into all the haunts of vice, and come to learn
that Habana is a port where vessels from the four
quarters of the world drop anchor. He will learn that
the toleration which is everywhere extended to sailors
ashore is not denied in Habana. With these sailors'
resorts and with its Chinese quarters, this Paris of the
Antilles is also the San Francisco of the West Indies.
Do all these things indicate that the blood of this people is hopelessly corrupt? Or are they the excrescences
which grow luxurious like all growths of the tropics,
but which may yet be rooted out? Not rooted out
entirely. The social vices do not have the germs frozen
in the temperate climates; they are not even chilled in
the border tropics.

The austere moralist may look upon it as a hopeless,
almost incurable, condition of depravity. The cynical
man of the world is a better judge. He will not be apt

to condemn without knowledge of other cities than Habana, nor will he accept unreservedly the verdict of the Habana residents regarding themselves. Probably the man of the world knows that the recruits for iniquity are not furnished by Cuban homes. He may know something of imported immorality—that more than 50 per cent of the outcast classes come from Mexico, from the Canaries, and from the peninsula. If he were in Cuba during the insurrection, he will know that misery did not conquer chastity. He may see hope for the future among a people where wives do not refuse the office of maternity. He may be cynical over the tolerance which permits the knowledge of male infidelity, but he will not fail to pay an honest tribute to the domestic life which withdraws the wife and mother from the social sphere and centres her life in the rearing of children. It narrows her intellectual horizon, but it enlarges her usefulness in the domestic circle.

The casual visitor may not understand this state of tolerant morals for the men. Its existence may strengthen his conviction that all is bad. His other experiences may not undeceive him. He goes to the best theatre which is attended by a refined audience. Broad references to delicate subjects are made on the stage. He expects to see the fans which the Cuban and the Spanish women use with such coquettish dexterity instantly covering their faces. His surprise is great to find them utterly unconcerned, no lull in their talk, no embarrassment on their part or on the part of their escorts. And in social gatherings he will hear topics discussed which in polite society in the United States would cause a panic. Certain domestic subjects are treated with the same familiarity as in German households. Is all this an indication of immorality? Was it so a century ago in the new American commonwealths? Has Anglo-Saxon morality improved so vastly since Chesterfield's maxims were published, or has conventionality simply been veneered?

Personal immorality does not muffle its face in Habana—does not even veil itself. The American fresh from his own social environment prefers the hypocrisy of veiled vice, yet he can hardly sit in judgment among those who do not draw the curtains. What is good in Cuban social life is open. What is bad is not hidden. In time some of the conventionalities to which Americans are accustomed will come. In time conventionality will clothe the naked children; but their nakedness is that of custom and not of immorality. Modesty will take the place of indifference. All this may happen without a real change in the innate morals of the people. Surface morality, if I may so call it, will improve. Houses of tolerancy may cease to be protegés of the municipality. Outward public decency will undoubtedly spread. Yet these things will not in themselves mean a radical change in the morals of the topics.

The hope of the Cuba of to-morrow for a sound public morality and for improved private morality lies deeper than the surface. It lies in the removing of the causes of past and present demoralization. The relation is an intimate one to the future population of Cuba. Is it to be of mongrels, negroids, abhorrent to civilization? In discussing future immigration and colonization, something has been said on this subject. It bears development. The race mixture that grew out of slavery has not been prolific, although the unmixed illicitness of the colored race is declared not to be so sterile as that of the white race. A barren or a sterile population would make Cuba forever a stunted growth of a commonwealth, the stump of a state without branches and without foliage. The black race is prolific, but the families of the blacks are not relatively much larger than those of the whites. The Cuban family, of whatever color, usually has its half dozen blessings, and sometimes there are a round dozen of them. So we may go out and beyond that phase of the subject, and ask again whether the morals of the tropics are indigenous or whether there is something exotic in them which may be corrected and improved.

The condition which has prevailed in Cuba for centuries was not indigenous. The men outnumbered the women. The Spanish occupation for four hundred years was a male occupation. This was not alone in the military garrisons. It was also of the civil classes—the officials, the merchants, and even the laborers. They were in Cuba to make money and return to Spain, not to settle and bring up families. Those who did settle and marry raised Cuban families who became hostile to Spanish Government. Of those who had families in the peninsula, few thought of bringing them to Cuba. They were conveniently forgotten during the residence on the island. Little distinction was shown in this regard between the husband and the bachelor. Inquiry was rarely made. They were single in Cuba, and custom tolerated their taking a mistress. The Cuban woman would not become the unlawful companion of the Spaniard. The Cuban home did not encourage degradation. The Spaniard had no choice except as between the mulatto and the black woman. Usually he chose the black woman because she would work, and she did not demand the finery that the woman of the chocolate complexion wanted. The latter occupied more the position of the Louisiana octoroon. She demanded that the title of a house or a small piece of property be vested in her. The Spaniard, thrifty in his personal vices, therefore took the black woman for mistress.

The statement of this condition is revolting, but it was recognized. It is stated here because with the end of Spanish control this condition begins to end. Its prevalence can be judged from census figures. In 1860 the population of the island was 1,396,470. Of these, 800,575 were men and 595,895 were women. By Spanish nativity the total was 83,000, of whom 66,000 were men and 17,000 women. Of the Cuban-born it should be noted that the women were slightly in excess, the total standing 513,461, of whom 254,193 were males and 259,268 were females. Further subdivision and analysis show that the black males outnumbered the black females. Therefore the excess of white Cuban women over white Cuban men was greater. In 1860 the foreigners, including Europeans and Americans, numbered 7,725, of whom 5,673 were men and 2,052 were women. Many of these foreigners were married to Cuban women. Many of the Spaniards also married Cuban women; but the significant fact is that there was only one Spanish-born female to four Spanish-born males.

The census of other years does not give the Spanish residents by sexes, but the figures apparently indicate that this relative proportion was not changed. In 1877 55.88 per cent of the inhabitants were males, 44.12 females. In 1887 the ratio was 54.70 males and 45.30 females. The variation is too small to be of moment when the uncertainty of all Spanish censuses is remembered. Early in the nineteenth century Humboldt observed that between one-fourth and one-fifth of the population of Cuba was condemned to live in celibacy. He meant more especially the negroes. He might have added that such Spaniards as were condemned to celibacy modified it by concubinage, and the irregular female classes by polyandry. Under the new era the parasitic and bureaucratic class of Spaniards disappears forever from Cuba. The demoralization which their presence and their mode of living caused disappears.

It has been noted that the majority of tradesmen and their clerks in Habana and the larger towns were Spaniards who expected to return to the peninsula. Few of the clerks, who were numbered by the thousands, married till late in life. They helped to swell the disproportion between the sexes of Spanish birth. The change in political and commercial conditions will gradually alter this unhealthy social state. Future censuses will show no such great disproportion as formerly existed between males and females born in the peninsula. For various causes, such as in the first stage of immigration men coming without their families, the disproportion will not wholly disappear. The removal of this cancer may not insure the social regeneration of Cuba, but it does assure an improvement in morals.

It might be said that for thirty years the social demoralization of the island has been continuous, due to war. The ten-years' struggle from 1868 to 1878 kept a large armed force on the island. The entire body of troops was not moved until long after the peace of El Zanjón, for the insurrectionary spirit was not quelled in the eastern provinces. When the last insurrection broke out, in 1895, the Spanish garrisons numbered 20,000 soldiers, chiefly single men. These 20,000 single men could not be accounted a healthful moral influence. Then came the 200,000 soldiers from the peninsula to crush the revolution. All this is gone forever. With an approach to normal industrial, political, and social conditions, there should be an approach to normal morality. These are the signs to watch, rather than the surface moralities.

Nor is Habana ever to be taken as a type of the whole island. Being the chief city, it will always have both the cream and the dregs of vice, and these will always be on exhibition. The country is seen to better advantage, and the virtues of the people are not obscured by the vices of individuals. Glimpses, too, may be obtained of the secluded home life, and the domestic qualities which have their foundation in the family. This home life is the answer to the supposed lack of morals in the tropics. Reinforced by family immigration, it is the hope of the future; and the prospect for bettering the state of *unmorality* may reasonably be assured in the circumstances which have taken the monopoly of marriage away from the grasping Spanish priesthood. From now forward both Protestantism and Roman Catholicism may be expected to diminish the statistics of illegitimacy by the encouragement which they give to lawful marriage.

These are mere incidents in the moulding of morals in the border tropics. The beginning of improvement is in the disappearance of the conditions which maintain an excessive male inhabitancy. The continuance of improvement lies in family immigration.

CHAPTER XVI

American Military Control

American authority in Cuba began with the surrender of Santiago by the Spanish troops in July, 1898. It was not complete until the formal yielding of sovereignty in Habana on January 1st, 1899. Its basis was purely the military power of the United States in foreign territory. This was set forth after the surrender of Santiago in the proclamation of President McKinley, which provided for the military government of that section of the island which was surrendered. Former political relations were severed and the new political power, that of the United States, was established.

The municipal laws of the conquered territory—conquered so far as related to Spain—such as affected private rights of persons and of property, were considered as continuing in force. The judges and other officials connected with the administration of justice, on accepting the supremacy of the United States continued administering the ordinary law of the land, as between man and man, under the supervision of the American commander-in-chief. The commander-in-chief had the reserve power to replace or expel the native officials, to substitute new courts of his own constitution, and to create new or supplementary tribunals. The treatment of property and the collection and administration of the revenues was declared to be one of the most important and practical problems, and the moneys collected were to be used for the purpose of paying the expenses of government under military occupation and for the payment of the expenses of the army. All ports in Cuba in actual possession of United States land and naval forces were open to the commerce of neutral nations. Following the surrender of Santiago and the executive proclamation came the protocol in which Spain relinquished all claim of sovereignty over and title to Cuba.

The exercise of American authority began first in the province of Santiago, because the United States was earliest in possession there. Subsequently jurisdiction was taken in the provinces of Puerto Príncipe and Pinar del Río, and on the first of January in the provinces of Habana, Matanzas, and Santa Clara. In Santiago the fixing of a new customs tariff was the first act of American sovereignty. It was followed by measures of local government under the direction of General Leonard Wood as commander-in-chief and military governor of the province. By virtue of his authority he issued a bill of rights which was in the nature of a provisional constitution. It consisted of ten articles.

The first section guaranteed to the people the right of
assembly for the common good and of applying to the
authorities petition or remonstrance for the redress of
grievances. The second guaranteed freedom of worship
according to individual conscience, provided that there
should be no interference with existing form of worship
and assured protection to all Christian churches. The
third article directed that the courts of justice should be
open to all, and that no private property should be
taken for public use without compensation. The fourth
article, dealing with criminal trials, invested the accused
with the right to be heard himself or by counsel, and
to have compulsory process to secure the attendance of
witnesses in his behalf. The fifth said that no person
accused of crime should be compelled to give evidence
against himself or be deprived of life, liberty, or property, except in accordance with the laws of the country.
The sixth section declared that no person once acquitted
should be tried again for the same offence. The sev-
enth provided that all persons charged with crime
should be entitled to bail, except in cases of capital
offence, and that the writ of habeas corpus should not
be suspended except when the commanding general
deemed it advisable. The eighth section declared that
excessive bail should not be required, and that excessive
fines or cruel or undue punishments should not be in-
flicted. Article nine provided that every citizen should
be guaranteed in his business, person, papers, house,
and effects against every registry and embargo unjustifi-
able while the probable motive of culpability had not
been declared under oath. The tenth article declared
the right of writing or printing freely on any matter

whatever, subject to responsibility for the abuse of the right. The municipal laws were to be administered in accordance with these declarations, subject to modifications which in the judgment of the commanding general would be beneficent and would promote the principles of enlightened civilization. Though some of the principles were new, these declarations found in the Castilian tongue a sufficient medium of expression.

This promulgation of the bill of rights was followed by a new constitution of the judicial tribunals, by local administrative measures, the most efficient of which was sanitation, and by reconstructing the municipal governments in the various towns of the province. Among the first municipal orders in Santiago was one prohibiting gambling and lotteries.

The general plan of American military control was set forth by executive order on December 15th, 1898. This created the military division of Cuba, and designated Major-General John R. Brooke as commander-in-chief and military governor of the island. General Leonard Wood was commander in Santiago de Cuba, General L. H. Carpenter in Puerto Príncipe, General J. C. Bates in Santa Clara, General J. H. Wilson in Matanzas, General George W. Davis in Pinar del Río, and General Fitzhugh Lee in Habana province. The character of government was indicated in the proclamations and decrees which followed the assumption of office. Thereafter the acts of the American authorities in the different provinces were simply the carrying out of a general policy applicable to the whole island. Habana city was erected into a separate military department with General William Ludlow as the military governor, but subject to the same supreme authority as the others. Subsequently, when the American volunteers were withdrawn, the departments were consolidated in the military administration; but for civil administration and purposes of local government the six provinces and the city of Habana, which might be called a municipal province, remained unchanged.

Following the exercise of American authority over the entire island, by direction from Washington a new customs tariff and new regulations for the coasting trade were promulgated. Fiscal adjustment to the new conditions was made by proclamation of the American Executive, fixing the parity of money to be received from customs duties and paid out in salaries and for other purposes. Thus was the highest prerogative of sovereignty affirmed. The basis of value was American money, and French gold and Spanish gold and silver coins in circulation were measured with it as the standard by their bullion value, allowance being made for exchange and for transportation charges.

Under the American control, the actual functions of internal administration were exercised by the military commanders of the various departments, while the customs revenues, the telegraph lines, and the postal service were administered directly through the general-in-chief as Governor-General of the island. With the exception of the postal administration, all branches of the government were under the supervision of army officers. The post-offices were administered as a branch of the department in Washington, with E. G. Rathbone, an experienced official, as director of posts. The customs districts were established by executive order from

Washington, Colonel Tasker H. Bliss becoming collector at the port of Habana.

All the commanders of the departments on assuming their offices issued addresses to the people, explaining the policy of the United States and inviting their co-operation. Governor-General Brooke, on recommendation of the military commanders, appointed civil governors, alcaldes of the towns, and other officials from among the natives. The acts of these officials were subject to the approval of the military commanders. Between the supreme power exercised by the Governor-General and the authority exercised by the military governors, many oppressive practices of Spanish rule were abolished and some of the laws were modified. One practice which was abrogated was the requirement for passports and the cedula or personal tax certificate for transit from one part of the island to another.

Police regulations and municipal administrations were moulded to the new conditions. The internal taxes, as distinct from local or municipal taxes, were regulated by the central adminstration of the Governor-General. After a strong protest had been made against letting the Spanish Bank of the island of Cuba collect the taxes, as had been done under Spanish dominion, the War Department revoked the agreement with the bank, and on the request of the military authorities, left them free to establish an independent fiscal system. This was done, and subsequently an entirely new basis of internal taxation was promulgated by authority of the Governor-General.

An advisory cabinet of four natives of the island was selected by Governor-General Brooke. It was composed of Pablo Desvernine, secretary of the treasury; Adolf Saenz Yañez, secretary of public works, agriculture, industry, and commerce; Domingo Méndez Capote, secretary of state and government; and José Gonzales Lanuza, secretary of justice and education. Geographically the cabinet was open to criticism because all its members were from Habana. Their preliminary work consisted chiefly in reconstructing the administrative personnel of their departments and in reducing the number of place-holders that had cumbered the official lists under Spanish rule. These cabinet secretaries were also given latitude in the matter of appointing their subordinates. The judicial system, after much care, was entirely reconstructed. A supreme court was appointed for the entire island, which took the place of the former court of final appeal in Madrid.

In every act of the United States Government, scrupulous regard was had to the temporary nature of the military occupation. The American Executive acted within the narrow limit of those powers. No public franchises of any kind were granted. This policy was determined in the beginning and was adhered to without modification. Mr. Griggs, the Attorney-General, in giving an opinion against granting permission to land a cable in Cuba, declared it would be inexpedient under all circumstances. The United States, he said, was exercising administration under the law of belligerent right, and the matter was under control of the War Department, but the Executive Department had taken the ground that in view of the circumstances under which the United States came into control of affairs in Cuba, and in view of the declared purpose of the American Government to retire and leave the government to the inhabitants, it would be inexpedient to grant applications for concessions except in case of absolute necessity. The Attorney-General did not concede that what was known as the Foraker amendment to the army appropriation bill directing that no property, franchises, or concessions be granted by the United States, or by any military or other authority whatever in the island of Cuba, during the occupation thereof by the United States, was mandatory upon the Executive Department. He intimated that it could only be considered as advisory.

Since there was no difference in intention or policy between the Executive and Congress, the distinction between advisory legislation and mandatory legislation is not important. In demanding that Spain withdraw from Cuba, Congress by resolution disclaimed any disposition or intention to exercise sovereignty, jurisdiction, or control over Cuba, except for its pacification, and declared a settled determination when that was accomplished to leave the government and control of the island to its people. President McKinley, in his annual message of 1898, reaffirmed this doctrine, and indicated that the United States would withdraw when complete tranquillity should be established.

This is the framework of American occupation and administration in Cuba. It is an iron framework. It bridged chaos. Its strength was not so much in its flexibility as in its completeness. The conditions and the pledges under which the control of the United States in Cuba began have been regretted by many persons as an interference with the right policy and a hindrance to it. There need be no regret. The first duty, that of pacifying the island and maintaining public order, could have been fulfilled by no other agency so effectively. The foundations of political and industrial reconstruction could have been laid by no other means. The situation was one in which was needful supreme power, unquestioned by either judicial or legislative limitations. Circumstances had to govern. Nor could the measures of sanitation, which was the greatest of emergencies, have been carried forward with such success under ordinary conditions. The military authority was best adapted to cope with this emergency. It was almost as valuable in the establishment of an educational system.

The administration of Cuba was a fresh and untried field for the American military officials, many of them new to civil duties and responsibilities. The discipline of the camp and garrison was not such as to fit them for the exercise of power that could be questioned. This authority in the main was exercised with tact and discretion. There was army politics with ramifications in Washington, but these personal ambitions did not interfere with the discharge of official duties, and did not affect the relations of the army officers towards the inhabitants with whose government they were charged. Though the tongue was foreign to most of them, and though they were among a strange people, they showed quick adaptability to their surroundings. They were not alien governors of conquered inhabitants.

It was given to the American officials in Cuba to walk within the temple of corruption erected by Spanish bureaucracy while the ruined walls were yet standing. They might have misgivings about the capacity and the ability of the Cubans to maintain an independent republic, and their doubts might sometimes find utterance. But they were all impressed with the conviction that the rotten structure of Spanish administration could not have continued and could not have formed the basis of a stable edifice of government, whatever changes in the system might have been made. Like all the world that saw the temple from within, their wonder was that it lasted so long. Their own administration has been an example of American institutions. The shrillest want of Cuba in the future, the one that cries out in the wilderness of chaos and corruption, is that of official integrity. The American officials have set the example. Their standard of integrity is the lesson of to-day, but it will not be learned in a day. It should be continued to-morrow. The same sense of responsibility and of a high conception of duty has been shown in other administrative relations. It was an experiment. The experiment has been a success in demonstrating American capacity and adaptability to administer government among other peoples accustomed to other institutions.

In a general sense it may be said that the plan of American administration in Cuba was reconstruction both industrially and politically. In the midst of passing conditions it is not worth while to examine in detail experiments in fiscal systems. Being experiments, they can be rejected when found unsatisfactory. And the industrial recuperation is a manifest witness for itself. If it fails to make known its presence, searching for it between the covers of a book would be fruitless.

The political reconstruction, the operation of the civil machinery, is apart and of itself. It can be followed in all the intricacies of administration. The strength of the American military control was demonstrated in its way of meeting emergencies and in the impress of official integrity and fidelity which it made. It stamped its mark so deeply that the impress will not be lost whatever government obtains. But there are defects in military control. The very success of the administration in its initial stages makes these defects the earlier apparent. To change the laws to which people have been accustomed for a long series of years is in all circumstances a doubtful experiment. The best that the wisest jurists would hope for would be to correct flagrant abuses and trust to finding suitable judges to construe the laws not oppressively, but beneficently. The abuses were flagrant enough. They were part of the Spanish political system.

The substance of the provisional bill of rights first promulgated in Santiago province was incorporated in the decree of the supreme American military authority regulating court practice and inculcating various desirable reforms in procedure. The tyrannical practice of keeping accused persons incommunicado — without means of communicating with friends or counsel—was abolished, and provision was made for giving the accused person an opportunity to know the charges against him in the preliminary hearing. These changes were opposed by some of the Habana lawyers; but they will stand because they are guarantees of personal liberty which were lacking under the Spanish system of government.

But a disposition was shown to go far beyond such simple provisions. The Roman law and its adaptation in the Code Napoleon do not suit a people who are used to the common law. Americans would not put up with it. Therefore the assumption was that under the new American relation to Cuba the Latin law must be rooted out, though a million or more inhabitants were accustomed to it, and what understanding of judicial systems they had was based upon it. When a purpose to reform the system of laws was first intimated, the College of Abogados—the bar association—of Habana was invited to make suggestions. The association was composed mainly of Cuban lawyers. Many had suffered exile for their opposition to Spanish misrule, all knew the oppressiveness of the Spanish laws. But they venerated the Latin principles of jurisprudence. The issue was raised that a concealed purpose existed to supplant the Latin law by American law. Dr. Gener, the president of the bar association, supported the suggestion that reforms be outlined by the association. Though the common courtesy was to re-elect the president, he found the opposition to his course so strong that he declined to be a candidate. Domingo Méndez Capote, who afterwards became a member of General Brooke's advisory cabinet, was chosen president of the bar association on the issue that radical changes in the laws were to be opposed.

Months afterwards, when the military authorities decreed some reforms, the Spanish lawyers met and organized an association to uphold the excellence of the

Latin law over the common law. The American military power had the advantage, for it could decree not simply changes in the law, but could enforce the changes, nominally at least. Nevertheless the lasting force of all the changes cannot be judged in the midst of fleeting conditions. For a temporary governing authority of a military character to reform a permanent system of jurisprudence is a huge task. The extent to which the system is reformed cannot be judged until the military power is withdrawn and the reorganized system is left to stand on its own support among the people of whose institutions it is a part. Codifying commissions in the States which find years of laborious work rejected might sigh for the military authority to enforce the acceptance of what they know are beneficent legal reforms; but the worth of a codification which rested on that basis is readily estimated.

An illustration which better fits the case of Cuba is that of Louisiana. If in the reconstruction period following the civil war the military commanders had undertaken to destroy the Code Napoleon and to bring Louisiana's system of jurisprudence to the basis of the common law in other States, the effect could be judged. And this is another way of affirming the author's belief that while provisions guaranteeing personal rights will stand, the bulk of changes in the laws made by direction of the American military authority are too transitory to call for detailed analysis.

After a few months' experience there was less disposition to hasten the introduction of new and strange principles of jurisprudence. Conservatism took the place of enthusiasm. Events showed the need of going slow.

The criminal laws required amendment, and the changes in the penal code, as well as in the court procedure, were salutary. Reforms in prison management were made with good results, especially in Habana under the vigorous direction of General Ludlow. Yet even in the criminal law reforms a halt was necessary. The most ardent military reformer did not advocate projecting grand juries and trial juries on a people to whom even the statutory jury of other Latin countries was unknown.

It was, however, in the domain of civil laws that the gravest shock to the progressive spirit was felt. The most troublesome question affecting the industrial reconstruction of Cuba is that of mortgages. By direction from Washington an extension of two years from May 1st, 1899, for the payment of mortgages on realty then due or which might become due within that period was granted. The extension was necessary in order to save a vast amount of property from becoming prey to the mortgage sharks. It was far from being what the debtors asked. It was more than the creditors conceded. No government can expect to please both debtors and creditors. In displeasing both classes the American authorities felt that they did substantial justice. But the discussion of the mortgage law and the legal rights of debtor and creditor and the changes proposed brought up the whole question of the civil laws. It showed how one change must lead to another until the entire system of civil jurisprudence should be reconstructed. Though the American military officials had Latin jurists for pilots, they wisely hesitated to enter upon these unknown seas. Perhaps they were conscious that a few months' tutelage could not make army commanders masters of jurisprudence. The strength of military administration is in its executive capacity, and not in its ability to construe abstract laws. It could and did correct abuses in practice, and endeavored to find the right individuals for the discharge of judicial duties. The wisest way is to stop there. The Latin laws will shape themselves to the new political institutions. American military authority cannot mould them too far in advance of the political institutions that are to prevail.

What is true of the laws is true of customs and usages. The zealous social reformer might sigh for the power of the military reformer in Cuba. If the latter sometimes gave way to his zeal he may be pardoned his weakness. So much there was to be reformed that the temptation was great to seek to do it all at once. Many communities in the United States would perhaps be better if a power from above such as the military arm of the general government were to regulate their affairs, but the communities would not tolerate reforms coming in this manner. In Cuba there is danger of too many sumptuary reforms by the American military authorities overriding long-established local usages.

When the American control began, the clerks in Habana petitioned Governor-General Brooke for the early closing of the shops and stores, and also for Sunday closing. Their hours were very long, and they were required to be on duty till ten o'clock at night. The first intimation given was that to grant their petition was beyond the powers of the military government. The shopkeepers were opposed to the change from motives of self-interest, but the habit of evening shopping was not without reason in a country where the heat of the midday and of the afternoon causes almost a suspension of trade. Ultimately the shops were ordered closed nights and Sundays after ten o'clock in the morning, and the closing was enforced by General Ludlow as military governor of Habana. A few weeks or months of the enforced experiment will hardly furnish sufficient basis for complacent congratulation about the observance of an Anglo-Saxon Sunday or a New England Sabbath in a Latin community. Left to itself, the agitation would probably have resulted in a compromise arrangement. Under military pressure there could be no compromise. When civil authority becomes supreme it will be time enough to judge of the experiment. Meantime the Anglo-Saxon Sunday should not be taken in too liberal a sense.

There are other customs which in the end would be better regulated by local regulations than by the military power of the United States. In a previous chapter I have given the reason for believing that the bull-fight is a dead institution—for this generation at least. If it were not so its formal prohibition by the American Governor-General of the island would not be apt to change the nature of the people who delighted in it.

In the old days the Governor-General laid down iron-clad regulations for the cocking-mains. By a decree promulgated in February, 1882, they were only permitted on Sundays, Church holidays of two crosses, and the day fixed in each town or village for the celebration of its patron saint. Subsequent dispositions of the Governor-General prohibited rival cocking-mains on the same day; required the owners of the game fowls to alternate the lidias, or exhibitions, and reaffirmed the prohibition on other than Sundays and the Church holidays which were specified. The idea was not to permit the sport to be held on regular working days because it would interfere with the industry of the laboring population.

Probably in its effort to free itself from the past abuses the Catholic Church will exert its moral influence against Sundays and saints' days as the occasion for cocking-mains and similar sports. This influence is also likely to be exerted against the amusement on any day of the year. With such encouragement, local public sentiment might be depended on to wean the people gradually from their liking for these sports, so that municipal regulations could be enacted and enforced. But the circumstances in Cuba are not so exceptional as to require the supreme military power of the island to issue edicts regarding this sport and similar amusements grounded in habits and customs because the customs are not in conformity with American notions. A proclamation against dog-fights by the governor of a great State such as New York or Illinois would be no more absurd.

There is extant the decree of a Spanish Captain-General prescribing the manner in which the legs of chickens should be tied when they were carried to market. The purpose was a humane one. If the highest military authority under American occupation is to be concerned with regulating the amusements and customs of the people it might with justice be asked to reform the customs of marketing and revive this humane decree. Against this it may be urged that police regulations should be sufficient. So they should be in innumerable other matters which were taken up by the higher authorities for regulation and enforcement under military decree. It is as if Connecticut were to regulate the habits of California, or Montana to prescribe the usages of Massachusetts.

These comments are made almost with apology for their triviality, but this tendency towards sumptuary and arbitrary regulation of the customs of a different people became a feature of the power exerted by the American authorities. It could not, therefore, be ignored. Errors of this kind may be made, yet they do not affect the American military control in its broadest sense. The example of official integrity and of earnest effort in good administration remains. When the military trusteeship ends it will be a creditable ending, with results to show which will justify the confidence of the American people.

CHAPTER XVII

POLITICAL APTITUDES

MECHANICAL aptitudes are usually inherited. Political aptitudes may be either acquired or inherited. Propensity for revolution may exist without a grasp of the
fundamental principles of free government.

Of the Cuban people as a people, it cannot be said
that they have an inheritance of political aptitudes from
their grandfathers, and atavism in political government
is a phenomenon not to be expected, because the right
use of civil liberty is a growth and not a miracle.
When so vast a majority of the human race has not
advanced far enough in civilization to find chairs either
a necessity or a luxury, it should not cause surprise
that a people whose habitation is the border tropics
cannot boast of inherited disposition for constructive
government. What they do have is the acquired aptitude. This is another way of saying that their training

has begun. The extent to which it has progressed and the influences affecting it may be studied.

From the knowledge of what has gone we gain the knowledge of what remains. In brief compass of a few chapters the autonomist agitation and régime were narrated chronologically as an expisode of Spanish history in the Antilles. From that narration the idea may be had of the degree to which the movement served the purpose of political education. The basis of free institutions is free discussion. Under the limitations of free print and free speech imposed by the Spanish dominion, this basis could not be a broad one. But Spanish Captain-Generals had one quality that was not bad. While they occasionally deported journalists and suppressed journals whose outspokenness was uncomfortable to the Government, they were tolerant of abstract discussions of political principles. Liberty in the abstract, the theoretical bases of civil government, were beyond their ken or care, and discussion on this line was treated with contempt. It was only when abuses and misgovernment were attacked specifically that the iron hand was shown.

These conditions strengthened a natural disposition towards speculative discussion, and speculative political philosophy forms a leading part in the programme of all the political leaders in Cuba. But in the days of repression, under its disguise real progress was made to a greater degree than was known. The terms "meeting," "mass meeting," "self-government," "home rule," had no equivalent in the Castilian language. Autonomy was not the translation of either self-government or home rule. That all these terms were incorporated into the idiom and are to-day current is the best evidence that the meaning of free discussion and free government is understood. The town meeting is not known because the town as conceived in New England did not exist. Besides, the discussion of local measures and of local officials would necessarily have been too concrete for the comfort of Spanish authority, and would have been treated harshly. But the town meeting is coming in Cuba. The aptitude for it is an acquired one—acquired from the mass meeting of the days of the Autonomist movement.

In the revolution of 1868 it was stated that a few wealthy and influential Cubans took their families, their dependents, and their slaves into the field, and thereupon Spain had a Ten-Years' war on her hands. In the last insurrection the influence of a few leading Cubans was also very great; but all they could do was to sustain a revolution that already had the support of the masses. The autonomist propaganda was the work of a group of talented and cultured men. They laid down their principles, and a grouping of personal followers accepted the dictum. When the principles were shifted the followers waited until the chief formulated the changed issues. Then they fell in line.

During the later years of the autonomist propaganda, when it gained its greatest strength as a popular movement, less disposition was shown to heed the formulas of the leaders; but these men did not know it. They were going with the crowd, and they thought the crowd was going with them. When under Blanco the autonomists who did not go into the field issued their allocutions and manifestoes accepting the new regimen, it was disclosed that old things had passed away. Neither whistle nor trumpet could bring back the followers who had once sat at the feet of the prophets. This was in part indisputably due to the presence of so many of them with the insurgents in the field. But it was also due to an advance in political education.

When peace was affirmed, manifestoes, addresses, and allocutions fell like autumn leaves. Some were from old-time Autonomists who had kept out of the insurrection, some from insurgent generals, and some from the Cubans who had been identified with the revolution on its civil side. They all had programmes and formulas. To the disappointment of their authors, little heed was paid to these allocutions. It was manifest that the people were thinking of their own concern and did not care for ready-made formulas. This does not mean that they had ceased to be responsive to good leadership. It is questionable if anywhere a people can be found who are more responsive to good leadership; but that leadership must interpret the sentiments and aspirations of the people; and the authors of the allocutions were not doing it. Their prepared formulas were not the thing, and the majority of the Cubans had become apt enough in political intuition to know it.

While the manifesto of the leader to his followers lost much of its importance in the later years, another outgrowth of the autonomist movement gained fresh vitality. This was the organization of juntas or committees. The Autonomist party rested on local juntas or clubs. So did that of their vigilant opponents, the Union Constitutionals. These local clubs delegated their functions largely to a central committee, a junta magna or junta directiva, as it was named. This body was in reality a directory of the entire organization, and it directed in a far greater degree than the central committee of a political party in the United States. At a period when a few prominent men dominated the Autonomist and Union Constitutional parties respectively, they were able to have their allocutions and manifestoes adopted by the directories, and the local juntas accepted the creed prepared for them without question. Though the later development of popular sentiment, whether intransigente or autonomist, made the central committee more the organ than the moulder of opinion, the idea of a directory for a political party was not entirely lost. It has survived intervening events and exists to-day in a modified form.

After the re-establishment of peace, great activity was shown in the formation of juntas or clubs. Usually they took the names of the heroes of the insurrection. They furnish the means for political activity and agitation. They also furnish the field for exercising the ambitions of young Cubans. In the period before the insurrection the lyceum was the institution in which young Cubans found vent for their literary and dramatic as well as their social ambitions. The lyceum existed in every town. It was an offset to the Spanish casino, the casino being to the Cubans the token of a favored and intolerant oligarchy. After the ending of hostilities the lyceum reappeared everywhere; but it did not take on a political character. A common feeling obtained that it should continue what it had been, and that political effort should take a different form. So the membership in the political clubs grew.

In the gradual development of parties the clubs will be the basis of them all. They are the existing political units. They are the medium of party organization and promotion. They will not be able to control public sentiment, but they promise to be its interpreters and thus preserve their influence. The primaries are yet to come. The germ of the caucus is already in evidence. It is likely to take the place of the directory. Cuban politicians who were identified with revolutionary juntas in the United States have shown a leaning to the caucus, though not under that name.

The newspaper, even under the restricted liberty of the press which was permitted by Spanish institutions, showed an aptness for political discussion. Though pamphleteering always prevailed, the journals were the most sought-for mediums of promulgating opinions. They conformed to all the traditions. Each journal represented a party, a group, or an interest. No one ever picked up a leading paper curious to see what stand it would take on a given question. The only curiosity was as to how it would champion or defend its side. The journals announced themselves as the organs of one set or another set of opinions. They took a serious view of their mission. Discussion was to them an intellectual tournament, and they recognized that there could be no tournament without the knights of the contrary opinion in the lists. Invariably their leading articles were well considered.

No great change was worked by the revolution except that with the end of the press censorship discussion was free. It is still possible to judge the probable course of the Spanish colony by reading two or three

Spanish newspapers. The views of the moderate Cubans are reflected in journals which announce themselves as organs of moderate opinion, while the feelings and purposes of the radicals may be easily gleaned from journals which carry their own designation. It is in the new and changing conditions that the traditional organs are confused and lost. The manner in which the newspapers find their way through this wilderness will be a valuable guide for those who are watching the march of circumstances in Cuba. They may be depended on to reflect the aspirations as well as the perplexities of the Cuban people. And their aptitude for discussing the problems which surround them may be accepted as an index of the aptitude of the people for free institutions.

They are keen in retort. Some well-meaning Americans on their arrival in Cuba believed they had a mission among savages of various degrees of gentleness. . They thought to impress the natives that they came from a land of perfect government. Their mistakes were corrected by the watchful press. The wretched bickerings among the insurgent leaders over the payment of the troops, the personal rivalries, were made much of in the United States as proof of Cuban incapacity for independence. The Habana newspapers had their campaign argument in reply. They gave instances of discord among the American officials which showed just as much jealousy, factionalism, and selfish ambition. The American officials in the midst of their discords could not fail to admit the fairness of the retort.

To the talk of crime and especially of brigandage as a reason for continuing military control, the newspapers replied with full accounts of the train robberies in the Western States, the daily crimes of the cities, the scenes of violence at the strikes, and the lynchings. Nor did they fail to exploit the occurrences, unfortunately too frequent, which were discreditable to individual Americans in Cuba. These are passing incidents. They serve to show that while Americans insist on a searching scrutiny of everything that happens in Cuba, the inhabitants of the island are not inapt at measuring them with their own yard-stick. They have progressed far enough to make comparisons.

In the broader sense the discussion in the journals showed in a high degree the faculty of critical analysis. Some of the American officials were sensitive over the criticism they received; but it was no more personal and was usually less unjust than that which was visited upon them by badly informed newspapers at home. A full understanding was shown of the constructive work they were doing. The greater value of the newspaper comments and suggestions lay in the complete knowledge they showed of the close relation between the economic future of the island and the political system. Discussion of the Cuban tendencies was thoughtful. It is common to find in the journals a warning that the reality is coming to the Cuban people, a caution that they cannot live in the clouds. The enthusiasts are told that government is something more than writing poetical manifestos and making poetical addresses. The Spanish idiom is a flowing one. The sentiments which find utterance in the United States on the fourth of July, translated into the Castilian language, would be a stream of hyperbole. The Cuban patriot voices his feelings with more metaphors and more vivid imagery; but the press moderates his exuberance. It hints at the practical side of government suggestively, though not in a way to destroy his idealism. That is a rare aptitude.

From what has been written a fair conclusion may be drawn. Free discussion and political organization are not simply elementary ideas: they are a working basis for free government in Cuba. But it may be said that the discussion, which has been limited to newspapers and pamphlets and to public meetings which were necessarily select, cannot be looked upon as political education in an island a large proportion of whose population is unable to read or write. The assumption would be misleading in any circumstances, but especially so in Cuba. The commonest sight in the rural communities is to see the village oracle reading the newspaper to a group of listeners, among whom, it is easy to guess, few can read for themselves. But there has never been a wide gulf between the classes who could read and write and the ignorant classes whose aspirations they interpreted.

Rocking in the cradle of the revolution, in the midst of guerilla warfare, in the manigua, and in the hills, there was the semblance of a political training. The stern commander, Máximo Gómez, who understood the Cubans better than they understood themselves, enforced military discipline and civil obedience, while the camp-fire discussions were of free government. The systems of prefecturas in the regions held by the insurgents were lessons in military and civil training. The juntas or revolutionary committees in the towns had no educational qualification. They were a political education as well as a political conspiracy under the shadow of Spanish authority. The army had real elections of a kind, for it chose the delegates who formed the assemblies, which constituted the provisional government.

The aptitude of the guajiro, the countryman or Cuban peasant, for public affairs, when he must be led through the winding paths of intellectual reasoning, is not great. Mental processes are too abstruse. But he is an apt pupil when taught through the physical senses. And he is a tenacious positivist in his conclusions. Object lessons reach him. He found himself in the midst of a false artificial condition. He saw the Spaniards govern and take everything to themselves. He knew that he was a victim of oppression, cruelty, and tax-eating rapacity and corruption. He knew that in a dispute with his wealthier neighbor he had no rights, because the justice that sat on the magistrate's bench—justice in the choice of which he had no word—was open-eyed and keen of vision for the hand that stretched out the bribe. Where the guajiro was a negative character he became a pacifico, sympathizing mildly with the insurrection and aiding it like a sheep. Where there was sterner stuff in his make-up he became an insurgent and took to the brush. Once in arms, nothing could move him. His was not the sublimated patriotism of the intellectual classes. It was the simple grit of the peasant. The revolution, while it had the support of the educated and the wealthy Cubans, was the supreme work of the Cuban people as a mass. The mass was responsive to good leadership. It trusted its military leaders. It will trust leaders in civil life who are true to its instincts and unelfish in their devotion to its interests.

Americans who have watched the internal affairs of the island closely sometimes propound a query, either mentally or openly, whether the aptness which may be shown for decentralized government will not become a propensity for revolution by sections or provinces of the island. It is in line with the general question whether the defeated party will accept the verdict of the elections or will take to the woods. The question cannot be answered with full satisfaction until the experiment has been tried. In outlining the provinces as a federal framework I have given the opinion that sectionalism or regionalism will be less rampant in Santiago de Cuba and in Puerto Príncipe than is feared. This is a matter of impartial administration, and in giving no just ground for jealousy of Habana.

Should a forced test of annexation be made, Santiago might then drop out of line with the other provinces in the hope of being admitted as a separate State. But the ambitious chiefs will have little prospect of satisfying their ambition by taking a defeated faction to the woods in a single province. It is a pure assumption that this class of leaders would have followers at all. Moreover, General Máximo Gómez checked the possibilities of regionalism when in the first months of the insurrection he nationalized the cause of independence. His policy bore fruit, and one result of the revolution was more thoroughly to mix up the inhabitants of the different provinces. Some of the Santiago natives who marched west with Macéo to Pinar del Río settled and remained there. Some of those from Habana and Matanzas who went to Puerto Príncipe made it their permanent abiding place. Greater homogeneity among the Cubans as a people is the consequence. This has its bearing on future government. It helps to develop the aptitude of the whole people for homogeneous political institutions.

The political parties will not be essentially different from parties everywhere. As they exist to-day the line is not sharply drawn, because there is little chance to divide on domestic policies until the basis of division as a territory, state, or independent commonwealth exists. There is the National League, which is composed chiefly of the civilian elements; the Cuban National Party, which wants to absorb all the elements favoring independence; and the various factions which call themselves military parties. They are all following one line in sustaining schools for voting which are preparing the Cubans for the use of the ballot. There will be an anti-American faction composed of a few military chiefs. These will be continuously demanding the immediate grant of absolute independence and the withdrawal of the intervening power. It is not probable that this group will ever reach the dignity of a real political party. Some of its agitators fought successfully in the insurrection, but it is yet to be shown that they have followers. They are like the Autonomist leaders who issued manifestoes without getting responses.

In watching the development of sentiment in Cuba it is well to remember that the cigar smoke which rises from the cafés in Habana is not always the will of the Cuban people. Habana as a great city will naturally influence the politics of the island, but the controlling influence will not be with it. American officials in the beginning made the mistake of supposing that the metropolis was the whole island. Other Americans make the same mistake. What is best in Cuba is its town and country life. The influences, whether social or political, are more healthful there. They should always be sought before forming a judgment.

The growth of public opinion is something that is also to be noted, and it has its basis in the country. It frequently stilled the voices of the agitators who were demanding the immediate withdrawal of the American forces. When the factious Assembly was seeking to prolong the uncertainty about accepting the payment for the insurgent troops, public opinion compelled that body to dissolve itself. There is no reason to think that it will be less healthful in the future whenever a group of discontented leaders undertake to interfere with peaceful progress.

The radical group, as it is called, is composed mostly of generals who were antagonistic to Gómez during the insurrection. They were patriotic enough to control their resentments while the struggle lasted. Now they seek to find expression for it and to prevent the old commander dominating in civil affairs. They have among them some respectable figures such as Salvador Cisneros Betancourt, who can show a record as president of the provisional republic during the Ten-Years' war and also during the last insurrection. Despite their personal ambitions and resentments, it is not just to class all these men as unpatriotic. They want to see Cuba strong, maintaining friendly relations with the United States; but they want to be the ones who shall direct her destiny. Some of them may rebound so that in time they will become annexationists, for the honor of being American Senators and Representatives appeals powerfully to them.

Americans who sympathized with the insurrection and who are sincerely desirous for the success of the Cuban commonwealth admit to themselves a certain distrust in the virility of the character when it comes to be applied to public administration. Their own robustness is lacking. They also note that duplicity is a common trait. Often they may turn over in their minds the question of the strong hand for the Latin races; but a study of past and present conditions in the island satisfies them that the strong hand will never control the destiny of Cuba. Not even a progressive and patriotic Porfirio Diaz could make himself the master of this people. They have been educated to the point where they will not stand a dictator. It is also worth noting that while this lack of virility is manifest, sentiment is a most pronounced trait in their make-up. An appeal to sentiment rarely fails to achieve results. When their confidence is once obtained they are trustful and responsive. But with distrust implanted among them, no progress can be made.

The aim of intelligent and patriotic Cubans was to pattern the political institutions of the United States. They showed a hunger for information regarding local government as well as the methods of federal administration. The American control set the pattern before them. In every possible way Cuban administration was modelled after American methods. It is certain that with the entire power resting with themselves the Cubans will not do as well as the officials from the United States were able to do for them. In the beginning and at the various stages of progress these officials were discouraged and sometimes disheartened.

They had to meet one condition which was the outgrowth of the war. This was the tendency to regard all the offices as a Cuban club, with the discharge of the duties a mere incident. Unquestionably under Cuban administration more public servants will be required than under American control. But in time the people of the island will learn what every people learns—that the cost of managing public affairs comes from the producers.

It may furthermore be said that much fondness for office is shown by the Cubans. Whether this trait is really a racial one may be judged by the scenes at the White House in Washington in the months following the inauguration of a new President, or the crowd in the anteroom of the newly elected mayor of a big city or of the governor of a State. There is one difference: the Latin office-holder or office-seeker cares more for the dignity of the position than for its emoluments. The American office-seeker first wants to know how much it will pay. Nor are public affairs in Cuba left to the monopoly of one profession. The doctor, the dentist, the journalist, and the civil engineer mingle in politics as well as the lawyer.

Another inquiry which Americans make sincerely is to what degree respect for constituted authority exists among the people who respected it only when enforced by military government. They want to know whether the masses have a clear notion of the difference between liberty and license. They have curiosity to learn whether the decisions of judicial tribunals will be respected when there is nothing beyond the confidence in the tribunals themselves to enforce respect. These are questions that cannot be answered until the opportunity has been given to put them to the practical test of experience. The test cannot come under American military control. The most that can be looked for is some indications of an answer in the choice of a constituent, representative assembly to formulate the future government. That the political aptitudes exist for the choice of such a body and for its deliberations is affirmed in what has been said of the progress of free discussion and political organization. Here seems to be the basis of institutions that will develop and endure. Probably the first congress, or convention, will bear witness to the saying of De Tocqueville that a nation is always able to establish great political assemblies because it is sure to contain a certain number of persons whose intellectual cultivation stands them to a certain extent instead of practical experience. The fashioning of the rude materials of the local community is, as the French philosopher says, a more difficult task; but the beginnings of municipal government are already seen.

The originator of the revolution of 1895, José Martí, was a poet. He sealed his aspiration for the liberty of the land he loved with his death on the battlefield. Other poets before him perished ignominiously for their faith in free government. Menocal, an artist of European reputation, left his easel to join the ragged forces of Máximo Gómez. Cultured men were marched through the streets of Habana tied to common criminals. Loaded with chains and herded in the foul holds of vessels with these criminals, they were sent to the penal settlements of Africa. The clanking of these chains still echoes through many households. All this was for the crime of rebellion. College professors, learned men, educators, and writers went into voluntary and involuntary exile. These classes returned to Cuba. They are a part of its future. Some of them are dreamers. They dream with an apostle of liberty * of another island:

> "The dreamer lives on forever,
> The toiler toils for a day."

These men may prefer to dream of idyllic government in the ideal future rather than to work for the imperfect structure which must be set up by toiling day by day. Their fondness for speculative thought, their theorizing on the nature of liberty, may unfit them for the intensely practical business of government. Their ability to administer the customs houses will never be demonstrated. A poet or dreamer in a Latin custom house will be a failure. But the sentiments which inspire them, and which they seek to inculcate, will have a fruitful soil. The dreamers will have their place in the evolution of the Cuban commonwealth. The problem is to evolve a successful administration not only of the custom house, but of all public offices between the dreamers on one side, and on the other side the men who think that revolution is merely a change to enable Cubans to loot their own island instead of letting Spaniards loot it. The poets and the dreamers themselves would be out of place in the custom house, but they have their place in keeping alive the sentiment which demands honest administration.

In Pensacola are the ruins of an old Spanish fort.

* John Boyle O'Reilly.

At St. Augustine are the ruins of the oldest Spanish fort on the American continent. Near Kingston, Jamaica, are the ruins of what must have been an extensive, almost impregnable, Spanish fort. When the American troops landed at Daiquiri and Siboney the old fortress which was discovered in the jungle compelled their admiration. They might have thought, too, of the vengeance of history, if they had reflected that near Daiquiri landed the Spanish expedition from Hispaniola which crushed the native chief Hatuey and established four hundred years of Spanish dominion over Cuba. The defences of Santiago de Cuba called forth the praise of the keenest military engineers. The defences of Habana won admiration for their scientific thoroughness and for their mathematical exactness. If forts, moats, walls, castles, cannons, and batteries constituted a state, Spain never would have lost her American possessions.

Men, says Sir William Jones, constitute a state. And they would have constituted a colony. Battlements and walls and moated gates went down not because Spain lacked men to defend them; it was because she lacked men who knew that in themselves were the power and the majesty of the state. The lands from which the Conquistadores sought to draw only the gold that was yellow to the eyes, while neglecting that which renews itself with the turning over of the soil, could not constitute a state. All this has gone. The mediæval civilization of fortresses and cannons is buried when the twentieth century is opening its chrysalis of potentialities. The future commonwealth of Cuba must be built with sound principles of government at the foundation, and with men—real men of muscle and mind—for the builders. If they have not the faculties of government fully developed, they have acquired the primary aptitudes.

CHAPTER XVIII

TO-DAY

TRANSITION of institutions may be during a transit of flags. The standard of Spain is of yesterday. The emblem of Cuba may be of to-morrow. The flag of the United States is of to-day. The creation of a commonwealth is under its folds.

This does not mean an indefinite continuance of the American military occupation. Like other questions, the one as to the time of its withdrawal is better met frankly. No policy of avoidance will be successful in dealing with these problems. The pacification of the island may not be complete, but it is far enough advanced to look forward. It is in advance of industrial progress, though the latter is not lagging. The question of the near future is both when and how to end the American military control in Cuba. It is of to-day, though by to-day should be understood not a few weeks or a few months, but a definite period. To-day * is a year.

Pleas may be offered for indefinite control, but they fall away in the imperious presence of facts. Incentives to vagueness may be urged on the ground that the people are so far from being capable of self-government that they must be put through a long course of political training. All the arguments for indeterminate occupation would in a short time force the necessity of a declaration of such purpose, and such a declaration would mean ultimate and coercive annexation. Sifted through all evasions, this is what these pleas mean.

Before going further a restatement may be made of the position of the United States with reference to Cuba. That position is both of to-day and of all time to come. The United States is a continuous intervening power. In ending the Spanish misgovernment and the strife which grew out of it, the American nation pledged itself not to permit internal misgovernment in the future. Whatever shifting there may be of policies, it is pledged to prevent anarchy and intolerable internal conditions just as it ended those conditions under Spanish sovereignty. It is also a continuous protecting power for Cuba. Should an independent government be set up, no bullying European nation could seize a pretext of damages to its subjects and send war-vessels into the harbors of Cuba to enforce the claim without reckoning with the United States. Besides, in the obligations for good government which it incurred the United States became the protecting power for foreign subjects therein,

* October, 1899.

whatever their nationality. So in every view the American nation has a moral protectorate over Cuba.

The immediate question is whether good government shall come from above and without, or from within. The military authority in its ultimate analysis is similar to the control exercised under Spanish sovereignty. The difference is that it assures good administration, freedom from official corruption and from oppressive taxation. But there is no misunderstanding that it comes from above. In describing the military control, I have stated its strength and what the American authorities were able to accomplish through its arbitrary nature. If it were of indefinite continuance the merging of a government of law, order, justice, and equality into the imposition of American manners and customs would be hard to avoid, judging from the tendency that already has been shown. Don Gerónimo Valdés might literally walk abroad with his paternal bando amplified to the degree of regulating public smoking and the wearing of undershirts by the workingmen with reference to the habits of a few thousand strangers rather than of some hundreds of thousands of natives. And under American rule it would be made more than ever manifest that these regulations were in reality the regulations of the military power. It would be the army which compelled the teamster to wear his undershirt, for the local law officers who enforced that order would rest on the military authority and would carry out its decrees.

The complaints of the multiplicity of government and of rulers are a passing phase of the occupation. The number of officials might be reduced and still the civil authority would rest upon military power. The gradual widening of municipal government after the full framework of laws and regulations has been set up by the superior military commanders may be a progressive step, but it is not a decisive one nor one which meets permanent conditions. The test of the capacity and the willingness to respect authority—that is, lawful government—cannot come under army rule because it is the army which enforces that respect. The limitations of education in political self-rule under these conditions are obvious. In its essence the American military control is as much government by decree as was the Spanish authority. The difference may be a wide one between beneficent government by decree and oppressive government by decree, as is shown under the American administration. But the popular element cannot enter largely into it, and that is the weakness.

So thorough is my own conviction that this fact will be recognized, and so scrupulous has been the American Executive in affirming that the military control is of a temporary nature, that without further analysis I proceed to the subject of the transition from military control to something else. Undoubtedly before this point is reached there will be a further relaxation of the military administration, and the high standard of official integrity and fidelity shown by the American officials will be given a deeper impress.

In the transition from American military control to something else the preliminary step is to ascertain the will of the people. It may be said that instead of a constituent representative assembly to formulate their wishes in the shape of constructive government, it should first be determined whether the people of the island want annexation. The power to force a determination of that question before anything else is settled undoubtedly lies with the United States, and if it were attempted the verdict would be so overwhelmingly against annexation that the only thing accomplished would be to prepare for another election. There must unquestionably be a plebiscite in ascertaining both the aspirations and the wishes of the people of the island. The natural process would be the choosing of a representative constitutional convention. In that election the issues would determine themselves so that the opposing tendencies could be developed in the convention. Then the work would be submitted to the people for their ratification or rejection. This would be another plebiscite. As the United States is at once the intervening power and the only recognized authority, whatever elections are held must be under its direction. This may be done by direct Executive action or by the sanction of Congress. The only important point is that it be by civil instead of by military agency.

It is necessary to ascertain the basis of the plebiscite. The declarations are so clear that a stable government is to be formed by all classes that no question can arise on this point. But with the tendency of the Spanish colony, or the majority of its members, to continue as Spanish subjects, when the time comes it will be found that "all classes" who are entitled to participate in determining the form and the formation of the new government are largely and overwhelmingly the Cuban classes. The foreigners, whether Europeans or Ameircans, will doubtless exercise an indirect influence, but there can be no actual participation by them in the proceedings to determine the form of the commonwealth. It will develop that the only basis for the plebiscite is universal suffrage. Americans are appalled at this idea when they think of the illiteracy of the island. The saddest chapter in the history of Cuba has been said to be the educational chapter. It is in reality a blank. With this in their minds, and with the further thought that the blacks are the bulk of the illiterates, Americans draw back and ask if the mistakes of reconstruction are to be repeated in Cuba.

The cases are not parallel. In the chapter on the Race of Color I have sought to show that the blacks in Cuba have reached a higher plane than the negroes in the United States. Their situation is not similar to that of the American negroes after the civil war. The race of color in Cuba fought for the freedom of the island. The blacks acquired political standing by their part in the revolution. It assures the continuance of their civil rights, but that in itself will not be enough. They are not aggressive in demanding a share in civil administration, but with their record in fighting for freedom they will never be content with a government in which they have no voice simply because the majority of them in this generation may not be able to read and write.

If a qualification for suffrage should be required, there would be the question as to whether it should be an educational one or based on property, or both. A large number of the guajiros, or countrymen, are small property owners, but they cannot read and write. They have all the conservative instincts of the property owner. In the towns and cities where the vicious classes congregate, a fair proportion of these are not illiterate. An educational test would enable them to vote at the expense of the small landholders. Under the Spanish Government the voting was so manipulated that the influence of the small property owners was lessened, and the influence of the clerks and similar classes in the towns was augmented. Any efforts by the United States to restrict the suffrage would give rise to the feeling that the old Spanish practices were being restored. And the Spanish Government itself in the decrees proclaiming autonomy proclaimed universal suffrage. That was part of the autonomous constitution. In actual operation it would unquestionably have been nullified, yet it stands as an offer from Spain. The United States can do no less.

As to the blacks as a class, neither the white classes in Cuba nor the all-powerful American nation can deny them their rights. There was neither color line, property qualifications, nor educational requirement in the insurrection. There can be none in determining the future government of the island. An Australian ballot is not necessary. The method of voting by word of mouth, which until recent years prevailed in Kentucky and other Southern States, will answer every purpose. Various expedients will be suggested and various plans discussed for limiting the suffrage in Cuba on the theory that its exercise by all classes would be harmful to the people themselves. In the end these plans will fail, and the determination of the wishes of the Cuban people will be on the basis of universal suffrage because that is the simplest and the most natural way. It is also the just way.

It is an unpopular thing to suggest a doubt about the early Americanization of Cuba. Nevertheless I venture to suggest it in the sense which is commonly understood. The veneer of Americanism is one thing, and so is the varnish. There will be plenty of veneer. The prophets already see Cuba an English-speaking country. My vision does not see it. So much has been promised from teaching English in the schools that it is heresy to insinuate a doubt. Nevertheless the American who speaks Spanish will be the successful one in Cuba during the lifetime of this generation. The American who depends on English-speaking Cubans or Spaniards will be misled. In spite of the wave of English teaching that has swept over the island, the mass of people will not be touched. When country schools come to be established the wisdom of forcing English upon them is questionable. They will speak the tongue of their mothers, they will think in that tongue, and they will act in accordance with the customs and traditions rooted in that tongue. These young Latins, whether black or white, have waxen minds. They show a facility in acquiring a foreign idiom; but it will not be their thinking and acting medium of expression. The institutions of which they become part will be interpreted in their own language. And if the stream of immigration flows in from the Mediterranean or from the slopes of the Pyrenees, Castilian will be the native tongue and English the foreign language.

At one time the German colony in Habana and Western Cuba numbered one thousand members. After the war there were four hundred of them. Not half a dozen purely German families existed. The German merchants married Cuban women. Their children were gathered up into a school by the German consul-general. It was found that a very small number spoke the language of their fathers or had any knowledge of German customs. Americans and Englishmen who married Cuban wives generally had their children taught English; but the family talk was in Spanish, and the American talk was sometimes the broken language of the foreign country. Frenchmen, with more affinity between their own tongue and that of the Castilian, also had the same experience. The history of Louisiana for a century affords an example. Upper Canada, after one hundred and fifty years, is also an example. The leaven of genuine Americanism will be felt beneficially, but for a quarter of a century or more it will be only a leaven among a Latin people and an African population assimilated to a Latin people. Good schools do not mean that English will uproot the language which is native to the great majority of the inhabitants.

Probably before the political future of Cuba is fully unfolded, ten per cent of the inhabitants will be natives of the United States. There will be a winter colony whose numbers will grow year by year. Many wealthy Americans with the charm of country life ever present to them will purchase country estates on which they may enjoy the palm-tree landscape and the azure skies. Trades and mercantile business and small farming will afford further openings. Yet with these inducements the prospect is not increased that the field labor of the country and the day labor of the towns can be drawn from the States. This is what bids a pause to the loose talk of Americanization.

The Americans who settle in the island will intermarry among the Cuban women; their vitality will be replenished by fresh immigration, and perhaps by themselves revisiting the more life-giving climate of the North. Out of this intermixture will come in time the best product of the two civilizations. Types of it may be seen in Cuba to-day where Americans, Englishmen, and Germans have married Cuban women. The rule is general enough to be accepted as a principle that their offspring combine the moral fibre and the physical stamina of the fathers with the domestic traits and virtues of the mothers. But these are only types. It will take fifty years or two generations to develop the tropical American. When he is developed all the problems of government in the Antilles will be solved. Meantime it is not well to assume that the tropical American is already evolved or that a Latin people need Americanization in the sense of losing their language, their habits, their customs, and their own institutions. Many plants that flower in the temperate climates wither when transplanted to the tropics. The same may prove true of customs and laws.

Nor are the un-American influences to be overlooked. Were the United States to be judged solely by its official representatives, military and civil, the influence would be without exception a healthy one. But the nation has to be judged by all classes of its representatives. The buzzards and the vultures trailed their flight in the van and in the wake of the American occupation. The adventurer from the Southwest who had failed in everything at home, and drifted into Mexico long enough to get a smattering of the tongue, appeared and told his contempt of Latin civilization. He talked of dagoes, gringoes, greasers, and mongrels, the superiority of the Anglo-Saxon race, the necessity of "our folks" taking hold of Cuba and running it so the country would be made to pay "us." Often he declared his preference for the gringoes, because the intermixture of blood in Mexico was Indian, while in Cuba it was "nigger."

American promoters, with experience in securing franchises and concessions from city councils and State legislatures, put in a prompt appearance. They knew what the Spanish system had been. They were ready to offer "gratifications"—bribes—with more effrontery than had been customary under the old rule. They sought out the insurgent leaders and opened negotiations on the theory that these men would have franchises and privileges to sell. Usually they proclaimed loudly that their investments were contingent upon Cuba seeking immediate annexation, but sometimes they became partisans of early independence.

When the custom-house passed under American control it was brokers from the United States who went about whispering their ability to keep up the old fraudulent practices in new ways. It was American agents who sought out the merchants with promises of bargains based on the assumption that goods could be imported fraudulently through connivance of the quartermaster's department of the army. Sometimes, too, it was an American officer who heard of this proceeding and kicked his countrymen out of doors. American firms were the first ones caught in actual smuggling. American strumpetry drove through the streets of Habana in blazoned coaches and proclaimed its presence. American drunkards also reeled through the streets of a city in which drunkenness was so rare as to be a genuine novelty. Habana saw more drunkenness in the six months following American occupation than it had seen in sixty years. American gamblers sought to dispute by new devices the lean pickings of the gaming table with the native gamblers. Americans first raised the color line and appealed to race prejudice in the cheapest and most blatant form. American braggarts swaggered through the town with their hands in their pockets and their hats tilted back. They shamed their fellow-countrymen who were there on legitimate business into silence and seclusion. They voiced their coarse criticisms of the domestic customs of a people of whose home life they could know nothing. The whole class of the buzzards abused the American officials who refused to recognize them as coadjutors in the work of uplifting Cuba. They almost justified the bitter comment of one commander that American military control was necessary in order to protect the island from American harpies.

Americans understood this phenomenon of the scum floating across the gulf before the healthier undercurrents reached the shores of the island. They sought to bear it with patience. Cubans who had lived in the United States also understood it. Those whose home always had been on the island, and the Spanish classes least of all, failed to understand it. This class of Americans is both of to-day and of to-morrow. They always will be of the same type, claiming kinship in the American nation, proclaiming the need of civilizing the Latin races and offering themselves as missionaries of the higher civilization. If at times there is in Cuba a disposition to doubt the superiority of Americanism, the presence of these adventurers may help to account for it.

Persons who visit Cuba for a week, especially if they happen to be officials, are impressed with the idea that the majority of the property holders and educated people, as well as a considerable number of the masses, want annexation. The sugar planters and the business men who want it call on them and tell them so. That the sugar planters long for the assurance of a market for their sugar the same that Hawaii has, does not require much argument. The Spanish financiers and merchants who want the American authority without the Americans to compete in business tell them that a stable government cannot be maintained except under the direct control of the United States.

The Latin doubters confide their doubts to the inquiring and receptive visitors. These are educated and generally property-owning Cubans. They see with the clearness of intellectual perception the dangers and the uncertainties of the future. They tell of the quickness with which the Latin blood mounts to the head, and they distrust the capacity of their race to maintain free government. They also saw the hopeless corruption and oppression of Spanish authority; but while sympathizing with the aspirations of their people, they doubted whether anything better could come of revolt. While they were doubting, the blacks and the guajiros and the educated Cubans who were not given to doubting carried the insurrection forward. These Latin doubters tell American visitors truly that a momentary agitation against annexation should not be taken as the deliberate conviction of the Cuban people. But their own influence is no greater than that of the doubter in other places and in other circumstances. It is certain that American officials will hear all the arguments and pleas for annexation, but it is not always creditable to their judgment that they go no further. For one thing, they do not seem to understand that the classes who oppose annexation do not call upon them.

Another point is thoroughly misunderstood. Of the Cubans who lean to annexation not one has the idea other than of immediate Statehood. The Cubans who have lived in the United States have been residents for a great part of Florida, Louisiana, and New York. They know nothing of territories. Those of them who advocate annexation have no notion that if they were to seek admission into the Union it could be on any other basis than that of equality. The island could furnish accomplished Senators and Representatives in Congress familiar with the language and the laws of both countries and ambitious of distinction. The honor of sharing in the government, of taking part in the elections for President, and possibly at a not remote period of having a member of the Cabinet appeals to all the ambitious men. With $100,000,000 of commerce, there would also be that element of power. It is so improbable that annexation sentiment in Cuba could be based on anything short of Statehood that I have not stopped to discuss the prospect of the island asking territorial form of government. If such a thing should happen it would not be a twelvemonth before the $100,000,000 of commerce would be demanding recognition, and the agitation for Statehood would be intense and ineradicable.

With the greatest faith in the capacity of the mixed nationalities in Cuba to work out their own destiny as a people, and with the determination to encourage and help them, it is very doubtful whether the people of the United States are ready to-day to share with them the full glory of American institutions. Manifest destiny can wait a quarter of a century, but in discussing the earlier future in Cuba there should be no misunderstanding. People of the United States should not turn their thoughts to annexation when by it they understand only limited territorial government, while the people of Cuba who are turning to annexation understand only full Statehood and equality in the American nation.

It has been noted frequently that the leaders in the last insurrection were veterans of the Ten-Years' war—Macéo, Gómez, Calixto García, Masó, and others. The young men never guided its fortunes. Many of them, especially those who have lived in the United States, are annexationists. Some of the older leaders want to see the flag of free Cuba floating for a while and then see a new Antillian star in the American firmament. The majority of them still believe that the ultimate destiny of Cuba is to be a part of the republic, but they say not now. But if a change of feeling should come upon the people and the drift should be toward annexation, neither old leaders nor Americanized young Cubans would be found supporting a policy that was not based on Statehood.

In the immediate future, during the transition from American military control to something else, the formation of Cuban parties may be on the line of Gómez and anti-Gómez, though the National League may become strong enough to retain an independent existence. Gómez is an old man. He gave his indomitable spirit to the winning of the freedom of Cuba. That he may live long enough to see in what form it shall be conserved, and to have a potent influence in determining that form, is possible. The Spanish blood in him is that of the conquistadores devoted to human liberty instead of to oppression. That he is capricious and dictatorial in his temperament is true. That his ambition was to be a dictator never has been justified by his history. He has experienced both the gratitude and the ingratitude of the people whom he served. The culmination of his influence was when he entered Habana on the fourth anniversary of the insurrection, and was received with honors by the American military authorities and with acclaim by the Cuban people. Their confidence in him was shown when they overwhelmingly repudiated the action of the Assembly in removing him from the command of their dissolving army.

General Gómez has been called a soldier of fortune, a mercenary adventurer whose sword was at the disposal of the highest bidder. Yet Spain unavailingly bid millions for it. Agents of sugar planters vainly sought the privilege of placing to his credit hundreds of thousands of dollars in the banks of London and Paris if his orders for the burning of sugar-cane and against the mills grinding were not enforced. No South American dictator could have levied such a tribute. The son of Gómez fell by the side of Macéo. His own life was risked countless times, but it was fated that the offspring who was his pride and his hope should be the sacrifice. There has been no change in the position of General Gómez regarding the future. He declared that Cuba was neither free nor independent so long as the United States administered its government. After coming out of the woods he threw the weight of his influence in support of the American authority and in deprecating the agitation for its immediate withdrawal. At all times he showed his comprehension of the industrial conditions which underlie the political progress of Cuba. But he is not for annexation.

The belief that immediate annexation is not likely to be an issue during the transition from military control to something else, has been indicated throughout this chapter. While this opinion is put forth with diffidence in the face of confident contrary views, I venture to follow it up and to indicate the possible lines on which the division may take place. The mass of Cubans have not changed their aspirations and their ideals. They are, as when an American statesman * visited them during the dying days of Spanish sovereignty, united in their purpose. The prediction of General Gómez came true to them, and as an outcome of the struggle for independence every household had its martyr. But these aspirations, while clear, are not aggressive and unreasoning.

It is my own conviction that while the overwhelming majority of Cuban people are not thinking of early annexation, they are not in a hurry to cut themselves adrift. They recognize that the moral protectorate of the United States is a fact. They have given more thought than is commonly credited them to what it means to create an army and a navy. The fondness for military show may be part of the Latin character, and there will always be that desire for military honors.

* Senator Redfield S. Proctor.

But this desire is not an insatiate one, and it may find expression in the creation of a rural police. A navy is not being thought of at all, and yet the navy is a part of an island nation.

There is another basis. This is the financial one. Under any conditions when the military control is withdrawn and a different government is set up, the new commonwealth will need money. The United States advanced $3,000,000 for the insurgent troops as a loan, and not as a gift. Further advances may be made for the internal improvements under similar conditions, with a lien on the customs receipts. It is an individual opinion, but I put it forth that this moral control and this lien on the customs and the guarantee of Cuba's protection from European aggression is for years to come all that is desirable by the United States. And it need not be surprising if Cuban public opinion takes this channel. Its opponents may charge that this is disguised annexation, but the disguise is so thorough that annexation would not recognize itself.

A protectorate would be something more than autonomy. It would be an independent government for Cuba in her internal affairs and in consonance with her aspirations. Many years would pass before such a government would be administered as well as the United States could administer it, but that is not the question. The certainty is that in determining the method of transition from military control to something else, the Cuban people as they approach the reality will be the less anxious to withdraw absolutely themselves from the American influence, though they will justly and properly oppose indefinite delay in ending the military nature of that influence. In these circumstances the Cuban public opinion which turns to a Protectorate may be left to controvert the public opinion which demands absolute severance of the relations with the United States. All that the intervening power can do is to assure the untrammelled utterance of these opinions; and if the ultimate sentiment should develop for a complete severance from the United States, it must be respected.

To-day there are two opposing tendencies. On the surface they seem political and social. In their depths they are economic. Commercialism antagonizes the instinct of nationality. Legitimate capital thinks it sees quicker industrial recuperation and political stability under immediate annexation by whatever means brought about. Speculative capital has no chance of exploitation unless Cuba is made part of the United States. It sees chiefly that annexed Cuba would mean free sugar. If free sugar were sure, the present mortgages on the cane lands would be easily lifted. Their value would increase at a bound. There would be an unexampled era of investment in plantations. Money that was seeking outflow in coffee culture, fruit raising, dairy farming, and in timber lands would change its course. It would all flow toward sugar-cane production. Tobacco would be the only agricultural industry not affected. Then the agitation would begin for more radical tariff legislation by the United States to destroy the European beet-sugar bounties. With a profitable market gained, the next question would be the cultivation of the inexhaustible cane lands. The first inquiry would be for cheap labor in a mass. Efforts to get Chinese coolies would probably be defeated because of the exclu-

sion policy of the United States. Some negro colonization might be attempted, and the dregs of miscellaneous
labor would be gathered up in all quarters. This would
not be an encouragement to family immigration. It
would be harmful socially and politically. Ultimately
the planters would have to turn to the provinces of
Spain, but not until they had demoralized the whole
island. The end would be a Latin plantation as one of
the States of the Union.

The United States by force of circumstances made an
investment in Cuba. The investment is the promise of
a people who are capable of self-government. Whether
these conditions are met by encouraging a sugar craze
which has no definite source of labor supply back of it
can easily be judged.

Against this tendency of commercialism is the aspiration of the Cuban people. Its impelling force, though
not always clearly discernible, is the hope to have the
country populated by small landowners. The labor
which is looked for is not servile or cheap. The immigration which is sought is the immigration of the family
from sources which give promise of constant freshening.
It is not assured that the Cubans can maintain a government which will invite immigrants and insure the
repeopling of the island. That is part of the experiment which must be tried and which may fail. But it
is no more doubtful than the experiment which inevitably leads to the exploitation of Cuba as a huge
plantation, and which insists on settling the political
status before an approach has been made to securing an
industrial population that will be in harmony with the
political institutions.

Foreign capitalists, especially the English and Spanish, are not concerned with the difficulties of government which may perplex the United States. They are transients. They do not expect to be of the island and of its people. Naturally they lean to the annexation idea, and do not encourage small landholdings. Viewed as a billion-dollar plantation, Cuba seems to offer greater profit to foreign investment than as a country in which the cane lands are to be diversified by the lesser agricultural occupations.

The Cubans are sometimes vague in their utterances. They do not put forth clearly the reasons which govern their motives. They realize the infinite richness of the sugar lands, but they also realize the importance of diversifying the cane-sugar industry and increasing the number of small landholders who will not be dependent on the market for sugar. Their instinct is correct. The interests of the American people seem to lie with the interests of the Cuban people. Industry and commerce must be encouraged, but they do not need to be stimulated artificially in order that great fortunes may be made by speculation in cane lands or in other projects. The American people want the civilization of the church, the home, and the school to obtain in Cuba. They will seek the foundation for these in the economic conditions which develop the independent life of the small capitalists and landowners. Their patience will be tried. They may be sure that in the various stages of Cuban government human nature will be shown at its ordinary level, and not at loftiest heights. But the end will justify their patience. When the mass of Cubans know that they are not being dispossessed from the country that is theirs, they will turn with intelligent judgment to determine the ultimate relation of the island to the United States.

These are the natural processes. They are also the healthier ones. They give time for the closer knowledge and understanding of popular government in the United States which should be the indispensable requirement for sharing in that government. Americans on their part should not be deceived. They should keep in mind that the civilization of Cuba is Latin. They should not blind themselves to the fact that the streams of white immigration which are to freshen and renew the population of the border tropics must continue to flow from Latin countries. American contact and example may modify and mould this civilization, but cannot change its nature in a single generation. For half a century Cuba is to be understood as a Latin commonwealth, whether it be an independent nation, a protected republic, or a State of the American Union.

In conclusion, if the majority of the people in Cuba reject the idea of a protectorate and want to try the experiment of nationality, separate and distinct, with all its perils, they must be allowed to try it. That a government of this kind would be more than an experiment its most earnest champions and its well-wishers would not assert. The first step toward testing the sentiment and toward solving the problems and the responsibilities with which the United States is confronted lies in the election of a constituent representative convention on the basis of universal suffrage. The island is for its people. Their welfare must be trusted to an assembly of their own free choice.

APPENDIX A.

BIBLIOGRAPHY.

SPANISH colonial history begins in the pages of Prescott and Irving. Three centuries of its record are almost barren. The student who wishes to know its outgrowth may start with the nineteenth century. He cannot do better than to begin with Humboldt. He will find there a survey of the state of Cuba which covers its physical, political, social, and economic phases. Unfortunately Humboldt, as presented in English, was the victim of a zealous editor who imposed on American readers a long preliminary essay and followed it with copious argumentative notes. This was during the period of the slave controversy, and the editor was a partisan. It is possible to extract the real Humboldt from a mass of irrelevant matter, but a simpler way is to consult the original French edition or an excellent translation into Spanish which was published in Paris. After Humboldt comes a long list of Cuban and Spanish writers whose works are both historical and controversial. The official history of Spanish rule in Cuba may be found in the Gazettes of the Captain-Generals and the Bulletins of the provinces. A summary of these was published two or three times a year as a collection of decrees, orders, and dispositions of the general Government.

The insurrectionary period of Cuban history, as well as the political agitation, is reflected in current newspaper literature for the last thirty-five years and in an avalanche of pamphlets. What may be called the Cuban special pleading is found in a series of volumes which were issued in the United States. The genuine insurgent literature, from which the spirit animating the revolution may be gathered, appears in some publications which came from the printing-press in the woods, and in a small newspaper *Las Villas*, which was the medium of the official orders, appeals, and addresses of the insurgent military chiefs. Necessarily the times of publication were irregular, but the journal had an existence, and its files are valuable. When peace came the old book-shops of Habana also gave up insurgent literature, which is an aid in helping to an understanding of the struggle that ended Spanish rule.

The intellectual life of Cuba for a hundred years is found in the archives of La Sociedad Económica de Amigos del País—the Economic Society of Friends of the Country. These archives contain the history of four centuries. From them was drawn the material for the most valuable works that have been published. Learning breeds sedition, and the society, if not under the ban, was often under the frown of the Government. But it proved that it was composed of true friends of the country. Its memorials, or reports, are of unusual value. A modern librarian would be appalled at the confusion in which the records and archives appear, but the honorable poverty of this learned society does not impair its usefulness.

On what may be called the American side it is not necessary to recapitulate the Congressional and Executive documents which define the attitude of the United

States toward Spain. They are all accessible. Economic tendencies contemporary with Spanish political rule are set forth for a series of years in the reports of Consul-General Ramon O. Williams. Concerning the present military government in the island, its acts are fully recorded in *The Official Gazette*. The industrial and commercial conditions, as well as the financial system which are the basis of the tariff and other regulations, are discussed in the reports of Mr. Robert P. Porter, special commissioner. Information regarding the customs duties, the laws of mortgages, railroads, public works, and other matters of interest are given publicity in pamphlet form from time to time by the insular division of the War Department.

Since the guardianship of the United States over Cuba was assumed, many American libraries have been adding to their shelves by books obtained in Madrid and in Habana. It is with the belief that most of those which I have consulted may be available to the student that I indicate the following list of references:

Antiguos Diputados de Cuba (Los). D. Eusebio Valdés Dominguez. Prólogo de D. Rafael Montoro. Habana, 1879.

Almanaque Bailly-Baillierie, Madrid, 1897-98-99. (Contains special chapters with reference to Cuba.)

Asturianos (Los) en el Norte y los Asturianos en Cuba. Ramón Elices Montes. Habana, 1893.

Bando de Gobernación y Policía de la Isla de Cuba expedido por el Excelentísimo Sr. D. Gerónimo Valdés, Presidente Gobernador y Captain General. Quinta edición. Habana, 1875: Imprenta del Gobierno. (The famous code of paternal despotism.)

Cuba with Pen and Pencil. Samuel Hazard. Hartford, 1871. (The best book in English descriptive of the country and its people. Thirty years have not lessened its value as a mirror of customs and habits.)

Cuban Sketches. J. W. Steele, former consul at Matanzas. New York, 1881.

Cuba y su Gente: Apuntes para la Historia. Francisco Moreno. Madrid, 1887.

Cuba y sus Jueces: Rectificaciones Oportunas. (Answer to the above.) Raimundo Cabrera. Sexta edición. Prólogo de D. Rafael Montoro. Habana, 1889.

Cuba por Fuera: Apuntes del Natural. Tesifonte Gallego García. Habana, 1890.

Cuba en la Cartera. Antonio E. Menendez. Habana, 1895.

Cuba: Monografia Historica. Antonio Bachiller y Morales. Habana, 1883.

Cuba ante la Historia y el sentido común. M. Benitez Veguillas. Habana, 1897.

Cuba para los Cubanos: Folleto Político. Alvaro de la Iglesia. Habana, 1898.

Cuba y la reforma colonial en España. Rafael Delforme Salto. Madrid, 1895.

Cuba: Physical Features of; her Past, Present, and Possible Future. Fidel G. Pierra. New York, 1896.

Centro Gallego—Memorias de la Junta Directiva. Habana, 1898.

Centro Gallego—Memoria de la Sociedad de Beneficiencia. Habana. 1898.

Cuestión de Cuba (La): Historia y Soluciones de los Partidos Cubanos. Juan Guálberto Gómez. Madrid, 1885.

Crónicas de la Guerra de Cuba. Habana, 1895-96-97.

Crimines y Criminales de la Habana. Ignacio D. Ituarte. Habana, 1893.

Control of the Tropics (The). Benjamin Kidd. New York, 1898.

Cuestión Social en las Antillas Españolas (La). Rafael M. de Labra. Madrid, 1874.

Collección de Reales Ordenes, Decretos y Disposiciones. Habana. 1898. 3 tomos. (Contains the Decrees of Autonomy.)

Compilación de (los) Articulos con Relación al Ramo de Loteria. Habana, 1873.

Chinos fuera de China (los) y el Antagonismo de Razas. Federico Ordas Avecilla. Habana, 1893.

Código penal para las Islas de Cuba y Puerto Rico. Madrid, 1894.

Diccionairo geográfico, estadístico, histórico de la Isla de Cuba. Don Jacobo de la Pezuela. Madrid, 1863. 4 tomos. (The fountain of much valuable information.)

Due South: Cuba, Past and Present. M. M. Ballou. Boston, 1885.

Ensayo Político sobre la Isla de Cuba. El Baron A. von Humboldt. Obra traducida al Castellano. Paris, 1827.

Esclavitud en Cuba (De la). F. de Armas y Céspedes. Madrid, 1866.

English in the West Indies (The). James Anthony Froude. London, 1888.

Froudacity: West India Fables Explained. J. J. Thomas. Philadelphia, 1890.

Folletos escritos contra la Anexión de la Isla de Cuba á los Estados Unidos. Antonio Saco. Nueva York, 1856.

Guía Geográfica y Administrativa de la Isla de Cuba. Don Pedro José Imbernó. Habana, 1891. (A valuable summary of the condition and resources of the island.)

Guía de Forasteros de la Isla de Cuba. Habana, 1872, etc.: Imprenta del Gobierno.

Guía de Gobierno y Policía de la Isla de Cuba. Don Francisco García Morales. Segunda edición. Habana, 1899.

Guía de los Ayuntamientos. Habana, 1891.

Habana Antigua y Moderna (La.) D. José Maria de la Torre. Habana, 1857.

Historia económica, polític,a intelectual y moral de la Isla de Cuba. Remón de la Sagra. Paris, 1861.

Historia contemporanea de la Isla de Cuba desde 1801 hasta 1896. P. Giralt. Habana, 1896.

Historia de Matanzas. D. Pedro Antonio Alfonzo. Matanzas, 1854.

History of the British Colonies in the West Indies (The). Bryan Edwards. London, 1807. 3 vols.

Insurrección de Cuba (La). Vicente Torres y Gonzalez. Madrid, 1896.

Insurrecciones en Cuba (Las.) Apuntes para la historia política de esta isla en el presente siglo. J. Zaragoza. Madrid, 1872–73. 2 tomos.

Isla de Cuba: Recuerdo de dos Epocas. Don J. M. de Andueza. Madrid, 1841.

Ile de Cuba (L'). J. B. Rosemond de Beauvallon. Paris, 1844.

Isla de Cuba: Inmigración de Trabajores Españoles. D. Urbano Feyjoo Sotomayor. Habana, 1853.

Libro del Ciudadano Español (El): Derechos Políticos y Administrativos. José Sedano y Agramonte. Segunda edición. Habana, 1889.

Leyes de las Indias. Madrid, 1847. 4 tomos.

Llave del Nuevo Mundo. Arrate. Habana, 1830.

Ley de Enjuiciamiento Civil, reformada para las Islas de Cuba y Puerto Rico. Madrid, 1894.

Legislación Autonómica. José Raul Sedano. Habana, 1898.

Manual de la Isla de Cuba. Su Autor D. José García de Arboleya. Segunda edición. Habana, 1859. (A valuable compendium of information regarding the Cuba of half a century ago.)

Memorias sobre el Estado Político, Gobierno y Administración de la Isla de Cuba. D. José de la Concha. Madrid, 1853.

TO-MORROW IN CUBA.

Memorias de la Sociedad Económica de Amigos del País. Habana, passim.

Muerte del General Macéo. José Miró y Argenter, Brigadier, jefe de Estado Mayor. Campamento de Manajanado, Diciembre 22 de 1896. (Imprenta insurrecta.)

Masoneria (La) pintada por sí misma. D. Rafael de Rafael. Prólogo de Don A. J. de Vildósola. Madrid, 1883.

Masoneria (La) Apuntes Históricos sobre el origen en la Isla de Cuba. Compilados por Manuel Ruiz Inza. Habana, 1891.

Masoneria (La) Procedimientos de la gran Logia. Habana, 1878.

Negro in Cuba (El). Por un Amante de la Verdad. Habana, 1866.

País de Chocolate (El): La Inmoralidad en Cuba. Francisco Moreno. Madrid, 1887.

Pasado y Presente de Cuba. El Brigadier D. Francisco de Acosta y Albear. Madrid, 1875.

Peninsulares y Cubanos. Aurelio C. Silveria y Córdova. Habana, 1891.

Partido Liberal: Segundo Anniversairo. Habana, 1880.

Partido Liberal Autonomista: Procedimientos para la Elección de Representantes. Habana, 1893.

Presupuestos Generales de Gastos e Ingresos de 1898–99. Habana, 1898. Imprenta del Gobierno.

Penal Code (The) of the Islands of Cuba and Puerto Rico. Translated into English. Habana, 1893.

Prostitución (La) en la Ciudad de la Habana. Dr. Benj. de Céspedes. Habana, 1883.

Restauración Teocratica (La). Fernando Garrido. Segunda edición. Madrid, 1881.

Revista Cubana (La). Habana, passim.

Sistemas Coloniales. Rafael M. de Labra. Madrid, 1874.

Los Yankees en Cuba: Pro Patria. Antonio P. Rioja. Habana, 1897.
La Guerra con los Estados Unidos. Adolfo Llanos. Habana, 1897.
La Invasion Norte Americana. Antonio P. Rioja. Habana, 1898.
(These last three pamphlets give an excellent idea of the feeling of the ultra-Spanish classes towards the United States when war was known to be inevitable.)

APPENDIX B.

EXPORTS and imports are a good means of showing the resources of the island and the opportunities it offers for American markets. Joined with these statistics are the possibilities of commerce as shown in the vessel clearances, and the sources of revenue as exhibited in the customs and similar receipts. Those persons who are specially interested in knowing what the inhabitants of Cuba are buying and what they are selling will be able to keep abreast of the subject by following the monthly and quarterly statements published in the newspapers. A general survey may be had from a summary of the first six months of American control. This information, together with that regarding the articles of export and import, is supplied in the following official statement. I am indebted for it to Colonel Tasker H. Bliss, collector of customs at Habana, under whose efficient administration the opportunities of Cuban commerce have been demonstrated.

OFFICIAL STATEMENT.

The principal exports of Cuba are sugar, tobacco, cigars, honey, molasses, aguardiente (cane rum), wax, sponges, fruits, minerals—principally manganese, iron, steel, etc., from the province of Santiago; wood from

Santiago and Puerto Príncipe; cocoanuts and bananas, the latter two articles principally from the ports of Banes and Baracoa.

The principal imports with their sources are as follows:

Rice, mostly from England and Germany.
Mineral waters, from France and Germany.
Oats, barley, and hay, from the United States and South America.
Olive oil, from Spain and France.
Codfish, from Norway and Canada.
Varnish and turpentine, from the United States.
Beer, from the United States, England, and Germany.
Cement, from the United States, England and France.
Coal, from the United States and England.
Coffee, from Puerto Rico and some from the United States.
Shoes, from the United States and Spain.
Onions, from the United States principally, some from Spain.
Preserves, from the United States, Spain, and France.
Drugs, from France, United States, and Germany.
Beans, principally from Mexico, some from the United States.
Cattle, from the United States, Mexico, and Central and South America.
Wheat-flour, from the United States.
Hams, from the United States and Spain.
Condensed milk, from the United States.
Crockery and crystal ware, from the United States, England, Germany, and Spain, principally from England.
Woods, from the United States.
Furniture, from the United States, France, and Germany.
Butter, from the United States, Spain, and England.
Corn, from the United States.
Lard, from the United States.
Machinery, from England principally, some from the United States.
Metals, from England and Germany, some from the United States.
Paper and pasteboard, from the United States, Germany, and France.
Hides, from the United States, France, Germany, and Spain.
Paint, from the United States, England, Germany, and Spain.
Petroleum, from the United States.
Chemical products, from the United States, France, England, and Germany.
Potatoes, from the United States, England, and Spain.
Cheese, from the United States and Holland,
Silk, from the United States, France, England, and Germany.

TO-MORROW IN CUBA.

Canned sardines, from Spain.
Hats, from the United States, England, and Spain.
Jipijapa hats, from South America.
Salt, from England and Spain.
Linen tissues, from England and Spain.
Woollen goods, from the United States, England, and France.
Cotton goods, from the United States, France, and England.
Bacon, from the United States and Spain,
Dried beef ("tasajo"), from Uruguay and the Argentine Republic.
Wines and liquors from Spain, France, and the United States.
Eggs and poultry, from the United States.

[Author's Note.—The importation of these last two articles will probably disappear with the reconstruction of the country. The possibility of the Southwestern States securing a share of the trade in tasajo, or jerked beef, is worth following up. Dried beef, from the nature of the climate, will always have a market in the tropics. In Cuba it is consumed chiefly by the negroes and laboring classes generally, partly on account of its cheapness and partly on account of its toughness, which renders it difficult of digestion, and for this reason especially preferred by those who perform hard physical labor. Any one who travels in the interior learns to value its nutritive qualities. The consumption is chiefly in the tobacco regions of Pinar del Río and Habana provinces in Matanzas, and in a section of Santa Clara where live beef is hard to procure. The price is eleven cents per pound in American money. During the last year the consumption has been about 12,000 hundredweights per quarter; but this is below the normal amount, and is due to the poverty of the people. Lately much of the importation has been by way of New York. Spanish ship captains, both of steamers and sailing vessels, were in the habit of buying large quantities of tasajo for sale in Cuba on their return voyages from South America. Minister W. I. Buchanan, in a recent report to Assistant Secretary of War Meiklejohn, leans to the belief that some of the trade can be transferred from Argentine and Uruguary to the United States, though he says the cheapness of stock raising in South America makes competition difficult. The process of salting and drying the raw beef in the sun could be followed as well in the Southwest as in Uruguay.]

The following data furnished by Collector Bliss with regard to receipts of customs funds are instructive:

Total receipts, sixteen ports from January 1 to July 1, 1899, were $6,983,705. Of this amount there was collected at the port of Habana $5,146,162.

Of the above-mentioned total receipts at all ports, the

import duties were $6,229,905, and the export duties were $388,960, the balance being from tonnage dues, fines, harbor improvement taxes, capitation taxes, cattle inspection fees, etc.

At the port of Habana during the six months the import duties amounted to $4,537,348, and the export duties to $386,114.

The order of the ports in the amount of collections was as follows: Habana, Cienfuegos, Santiago, Matanzas, Cárdenas, Nuevitas, Sagua le Grande, Manzanillo, Caibarién, Gibara, Guantánamo, Baracoa, Trinidad, Tunas de Zaza, Batabanó, and Santa Cruz.

During the six months there entered at the sixteen ports of the island, 2,227 foreign vessels and 4,487 coastwise vessels, making the total number entered 6,714. During the same period there cleared from all ports 2,125 foreign vessels and 4,524 coastwise vessels, making the total number of clearances 6,649.

At the port of Habana during the six months, the number of foreign entries was 1,031, coastwise, 889; total entries, 1,920. The total number of foreign clearances was 953, coastwise 850; total clearances, 1,803.

The total tonnage entered at all the sixteen ports of the island was: foreign vessels, 2,477,562 tons; coastwise vessels, 735,696 tons. The total amount of tonnage cleared was, of foreign vessels 2,351,936 tons, and of coastwise vessels 707,152 tons; making the total amount of tonnage entered of 3,213,258 tons, and the total amount of tonnage cleared of 3,069,080 tons.

At the port of Habana the total amount of tonnage entered was, of foreign vessels 1,292,960 tons, and of coastwise vessels 124,420 tons. The total amount of tonnage cleared was, of foreign vessels 1,227,234 tons, and of coastwise vessels 99,291 tons; making a total amount of tonnage entered during the six months of 1,417,380 tons, and a total amount cleared of 1,326,525 tons.

The course of commerce, foreign and coastwise, is exhibited at a glance in the following official tables:

STATEMENT OF FOREIGN VESSELS ENTERED AND CLEARED, PORT OF HABANA, CUBA, JANUARY 1st TO JULY 1st, 1899.

ENTERED.

MONTHS. 1899.	STEAM.				SAIL.				TOTAL NO. ENTERED.
	United States.	Spain.	Other Countries.	Total.	United States.	Spain.	Other Countries.	Total.	
January..	61	27	69	157	44	7	9	60	217
February.	58	17	47	122	32	1	5	38	160
March ...	64	25	61	150	43	1	6	50	200
April.....	53	0	61	114	27	0	12	39	153
May......	56	0	76	132	28	0	6	34	166
June	47	17	47	111	10	7	7	24	135
Totals..	339	86	361	786	184	16	45	245	1031

CLEARED.

MONTHS. 1899.	STEAM.				SAIL.				TOTAL NO. CLEARED.
	United States.	Spain.	Other Countries.	Total.	United States.	Spain.	Other Countries.	Total.	
January..	56	26	62	144	28	1	8	37	181
February.	45	16	47	108	26	1	6	33	141
March ...	57	24	54	135	33	1	5	39	174
April.....	49	0	69	118	38	0	4	42	160
May......	52	0	74	126	19	0	7	26	152
June	49	17	49	115	20	3	7	30	145
Totals.....	308	83	355	746	164	6	37	207	953

STATEMENT OF FOREIGN AND COASTWISE VESSELS ENTERED AND CLEARED, PORT OF HABANA, CUBA, JANUARY 1st TO JULY 1st, 1899.

FOREIGN.

		Jan.	Feb.	March.	April.	May.	June.	Total.
Entered	Steam.	157	122	150	114	132	111	786
	Sail ...	60	38	50	39	34	24	245
Total........		217	160	200	153	166	135	1,031

		Jan.	Feb.	March.	April.	May.	June.	Total.
Cleared	Steam.	144	108	135	118	126	115	746
	Sail ...	37	33	39	42	26	30	207
Total........		181	141	174	160	152	145	953

COASTWISE.

		Jan.	Feb.	March.	April.	May.	June.	Total.
Entered	Steam.	22	25	20	20	24	26	137
	Sail ...	88	114	130	135	161	124	752
Total........		110	139	150	155	185	150	889

		Jan.	Feb.	March.	April.	May.	June.	Total.
Cleared	Steam.	10	21	14	17	18	27	107
	Sail ...	110	96	125	147	140	125	743
Total........		120	117	139	164	158	152	850

Supplementary to these tables is the following information relative to the arrival and departure of passengers. It should be noted that the departures during the months from April to October always have been considerably in excess of the arrivals.

TO-MORROW IN CUBA.

PASSENGER STATEMENT, ARRIVALS AND DEPARTURES,
HABANA, CUBA, JANUARY 1st TO JULY 1st, 1899.

ARRIVED.

	Jan.	Feb.	March.	April.	May.	June.	Total.
United States ...	3,618	3,486	2,634	1,675	1,329	951	13,693
Spain	369	446	1,106	342	745	613	4,565
Other Countries.	1,074	1,023	609	689	716	454	3,621
Total..	5,061	4,955	4,349	2,706	2,790	2,018	21,879

DEPARTED.

	Jan.	Feb.	March.	April.	May.	June.	Total.
United States ...	1,423	2,215	5,243	2,492	2,124	998	14,495
Spain	769	577	1,031	1,757	2,084	1,749	7,967
Other Countries.	231	235	256	869	243	122	1,956
Total.........	2,423	3,027	6,530	5,118	4,451	2,869	24,418